The Furies

The *Furies*

Irving McCabe

Matador
9 Priory Business Park,
Wistow Road, Kibworth Beauchamp,
Leicestershire. LE8 0RX
Tel: (+44) 116 279 2299
Fax: (+44) 116 279 2277
Email: books@troubador.co.uk
Web: www.troubador.co.uk/matador

ISBN 978 1785891 021

British Library Cataloguing in Publication Data.
A catalogue record for this book is available from the British Library.

Printed and bound by CPI Group (UK) Ltd, Croydon, CR0 4YY
Typeset in 11pt Aldine by Troubador Publishing Ltd, Leicester, UK

Matador is an imprint of Troubador Publishing Ltd

Table of Contents

PART TWO 1915–1916

PART THREE 1919

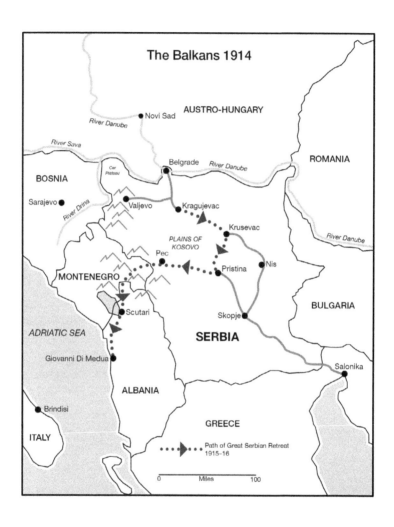

PART ONE

1914–1915

POLICE RAID THE
TWENTIETH CENTURY FURIES

The Police momentarily took the offensive in the war against the "Twentieth Century Furies", as the militant suffragettes are now called, raiding the London offices of the Women's Social and Political Union yesterday morning.

Boston Evening Transcript, Saturday May 23rd 1914

FURIES TRY TO MOLEST THE KING

Two Furies made an attempt to molest the King and Queen as their majesties were driving to an inspection yesterday morning. One threw a parcel of leaflets which fell into the Royal carriage. The women were surrounded by an angry crowd, before being arrested by the police. They will be brought up today, charged with insulting behaviour.

The Daily Mail, Monday June 29th 1914

1

London, Thursday 11th June 1914

Although she had originally agreed to take part in the mission, Dr Elspeth Stewart wasn't sure she had the courage to go through with it.

However, on the surgical ward that morning, Sylvia had told her the attack was planned for later that afternoon. Despite her misgivings, Elspeth kept her word and returned early to the terraced house in Paddington where she lodged. Sylvia had also promised to be there by three o'clock but it was almost four before she arrived, an embroidered canvas handbag slung over one arm and a pink feather boa around her neck. Elspeth led her upstairs and into the bedroom, locking the door behind her as Sylvia gently set the bag on top of the small bedside table. Elspeth saw the slight tremor in Sylvia's hands as she carefully removed a linen-wrapped bundle from the bag, loosening the fabric bindings to reveal a corrugated metal pipe, both ends crimped flat, a stub of wick jutting through the side. Then, like a priest raising the Holy Sacrament, Sylvia held the device aloft.

Elspeth's previous idea of a bomb – a caricature black cannonball with a long, fizzing fuse – had come from newspaper cartoons. But there was something almost animate about the ribbed grey shell, which seemed like the fossil of a prehistoric worm, or the chrysalis of some giant exotic moth. She took the bomb from Sylvia's hands, hefting the cool and surprisingly heavy weight in her fingers, the faint scent of iron in her nostrils, the tang of gunpowder at the back of her throat. 'It's not how I expected it to look,' Elspeth finally said.

'What did you think it would look like?' Sylvia unwound the boa from her neck and laid it on the bed.

Elspeth shrugged. 'I don't know,' she said in her soft Scottish brogue.

'It's a pipe-bomb. Vera and I made it in the workshop at her parents' farm. We found this length of old pipe and packed it with powder from her father's shotgun cartridges. Then we crimped both ends shut, *et voila*.'

'And how does Vera know how to make a bomb?' Elspeth asked as she examined the device, turning it over in her hands.

'Anya told her. She said they're easier to make and more reliable than the battery-triggered devices.' Sylvia paused. 'Anya says they're deadly.'

Deadly? Elspeth looked up quickly, but below her blonde fringe, Sylvia's green eyes were calm and steady.

'No one's going to get hurt, Ellie. What Anya means is that a bomb this size will destroy the chair, that's all.'

But Elspeth still felt a frown of worry crease her brow. Sylvia placed a reassuring hand on her shoulder.

'Ellie darling, nobody will be injured. But the Coronation Chair symbolises a King who has ignored our cause. It's almost exactly a year since Emily died under his horse, so it's right and proper the chair should be attacked, trust me.'

Elspeth looked at the bomb again. Of course she trusted Sylvia, but platitudes were not what she needed. What she needed was to understand the device: how it worked, what it was capable of. After a further period of silent scrutiny she lowered it to the bedside table, then sat on the bed and looked up at Sylvia 'The last bomb the WSPU planted, at St Paul's Cathedral, didn't explode,' she said. 'So how do you know this one will work?'

Sylvia sat next to Elspeth, rested her hands neatly in her lap, smiled patiently. 'The St Pauls bomb was more complicated, with a battery and electrical detonator that failed; our device is simpler. And just to be sure, Vera and I made two bombs and tested the other on Sunday while her parents were at church. The wick lasted thirty seconds and the explosion blew several roof tiles off her parents' piggery. Have faith, Ellie, it will work.'

'Thirty seconds…?' Elspeth narrowed her eyes. 'That's not a lot of time.'

Sylvia folded her arms across her chest. 'Well, we don't need much time.' She sighed. 'Look: if we leave too long a fuse, there's a danger someone might come into the chapel and get injured. All we need do, is be sure there's no one there, light the fuse, and casually walk out to join the other visitors. Thirty seconds later it explodes. In the meantime, we've slipped away in the confusion.' She placed a hand on Elspeth's wrist. 'Honestly, darling, everything will be fine.'

Elspeth felt the cool touch of Sylvia's fingers on the skin of her forearm. 'And it's this evening?' she asked.

'Yes. Vera suggested after evensong, just before the Abbey closes. I was meant to do a late shift at the hospital but I swapped with Sister Hughes. You're not on call, are you?'

'No.'

'Well then.'

Elspeth stared down at the device, as if staring at it might help her decide. Then she glanced at Sylvia – ward sister Sylvia Calthorpe – who had befriended Elspeth when she had first arrived at St Mary's Hospital and subsequently recruited her to the WSPU arson squad. At first the idea of placing a bomb had seemed insane and went against Elspeth's every instinct. But then she'd thought about it at length: two decades of lawful civil protest by the suffragists had failed, and nothing that the suffragettes had tried so far had made any difference.

Sometimes, instincts had to be ignored.

'All right,' Elspeth finally said. 'I'll do it.'

Sylvia's face lit up as she leant forward to give Elspeth a hug. 'It wasn't an easy decision for me either,' she said, as she pulled away. 'But I know we're doing the right thing.'

'And you're sure about Vera and Anya, that they're happy it should just be the two of us?'

'Apparently Anya was desperate to place the bomb herself. But Vera told me she overruled her. She says we'll attract less attention. You know how unconventional Anya is... the foreign accent and the dress sense.'

Yes, thought Elspeth, Anya could appear a little eccentric.

'And Vera's height makes her stand out in a crowd,' Sylvia continued. 'You and I are much less likely to be viewed with suspicion. So it's decided; it's just us.'

Elspeth – her decision made – exhaled deeply and felt her shoulders relax.

'After all,' Sylvia said, an impish look on her face, 'Who would suspect two such delicate members of the feebler sex,' – she mock-fluttered her eyelids, placing the back of one hand on her forehead, the palm of the other on her breastbone – 'of such a fiendish plot?'

'Stop larking about,' Elspeth said. Much as she loved Sylvia, at times her frivolity could be exasperating. 'This is serious, and anyway Mrs Evans might hear us.' She picked her pocket watch up from the bedside table. 'And if we're going to do this today, we need to leave right away, don't we?'

Sylvia glanced at the watch in Elspeth's hand. 'Yes, we should go,' she said, her expression now solemn as she re-wrapped the bomb and slid it back inside the bag.

Elspeth rose and crossed the room to her wardrobe. She opened it, took out her beige jacket and put it on, then reached behind her head to adjust a mother-of-pearl clasp that kept her shoulder length dark brown hair in check. There was a full-length mirror on the inside of the wardrobe door, and for a moment she studied her appearance: her eyes – the blue of water over a sandy beach – were darkly under shadowed, a sign, she recognised, of her uncertainty. She picked up her purse from the bed. Sylvia was already standing by the door, the handbag casually hooked over one arm. 'Ready?' she said to Elspeth.

Elspeth took a deep breath. 'Ready.'

★★★

They left Elspeth's lodgings – saying goodbye to Mrs Evans, her landlady on the way out – and walked the short distance to Paddington railway station. There was already a queue of travellers waiting at the taxi stand, so Elspeth hailed an empty four-wheel growler as it swung into the station forecourt.

'Westminster Abbey please, driver,' she said, climbing up to sit opposite Sylvia. The driver gave a nod and flick of the reins, and the carriage clattered over the cobbles into the late afternoon traffic.

For the first few minutes of the journey Elspeth fiddled nervously with the brass catch of her purse. Then she caught sight of a discarded copy of the *Daily Mail* under Sylvia's seat and leant forward to pick it up. The main headline was on home rule for Ireland, but on the third page she found an article on Mrs Pankhurst's WSPU – the Women's Social and Political Union – and the increasing violence of the "The Furies", as the newspapers now called the suffragettes. The article stated that because of attacks on paintings, women would only be allowed to enter London's art galleries if they had a personal letter of recommendation from a man. Elspeth lowered the paper to her lap and gently bit her lower lip: what if the authorities had decided to do this for the Abbey? Then, aware she was worrying needlessly, she scolded herself, folded the paper and pushed it aside, and leant back against the seat.

Sitting across from her, Sylvia looked elegant in a lavender skirt and jacket, the feather boa around her neck, the canvas handbag resting innocently on her lap. To the casual observer she would appear poised and composed. But Elspeth could see the slight frown of concentration that told her maybe – just maybe – Sylvia was not as carefree about their mission as she would like to appear.

The steady clop of horse hooves and gentle sway of the carriage was soothing, and as they rode past St James's Park Elspeth tipped her head back against the leather seat, shut her eyes, and allowed her mind to drift. Was this mission really worth the risk? She thought about her parents. Perhaps it was just as well that they were no longer alive; they would have been horrified that their daughter – the first woman from the Isle of Skye to qualify as a doctor at Edinburgh Medical School – was now part of an arson squad and about to plant a bomb on the Coronation Chair in Westminster Abbey. And what about Elspeth's mentor in Edinburgh, Dr Elsie Inglis, who had helped her obtain the position of assistant surgeon at St Mary's? She would be appalled if she knew what Elspeth was about to do…

'That'll be half a crown please,' said the cabbie as the carriage jolted to a halt. Elspeth opened her eyes, feeling the prickles rise on the nape of her neck as she saw the twin-steepled front of Westminster Abbey before her. Sylvia – back to her usual – was smiling confidently. 'We're here, darling,' she said to Elspeth. 'Will you settle the fare?'

Elspeth paid the driver, gazing up at the stone façade of the Abbey as she stepped down onto the pavement of Broad Sanctuary. It was an impressive view – the high towers, the carved stone, the stained-glass windows – but looming behind the Abbey roof was the daunting sight of the Houses of Parliament; Big Ben to her left and Victoria Tower to her right. She lowered her gaze, now taking in the formidable aspect of the west door of the Abbey. This, she knew, was the main entrance to the Abbey, the door through which every British monarch over the past five hundred years had passed on his or her way to the Coronation Chair.

And she and Sylvia were about to walk through that door, and plant a bomb on that very chair.

An ember of anxiety began to glow hot in Elspeth's chest. She took a deep breath to try and calm her racing mind, and then became aware of Sylvia's presence by her side. Looking down to see her friend's self-assured smile, Elspeth managed a half-smile back. She slipped a hand inside Sylvia's elbow, and together they went forwards.

As they approached the entrance, Elspeth saw with relief that no one was being stopped or searched. But once through the door and inside the nave she received a shock: good Lord – the place was heaving with people! According to Sylvia, Vera had suggested they plant the bomb half an hour before the Abbey closed, on the assumption the building would be almost empty. Yet Elspeth saw that the nave was still full of visitors, some sitting in the pews in silent contemplation or prayer, while others strolled between the giant stone support columns, gazing up at the marble statues and busts of the famous dead. The murmured hush of voices echoed from the stone walls around her, the aroma of incense and burning candles strong, as Elspeth looked up at the vaulted ceiling high above her head, feeling dwarfed by the imperiousness of it all. Could she and Sylvia really go through with this... sacrilege, this desecration? She took another deep breath as she fought the urge to turn around and walk straight out of the building, to just admit she hadn't got the courage to go through with it. But she managed to hold her nerve, concentrating only on the reassuring feel of Sylvia's arm, trying to control the growing sense of panic as she pretended she was, quite simply, just another visitor.

Her hand still hooked inside Sylvia's elbow, Elspeth walked up the centre of the nave, the stone floor beneath her feet lit by splashes of coloured light from the stained-glass windows high above. Directly ahead of her were the stalls of the choir. To her left was the marble figure of Sir Isaac Newton, and just beyond his statue, a ticket desk and entrance gate.

'There, just past Newton's monument,' Sylvia whispered, 'is where we pay to gain admission to the inner areas of the Abbey.'

Elspeth followed Sylvia past Newton's statue and up to the desk, where she purchased two visitor tickets from a pale-faced, ginger-haired verger dressed in a dark blue cassock.

'We close in half an hour,' the verger said. 'I'm afraid you've missed the last guided tour, so you'll need a guidebook if you want to know about the exhibits.'

Elspeth paid for the book and then followed Sylvia through a door-sized metal grille and along a short passageway into the central open space at the heart of the Abbey. Directly ahead of her she could see the Abbey's high altar, behind which lay an ornately carved stone screen.

'Edward the Confessor's chapel is behind that stone screen,' Sylvia whispered, 'and the Coronation Chair is inside the chapel.'

She led Elspeth across the central space, bearing left to enter another gently curved passageway. After a short walk along this passage they arrived at a short wooden staircase; eight oak steps leading up to a stone archway.

'The chapel entrance is through that archway,' Sylvia whispered, pointing up at the top of the staircase. She mounted the first step: but at that precise moment another blue-cassocked verger – a blond-haired, good-looking youth – appeared at the top of the staircase. Sylvia hesitated, then stepped back again while the youth, followed by a group of visitors, began to descend. With each footfall, the steps of the staircase let out a low moan, like the throaty croak of a bullfrog. Elspeth moved aside as the group arrived at the passage floor, the verger flashing her a smile of thanks before leading the visitors back towards the central space.

'It's much busier than I thought it would be,' Elspeth whispered to Sylvia when the group were out of earshot.

'Yes, but most of the visitors are leaving,' Sylvia replied. 'I expect it'll be empty now – come on, let's go up.'

Elspeth mounted the staircase, each step creaking loudly as she climbed. The noise was unnerving, almost as if the staircase was sending out a warning, an absurd notion she quickly dismissed. Arriving at the top of the steps, she followed Sylvia through the archway.

They were at last inside the chapel, a space bordered by the tombs of five kings and queens. In the middle of the room stood a tall, gilt-trimmed shrine, and according to the guidebook, St Edward was buried beneath it. But Elspeth wasn't interested in that fact; she was much more concerned with who else might still be in the chapel.

And with dismay, she now saw an older couple reading an inscription on the side of the shrine. She walked deeper into the room, her heart sinking further as she caught sight of a third person; an unkempt, bearded young man drawing on a sketchpad. A few more steps and the rear of the chapel – the back of the carved stone screen – came into view. And then finally, resting against the stone screen, she saw the target of her mission: The Coronation Chair.

Elspeth's first reaction to the modestly sized wooden seat was one of disappointment: the chair did not look particularly grand or regal; indeed, at first appearance it seemed rather ordinary. For it was only as she drew near that the intricate engravings and graffiti on the darkly varnished oak frame hinted at the chair's turbulent history. And resting beneath the seat was her own country's Stone of Scone, the red sandstone encaged in a metal cradle, guarded by four gilt lions—

'The English on top of the Scots, as always,' Sylvia whispered, interrupting Elspeth's train of thought. She turned to see the mischievous grin on Sylvia's face.

'Then we'll be striking a blow for Scots, as well as for women, won't we,' Elspeth whispered in reply, before turning her attention back to the chair.

Where to place the bomb? After some consideration she decided she would loop the bags' strap over one corner of the seat's high backrest, allowing it to hang down behind the chair. Then she would light the bomb inside the bag, so that the explosion would occur between the stone screen and back of the chair, reducing the risk to anyone who might inadvertently walk into the chapel. Feeling more confident with this plan in mind, she tried to act like an ordinary visitor, casually flicking through the guidebook and then wandering back to the shrine. A number of purple velvet knee-cushions were scattered around the altar's base, and with Sylvia beside her Elspeth knelt, positioned so she could see the entrance archway and chair at the same time.

Her hands clasped as if in prayer, Elspeth discreetly monitored the other occupants. The elderly couple were now standing in front of the chair. They both appeared frail: the husband – bald and stooped – reading from a guidebook, while his wife – white-haired, painfully thin – holding onto his arm, her head tilted slightly towards him. To her right Elspeth could see the young man with the goatee gazing at the top of the shrine, making deft strokes on his drawing pad with a piece of charcoal. With scruffy shoes and clothing he looked to her like an art student.

Elspeth pulled out her pocket watch; only twenty minutes before the Abbey was due to close. A sudden movement caught her attention; glancing aside she saw the older couple turn away from the chair and – arm in arm – shuffle towards the archway. A moment later Elspeth heard the creaking of wood as they descended the stairs. Good, she thought; only the art student left.

But now he moved to stand in front of the chair, and for the next few minutes remained engrossed with his drawing. Elspeth tried to stem her rising frustration. The Abbey would be closing soon; how much longer was he going to be? In exasperation she stared at the back of his head, silently willing him to leave. But her annoyance distracted her, for as she quietly cursed him, he unexpectedly turned his head in her direction and – with a smile – made eye contact. She quickly bowed her head, feigning not to have seen him, trying to pretend she was taken in prayer. But she could feel his gaze on the crown of her head, and so she allowed a full minute to pass before she dared look up again, to see him once more absorbed with his drawing. Now a wave of nausea passed through her because if he didn't go soon… well, they would have to abort the mission. And could she go through all this again? She was not sure she had the nerve.

The noise of creaking wood startled her, and looking towards the archway she saw a ginger head appear. 'Just to let you know, the Abbey closes in fifteen minutes,' said the verger who had sold them their tickets, glancing first at Sylvia, then at Elspeth, and finally the student.

'Almost finished,' the art student replied. Elspeth nodded to the verger and watched him disappear. She bowed her head again. A few minutes later she heard footsteps as the student walked away from the chair, followed by the groaning of the wooden staircase, and then finally silence.

'Thank goodness,' Sylvia whispered. 'I thought he'd never leave.'

'We need to hurry,' Elspeth replied as she rose to her feet. 'There's very little time left.'

With Sylvia close behind she hurried back through the archway, leaning over the top of the staircase and craning her neck to look back towards the Abbey's central space. The passageway below seemed empty, but because of the gentle curve she couldn't see all the way to the end. Were there still visitors further up? She looked across at Sylvia and shrugged her uncertainty.

And now a furrow of determination appeared on Sylvia's face as she unslung the feather boa and handbag – handing both to Elspeth – before lifting the hem of her skirt and skipping lightly down the stairs. Elspeth's heart began to pound as she watched her friend disappear along the passageway. Thirty long seconds later, Sylvia reappeared and hopped back up the steps.

'Can't see anybody,' she whispered, breathing heavily. 'I think it's all clear.'

'Good. Stay here and keep watch. If anyone appears, cough loudly to warn me.'

'All right, but be quick.'

Elspeth hurried back through the archway and across to the chair. She placed the guidebook and feather boa on the floor and then opened the handbag; a yellow box of Swan Vesta matches lay on top of the linen bundle. She was just about to remove the matches when Sylvia suddenly coughed, and Elspeth turned to see her friend scampering back through the archway, her green eyes wide with alarm, the familiar noise of creaking wood following her. A moment later the face of the blond verger appeared behind her.

'Ten minutes to closing,' he said to Sylvia, who smiled at him before resuming her sham fascination with the carvings on the shrine. Then he looked at Elspeth – standing paralysed with surprise beside the chair – and smiled at her. She had already taken a step forward to hide the boa and guidebook lying on the floor. Now she stood with the bag clutched to her chest and – swallowing hard – forced a smile back at him. He nodded at her and turned away. Again there was the sound of creaking wood and then silence. Sylvia turned to Elspeth, a hand held over her breastbone.

'Oh my Lord, Ellie,' she whispered. 'He must have been in one of the alcoves off the passageway.'

Elspeth – who had held her breath throughout his appearance – exhaled, her heart thumping furiously as her hands began to shake with delayed surprise.

But Sylvia had already followed the verger through

the archway. And yet another precious minute passed – allowing Elspeth's racing pulse to slow – before Sylvia reappeared.

'He's gone,' Sylvia whispered breathlessly, 'and I've thoroughly checked all the alcoves. I'm really sure it's clear now. Go on, Ellie – do it.'

Elspeth took a deep breath to compose herself again, and cleared her mind of everything except the task ahead. She opened the bag once more, removing the box of matches and unwrapping the linen bundle that lay underneath. She turned the bomb so that the wick was pointing up, then looped the handbag's leather strap over the left-hand corner of the seat's backrest, before draping the open bag down the back of the chair. One final glance at Sylvia – who swivelled her head to look through the archway before turning back and whispering, 'Still all clear,' – and Elspeth knew the moment had come.

She struck a match against the side of the box, watching it flare with a hiss, the bright phosphor flash dazzling in the gloom of the chapel. With the after-image of the flame still black on her retina she lowered the match to the oily wick.

There was no going back now.

The wick immediately took fire with a flame that leapt a good two inches in the air, and Elspeth knew instinctively that something was wrong, that this was more than expected. She sprang away from the bag, dropping the box of matches as she ran towards Sylvia, taking her friend by the hand and pulling her back through the archway.

They practically flew down the staircase to the floor below, Elspeth lifting the hem of her skirt as they dashed along the passageway, her heart hammering in her chest as they arrived at the central space, their shoes skittering on the stone floor as they came to a halt and were forced to casually saunter between the visitors still present. Every nerve in Elspeth's body seemed to scream at her to hurry, to escape, the blood pounding in her head as she fought the urge to run through the open space as fast as possible.

And it was only now she realised she had been silently counting the seconds since the wick was lit:

Ten: as they casually sauntered across the central space towards the exit grille alongside the choir.

Twelve: remembering she had left the feather boa and guidebook beside the chair – too late to worry about that now.

Fourteen: as she fought down a wave of panic when they had to stop behind a group of visitors slowly filtering through the grille back into the nave.

Eighteen: tensing with frustration at the precious seconds wasted before they began to shuffle forwards again.

Nineteen: why were they going so slowly?

Twenty: knowing that the faster-burning wick meant the bomb would explode sooner than thirty seconds.

Twenty-one: but how much sooner?

Twenty-two—

An ear-splitting crack rent the air, like thunder directly below a lightning strike.

Even though she had braced herself for the explosion, the shocking intensity of sound stunned Elspeth, weakening her knees and causing her to drop to the stone floor. A cacophony of echoes still rang about her as she lifted her head and looked back to see a cloud of dirty grey dust billowing towards her, a wobbling disc of black smoke spiralling up to the high ceiling above. Sylvia crouched beside her as the cloud of debris reached them, the noise of the blast still reverberating around the Abbey walls. Elspeth's ears were ringing as the blond-haired verger ran towards her.

'Are you all right, miss?' he shouted to Elspeth as he helped her up.

'I'm fine,' she replied, brushing dust from her skirt and shaking her head to try and clear the noise from her ears. And then, remembering to stay in character, 'What's happened?'

'It's a bomb I think,' he answered, and then hurried past her towards the smoke.

Through the dusty haze Elspeth could see other visitors slowly getting to their feet, coughing, blinking, rubbing eyes and ears. And then ahead of her she noticed the elderly couple that she had first seen in the chapel: both appeared bewildered; the frail woman's face pallid and drawn, the old man leaning against the passage wall for support. Sylvia had already gone forward to help the woman: Elspeth – now filled with a sudden, awful remorse – hurried towards the man. He looked at her with surprise as she took his arm; then smiled with gratitude as she gently led him towards the exit grille and into the nave. Glancing back she saw that Sylvia had her arms about the man's wife, supporting the frail, older woman as she slowly tottered along beside her. And now Elspeth felt truly racked with guilt, for she had only considered the physical injuries from the bomb, not the fear, nor the panic that might ensue.

Steering the man slowly down the nave, Elspeth arrived at the west entrance. To her concern she saw a crowd of visitors blocking her exit. Above their heads she could see that the door was open: why had they not left the Abbey? Stretching herself up on her toes to peer over the crowd, she saw two police constables with outstretched arms holding back the visitors. Her unease grew: how had they gotten here so quickly? Then she remembered that the Houses of Parliament were nearby and guessed that the unexpectedly loud noise of the explosion must have quickly drawn them to the scene.

Sylvia and the woman were now by her side, and leaving the old man with them, Elspeth wormed her way around the side of the crowd towards the door, keeping her body out of the policemen's line of sight.

'... No, I'm sorry, but you'll have to wait until Inspector McCarthy arrives,' one of the policemen was saying to an agitated-looking visitor trying to leave. 'Scotland Yard is only two minutes away, so he should be here shortly. Our instructions are to keep everybody in the nave. The culprits might still be inside, you see. Ah, that looks like him now.'

Another man appeared: very tall, ginger mutton-chop sideburns and moustache, dressed in a black suit and bowler hat, collar and tie. There was an imposing authority about him, thought Elspeth, leaning further back inside the doorway and straining her ears to listen.

'Right, constable, you can let them out, but I want names and addresses.' The inspector lowered his voice and spoke in hushed tones, which Elspeth could just catch. 'Keep a look out for any suspicious women. This'll be Furies again.'

Elspeth felt a knot of tension rise in her abdomen, but instantly quelled it: I must not panic, she told herself. Turning round, she saw Sylvia and the elderly couple standing behind her and motioned them to come forward. Taking the man by the elbow, she guided him through the doorway and out into the early evening daylight.

Both constables were busy taking the names and addresses of the first visitors to have left the nave; the inspector stood to one side, watching the crowd. But as soon as Elspeth came into his field of view she saw his head swivel in her direction, and a moment later he was striding towards her.

'Do you know each other?' he asked, waving a finger at her and the man.

'Yes. We were together when the bomb went off,' Elspeth said.

'That's not what I asked.'

She looked him directly in the eye, knowing that to look elsewhere would appear evasive. 'As I've just stated, inspector, I was with this gentleman and his wife,' she said, turning to indicate Sylvia and the older woman coming through the doorway behind her, 'when the explosion occurred.'

The inspector's expression did not change as he turned to the man. 'Do you know this young woman, sir?'

The man hesitated as he looked at Elspeth, then back at the inspector. 'No, but she was near us when the bomb went off.'

'So she didn't go into the Abbey with you?'

'No...' The man's eyes flicked uncertainly between Elspeth and the inspector. 'But the young lady has been of great assistance to me, sir.'

The other visitors appeared to have noticed Elspeth's interrogation by this authoritarian figure, and she could feel their curious looks just as Sylvia and the frail woman arrived alongside her.

'Is there a problem?' the older woman asked with a look of concern.

The inspector merely glanced at her before his gaze fell upon Sylvia. 'There's no problem, ma'am. However, it's more than likely this bomb was planted by suffragettes.' The implication was clear, as his eyes were now firmly fixed on Sylvia: she, in turn was staring confidently back at him.

There was a moment's stunned silence. Then: 'Suffragettes?' The old woman's shock seemed to have completely evaporated. 'Oh, inspector, these young ladies are not suffragettes!' she continued, her indignant tone clearly indicating how ridiculous the inspector's suggestion was. 'No, no, they've been of great help to my husband and I.' Still holding Sylvia's arm, she squeezed it with affection and turned to smile at her. Sylvia returned the smile and then, with a slight tilt of her head, turned back to the inspector, giving him her most coquettish of looks.

'Hm.' He rubbed his chin between his index finger and thumb. 'So you can confirm that neither of you are members of any suffragette organisations?'

'I assure you we're just visitors,' Elspeth replied, 'helping this gentleman and his wife, who were affected by the violence of the explosion. There are no signs of physical injury, but they are both shaken by the experience.'

His eyebrows narrowed as he looked at Elspeth without reply. Finding his silence unsettling, she suspected her answer might not be specific enough and so she continued.

'No, sir, we are not members of any suffragette organisation,' she said, holding his gaze as confidently as she could.

He continued to stare at Elspeth for several long seconds before replying. 'Very well. Leave your names with one of the constables before you go.' Then he turned away, his eyes already on other visitors filtering through the doorway.

Elspeth escorted the old man to the nearer of the two constables, who jotted his name and address in his notebook before asking for Elspeth's details.

'It's Agnes Smith, of three Manor Court, Ealing.' She waited for him to finish writing. 'Now, constable, this has been very distressing for this gentleman, and his wife.' She pointed at the older woman, standing beside Sylvia as they gave their addresses to the other constable. 'Could I trouble you to summon that taxi cabriolet over there, so that we can get them home?'

She nodded towards a taxi idling in Broad Sanctuary, the driver leaning out of his window as he stared at the crowds on the Abbey forecourt.

The constable looked at the man and his wife for a moment before snapping his notebook shut. 'Of course, miss.' He walked across and spoke to the cab driver; the taxi slowly motored towards Elspeth as Sylvia and the older couple arrived at her side.

'The constable has kindly arranged a taxi to take us home,' Elspeth said to Sylvia with a meaningful look as the cab stopped beside them.

'How very thoughtful of him,' Sylvia replied.

While Sylvia helped the couple into the cab, Elspeth glanced back at the crowd standing outside the west door. The inspector was still visible – his bowler-hatted profile jutting high above the crowd – but standing in front of him now she could see the blond-haired verger, the ginger-haired verger, and the art student, all of whom had seen her in the chapel just before the explosion. The knot in her abdomen reappeared as she followed Sylvia into the cab and sat beside her, immediately behind the driver in backwards facing seats. Hurriedly, Elspeth turned and tapped on the glass partition. The driver – a hollow-cheeked man wearing a thick pair of spectacles – slid the partition open.

'Yes, miss?'

'Islington Road, driver,' Elspeth instructed. 'As quick as you can, please.'

'Righty-ho, miss,' he said, blinking at her through bottle-bottom lenses, before turning forward.

The elderly couple were sitting at the rear of the cab. 'That is the address you gave, isn't it?' Elspeth said to the man.

'Yes,' he replied, 'and thank you for your kindness, miss.' He looked across at Sylvia. 'And you too, miss. There are so many newspaper reports of young women breaking shop windows and damaging property, so it's a real pleasure to come across two such helpful young ladies. Isn't it, dear?' he said, turning to his wife.

'Yes, Arthur,' she replied. 'Suffragettes indeed: how preposterous.'

'Oh it's our pleasure to help,' Sylvia replied as she leant forward to pat the old lady's knee.

Elspeth forced a smile, but glancing through the side window she saw the two vergers and the student artist in animated discussion with the inspector. Why hadn't their taxi started to move yet? She turned round again and saw the driver fiddling with the mirror above his head and she tapped on the partition to attract his attention. 'Is there a problem, driver?' she asked, as he slid the glass open.

'It's a new rear-view mirror the company have installed, miss,' he replied, 'although why they wants me to see what's behind me, when I'm driving forwards—'

'Yes, all right, just *drive* please,' Elspeth snapped, dread growing in her chest. Then she glanced back and saw the elderly couple's surprise at the sharpness of her reply. An uncomfortable silence hung in the cab as she turned once again and saw the driver looking at her, his sulky brown eyes magnified in the lenses of his glasses.

'I'm sorry,' she said, using as mollifying a tone as possible. 'I just want this gentleman and his wife home as quickly as possible. They've been quite shaken by the explosion.'

The driver mumbled under his breath before sliding the partition shut and turning forward again. Finally the taxi began to move.

But the vehicle was pointing in the wrong direction for Islington and Elspeth's frustration was almost at breaking point as the driver steered the taxi into a slow circle-turn. With an increasing sense of trepidation, Elspeth looked through the side window and saw the inspector suddenly raise his arm and wave the two constables towards him. Agonizingly slowly, it seemed to her, the taxi eventually completed its turn and began to putter sedately away from the Abbey. But now, looking back over the heads of the old man and his wife, Elspeth saw the bowler hatted profile suddenly move, and a moment later the inspector ran out of the crowd and into the road, followed an instant after that by the two constables, all three men waving their arms and – evident from their open mouths and facial expressions – shouting in fury. Elspeth half-turned and saw the driver glance up at his mirror. Immediately she rapped on the glass partition and slid it open as he swivelled his head in her direction.

'Now, driver,' she said. 'I'll give you an extra guinea if you can get us back to Islington inside ten minutes…'

2

Sarajevo, Sunday 28th June 1914. Morning

In the middle of Sarajevo, in the largely old Islamic area close to Gazi Bey's mosque, sits a two-storey redbrick and sandstone building. It is the living quarters for the army surgeons who work in Sarajevo's garrison hospital, and shortly before half past nine that Sunday morning, the main entrance door opened and a tall, slim young man dressed in a pale blue uniform stepped out onto the street.

Captain Gabriel Bayer, regimental surgeon for the Austrian 6th Army, stopped for a moment to remove his cap and run his fingers through thick black hair. He replaced the cap and adjusted it to fit, then pulled the door closed behind him and began to stride purposefully along the street, a copy of the *Boston Medical and Surgical Journal* tucked under one arm.

Gabriel glanced up at the sky. Although the day had started out wet, a dazzling sun had burst through the clouds half an hour earlier and already a gentle steam was rising from the pavement beneath his feet. He hoped this was a good omen for the day ahead, because in a few minutes the Austrian Archduke Franz Ferdinand and his wife, the Duchess Sophie, were due to begin a royal visit of Sarajevo. For the past three drizzly days the royal couple had been staying in Illidza, a spa town twelve kilometres south of Sarajevo. But now, as if on cue, the sun had come out at the very moment their train should be arriving at Sarajevo central station, where they were due to be met by General Oskar Potiorek, the Governor of Bosnia.

The streets were unusually busy for a Sunday morning, Gabriel thought, impatient at a crowd of slower-moving people on the pavement ahead who were delaying his progress. It appeared as if much of Sarajevo was going the same way as him, south towards the Appel Quay embankment on the River Miljacka, presumably to find the best vantage points to view the royal procession which was due to pass there shortly. Gabriel's impatience was due to a headache caused by an uncharacteristic excess of wine the previous evening. As a consequence, he felt an urgent need for coffee, and the lure of Schiller's café on the embankment – only a minutes walk away – was strong. But just as he was striding past a dawdling couple in front of him, he heard a call from the street behind.

'Captain Bayer!'

He turned and saw the squat figure of Lieutenant Peter Flieger, his First Surgeon, hurrying towards him. Gabriel stopped and allowed the stream of pedestrians to flow past while he waited for Flieger to arrive at his side.

'Morning, Captain,' Flieger said as he drew near,

a large grin on his owlish face, bushy eyebrows partly hidden by round, silver-rimmed spectacles.

'Morning, Peter,' replied Gabriel. 'I take it that everything went well?'

Flieger's grin broadened. 'Yes, it was quite a short labour and Maria produced a son for me just before midnight.'

Gabriel reached out to shake the young lieutenant's hand. 'Congratulations, Peter, a son at last. Mother and baby doing well I hope?'

'Yes. I've left them with the midwife.'

'Shouldn't you be at home with them?'

Flieger waved a hand dismissively. 'No, they're fine, really. I'll just get in the way and Maria's sisters are there to help look after the other children. Anyway, I'm on duty for the royal visit.'

'Still, it's the birth of a son,' Gabriel said, walking again with Flieger by his side as they turned into Franz Josef Strasse, the embankment now quite close. 'I could do your shift for you if you want. Chief Fischer wouldn't mind.'

'That's kind of you to offer, Captain, but I'm quite happy to get away from all the women fussing at home.'

Gabriel smiled: four girls and now a son, he thought. Good Lord, how on earth did Peter manage time to study? Gabriel felt a tinge of sympathy for his friend, because it seemed that Peter's wife was in a perpetual cycle of pregnancy, only interrupted by brief interludes of labour. Without a wife or family to worry about, Gabriel relished the fact that he could devote all his time to his career, and for a moment his mind drifted towards the research paper he hoped to present at the Royal College of Surgeons in London in August: a study of methods for reducing infection after surgery for bullet wounds. He had already presented the work at a meeting in Vienna, and there had been a great deal of interest from surgeons as far afield as America and England. Having already spent some time in London and New York, Gabriel was hoping the research would help him find a good job once his time in the army was over. 'Well I hope you're not too busy, Peter,' he said.

Flieger shrugged. 'I don't mind being busy. And as it's St Vitus Day, there's always the possibility of a stabbing,' he said with a grin, briefly side-slipping a lone pedestrian coming the other way, before stepping back into stride beside Gabriel. 'Anyway, why are you in uniform on your day off?'

'I'm going to the hospital to finish writing up the results of my latest experiments,' Gabriel explained, 'and I need to catch up on the latest research from America.' He pulled the journal out and showed Flieger the front cover before tucking it back under his arm. 'But first, I'm breakfasting at Schiller's.'

'So you're not going to watch the royal couple as they drive past?'

'No… well…' Gabriel paused, and then gave an enigmatic smile. 'Actually, I met them both last night.'

Flieger's eyes blinked rapidly behind the lenses of his spectacles. 'What? You *met* them?'

Gabriel smiled. 'Yes. The chief was meant to

represent the garrison hospital at a royal banquet at the Hotel Bosna in Illidza last night. But his wife was unwell, so he deputed me to go at the last minute.'

'You attended the royal banquet?

Gabriel nodded.

'You mean you actually met the Archduke?'

Gabriel nodded again, and then smiled at the look of astonishment on his friend's face. But the real truth of the matter was that his introduction to the Archduke had been curt, almost to the point of rudeness. The chief – Dr Rudolph Fischer, chief surgeon for the 16th Corp of the 6th Army – had forewarned Gabriel that Franz Ferdinand was a stiffly unfriendly individual, unlikely to pay much attention to a mere regimental surgeon, and that had indeed turned out to be the case. But the remainder of Gabriel's evening had been most interesting, largely because he had sat between General Potiorek's adjutant, Colonel Merizzi, and Colonel Harrach, one of the Archduke's personal advisors. They were both entertaining conversationalists, and all three men had drunk a considerable amount of the local Blatina wines as they talked.

His tongue loosened by alcohol, Colonel Harrach had even spoken of his fears about the following day's tour: that the visit clashed with St Vitus Day – an important Serbian national holiday – which might provoke violent protests from Serb nationalists. Harrach was also concerned that General Potiorek had placed very little security along the route: only one hundred and twenty gendarmes and no military presence of any kind.

Colonel Merizzi, however, had vigorously defended Potiorek's handling of the occasion and Gabriel had found it all most revealing, offset only by the throbbing in his head this morning, a reminder of his unusual lapse in temperance.

'Yes, I was introduced to the Archduke, albeit briefly. He has quite a commanding presence.'

'The duchess looked beautiful?'

'She did indeed, Peter – very elegant.'

'It must have been magnificent,' Flieger said, a note of envy in his voice. 'And I suppose General Potiorek must be a very happy man.'

Ah yes, Gabriel thought sourly: General Oskar Potiorek. With his close-cropped grey hair, thin moustache and intimidating dark eyes, the normally solemn-looking governor of Bosnia had appeared unusually cheerful the previous evening. He had been dressed in a pale blue tunic with three gold stars on his collar and an impressive array of medals on his chest, and Gabriel had watched as Potiorek skilfully worked the room: one minute clapping old friends on the back, the next shaking hands with others, and then cracking a joke and laughing before moving on to the next person. He was clearly very pleased, as well he might be; he had invited the Archduke to Sarajevo for this three-day visit and so far it had all gone swimmingly. On the Friday and Saturday the Archduke had observed the two corps of the 6th Army undertake military exercises in the hills outside Sarajevo. The 15th Corp had defended the northern camp whilst the 16th held the southern one.

During competitive war games like these, mishaps were fairly common, but Gabriel was only called upon to deal with a few minor injuries: several sprained ankles from the rocky terrain chosen for the exercise, one broken arm and concussion when a gun carriage overturned whilst cornering on a steep track, a nasty perforated gangrenous appendicitis, which he had personally removed; and three cases of acute urinary distress due to venereal infection. Probably gonorrhoea, Gabriel thought, as all three soldiers had visited the same brothel whilst on leave the previous weekend. But apart from these incidents the manoeuvres had gone well.

'Yes indeed, Peter. General Potiorek seemed very pleased with the visit so far… ah, here we are.'

They had arrived at Moritz Schiller's café on the corner of Franz Josef Strasse where it intersected the Appel Quay embankment. The pavements on both sides of the embankment were already lined with spectators, and the Latin Bridge, which spanned the Miljacka River, was teeming with onlookers jostling for the best positions to view the royal couple. Gabriel could only see two uniforms on the bridge; Flieger scanned the crowd for a moment, and then turned to him with a quizzical look.

'Not many gendarmes on duty.'

'At the Archduke's request,' Gabriel replied, with a twinge of concern. 'It's the duchess's first royal tour and – according to Colonel Harrach – the Archduke thinks that too large a security presence might alarm her.'

Flieger looked surprised 'I'd have thought that too

little a presence would be more alarming.' He shrugged. 'Anyway I'd better go, or I'll be late.'

'Who else is on duty with you?'

'Major Arnstein.'

'Good. Well, enjoy your shift, Peter. I'll see you tomorrow.'

Flieger nodded, turning away before hurrying west along the embankment in the direction of the garrison hospital. Gabriel watched him disappear from sight and then stood on the corner for a moment, squinting slightly into the sunlight as he studied the crowd on the bridge ahead. He had, of course, been given a full itinerary for the visit but officially he was off duty. There was to be no fuss, General Potiorek had repeatedly emphasised to him and chief Fischer at their last meeting. However, Gabriel was still uneasy at the low-key security for the visit. As Colonel Harrach had said last night, it hardly seemed adequate. What if there were protests from Serbians in the crowd? Gabriel had felt slightly ill at ease on waking that morning and now, looking at the sparse police presence, he felt even more unsettled. But was there any point in worrying? Probably not. He and the chief had followed their orders to the letter. The garrison hospital was on full alert and Flieger and Arnstein – both capable surgeons – were on duty. Anyway, his priority now was caffeine. So he turned and walked into the café, hearing the gentle pinging of an entry bell as the door swung open, and being greeted with the delicious aroma of freshly ground coffee.

The café was unusually empty and only one table

was occupied, by two older women gossiping over cake and coffee. The walls of the café – which was also a delicatessen – were lined with shelves stacked with jars of preserves and tinned food, and behind the counter at the back of the café, an older, well-built man with thin grey hair and whiskers was talking to the waitress. He was wearing a short white serving apron, arms folded across his broad chest, and at the noise of the bell he looked up and nodded a silent welcome to Gabriel. Gabriel nodded back at Moritz, the owner, then walked towards a table just inside the front window. As he pulled a chair out from under the table, the waitress – an ample-bosomed blonde girl, with high-coloured cheeks – arrived by his side.

'A large coffee, please,' Gabriel said, as he settled himself into the chair. He often breakfasted at Schiller's before work, and the waitress – he knew her name was Eva – had always been particularly attentive towards him.

'Of course, Herr Doctor,' she answered unhurriedly. Gabriel felt the closeness of her presence as she stood by his table, her hand resting lightly on the back of his chair. 'Is there anything else I can get you,' she added with a smile.

Gabriel thought he detected a languid, almost wistful tone in her voice. He shook his head, noting that she held his gaze a moment longer than necessary before turning back to the counter. He frowned. He had always found it difficult to read women, their intentions, their meanings. Then inwardly he shrugged. There were more important things in life – like keeping abreast of the latest clinical developments. And so he unfolded the journal and began to read an article on surgical ophthalmology.

But after several minutes of staring at the page and finding it unusually difficult to concentrate, he lay the journal down on the table and tried to analyse why he felt so troubled. His musings were interrupted as Eva reappeared and placed the coffee in front of him.

'Thank you,' he said to her. But she didn't immediately leave and for a moment he felt awkwardly self-conscious, as if he was expected to say something more. 'You've not many patrons here this morning,' he finally said.

'Because, Herr Doctor, they're all waiting to see the Archduke go past. After that we will be busy.' She paused. 'But we're closing after lunch…' She hesitated. '… and so I have the rest of the day off.' She looked at him expectantly.

Gabriel blinked. 'Good… good,' he finally said, noting a strange half-smile play on her lips. 'Well, enjoy your afternoon off, Eva.'

She did not reply, but the smile wavered slightly before she turned away and walked back towards the counter. Peculiar girl, thought Gabriel: but he quickly forgot about her as he lifted the cup and inhaled the intoxicating aroma of fresh coffee. He took a sip, relishing the rich flavour flowing over his tongue, and then, still holding his cup, sat back in his chair as his thoughts returned to General Oskar Potiorek.

Because there was something deeply unsettling

about the man, Gabriel reflected. He knew that Potiorek – who had been appointed governor of Bosnia only two years earlier – was an intelligent individual with a good reputation as a strategic planner; his attention to detail and hard work ethos were much admired. But many of Gabriel's fellow officers worried that Potiorek was more of a theoretical soldier, a textbook strategist, better placed to produce a detailed war plan than actually carry it out. Despite the array of ribbons and medals on Potiorek's chest, he had little combat experience.

And then there was the ghastly issue of the skull that sat on Potiorek's desk: a barbaric and disgusting trophy. Was that how a civilised and intelligent man was supposed to behave? It had been a shock for Gabriel when he had first seen the skull in the Konak, the governor's Sarajevo residence. He and the chief had been summoned to discuss the Archduke's visit, and it was the first time Gabriel had been inside the imposing redbrick mansion. Four huge ionic columns supported the front of the building, the heavy oak entrance door – approached by a flight of white marble steps – guarded by two impressive stone lions. Gabriel and the chief had been ushered into the governor's office; Potiorek was sitting behind his desk, simultaneously speed-reading and signing a stack of letters. But what really caught Gabriel's attention was the ink-stained human skull resting on the desk. The top half of the skull had been removed and the interior filled with ink; watching Potiorek dip his pen in and out of it was most unnerving, almost grotesque. 'It's the head of an anarchist,' Potiorek had joked, confirming that the skull was indeed that of the Bosnian youth who had tried to assassinate the previous governor, two years earlier. It still sent a shiver down Gabriel's spine to think that the remains of a man, even a criminal, could be desecrated in such a manner…

The pinging of the entry bell broke his reminiscing and Gabriel looked up to see a man with the upright bearing of a military officer standing in the café entrance. Dressed casually in a dark green felt-edged hunter's jacket and trousers, he had neatly trimmed grey hair and beard, and intense eyes which scanned the room before they fell upon Gabriel and broke into a smile of recognition. As chief Fischer walked towards Gabriel, he glanced towards the back of the café. 'A large coffee please,' he called across to Moritz at the counter. Gabriel had already begun to rise from his chair, but the chief waved a hand to indicate he should stay seated. 'I thought I might catch you here,' the chief said as he sat opposite Gabriel. 'Did you have an interesting evening?'

'It was fascinating, chief… but first; has Frau Fischer recovered?'

'Oh, she's fine, Gabriel – just one of her migraines. She gets terribly nauseous and they affect her vision, so I prefer to be with her when they start.'

'Well it was good of you to suggest I attend the banquet in your place.'

The chief shrugged. 'I find these formal occasions tedious if I'm honest, so I wasn't too bothered to stay away. Anyway, I knew it would be a good experience for you. A successful career in surgery isn't all about books, you know.' He glanced at the open journal on the table. 'In Austria, in any professional field, *who* you know is much more important than *what* you know if you want to get on.'

The chief had often made this point, which Gabriel knew to be true, yet felt so wrong. 'Well, thank you for the opportunity, chief.'

The older man slipped a hand inside his jacket pocket and took out a smoker's pipe. 'So, did you talk to anyone of importance?' he asked, pulling a pouch of tobacco from the other pocket.

'I sat next to Colonel Merizzi, Governor Potiorek's adjutant.'

The chief nodded, looking suitably impressed. 'Good man Merizzi.' He began to fill the pipe with tobacco.

'And Colonel Harrach, one of the Archduke's advisors.'

The chief frowned. 'Mm, can't say I've come across him before. What was he like?'

'A very interesting fellow, but quite concerned about the Archduke's safety…' Gabriel stopped talking as Eva arrived at the table.

'Thank you,' the chief said with a smile, as she placed a cup of coffee and glass of water on the table in front of him. She smiled back at him and turned away from the table, but not before throwing a quick half-glance towards Gabriel. The chief appeared to have noticed this, because as she walked back towards the counter he looked across at Gabriel and grinned.

'Pretty young thing, isn't she?'

Gabriel shrugged and the chief's grin widened. 'And she seems to like you,' he said. Gabriel felt the heat rise to his face and fidgeted in his chair; the older man gently laughed. 'You're spending far too much time with your head stuck in those journals of yours, Gabriel,' he said, teasingly.

Gabriel smiled shyly, and then lowered his eyes and drank some of his coffee. For some time now the chief had been encouraging Gabriel to 'develop his social skills', by which Gabriel understood him to mean 'find a bride'.

'And how is Dorothea?' the chief asked, almost as if he could read Gabriel's mind. Dorothea was the unmarried daughter of Georg Roth, who owned a munitions factory on the outskirts of Vienna. Gabriel was carrying out part of his research in Roth's factory, and it was here that he had first met the wealthy businessman's attractive daughter.

Gabriel paused before replying. 'Actually chief, I was going to talk to you about her—'

But at that very moment, a sudden explosion from outside the café made the windows rattle, and a gasp of surprise came from one of the women sitting at the other occupied table. Gabriel had also been startled at the sound, and in the short silence that followed the detonation he heard the rapid fluttering of wings as pigeons roosting on the roof of the café flew away. A moment later a second bang was heard, and then a third, and suddenly Gabriel realised what was happening. A startled-looking Moritz had already hurried over to the window to see what was going on, but the chief calmly pulled out his pocket watch, nodding his head as the explosions continued.

'It's all right, Moritz,' the chief said. 'It's not an anarchist attack, but the start, precisely on time, of the twenty-four-gun royal salute, from the cannons on the fortress.'

'Ach, what a fright,' Moritz replied, his hands on his hips as he looked down at Gabriel. 'It would have been nice if they had warned us they were going to fire the artillery. And on a Sunday morning as well.'

Gabriel gently laughed at the look of indignant relief on Moritz's face while the chief continued to concentrate on the cannonade. 'Twenty-two, twenty-three, twenty-four,' the older man counted aloud, and then the echoes faded away to silence. 'There you go, Moritz,' he said. 'Twenty-four royal accolades for the Archduke. That will have scared the pigeons away for a bit—'

But now another explosion – sharper, louder, than the others – split the air, and the café windows shuddered more violently than before. Gabriel – realising that something was seriously wrong – stood up from the table.

'Forgotten our maths, have we, chief?' Moritz teased. Gabriel could hear shouts and screams from outside, and the smile on Moritz's face vanished as he and the chief pushed past him, and hurried out of the café.

On the opposite side of the embankment, near the bridge, the two gendarmes Gabriel had seen earlier were struggling to wrestle a man to the ground. A smell of cordite and burning oil hung in the air, and fifty yards west along the embankment a stationary red-and-black open-top car was slewed diagonally across the road, greasy black smoke coming from the bonnet. Gabriel stepped into the road and was hurrying towards the vehicle, when he heard the high pitched revving whine of a motor engine under strain, and saw another car accelerate past the burning vehicle on a direct line towards him. To avoid being run over, Gabriel had to hop back onto the pavement just as a dark green open-top convertible sped past him. He could see General Potiorek sitting behind the grim-faced driver, while in the rear of the vehicle – wearing his distinct, green-feather-plumed ceremonial helmet – was the visibly unharmed figure of the Archduke; the duchess next to him was also uninjured. Gabriel watched the vehicle disappear from view as it travelled east towards City Hall. Then he sprinted towards the burning car.

★★★

Arriving beside the vehicle, Gabriel saw a gendarme attending a uniformed officer who lay in the road nearby. From the Prussian moustache and red-cheeked face, Gabriel recognised the officer as Colonel Merizzi, Potiorek's adjutant, the jacket of his pale blue army uniform heavily stained with blood, a deep gash running across the side of his head.

'Captain Bayer – I'm so glad you're here,' Merizzi said through gritted teeth. He looked to be in severe pain. 'Some idiot threw a grenade at the Archduke, but it missed his car and blew up under mine.' He turned his head to one side; and as he did so, Gabriel saw the colour drain from his face. 'The pain is unbearable,' Merizzi muttered, just as his eyes rolled back in his head and his eyelids closed. Gabriel quickly knelt beside him and was feeling for a pulse just as the chief arrived at his side, breathing hard from his run along the embankment.

'It is serious?' the older man asked, kneeling beside Gabriel.

'No, but he's fainted with the pain,' Gabriel said. He had noted Merizzi's steady pulse and regular breathing. 'It's a shallow shrapnel injury to the scalp, chief, but it's bled a lot. He'll live, but we need to get him to the garrison hospital as soon as possible.' He began to apply pressure to the head wound with a folded handkerchief he had found in his jacket pocket. The chief reached over Gabriel's hand and took control of the temporary pressure bandage

'You're younger than me Gabriel: I'll tend to the Colonel while you run back to the café and use Moritz's phone to call Arnstein and Flieger; get them to come down here with an ambulance.'

Gabriel nodded and quickly got to his feet.

'And tell them to bring a surgical pack,' the chief shouted as Gabriel slipped away between the gathering crowd and hurried back towards Schiller's café.

***

It took Arnstein and Flieger five minutes to drive down to the quay in an army ambulance, by which time Gabriel and the chief had ascertained that there were no other injuries to Merizzi. Two other spectators standing on the embankment pavement had also suffered minor wounds when the grenade had exploded, and, using the surgical kit, field dressings were applied to their wounds. Colonel Merizzi was given an injection of morphia to ease the pain, placed on a stretcher, and lifted into the ambulance. Gabriel had automatically assumed that he and the chief would join Arnstein and Flieger in escorting Merizzi back to the garrison hospital. But just as Gabriel was clambering up to join the chief in the back of the ambulance, the colonel finally opened his eyes.

'Is the Archduke injured?' were his first words.

'I personally saw the Archduke and duchess drive away,' the chief replied, 'and both are unharmed.'

'And Oskar... I mean General Potiorek... is he all right?'

'Also unharmed, Colonel.'

'Thank God,' Merizzi sighed.

'Don't worry,' Gabriel said, squatting beside him. 'Chief Fischer and I will accompany you to the hospital where you'll receive—'

But Merizzi levered himself up from the stretcher. 'No, please, Captain, I'm not seriously injured. I'm worried for the Archduke and General Potiorek. I have to go to City Hall to make sure they're safe.' He tried to get off the stretcher, but Gabriel gently restrained him.

'No, you're not well enough, Colonel Merizzi. You need to go to hospital—'

'Please, I beg you, Captain Bayer, let me go, or if not, please – both of you – stay with the general in case there are further assassination attempts.'

Gabriel saw the distress in Merizzi's eyes and looked up at the chief with a questioning shrug. The chief's expression was grave as he stared down at the colonel, but after a moment his face softened and he smiled.

'Of course, Colonel,' the chief said soothingly. 'Captain Bayer and I will stay close to the Archduke until he is safely back in Illidza. But you need treatment at the hospital. So please lie back and don't worry. Major Arnstein and Lieutenant Flieger will go with you.'

Relief appeared on Merizzi's face as he nodded, closed his eyes, and his head sank down onto the pillow again.

Followed by the chief, Gabriel stepped out of the ambulance, secured the rear door, and nodded at Flieger, who cranked the vehicle's starting handle, bringing the engine into life. Gabriel watched Flieger climb into the drivers' cab, and – with a spurt of exhaust – the ambulance bounced into motion and began to drive west towards the garrison hospital.

'So what do we do now?' Gabriel asked.

The chief's expression was sombre as he pulled out his pocket watch. 'The next scheduled part of the royal tour is a visit to City Hall, where the Archduke is due to be welcomed by the mayor of Sarajevo. But after this incident…' He shook his head. '…I hope they'll cancel the visit and head straight back to Illidza.' He looked east along the embankment, past Schiller's café and the Latin bridge opposite. 'I suggest we go to City Hall to find out for certain. It's only five minutes from here.'

Gabriel nodded and followed the chief back onto the pavement. They began to walk briskly back towards Schiller's, but nearing Franz Josef Strasse the chief suddenly stopped and pointed ahead. 'Wait a minute… isn't that the Archduke's car?'

They were now only thirty yards from Schiller's, and just as the chief had said, Gabriel saw a dark green convertible driving fast along the embankment road towards them. As it neared the junction with Franz Josef Strasse, Gabriel could see the green feathers of the Archduke's helmet and the duchess's white dress in the back of the car, General Potiorek sitting in front of them, just behind the driver. Standing on the silver running board outside the vehicle was an officer in a pale blue uniform; Gabriel recognised him as Colonel Harrach, the Archduke's advisor. Another car, a dark blue convertible with two men seated in the front and two women in the rear, followed behind.

'Thank goodness,' the chief said, and Gabriel saw his smile of relief as the two-car convoy approached. 'It looks as if they're heading back to Illidza.'

But as it drew level with Schiller's café and the Latin Bridge, instead of carrying straight on the embankment road towards them, the Archduke's car slowed and turned into Franz Josef Strasse. Gabriel was surprised: why on earth were they going that way? Then he saw

General Potiorek lean forward and speak to the driver: the car came to a sudden stop, on the corner directly outside Schiller's café.

'You bloody idiot,' Potiorek shouted, and even at this distance Gabriel could hear the anger in his voice. 'You should have continued straight along the Appel Quay. Hasn't anyone told you the tour is over?'

Apparently not, thought Gabriel, feeling sorry for the driver, who seemed genuinely surprised and flustered at Potiorek's tongue-lashing. Gabriel watched as the poor man tried to reverse the car into the embankment again, the dark blue convertible behind also backing up to give him space to manoeuvre.

And then everything seemed to happen in slow motion.

The entrance to Schiller's café swung open with a clatter, the entry bell clanging violently as the door slammed against the frame.

A slim young man in a scruffy dark suit rushed out of the café and ran up to the car.

The man lifted his hand and pointed a small black pistol at the car's occupants.

There was the sharp crack of two shots fired in quick succession.

A woman on the pavement nearby screamed and several bystanders rushed to overpower the man.

Potiorek was gesticulating wildly and Colonel Harrach was leaning protectively over the Archduke as the car's engine howled and the vehicle turned back into the embankment. Then with a screech of rubber it drove towards the Latin Bridge and accelerated south over the Miljacka River, followed a moment later by the second car.

Gabriel – in shock – turned to look at the chief. 'My God, do you think he hit anybody?'

The chief's eyes were wide, his face pale. 'I'm not sure… he was only a few feet away from the car.'

'Where have they gone? That's the wrong way for the hospital.'

The chief had already begun to jog towards the Latin Bridge. 'I think they must have driven to the Konak,' he shouted as Gabriel ran after him. 'I can't think where else they'd take them.'

'I'll go ahead,' Gabriel said, as he sprinted past the chief and onto the Latin bridge. He ran across to the far side, and then another fifty yards along a narrow street, before ducking left into a side alley that he knew led past the Emperor's Mosque. With the green dome and spire of the mosque behind him now, he ran through a small side street that brought him to a set of open metal entrance gates and the grounds of the Konak.

Running across the oval lawn in front of the building, Gabriel saw the dark green convertible parked askew at the bottom of the short flight of steps that led up to the Konak entrance. Nearing the vehicle he saw it was unoccupied, doors ajar, engine still running. He stopped for a moment, saw a bullet hole in the rear passenger door, green feathers scattered on the rear leather seat, bloody footprints on the silver running board outside the car. Someone had definitely been wounded. Was it Colonel Harrach, who had been standing on the running board when the shots were fired? Gabriel heard a shout and turned to see the chief jogging across the lawn towards him, the older man puffing heavily as he tried to keep pace.

'There's blood in the car,' Gabriel shouted back before striding up the white marble steps that led to the Konak entrance. And now he saw that there was more blood on the steps; glistening fat clots of it, like some strange species of slug, a macabre purple against the brilliant white of the stone.

He ran to the heavy oak door, which was ajar, and hurried inside the building. The white tiled surface of the Konak's lobby was streaked with blood and a single ladies' dress shoe lay forlornly in the middle of the floor. A staircase at the back of the lobby was also splashed with blood and Gabriel followed the trail, taking the steps three at a time.

He was breathing hard by now, and on the landing at the top of the steps he took a moment to catch his breath. But then he heard voices coming from an open door nearby, and he hurried through to find himself inside a bedroom. From the oil portrait that hung on the wall Gabriel guessed it was General Potiorek's bedroom. But it was the bed that grasped his attention, for lying on top of the bedspread, in a heavily blood-stained white silk dress, was the wife of the Archduke.

Two aides were attending her. The first, an older woman with a tear-streaked face, was leaning on her abdomen, pressing down in an attempt to staunch the flow of blood. The other aide, a younger man, was hunched over the duchess's face, his ear close to her mouth.

'I'm a surgeon,' Gabriel said as he approached the bed.

The aide lifted his head to look at Gabriel. 'Thank God you're here... I can't hear any breathing,' he said, his voice filled with panic as Gabriel reached past him to feel for the carotid artery in the duchess's neck. Gabriel tried his fingers in several different positions, but he couldn't find a pulse and when he lifted her closed eyelids he saw the already-glazed, dilated pupils. Gabriel felt strangely calm now; the shock of finding blood in the car had already passed and his surgical instincts had taken over.

'I'm afraid she's dead,' Gabriel said quietly to the young man. The woman pressing on the duchess's abdomen sat back on the bed, let out a low moan, then began to sob uncontrollably. Another aide – Gabriel hadn't noticed her at first – was kneeling on the far side of the bed and she now began to pray and weep at the same time.

The young man pointed at an archway across the room. 'The Archduke's through there,' he said. 'You must try to save him.'

Gabriel hurried through the archway and found that it led into a separate annexe, a small dressing area off the main bedroom. In the middle of the annexe was an ornately embroidered red-and-gold Ottoman couch. And lying on his back on the couch, with his eyes closed as if asleep, his hands resting on his lap, his gold-buttoned blue tunic heavily stained with blood, was the Archduke.

Standing above him was General Potiorek, his face a mask of disbelief as he looked down at the wounded man. Kneeling on the floor beside the couch was Colonel Harrach, his clean-shaven cheeks splashed with blood. Standing next to Potiorek was another of the Archduke's aides, a frantic look in the man's eyes as he waved a small pocket-knife in the air.

'I'm sorry,' Gabriel heard the aide say to Potiorek, 'but the buttons are only for decoration: the Archduke always insists on being sewn into his tunic.'

Potiorek and Harrach both looked up as Gabriel entered the annexe. 'Captain Bayer – thank God you're here,' Harrach said as Gabriel knelt beside him.

'Please, good doctor, can you save him?' Potiorek said, the pitch of his voice raised in desperation as Gabriel took hold of the Archduke's wrist. 'He must not die…'

Gabriel could feel a fast, slender pulse at the wrist bone. 'He's still alive… just,' he said, looking up at Potiorek, 'but he's lost a lot of blood.' He turned to Harrach. 'Where's he been shot?' he asked.

'In the chest, I think,' said Harrach, just as the chief appeared in the archway behind, breathing heavily.

'Good God!' the chief exclaimed.

Gabriel looked up at him. 'He's still alive but bleeding badly.'

The chief knelt beside Gabriel as they tried to find the bullet entry hole. Gabriel could see a large gash had been made across the left side of the Archduke's tunic; unsuccessful attempts by the aide to cut the jacket open, he realised. But the right side of the tunic was more blood-stained and there was a small hole in the right side of the collar…

'There,' Gabriel said, pointing to the rent in the collar.

The chief reached across and lifted the collar: and immediately a small fountain of blood gushed from a hole at the base of the Archduke's neck; Potiorek gasped at the sight. The chief quickly pushed the collar back into place: at the pressure of his hand the Archduke's eyes flickered open, then closed again.

Gabriel looked up at the aide. 'Give me the knife, quick,' he ordered. As he took the penknife he turned to Harrach. 'Get him on his side. I'll cut the jacket open at the back.'

While the chief kept his fingers on the neck wound, Harrach and the aide rolled the Archduke onto his side. A stream of blood trickled from the wounded man's mouth: his eyes opened again and his lips began to move. 'Sophie… don't die… please… for the children…' He began to cough and splutter.

'Keep him on his side,' Gabriel said, concerned the Archduke might choke on his own blood. He slit the back of the jacket from hem to collar, then watched Harrach and the aide pull the tunic off from the front. More blood spurted from the wound when the tunic was removed, only stemmed when the chief applied more pressure with his fingers.

With the Archduke positioned on his side, Gabriel leant over the body to examine the wound. He couldn't see an exit hole – only the entrance wound just above the right clavicle – but when the pressure of the chief's hand was eased, the flow of blood coming through the hole was heavy and suggested a major vessel was involved. Could it be the subclavian vein, which lies close to the lung? It would explain why the wounded man was coughing up blood. For a moment Gabriel's hopes rose; the Archduke might survive a subclavian vein wound. But when the chief removed his hand and Gabriel slipped his little finger into the gushing hole, he felt the track pass away from the lung and up towards the base of the skull. The Archduke must have been leaning backwards when the shot was fired, as the bullet had travelled upwards once it entered the neck. And that meant that either the jugular vein or carotid artery had been injured.

In a battlefield situation a wound like this would normally be considered fatal, and any attempt at surgery would almost always result in death. Gabriel knew the situation was beyond serious, almost certainly hopeless, and he looked across at the chief. He could tell by the expression on his mentor's face that he thought the same.

In any case, what more could he do? He had no surgical kit, no bandages, no instruments apart from a penknife. The aide had cut a piece of linen shirt into strips, and in desperation Gabriel used the blunt end of the penknife to stuff a piece of this ad-hoc dressing into the wound to try and reduce the blood loss. But the wound track was long – longer than the four-inch hilt of the penknife – and Gabriel suspected that the bullet was embedded deep at the back of the neck. Within a few seconds, blood was again seeping through the exit hole. More ominously, Gabriel heard the Archduke's breathing change to shorter gasps with longer pauses between each breath.

'Can't you do something more?'

Gabriel looked up to see Potiorek staring down at him, the look on the General's face one of utter desperation.

'Can't you operate, stop the bleeding?' Potiorek persisted.

Gabriel's eyes flicked towards the chief and they exchanged glances. The chief looked up at Potiorek.

'General, I'm afraid this is a fatal, untreatable wound.'

Even though the chief's words only confirmed what Gabriel knew to be the truth, hearing them filled him with dismay. It was always horrible when – in spite of your best efforts – a patient died under your care. But this, Gabriel thought, was different. The second most important man in the Austro-Hungarian Empire was going to perish right in front of him and there was nothing more he could do. He tried to suppress his rising anger. Why were they here at the Konak? Why hadn't they driven to the hospital? He heard the Archduke mumble a few indistinct words, and then there was one final, drawn-out, sighing exhalation – almost a farewell: then silence.

The chief felt for the carotid pulse on the other side

of the neck, then looked across at Gabriel and shook his head. Gabriel knew it was over and sat back on his haunches, the desolate feeling of losing a patient already beginning to well up inside of him.

And now – just as he was about to stand – a hand grasped the collar of his jacket and Gabriel felt himself being pulled backwards. He turned his head and found he was eye-to-eye with General Potiorek who was staring down at him, flecks of spittle at the corners of his mouth, lines of tension radiating across his cheeks as he gripped the back of Gabriel's jacket. 'For God's sake,' Potiorek said, 'there must be something more you can do?'

Gabriel was at first stunned, then angry at being manhandled. But before he could react, he heard the chief's reprimanding tone – 'Herr General!' – and saw Potiorek turn towards him. 'There is nothing that God or any man can do,' the chief continued.

Potiorek seemed to come to his senses and released his grip. Gabriel pulled away, shrugging his jacket back into place as he stood up and stepped away from the couch. Colonel Harrach – standing beside him – looked embarrassed at Potiorek's outburst.

'The Archduke is dead, Herr General,' the chief reiterated. 'It's over.'

For several seconds Potiorek stood motionless. Then his head dropped onto his chest, his shoulders slumped, his body swayed, and for a moment Gabriel thought he was about to collapse. But then he reached out to grasp the side of the chaise longue, steadied himself, and slowly sat down on the edge of the couch, by the dead man's feet.

The room was completely silent, broken only by the sound of sobbing coming through the archway. Gabriel walked back through into the bedroom, where the body of the duchess still lay on the bed, her aides weeping beside her. He felt numb as he stood mindlessly watching this pitiful tableau. Then another hand touched his collar – softer this time – and when he turned, the chief was standing beside him.

'You did your best, Gabriel,' the chief said, mopping his brow with a handkerchief.

The words of kindness should have consoled him, but strangely Gabriel had felt better being angry. He watched the chief walk back into the annexe to speak to Harrach, Potiorek still sitting on the end of the bloodstained chaise longue, his elbows on his knees, his head in his hands. Gabriel turned to look at the sunlight streaming through the bedroom window and for a moment felt lightheaded. Then he remembered he hadn't eaten anything, hadn't had his breakfast yet. He walked forwards and leant on the windowsill. Through the glass he saw an army ambulance speeding through the entrance gate to the Konak and pull up beside the Archduke's convertible. The top of Flieger's head appeared as he jumped out from the driver's cab and, accompanied by Major Arnstein, he ran up the steps to the Konak's entrance. Too late, thought Gabriel as he lifted his gaze to look at the cypress trees at the edge of the compound. A sapphire-blue sky heralded the prospect of a beautiful summer day, and a flight of swallows swooped into view, darting and diving between the trees. Gabriel slipped a hand inside the pocket of his bloodstained jacket, pulled out his pocket-watch, and flipped open the lid with his thumb: it was only eleven-fifteen in the morning.

3

Summer had finally arrived in London and Elspeth had the warmth of the sun on her back as she walked beside the Serpentine in Hyde Park. She was due to meet the rest of her arson squad later that afternoon, but as Sylvia was on duty in the hospital that morning, Elspeth had decided to take a stroll in the park on her own first.

The previous Sunday a group of suffragettes had held a meeting near the Serpentine. Elspeth and Sylvia had gone to watch the event, which the suffragettes had called a 'Water Carnival' as they were banned from holding demonstrations in the park. In fancy dress as dominoes, the women had paraded around the lake, each wearing a letter on her chest that spelt out the word 'suffragettes'. The parks' office of works had expected this protest and had lashed the boats together in mid-water to prevent their use. But the women had flung off their wraps to reveal bathing costumes and then swum out to the craft to cut them free. Elspeth and Sylvia had gleefully watched all of this unfold from a distance – a sensible precaution, it turned out, because the police soon arrived to arrest the women and take them, dripping wet, to Paddington Green police station.

On this Sunday afternoon, however, there were no suffragette activities taking place and, after a stroll round the Serpentine and an ice cream in the park café, Elspeth decided to return to her lodgings. Sylvia would have finished her shift by now, and Vera and Anya – who had spent the weekend at Vera's parents' farm in Oxfordshire – should be arriving back at Paddington station shortly.

As she walked home, Elspeth thought about the past two weeks. The day after the Abbey bombing, she and Sylvia had gone back to St Mary's Hospital and carried on with their work as if nothing had happened. Sylvia was euphoric over their success but Elspeth had mixed feelings: a sense of pride she had struck a blow for women's emancipation, but also unease about the violence of their method, the distress it had caused the older couple, and the consequences if they had been caught. It had been a close-run thing: if she had not been successful in diverting the cab driver's attention from his rear-view mirror… Well it was just too awful to contemplate.

The day following the event *The Times* and the *Morning Post* had articles about the 'suffragette bombing outrage' stating that a feather boa and guidebook had been found at the scene and that although the Coronation Chair had been badly damaged, it was repairable. Other newspapers specified that two women had been questioned leaving the Abbey, but no suspects had yet been identified. She knew she should feel pleased, but Elspeth could not shake off a nagging sense that they had been fortunate to get away with it.

Then, two days ago, Sylvia had taken Elspeth into the ward sister's office. 'Vera wants to meet to discuss further attacks,' she whispered. 'And Anya has some interesting ideas as targets. Can we meet on Sunday afternoon? Vera is taking Anya up to her parents' farm for the weekend, but they'll be back by mid-afternoon. And guess what: Vera says that the Pankhursts have sent us personal congratulations. Isn't it fabulous, Ellie? We're famous!'

Although reluctant to discuss another attack, Elspeth had agreed to the meeting. But walking back from the park she found herself dreading it. She had always supported the suffrage cause, and it was her frustration with the lack of progress of the suffragists that had pushed her to join the arson campaign. But was it worth the risk to the most important thing in her life – something she had wanted for as long as she could remember – her vocation as a doctor? She had worked hard at her career, harder than the men around her, for as a woman, it was not easy to get the best training and experience. And Elspeth had chosen surgery, one of the more demanding branches of medicine. However, the years of hard work had paid off and she was making good progress in her chosen profession, honing her surgical skills in a prestigious London teaching hospital. Now she was jeopardising all of it with the arson strategy. Surely there must be some other, less destructive way to advance the suffrage cause?

As she turned into the quiet side street and walked

towards her lodgings, Elspeth was surprised to see Mrs Evans on her knees, scrubbing the doorstep with a two-handled brush, a bucket next to her filled with milky-looking water. Elspeth's landlady was a plump, kind-faced woman with small eyes that vanished into the folds of her face whenever she smiled.

'Cleaning the doorstep on a Sunday, Mrs Evans?' Elspeth asked. 'You dear woman, don't you ever have a day off?'

Mrs Evans stopped her scrubbing, sat back on her haunches, then wiped a trickle of sweat from her brow with the back of a forearm. It had always been obvious to Elspeth that Mrs Evans loved having her as a lodger, probably because she was the first female doctor ever to board with her. She smiled up at Elspeth.

'I dropped a bottle of milk on the step just after you went out, Dr Stewart, and if I don't clean it up now it'll be stinking to high heaven by this evening.'

'Och well, just be careful. Don't overdo it in this heat.'

'I'm almost finished. By the way, you have a couple of visitors: Sister Calthorpe and one other lady I don't rightly know.'

One other lady? That was odd, thought Elspeth: Vera and Anya should have arrived together.

'I let them both up to your rooms,' Mrs Evans continued. 'Sister Calthorpe said you wouldn't mind?'

'No, of course not.' Elspeth glanced up at her open bedroom window and caught a glimpse of a rosy-cheeked face surrounded by curly brown hair. 'And that'll be Vera,

Mrs Evans. She a friend of Sister Calthorpe's and mine. There'll probably be another lady joining us shortly.'

Mrs Evans shuffled to one side and Elspeth stepped past her into the cool, dark interior of the hallway, into a lingering smell of floor polish and boiled cabbage. As Elspeth reached the bottom of the stairs, Mrs Evans called up after her.

'I could do some iced lemonade for you ladies, if you'd like?'

'That's very kind, but there's no need to go to any trouble,' Elspeth called back as she began to climb the steps. She reached the top of the landing, then walked towards her bedroom door and turned the handle.

'Ah, the wanderer returns,' Sylvia said as Elspeth entered the room. She was sitting on the edge of the bed and had changed out of her nursing uniform into a white summer blouse and red skirt.

'Hullo, Ellie,' said Vera, standing by the open window, as if she had been looking out for something, or someone. Her hair was – as usual – uncombed, but her tall figure looked unusually smart in a matching grey traveller's jacket and skirt. 'We wondered where you'd got to.'

'Just enjoying the sunshine in Hyde Park, Vee.'

Sylvia had already risen, and now gave Elspeth a hug of greeting. 'And anything of interest taking place today?' she asked.

'Nothing,' Elspeth said as she returned the hug. 'No water carnivals, no demonstrations, nothing like last Sunday,' she said sweetly, and Sylvia laughed in response. They pulled apart and Elspeth turned to face Vera.

It was the first time they had met since the Abbey bombing. But there was no mistaking the pride on Vera's face as she came forwards and placed her hands on Elspeth's shoulders, then leant forward to kiss her on both cheeks, almost, Elspeth thought, as if she was some Amazonian warrior princess returning from battle. For a moment Elspeth felt awkwardly self-conscious at this display of melodrama, but then could not help grinning as Vera encircled her in her arms and lifted her off the floor, spinning her around in a hug.

'Very well done, Ellie,' Vera said, and Elspeth laughed at the sheer spontaneity of Vera's embrace. Lowered to the floor again, Elspeth smoothed her ruffled skirt, then sat back on the edge of the bed and looked up at her two comrades.

She had always been intrigued about Sylvia and Vera's relationship because – on the face of it – they seemed such polar opposites.

Lady Sylvia Calthorpe was the epitome of elegance and good breeding. Having initially come out as an Honourable, her wealthy family were aghast when she had announced that she'd been inspired by Florence Nightingale to devote herself to a career in nursing. Currently the sister on the female surgical ward at St Mary's Hospital, the blonde, green-eyed beauty was a magnet for many of the younger doctors. But they vied for her charms without success, because Sylvia just didn't seem interested in any of them, using her professional manner and wit to disarm them with ease. Most of the beautiful women that Elspeth knew relied solely on their looks to succeed in life. But Sylvia had also been blessed with intelligence and a lightness of spirit that had soon caught Elspeth's attention. They had quickly become firm friends and Sylvia was now Elspeth's closest companion.

Vera, however, was big-boned and well fleshed, and a good head taller than Sylvia. With her square face, red cheeks, and wavy dark brown hair cut boyishly short, she looked every inch the farmer's daughter she was. 'There's nobody more loyal,' Sylvia had said of Vera, before introducing her to Elspeth at a WSPU meeting. 'And she's very practical-minded.'

Vera did indeed seem very down-to-earth, thought Elspeth, who had not been surprised to learn that she was the leader of an arson squad. However Elspeth had been most surprised when Sylvia told her that she was also a member of the squad, and then had invited Elspeth to join them as well.

As if she knew Elspeth was thinking about her, Sylvia now came and sat on the bed next to her. Vera stood on a Turkish rug in the middle of the bedroom, smiling down at them both.

'Well done, girls,' she said. 'The Pankhursts are thrilled at your achievement. I saw Emmeline in Holloway yesterday and she sends her personal greetings, while Christabel has sent a letter of congratulations from Paris. All the sisters are proud of what you did.'

Elspeth felt Sylvia's arm slip inside the crook of her elbow and turned to see the smile of satisfaction on her friend's face. Then she looked back at Vera and gave a shy grin.

'Well it was your and Anya's bomb that did it, Vee, even though it nearly blew us up.'

Vera laughed. 'Well, next time we'll use a longer fuse.'

Elspeth swallowed and her grin disappeared. 'Yes. Well. Anyway where's Anya?' she asked, quickly changing the subject.

Vera's smile faded. 'Oh…' She hesitated. 'She should be here in a minute.' She turned away from Elspeth and walked back to the open window to peer into the street below.

'But I thought you both took the train back from Oxford?'

'We did,' Vera said, still looking out of the window. 'But…'

'But what?'

Vera sighed; then pulled her head back into the room and looked at Elspeth. There was a strange expression on her face. 'Well…' she hesitated as she glanced at Sylvia and then back at Elspeth again. 'Anya thinks…' she hesitated again '… Anya thinks our squad is being followed.'

For a moment Elspeth felt nothing. And then her eyes widened as a queasy sensation rose in her belly. She quickly pulled away from Sylvia and stood up from the bed, but Vera was already by her side, palms up in reassurance.

'No, don't worry, Ellie. I'm sure she's mistaken. Sylvie and I haven't seen anything to concern us.'

'But who does Anya think might be following us?' Elspeth demanded.

'Well…' Vera grimaced, then ran her fingers through her tousled hair, '… she's mentioned several possible groups.'

'Several?' Elspeth felt bile rise into the back of her throat. 'Like who?

'Well…' Another grimace, another beat of hesitation. 'Special Branch, for one.'

The words Elspeth did not want to hear: her mouth felt as dry as sandpaper as she tried to find saliva and swallow. 'Who else?' she said, her voice a croaky whisper.

'The Austrian secret service.'

'*Austrian?*' Elspeth shook her head in confusion. 'What?… Why…?'

'Anya hasn't said why. But I think it's something to do with a relative who fell into trouble with the police over there—'

'But Anya's not Austrian… is she?' Elspeth interrupted. 'I thought she was originally from Poland or somewhere else in Eastern Europe. Is that not the case?'

Vera stepped forward and placed her hands on Elspeth's shoulders again. 'Look, Ellie,' she said reassuringly. 'It really doesn't matter where Anya's from. All that matters is that I'm certain we're not being followed.' She looked across at Sylvia for support.

'Vera's absolutely right,' Sylvia said. 'I haven't seen a thing.'

'So you're both certain we're not being followed,' Elspeth said. 'By Special Branch, or Austrian secret police, or anybody else for that matter.'

Both nodded their heads.

'But you say that Anya thinks we are. So what exactly are you implying, Vera? That she's imagining it? That she's delusional?'

Vera sighed. 'I think so. The trouble is, Anya's always been a little paranoid, Ellie. Which I think comes from her being an émigré, you know, seeking asylum—'

'And from which country,' Elspeth interrupted, 'is Anya seeking asylum?'

Vera shrugged. 'I don't know. She's always been vague about that. One of the Slavic states within the Austro-Hungarian Empire, I think.'

'But you don't know which one?'

Vera shook her head. 'I've asked her, of course, but she says she'd rather not say; that the less people know about her, the better.'

'So what *do* you know about her?' Elspeth said, unable to hide the irritation in her voice.

Vera stiffened. 'Well I only met her last year, when she joined the WSPU. Where she came from didn't seem to matter then. What was important was her commitment to the suffrage cause and of that there's no doubt. She knows lots of useful things, Ellie, like how to make a pipe bomb—'

'And where is she now?'

Vera looked awkward. 'When we arrived at Paddington half an hour ago, she told me she'd stay behind to watch if anybody might be following us. I imagine she's down on the street, watching the door as we speak.'

Elspeth strode to the window and strained to see as

far up and down the street as she could and then pulled her head back into the room. 'Well, I can't see her,' she said irritably. Is there anything else about Anya you haven't told me?'

'I've not been keeping anything back, Ellie,' Vera protested. 'I just didn't think it was important to tell you every last detail about her—'

'Now look here, Vera,' Elspeth interrupted. 'Sylvie and I planted a bomb. Innocent people could have been injured or worse. This is important. I need to know exactly who the members of our squad really are.'

Vera sighed. 'Look, I know that Anya entered Britain two years ago on asylum and for a while lived in a flat with a group of WSPU supporters, one of whom was called Grace. Anya and Grace developed a close friendship and become involved with the arson campaign – breaking shop windows, pouring petrol through letter boxes – that sort of thing. Then a year ago they were caught smashing the windows of a jewellers in Mayfair and were being held by the owner and his staff until the police arrived. Grace knew that if Anya was arrested she would be deported. So she threw herself at the owner to create a distraction that allowed Anya to escape before the police arrived. So only Grace was arrested and she was tried and convicted, then sent to prison.'

'Holloway?'

'Yes. She went on hunger strike and was force-fed, but there must have been a problem, because some of the feed went into her lungs and she caught pneumonia and died.'

The death of a close friend, Elspeth thought. That could certainly unhinge a person. Might even bring on delusional thoughts that they were being followed…

'Apparently for a while Anya was inconsolable,' Vera continued. 'I think she loved Grace very dearly. Anyway, a while after that I was asked by Christabel to form an arson squad and with Anya's previous experience she was an obvious choice. Then I asked Sylvie to join, and she of course recommended you and—'

Thump, thump, thump: the sound of the front door knocker. Vera stepped past Elspeth, looked out of the window, and waved at somebody below. When she pulled her head back into the room, there was a smile of relief on her face.

'It's Anya.'

'I'll let her in,' Elspeth said. She opened her bedroom door and hurried down the stairs. Arriving at the bottom, she saw Mrs Evans coming out of the scullery at the back of the house, wiping her hands on a kitchen cloth.

'Oh, it's all right, Mrs Evans. It's the other friend I mentioned.'

'You sure you ladies don't want some refreshments?'

'No, really, we're fine, thank you, Mrs Evans,' Elspeth replied.

Mrs Evans smiled and went back into the scullery while Elspeth went to open the front door.

With high cheekbones and a helmet of short, shiny hair, black as the wing of a raven, Anya regarded Elspeth with large brown eyes and a serious look on her angular face. A tall, wiry figure, she was dressed in a black skirt and off-white blouse, and carried a battered black suitcase in one hand. Perched on her head was a flat, red beret. She looked up and down the street for a moment, and then stepped over the threshold.

'Ellie,' she said in a deeply resonant Slavic accent. She kissed Elspeth on both cheeks and then stood back. 'How are you?' Before Elspeth could reply, Anya leant forwards and whispered in her ear. 'You did good job in Abbey.' She pulled away, gave Elspeth a wink, and then without waiting to be invited walked quickly past her and onto the stairs. Elspeth sighed and shook her head, then closed the front door and followed Anya upstairs.

When Elspeth re-entered her bedroom, Anya was already standing at the open window, gazing down at the street below, an awkward-looking Vera by her side. As Elspeth closed the door she glanced across at Sylvia, still sitting on the edge of her bed: she also looked uncomfortable with Anya's behaviour. After a moment Anya drew back from the window and walked across to Elspeth, putting a hand on her shoulder and giving it a friendly squeeze. Her grip – for someone so slender – was surprisingly strong.

'You did very good job, Ellie. Next time, we make bigger bomb, attack bigger target. Maybe Tower of London. Maybe Royal Albert Hall. What do you think?'

Elspeth brushed Anya's arm – and question – aside.

'What's this about being followed?'

Anya's eyes narrowed. Then she looked at Vera and back at Elspeth again.

'Vera told you?'

Elspeth nodded, her eyes not leaving Anya's face.

'Do not worry, Ellie,' Anya replied with a reassuring smile. She reached across to caress the side of Elspeth's face. 'I check carefully and I see no watchers. In my country secret police follows people. In your country Special Branch follows people. We must always be on look out.'

'What have you done that your secret police should want to follow you?'

'I have done nothing.' The smile faded. 'But my cousin Bogdan...' She sighed. 'He was only a boy, but very brave. He died for my country. Then secret police arrest and interrogate all our family and friends. I fled to Paris before they seized me. And then I crossed to Great Britain. This country is a good friend to people in trouble.'

'And what did your cousin do, to bring you so much trouble?'

'He tried to free my country.'

'And which is your country?'

For a moment a distant look appeared on Anya's face, as if she was picturing her homeland in her mind's eye. Then she lifted her chin and smiled, placing her hand on Elspeth's shoulder once more.

'I have said too much already, Ellie. But I have looked carefully and there is nobody watching us—'

'You're sure,' Sylvia interrupted from the bed, 'that nobody is following us?'

'Yes, I am sure.'

'Well, thank goodness for that,' Sylvia said as she

stood and went across to Elspeth and Anya, putting an arm around a shoulder of each. 'Now let that be an end of the subject. We've much more important matters to discuss – like what the next target should be.'

But Elspeth was exhausted from the strain of the discussion. There was a throbbing in the side of her head and Sylvia's arm did not comfort her, so she slipped out from underneath it. Sylvia appeared surprised but then her expression changed to one of concern.

'Ellie darling, are you all right?'

But Elspeth didn't answer. Her previous misgivings about the bombing campaign had been amplified by the discussion with Anya. This didn't feel right…

'You're not having doubts, Ellie, are you?' Vera said, and Elspeth saw the look of concern on her face.

'I just think we should take things more slowly,' Elspeth replied. 'That inspector almost caught us—'

'Oh, Ellie darling,' Sylvia said, an almost patronisingly confident smile on her face. 'We got clean away with it.'

'We were lucky, Sylvie,' Elspeth replied, 'and our luck may run out. Emmeline's in Holloway and Christabel's fled to France otherwise she'd be in Holloway, too. We all need to be careful.'

'But we can't stop now, Ellie,' Sylvia said. 'If we plant further bombs, the government will simply *have* to take notice of us.'

'I'm not sure about this strategy, Sylvie—'

'Look, there's going to be a WSPU meeting at Holland Park skating rink in two weeks,' Vera interrupted. 'The rumour is that Emmeline will time her release from

Holloway to attend the meeting. She's been on hunger strike for a while now, so they'll have to let her out soon. We all need to be there to show her our support.'

'I'm on duty that evening —'

'Oh, Ellie,' Sylvia interjected. 'You've done more than your share for those lazy house surgeons. Don't you worry. I'll charm one of them into covering for you—'

A floorboard in the corridor outside the room creaked, and Sylvia fell silent as all four women swivelled their heads towards the door. After a moment's silence they heard a hesitant tapping. Sylvia looked at Elspeth with wide, inquiring eyes, but Elspeth shrugged and then walked to the door and opened it to find Mrs Evans standing there.

'I know you said not to bother, Dr Stewart,' she said, holding a tray of glasses and a jug of lemonade before her, 'but it really is no trouble and I thought you ladies might be in need of something refreshing on such a hot afternoon.'

Elspeth forced a smile to her face. 'That's very sweet of you, Mrs Evans, but you really needn't have troubled—'

'Oh it's no trouble, darling, and I know how hard you doctors and nurses work. Sister Calthorpe was on duty this morning, she was saying, so it's the least I can do.'

Elspeth knew it would appear churlish to rebuff the offer and Sylvia must have thought the same, for she stepped past Elspeth to take the tray from Mrs Evans with a smile of thanks and an invitation to join them.

Elspeth took the jug – damp with condensation – and while Sylvia introduced Mrs Evans to Vera and Anya, she poured lemonade into the glasses. As the four women drank and Mrs Evans chatted to the other three, Elspeth thought about the forthcoming WSPU meeting. It wasn't as if they were going to plant another bomb, and at least it meant she had agreed to do something positive for the squad. Maybe it was a good idea to go?

4

Sarajevo, Sunday 28ᵗʰ June 1914. Evening

After the royal couple were pronounced dead, a Jesuit priest was called to administer the last rites. Gabriel had intended to stay at the Konak and assist the chief with the Archduke's autopsy. But news of the assassination spread quickly: street fights broke out as Hapsburg-friendly Bosnians began attacking Serbian shops and businesses, and Gabriel was summoned back to the garrison hospital to help Arnstein and Flieger with several stabbings. He was kept busy in the operating theatre for the rest of the day, and it was only much later that evening, having finished his last operation, that Gabriel finally found time to go to the doctor's mess for a late supper.

The room was empty as Gabriel walked up to an oak cabinet set against one wall and opened one of the side compartments. He was famished – he hadn't eaten all day – and he eagerly helped himself to a portion of bread and ham from the food locker inside the compartment. Then, with a large glass of red wine taken from a crystal decanter sitting on top of the cabinet, Gabriel went to sit in one of the wing-backed leather armchairs set in front of the room's bay window.

He quickly finished his meal. And he was quietly sipping his wine, when the mess door swung open and the chief strode into the room.

'Stay seated, Gabriel,' the chief called across as he walked over to the cabinet. 'I'll come and join you, but I need a drink first.'

He poured himself some wine, and then came across and flopped into the armchair beside Gabriel. He swallowed a mouthful of wine, then looked across at Gabriel and shook his head. 'What a damned fiasco,' he said.

It was rare for the chief to use profanity and Gabriel smiled as the older man continued. 'You don't know the half of it. A catalogue of mistakes *and* bad luck.'

'How do you mean?'

'Colonel Harrach is furious and holds General Potiorek personally responsible for this catastrophe.'

'Why?'

'Apparently, even after the grenade was thrown at the convoy, Potiorek carried on with the day's schedule as if nothing had happened. They went to City Hall, where the Mayor was meant to be giving a speech of welcome. But the Archduke was clearly upset after the attack and stated that the visit was over.'

'So why didn't they go straight back to Illidza?'

'Because Potiorek suggested the Archduke might want to visit the garrison hospital to see Colonel Merizzi. Colonel Harrach opposed this detour, but Potiorek was very keen and gave assurances it would be safe.'

'I see.' Gabriel puckered his brow. 'Well, after the

grenade attack, the possibility of other assassins in the crowd must have been obvious. With so few gendarmes on duty, getting the Archduke to a place of safety should have been the priority.'

'Exactly what Colonel Harrach said, but he was overruled by Potiorek. And then to make matters worse, their car took a wrong turning; the driver had not been told about the change of plan. As they turned into the wrong street, Potiorek realised the error and brought the car to a stop right outside Schiller's café.'

'And do we know how the assassin came to be inside Schiller's?'

'Plain bad luck,' the chief said before taking another sip of wine. 'Apparently, a few minutes after we ran out to help Merizzi, a depressed-looking man came into the café, and sat down at the very table we had just left. Moritz remembered he looked very out of place: furtive-looking, scruffy. So this man orders a coffee and sits there for twenty minutes, looking gloomy, and then outside the café a car comes to a stop. Moritz is curious to see what's happening, so he goes across to the window and sees it's the Archduke's car. Then this fellow leaps up from the table, barges past Moritz and runs out into the street. He pulls a pistol out of his coat pocket and… well, the rest of the story you already know.'

'Unbelievable,' Gabriel said, shaking his head. 'I almost feel sorry for Potiorek. He'll have to live with this for the rest of his life.'

'Well that's quite generous, Gabriel, considering what he did to you after the Archduke died.'

Gabriel flinched at the memory of Potiorek hauling on his collar. Then his face softened and he smiled.

'It's not the first time I've been assaulted by a distraught friend or relative of a patient of mine. That, I don't take personally. But I *am* angry that Potiorek took them to the Konak instead of the garrison hospital. Not that it would have made much difference, I suppose, but what was he thinking?'

'Colonel Harrach said that Potiorek panicked after the shooting. I suspect he was in shock, just not thinking straight.'

'Bad decisions all round,' Gabriel said. 'Not what you would expect from a good leader. Well, I suppose that's his career finished.'

The chief stroked his beard. 'It certainly doesn't look good for Potiorek: he invited the Archduke on St Vitus Day, the worst possible time; he was responsible for the inadequate security; he gave assurances for the Archduke's safety on the return trip to the hospital. There will be a court of inquiry of course but I suspect he'll resign or be dismissed as Governor. It'll be an ignominious end to his career.'

'And what about the assassin? Anything known about him yet?'

'A Bosnian youth by the name of Gavrilo Princip, apparently. According to Colonel Harrach, Princip's a member of Young Bosnia, an organisation dedicated to the creation of a Greater Serbian state. Harrach is certain that Serbian Nationalists are behind this.'

Gabriel frowned. 'Wasn't the youth who tried to

assassinate Potiorek's predecessor a member of Young Bosnia?'

'Yes. Some chap by the name of Zerajic, but he didn't do as well as Princip; it's his skull you saw gracing Potiorek's desk.'

Gabriel grimaced. 'Don't remind me – it was nauseating, like some gory trophy. I'm surprised at General Potiorek. What kind of man would do a thing like that?'

'You don't get to the top without being ruthless, Gabriel.' He paused. 'Anyway, you don't need much imagination to know what will happen next.'

'We're going to war, aren't we?'

'Yes,' said the older man, and Gabriel felt a flicker of anticipation. This was, after all, something he had been training for all these years: an opportunity to put to good use the skills he had so painstakingly acquired. 'I'm certain,' continued the chief, 'that Vienna will use the assassination as justification for sorting the Serbs out, once and for all. Ever since we annexed Bosnia, the Serbs have been nothing but trouble. And as our 6th Army is closest to Serbia, you can be sure we will be in the thick of it.'

'But we should easily defeat the Serbs, shouldn't we chief? After all, we have twice as many soldiers as they have.'

'Unless Russia gets involved. If they come to Serbia's aid, we'll have to divide our forces.'

'But if Russia supports Serbia, won't Germany come to our aid—'

'—which would bring Britain and France into the war,' the chief said. 'Don't forget; they're also Russia's allies. So you can see how delicate the situation is.'

Gabriel fell quiet. A war between Austria and Serbia had always been on the cards. But the idea of Russia and Germany – perhaps even Britain and France – becoming involved, seemed almost too much to take in. Gabriel's parents hadn't the money to send him to medical school, so the only way he had been able to train as a surgeon was to accept a military scholarship which had stipulated that he must serve a term of ten years in the army medical services. Gabriel had always been aware he might have to go to war some day and wasn't daunted by that possibility: indeed, he felt ready to deal with whatever a war might throw at him. But a war that might involve most of Europe…

'Well,' the chief said, interrupting Gabriel's chain of thought, 'it looks as though you will soon be given an opportunity to continue your wound research in men, rather than pigs.'

For a moment Gabriel was taken aback, but then he grinned at the older man's black humour. 'Mind you, chief, the way some of our men behave…'

Chief Fischer laughed. 'How is the research going, anyway?'

'Quite well, I think. The studies on pig cadavers are almost finished and I should have the results ready for the London surgical conference this August. Herr Roth has been most generous in allowing me to use the ballistics laboratory at his factory for the tests—'

'Which brings me back to the question I asked you this morning,' the chief interjected, 'which you were saved from answering by the terrorists grenade: how are you and Dorothea getting on?'

Gabriel smiled ruefully as he realised the older man had deliberately steered the conversation back to that question. He had first met Dorothea Roth a few months ago, whilst doing research on the wounding effects of different bullet shapes. The chief was a long-standing friend of Georg Roth, and after being introduced to Gabriel, Herr Roth had agreed to provide him with a supply of bullets and cartridges as well as the use of his factory's extensive ballistic testing facility. Over the past year Gabriel had often travelled to the factory to carry out his research and had frequently met Dorothea.

'Last time I saw her she was very well. Why do you ask?'

The chief placed the empty wine glass on the floor by his chair. 'Well, Gabriel, Dorothea's a lovely young woman – she'll make a good wife. And Georg tells me he really likes you.' He brushed a fleck of lint from his trousers and then looked up at Gabriel again. 'I think you ought to seriously consider asking him for permission to marry her.'

Gabriel fidgeted in his chair. Dorothea was a good-looking woman; there was no doubt about that. She had thick dark hair and an attractive figure, and Gabriel had been surprised to learn that she was not yet married. But although he liked her well enough, there was something missing, a vital spark that seemed lacking whenever they engaged in conversation. He knew the chief would have loved nothing more than for him to propose to her, but…

'I know Dorothea is a fine young woman,' Gabriel said. 'I also know she'll make a good wife for somebody. But I'm not sure that person is me. I'm so busy with my research right now—'

'You need to realise,' the chief interjected, 'that there's more to life than research, Gabriel. Dorothea is an eligible young woman, who will not wait for ever.'

Gabriel sighed and turned away.

'You are very gifted with the scalpel,' the chief continued, 'and you make good clinical decisions. But sometimes you can be quite naïve, particularly with women.'

Gabriel smiled to himself. He knew this last comment to be true, that because he was so focussed on the science and art of surgery, he had neglected to pay much attention to the social aspects of his profession.

'And career advancement is dependent on more than just ability,' the chief continued. 'The empire is not a meritocracy and you need to be seen to be doing the right things, with the right people, at the right time. I only have your interests at heart, and I'm telling you that people may well ask questions as to why a thirty-five-year-old surgeon has not taken a wife. They may come to a wrong conclusion.'

'But General Potiorek isn't married…' Gabriel said without thinking, and then immediately regretted his words as the older man gave him a look of warning. He realised that the chief must have also heard the rumours about Potiorek and Merizzi, but his mentor's expression told Gabriel this should not be discussed further.

'What I mean,' Gabriel said, trying to extricate himself, 'is that being married doesn't necessarily—'

'This Colonel Redl business,' the chief interjected, 'has made people very nervous. That the head of the Austrian Secret Service, no less, could allow himself to be blackmailed over his homosexual inclinations into spying for Russia has shaken Vienna to its core. That the poor man managed to salvage some dignity by shooting himself before it came to trial is a moot point.'

'Yes, but—'

'My point,' the chief interrupted again, and Gabriel could hear the fatigue in his mentor's voice, 'is that there is more to being a successful surgeon than simple surgical ability.'

Gabriel knew better than to argue. 'I know you have my interests at heart and I'm grateful for your advice. I'll think carefully about what you say.'

'That's all I ask.' The chief stretched his arms and yawned. 'And talking of wives, I must return to my own. It's been an eventful day.'

'Of course.'

The older man stood and wished Gabriel goodnight and then left the room.

And Gabriel was once more alone with thoughts from the morning, a collection of random images and sounds from the Konak: the Archduke calling for his wife, the blood-stained Ottoman couch, the look in Potiorek's eye as he hauled on the back of Gabriel's collar. But the most unsettling thought of all was that, very shortly, Gabriel would be going to war.

5

Another hot summer's day, but by early evening the streets of Paddington were beginning to cool as Elspeth left her lodgings to join Sylvia, Vera and Anya on the short walk to catch a tram for Holland Park. More than a month had passed since the Abbey bombing and it now seemed unlikely that the police would charge anyone with the crime. Although Elspeth had decided not to participate in further acts of militancy, she still wanted to support the WSPU, and in spite of her previous misgivings she was now looking forward to the public meeting that evening.

The quartet of friends arrived at Lancaster Gate where Elspeth saw a large group of women already waiting at the tram stop. Drawn from all ages, some held placards or furled banners, while others carried flags in the suffragette colours of purple, white and green. A few were wearing a white WSPU sash across their blouses, or, like Elspeth, had the WSPU badge pinned to their chests: a metallic green-and-red shield overlaid with a white chevron engraved with the words "Votes for Women". There were even two women holding large silver-painted wooden arrows, a sign that these militants had previously suffered imprisonment for their suffrage beliefs. It did not surprise Elspeth to see that Vera seemed to know them both, and gave both a nod of recognition.

A tram drew up at the kerb and Elspeth joined the other women as they pushed to get inside. The carriage was full of evening commuters and Elspeth had to stand in the central gangway holding onto the leather strap above her head as the carriage swayed on its route through west London, the overhead wires humming with electricity, the crackle of sparks flying from the tracks. After a short ride they arrived at Holland Park and dismounted to join a crowd of other women – old and young, some smartly dressed, others in their work clothes – who were walking towards the skating rink.

The rink was located in a narrow street full of shops and restaurants, and Elspeth could see the wide pavement in front of the entrance was already packed with supporters of the Pankhursts, many of them spilling off the kerb into the street. Placards had been raised, banners unfurled, and everywhere that Elspeth looked she saw the words 'WSPU' and 'Deeds not Words' swaying above the heads of the crowd. On the pavement on the opposite side of the street, a detachment of constables stood with folded arms and patronising grins. In the middle of the street, four mounted police officers leant on their saddles, watching the crowd with interest. Since the interrogation outside the Abbey, the mere sight of a police uniform sent a spark of apprehension through Elspeth. So she turned her face away and with Sylvia by her side followed Vera and Anya into the crowd, trying to blend anonymously in the sea of bodies.

And it was just as she was worming her way into the thicket of women, that Elspeth heard a cry of "she's here". She turned to see an ambulance stopping at the kerb, the excited women on the pavement surging towards it. Elspeth – almost swept off her feet by the pressure of the crowd – had to hold onto Vera in order to steady herself.

In spite of a group of women stewards – each wearing a white WSPU sash – trying to hold the crowd back, the ambulance was quickly surrounded. Two men in white uniforms stepped out of the cab and pushed their way to the rear of the vehicle; the back door was opened and the men climbed inside. A moment later a stretcher appeared, and a joyous cry erupted from the crowd when they realised the figure on the stretcher was Mrs Emmeline Pankhurst.

In spite of the warm evening Mrs Pankhurst was dressed in a red velvet robe and hat, her gaunt face testimony to the effects of her hunger strike. The men carefully manoeuvred the stretcher between two rows of stewards who had linked arms to create a corridor in the crowd, and carried Mrs Pankhurst towards the rink entrance.

Followed by Sylvia and Anya, Elspeth stayed close behind Vera as she used her height and strength to force a way through the crowd to the edge of the cordon. The stretcher passed directly in front of Elspeth and she looked over Vera's shoulder to see Mrs Pankhurst waving at her supporters as she was carried by.

And then, quite suddenly, Elspeth heard the piercing shriek of a police whistle from behind her. She looked across the street and saw that the policemen on the opposite pavement had begun to move towards the crowd of women.

'Bastards,' Vera cried out, the muscles in her jaw tight, her shoulders taut with indignant anger. 'She's only just out of Holloway and they're already going to re-arrest her!'

Cries of anger and shouts of frustration replaced the cheers of the women, and Elspeth steadied herself, clinging onto Vera as she tried to keep her feet in the surging crowd. Hearing the stamp of hobnail boots she turned to see a wedge of blue uniforms forcing their way into the throng. The police constables at the front of this spearhead – determined looks on their moustached faces and truncheons raised – broke through the stewards' linked arms. Now the crowd became a mob, booing and hissing as the police surrounded the stretcher-bearers, who lowered Mrs Pankhurst to the pavement. Another police officer elbowed his way past Elspeth and slipped through the ring of constables surrounding Mrs Pankhurst. The noise of the crowd faded as he held a piece of paper in front of his face.

'Mrs Emmeline Pankhurst,' he read. 'Under the terms of the Temporary Discharge for Ill Health Act, I am re-arresting you…'

But he was unable to finish his words as the women

resumed their baying. Elspeth saw that Sylvia and Anya were caught up in the crowd's rage, both yelling at the police, both red-faced with fury. A slightly built woman a few paces away from Elspeth tried to pull one of the policemen away, and was immediately struck with a truncheon and forced to the pavement. Elspeth clutched her throat and gasped with anger at the disproportionate violence of the constable's response.

And then, quite abruptly, her anger disappeared and was replaced by an uncomfortable feeling of danger, a feeling that someone was watching her. She turned her head to scan the crowds ahead. Beyond the broken cordon of stewards on the far side of the road she locked eyes with someone she knew, a tall man, with ginger sideburns, and a black bowler hat.

There was a smile of recognition on the inspector's lips as he spoke to a uniformed police sergeant standing by his side. Then both men began to push through the crowd towards her.

Sylvia suddenly spun around. 'Oh my giddy aunt Ellie, it's the inspector from the Abbey.'

Anya was looking at Sylvia with a puzzled frown, but Vera appeared to have grasped the situation because she turned her back towards the inspector and pulled Elspeth and Sylvia in front of her, shielding them from his view.

'That policeman – he saw you at the Abbey?' Vera shouted above the noise of the mob, and Elspeth nodded her head. 'Right, you and Sylvia need to split up. I'll delay him as long as I can. Anya, you can't risk being caught so leave this to me. We'll all meet at Ellie's in an hour. Now go, all of you, quickly,' she said, turning to face the inspector.

Elspeth turned away and tried to force a passage through the wall of women straining to reach Mrs Pankhurst. Her arms ached and her ribs were bruised and battered as she pushed against them. But eventually, like a swimmer wading into the sea against a breaking wave, she managed to find a way between them. As she neared the edge of the crowd she turned to take a final look behind her. She could just see the back of Vera's head, and beyond her distinct brown curls the approaching bowler hat of the inspector. Then she saw Vera lurch towards him and suddenly both disappeared from view. Good Lord, Elspeth thought, what has Vera done? But she had no time to think, because the police sergeant was still coming and so she turned round and pushed forward once more, until she finally found herself free of the crowd, standing on the pavement outside a greengrocers' shop.

Two mounted policemen were standing nearby. The sight of them – big-shouldered men on powerful-looking animals – filled her with fear, but she avoided looking at them as she walked along the street. Elspeth tried to act casually, trying not to run, nonchalantly turning around every few steps or so to check for signs of pursuit. Fifty yards along the street she turned once more, and this time saw two policemen break through the edge of the crowd. One of them was the sergeant and as he looked towards her he let out a sudden yell. 'You there, stop!'

Her heart sank. She hurried forward to reach an intersection where she quickly turned left into a row of terraced houses. With the shrill noise of a police whistle behind her, she lengthened her stride as much as the hem of her skirt would allow, and scurried along the pavement, all the time aware of the curious glances from pedestrians walking towards her.

More shouts and another blast from a police whistle followed – both louder, both nearer – and she realised she could not outpace the police. Dear Lord, they would soon catch her, or some diligent citizen might stop her. What should she do?

There was only one option: hide.

She saw an alleyway between the houses and slipped into it – she had no idea where it went – and blindly hurried to the bottom; it turned right into a brick-walled passage, which ran parallel to the main street. Wooden doors were built into the passage wall, presumably leading into the back yards of the houses, Elspeth thought, as she tried the handle to the first and found it locked. There were footsteps in the alleyway behind her and she quickly tried several more doors before finding a handle that responded: with a click the door swung open. She slid through and hurriedly closed it behind her, her heart hammering in her throat as she looked up to see a bolt and quietly slid it across. Then she turned round and leant back against the doorframe, trying to catch her breath and slow her racing heart.

It took her a moment before she realised that sitting on a chair outside the open back door of the house was a young woman with a small boy on her lap. The child – he looked about five years old – was dressed in pyjamas, with a book propped on his lap. Both looked frightened as the woman pulled him close to her chest.

A clatter of hobnailed boots, the rattle of handles, the thump of passage doors being shoulder-barged. The woman slowly lowered the boy to the ground, then took his hand, and, keeping her eyes fixed on Elspeth, began to back towards the open door of the house.

Elspeth saw her fear and took a measured step forward, holding her hands out in a gesture of supplication. 'Please, ma'am,' she whispered. 'I mean no harm to you or your child.'

As the woman watched her, Elspeth heard footsteps in the alleyway and turned to see the handle to the passage door rotate and then shudder as one of the policemen leant against it. Elspeth paused, holding her breath, waiting to see if his weight might force it open. But it held, and his footsteps faded as he walked further along the alleyway. She turned back to the woman, who was staring intently at the red-and-green WSPU brooch Elspeth had pinned to her blouse. After a moment the woman looked up, put a finger to her lips, and silently motioned for Elspeth to go towards her.

Elspeth quietly followed her into the house, stepping aside as the woman closed the door and turned a key in the lock.

Inside the small scullery kitchen Elspeth smiled at the boy, who was hiding behind his mother's leg, clinging to her skirt out of shyness or fear. The woman leant back against a small kitchen table, her arms crossed, her eyes wary. 'What's a smart woman like you doing running from the police?' she said. 'Is it something to do with the suffrage meeting at the rink?'

'Yes.'

'Why are you running away?'

'Mrs Pankhurst was there – they released her from prison two days ago under the cat and mouse rule.'

The woman nodded.

'Well, the police were waiting and re-arrested her before she could enter the meeting. She's a sick woman and the crowd were upset about it. They were – we were – protesting, which is our legal right. Then the police began to arrest us and I had to make a run for it.'

The woman thought for a moment. 'Well, I don't approve of law-breaking,' she said. Then she stared at the WSPU brooch again. 'But the way some women protesters are treated by the police is a scandal.' She smiled and looked down at the boy. 'What do you think, Tom? Shall we let her stay for a while?'

Seeing his mother smile, the boy looked up at Elspeth and, with a grin, came out from behind his mother's leg.

'Thank you so much,' Elspeth replied. 'If I could wait here for half an hour or so until the commotion has died down, and then I'll slip away without causing you any more trouble.'

'My husband won't be back until later, so it's no trouble. There's even a cup of tea if you like.'

'Really, there's no need to go to any bother—'

'It's no bother.' The woman turned away and took a

kettle from the table behind her. She held it under the tap, and as it filled she turned back to Elspeth. 'And for what it's worth, I support you girls. If I didn't have this little one to look after, I'd probably be at that meeting, booing the police with the rest of you.'

6

Gabriel, dressed in his pike grey service uniform, sat inside the cool of the Café Kaiserhof in the Ringstrasse, a cup of iced coffee on the table before him, that day's edition of *Neue Freie Presse* resting on his lap. It was a sweleringly hot afternoon, yet looking through the window he could see the pavement was packed with an enthusiastic throng of Viennese citizens, some waving Austrian flags, while others held placards which read 'Death to Serbia'. Inside the café the noise was intense: laughter, singing, animated conversations, all of which told him that the people of Vienna were thrilled to be at war. The patriotic fervour was almost palpable, Gabriel thought, as he watched anybody in uniform being praised a hero, clapped on the back, hands vigorously shaken. This included himself, and as the café was crowded with patrons, Gabriel was finding it almost impossible to read the newspaper without interruption.

And some of these people were so idiotic! Even though he was wearing a Red Cross armband, one buffoon had shouted across the café: 'Kill a Serb for me, Officer.' Gabriel was finding it all rather tedious, this sudden jingoistic flag-waving more than a little embarrassing. Although initially excited at the prospect of using the combat surgery skills he had so carefully acquired, over the past few weeks Gabriel had become increasingly uneasy about the idea of going to war. Several of Gabriel's friends and clinical colleagues in Sarajevo were Serbian, and many of them had now returned to Serbia to join their army medical services. It seemed more than a little strange to consider that they would now be labelled his enemy. He tried to push these doubts aside. It was the price to pay for the scholarship that had allowed him to qualify as a doctor. And it was his duty to care for the men in his regiment.

He tapped his fingers on the table and rechecked his pocket watch. Ten past two, and the train for Sarajevo left the Ostbahnhof at three. Where was the chief? He should have been here ten minutes ago. Gabriel picked up the newspaper. Below the stark headline 'War with Serbia' was an article that described how yesterday was the first time in history that a telegram had been used to notify a country that war had been declared on it. The news had come as a surprise to everybody – including Gabriel.

In the first three weeks following the assassination there was no response from the Austro-Hungarian government and life had carried on as normal. Gabriel, who only needed to make one final visit to Roth's factory in order to finish his research, travelled up to Vienna with the chief, who had been summoned to a three-day conference at the Army Medical Board. They had arrived in Vienna two days ago, but yesterday evening the chief had received a telegram stating that the Austrian army was being mobilised and they would have to return to Sarajevo the following day. And this morning the newspapers broke the news that Austria had formally declared war on Serbia.

Another loud cheer erupted near the front of the café, and Gabriel looked up to see Chief Fischer standing in the doorway, swamped by a small crowd of civilian well-wishers clapping him on the back and trying to shake his hand. There was a look of flustered irritation on the older man's face as he tried to escape this unwanted attention, glancing desperately around the room for sight of Gabriel. Gabriel waved a hand to catch the chief's eye, and then saw his mentor extricate himself from the mob and make his way between the tables to sink into the chair opposite.

'Unbelievable,' the chief said, his forehead shiny with perspiration as he loosened his collar. 'I've never seen anything like it.'

'Isn't it amazing how war can inspire a nation?' Gabriel replied.

The chief scowled. 'Only three months ago everybody in Vienna was complaining about unemployment and poor wages. Now all they want to do is enlist and take revenge for the Archduke.' He shook his head. 'People. Really.'

Gabriel laughed. 'Do you have time for a coffee?'

The chief pulled out his pocket watch. 'I think we have fifteen minutes or so but then we'll have to try to find a cab in this mob.' With a deft hand movement he caught the eye of a waiter, who arrived at the table and took an order for two iced coffees. After the waiter had gone, the chief looked across at Gabriel. 'Well, how did it go?'

'Very well I think,' Gabriel replied. 'I managed to tie up a few loose ends from the ballistic testing, so now I can finish writing the research paper—'

'No, no,' the chief interrupted in an exasperated voice. 'Not your research… did you speak to Georg?'

Gabriel hesitated before answering. 'No… ' He hesitated again. 'I… I decided not to.'

'Ah. I see.' Disappointment flickered across the older man's face. 'Well I hope you don't regret this, Gabriel. A wife and family bring great comfort to a man and Dorothea is a fine young woman. With Georg's Viennese connections you could have had a large private practice in Vienna, a big house with a maid and cook, a holiday chalet in the mountains—'

'I know, I know.' Gabriel sighed and then smiled apologetically. 'Look, I can't say exactly why, but it doesn't feel like the right thing—'

'Feel? That's interesting coming from you, Gabriel, a man of science.'

'I *do* have feelings,' Gabriel protested. 'And I do understand why you think Dorothea would be a good match for me, but…' He shrugged and fell silent, finding it difficult to express the instinct that told him that proposing to Roth's daughter would be wrong. He glanced at the other patrons in the café: at a nearby table he saw a young couple, an army reservist in his grey field uniform sitting with a young woman, probably his bride or sweetheart, Gabriel thought. They sat there with hands entwined and eyes locked on each other, utterly oblivious of their surroundings, clearly very much in love. The heat rose to Gabriel's cheeks as he watched them, feeling as if he was intruding into something private, something alien. He had never experienced a moment like that – with Dorothea or any other woman. He turned back to the chief, who had a resigned expression on his face.

'Well, maybe you're right,' said the chief as the waiter arrived and placed two glasses of iced coffee on the table. 'With war declared, perhaps getting married now isn't such a good idea after all. These are uncertain times.'

Gabriel – relieved his mentor understood his position, and now wanting to change the topic – slid the newspaper across the table. 'There's something you need to read.' he said, pointing to a column at the bottom of the front page. 'It's about General Potiorek.'

The chief picked up the paper. His eyebrows rose slightly as he read the article. 'So: he's been promoted to Field Marshall.'

'Yes. Isn't it astonishing?'

'Hm.' A wry smile now passed across the older man's face as he put the paper down and picked up his coffee. 'Well, maybe not,' he said with an indifferent shrug.

'What?' Gabriel felt bemused. 'Potiorek's carelessness contributed to the Archduke's death. Far from being promoted, he ought to have been sacked, court-martialled even.'

The chief took a drink of coffee, then leant forward and rested his elbows on the table. 'Actually, I think many people feel Potiorek has done the country a favour.' The chief motioned Gabriel closer. 'Look, it's quite simple,' he continued. 'Vienna now has the perfect excuse, and moral justification, for declaring war on Serbia. And let's be honest here.' He leant even closer and lowered his voice. 'The Archduke wasn't much liked. He had a venomous temper on him and no sense of humour. He wasn't popular with the average Austrian and there are no real signs of grief over his death, only anger at the boldness of the Serbs.'

'Still, it just seems wrong.'

'Well there are other, more practical reasons for Potiorek's promotion. It seems certain Russia will come to Serbia's aid, which means we face a war on two fronts. As Serbia is the smaller issue, it would be good if we could steal a quick victory over them, so our troops can be transferred to the Russian front. I suspect Vienna believes they don't have enough time to bring a new man into the job. Potiorek commands the 6th Army and knows the Serbian region well. I can see how Vienna probably thinks it's better to leave him in charge: better the devil you know, and all that.'

'So... he's been given an opportunity to redeem himself.' Gabriel mused aloud, trying to understand the politics that underlay such a seemingly perverse decision. 'A second chance. It's just so... so surprising.'

'And concerning.' The chief said, his voice now a whisper. 'Potiorek's mental state has worried me for a while. He appeared almost suicidal in the days after the Archduke's death, but last week he was telling people that it's his divine mission to beat the Serbs.'

Gabriel remembered the look in Potiorek's eyes during the attempt to save the Archduke. 'Well, if he's leading us into war, let's hope the decisions he makes on the battlefield are better than those he made during the Archduke's visit.'

The chief drained the last of the coffee and then pulled out his pocket watch. 'Anyway, we'd better try to find a cab—'

But he was interuppted by another loud cheer, followed by prolonged round of applause. Gabriel looked across the café and saw that a crowd had gathered around the army reservist and his sweetheart. The couple looked embarrassed as the well-wishers – some waving hats and handkerchiefs – surrounded the pair, the girl hiding her face in her hands. The soldier rose from his seat and saluted the crowd, opening his mouth as if he wanted to say something. At first he made no sound, appearing to struggle for words. But then suddenly, as if by inspiration, his face lit up and he began to sing.

'*God save, and God bless,*
His Imperial Majesty, and our country,'

To his surprise, Gabriel saw everybody in the café stand up and begin to sing the Austrian national anthem; men removing their caps as they sang, women holding their hands over their chests. Gabriel threw a cynical glance at the chief, but then saw the older man shrug his shoulders as if to say they had no choice, and so they both stood and joined the refrain.

'God and Blood for the Emperor,
God and Blood for the Fatherland,'

Through the front window, Gabriel saw pedestrians who had stopped on the pavement outside the cafe to sing the anthem. In the street beyond, he could see that the traffic on the Ringstrasse had come to a standstill. The café door opened and a wave of sound rolled towards Gabriel as the singing from outside merged with the voices from inside the café. Through the open door, Gabriel could see that an omnibus had stopped in the street right outside the cafe, and all the passengers and even the omnibus conductor were singing with gusto.

'Hail to the Emperor, hail to our Land,
Austria will stand for ever,'

The anthem finished and a thunder of applause began. After more than half a minute of continuous clapping and with no end in sight, the chief stood and dipped his hand into his pocket. He pulled out some coins and dropped them on the table, then turned to Gabriel. 'Come on,' he said. 'We'd better go if we're to catch that train.'

★★★

After a badly delayed journey, caused by military transport trains taking priority on the railway, Gabriel and the chief arrived in Sarajevo the following morning and took a taxi straight to 6th Army HQ in the centre of the city. On arrival at the old Islamic palace being used as 6th Army headquarters, they were informed that Field Marshall Potiorek was about to begin a briefing and told to go straight up to the meeting room on the first floor. Inside the high-ceilinged chamber, which had previously housed a Sultan's harem, they found fifty or so senior officers sitting in rows before a raised podium. Standing on the podium was Colonel Merizzi, the scar of the shrapnel wound on his head still visible as he unveiled a large chart supported on two easels. Across the top of the chart, written in heavy black capitals, were the words "INVASION OF SERBIA, AUGUST 1914".

Gabriel took a seat near the back of the room and gazed over the rows of epauletted shoulders in front of him. As well as his fellow senior officers from the 6th Army, he noticed several new faces, the insignia on their uniforms showing him they were soldiers from the 2nd and 5th Austrian Armies. Everybody was staring up at the map Merizzi had revealed. This clearly showed the positions of Bosnia and Serbia, with the river Drina as the natural border between the two countries. Thick black arrows marked the direction each Austrian army was expected to take during the invasion, and there was a murmur of anticipation as the officers in the room craned their heads, trying to get a closer look at the detail. Potiorek, dressed in the pale blue uniform and the gold ribbon and braid of a Field Marshall, stood motionless to one side of the easels, an aura of calm around him, like a teacher giving a class of not-so-bright children time to read a blackboard. As the hum of voices gradually diminished and the room fell silent, Potiorek began to speak, his voice quiet, the men in the room straining to listen. Gabriel sensed that some were holding their breath in case the sound of their breathing might mask his words.

'Fellow officers of the 2nd, 5th and 6th Armies: the emperor has charged me with leading you into battle against the war-mongering Serbs. My strategy will be to defeat the opposition in one week with a lightning attack of overwhelming force.'

He paused. 'I would emphasise that the essence of my strategy is speed. I therefore expect that all three armies will be battle-ready within three days. The attack will begin four days later, on the 7th August, which is one week from today.'

One week? Gabriel heard the mutterings and saw the quizzical looks that told him he was not the only officer in the room to think it overly optimistic – indeed, absurd – to expect an army of reservists to be ready so soon. But Potiorek did not appear to sense this disquiet as he continued his briefing, glancing down at General Appel, the commander of the 6th Army, who was sitting in the front row.

'The attack will begin with the 6th Army, who will move east out of Sarajevo, ford the lower Drina river and cross the western Serbian mountains, heading towards the strategically critical town of Kragujevac, which houses Serbia's military arsenal.'

Potiorek glanced down at two officers sitting beside General Appel, and Gabriel saw from the insignia on their shoulders that they were the commanding generals in charge of the 2nd and 5th Armies. 'But the shortest route into Serbia is from the north,' Potiorek continued.' The 5th Army will cross the upper Drina into northern Serbia, while the 2nd Army on the left flank will cross the Danube and take Belgrade. Then the 5th and 2nd will link up and thrust further south, towards Kragujevac. Thus the 6th Army coming from the west, and the 5th and 2nd coming from the north, will act as two arms of a pincer and trap the Serbian forces near Kragujevac, where they will be forced to surrender or be destroyed. If all goes according to plan, the war should be over by the end of the following week, the 14th of August.'

Gabriel heard more muttered whispers and saw heads turn together as the assembled officers looked at each other with obvious disquiet. He was no expert on military strategy, but even Gabriel could see that the plan was very ambitious; an advance through difficult terrain on an unrealistically short timetable, against a tough, battle-tested opposition. He was surprised that nobody had objected to the strategy, but then saw the commanding general of the 5th raise an arm.

'With respect, Field Marshall, although the northern approach is mostly flat terrain, there is the problem of the Cer heights: the enemy have fortified it with artillery. From this vantage, the Serbs can direct ordinance onto our troops below. Would it not be more sensible to first bombard the heights and neutralise their cannon—'

'A bombardment will take too much time,' Potiorek said, cutting through his words. 'A frontal assault on the

Cer heights is faster, more direct. It is important you capture it quickly, because the 2nd Army is needed against the Russian threat and will be transferred to the Galician front on the 15th of August.'

The general's face turned the colour of curdled milk. 'But, Field Marshall, that will leave my 5th Army alone—'

'I believe,' Potiorek said, again overriding his reply, 'that two armies should be more than enough to defeat the Serbs.'

This is madness, thought Gabriel. That would leave only the 5th Army in the north and the 6th Army in the east. He had read somewhere that an attacking force needed a two-to-one advantage in numbers in order to ensure victory over the defenders. Yet without the 2nd Army the Austrians would be fielding fewer soldiers than the Serbs.

'Casualties will be high,' General Appel said.

'Sacrifices will have to be made,' Potiorek replied. 'The empire assumes it. The emperor expects it.'

But the General did not reply as Potiorek continued. 'I believe that the Austrian soldier, led by the Austrian officer, can overcome any challenge.' He took a deep breath and puffed his chest out. 'And it is the emperor's birthday on the 18th of August, so I would like to present his highness the birthday gift of victory over Serbia by that day.'

Silence hung heavily in the hot and humid atmosphere of the room. Someone coughed; no one spoke. Potiorek scanned the room for dissenters, but there were none. The commanding generals sitting in the front row stared unhappily at the map, while other officers – their heads inclined – continued to whisper to each other. Gabriel was thinking about the difficulties of moving wounded men in the mountainous terrain when Potiorek spoke again. It seemed to Gabriel that at last, he might have picked up the undercurrent of unrest in the room.

'You must have confidence in my plan, gentlemen, because I believe it is my destiny to defeat the Serbs.' He paused before continuing. 'The assassin at Sarajevo said he was aiming at me. Yet from a distance of only three yards he missed, and his bullets fatally wounded the Archduke and his wife.' He paused again. 'There can be no other explanation, gentlemen; I was spared by God,' he lifted his gaze from the men below him and spread his arms wide, 'because my purpose, my calling, is to lead the Austrian army to victory over the Serbs.'

Dear Lord, thought Gabriel, did he really just say that? In the momentary silence that followed, Gabriel heard only the blood pumping through the arteries in his own head. He glanced at the faces of others in the room, and saw from their expressions that many were thinking the same as him. Potiorek seemed like a man possessed as he stood on the podium, a look of almost religious fervour still on his face as he lowered his arms and dropped his gaze to the ranks of men sitting below him. Princip's bullets may have physically missed Potiorek, thought Gabriel, but psychologically they had struck him hard.

'One final point,' Potiorek continued. 'This war

will take us into a country that has a fanatical hatred of Austria, a country where murder – as the catastrophe of Sarajevo has proved – is glorified as heroism. Towards such a country, all humanity and kindness of heart are out of place and might even endanger our troops. Thus, no consideration or mercy should be extended to the population. This instruction will be issued in the general orders to all our troops.'

An order to show no mercy or consideration to the civilian population? Gabriel had never heard of such a thing. A feeling of dismay rose from the pit of his stomach as Potiorek asked if there were any questions. Just as Gabriel was about to raise his arm, he saw the chief – sitting two rows ahead – stand up.

'Just for clarification, Field Marshall,' said the chief. 'When you say "population"; you mean the civilian population?'

Potiorek looked annoyed for a moment, as if being asked to repeat himself was a waste of his time. Then his face relaxed. 'It may appear harsh, but I must consider the safety of our troops. So to clarify: that order applies to both military and civilian personnel. Am I understood?'

The chief looked about to say something but then seemed to think the better of it; he nodded and sat down. Gabriel heard the shuffle of feet, some throat clearing from others in the room but no words. He reached up and loosened his collar as he was, by now, perspiring quite heavily.

Potiorek scanned the room. 'Any other questions?'

Again he was met by silence.

'No? Excellent.' Potiorek lifted his chin and pulled his shoulders back. 'One last point, gentlemen: the emperor wants every man to do his duty and expects sacrifices to be made. Make sure you and your men do not forget this.' Then he nodded towards Merizzi, who called the room to attention, and the synchronous clatter of clicking heels sounded as everyone in the room stood up. Potiorek stepped down from the podium and left the room, Merizzi close behind him.

As the other officers followed the two men out, the chief walked across to Gabriel. 'My God,' he whispered. 'The man's mad or a fool. We'd better get back to the hospital. There are a lot of preparations to make, and not much time to make them in.'

7

London. August 1914

'We have to shoot McCarthy.'

Anya's unexpected words hung in the heavy evening air above the small kitchen table. It had been another blistering day, and even in the shady kitchen at the back of the terraced house where Vera lodged, it was still oppressively hot. But Elspeth felt cold with shock as she stared across the table at Anya, the other woman's eyes shaded by the red beret slung low over her forehead. Vera, sitting beside Anya, appeared ill at ease as she shifted in her chair and avoided Elspeth's gaze.

'Did you just say we should shoot Inspector McCarthy?' Elspeth asked incredulously.

Anya folded her arms and leant back in the chair. 'Yes.'

My God, Elspeth thought; she's serious. She glanced at Sylvia sitting beside her – saw her lips parted in surprise – then turned back to Anya. 'This is madness, Anya. The arson strategy is directed against the property of the government and monarchy, nothing more. That's why I was prepared to plant the bomb on the Coronation Chair. But what you're proposing…

shooting someone… goes against everything the WSPU stands for.'

'McCarthy is the enemy,' Anya said, very matter-of-fact.

'You're talking about shooting a policeman…' said Elspeth. But she fell silent when she saw the watery sheen that appeared in Anya's eyes.

'He killed Grace,' Anya muttered, then dipped her head so that her face was obscured below the beret. A wet smudge suddenly flowered on the dry pine surface of the table below Anya's head as a teardrop fell from her eyes. Vera leaned towards her and stretched a comforting arm around her shoulders but Anya ignored her, merely wiping her eyes with the sleeve of her blouse. She sniffed once and then looked up at Elspeth again.

'Do not forget that women have died,' Anya said, her voice thick with grief. 'I saw Grace after a feed…' she shook her head as if to erase the memory, '… it should be a doctor to put the feeding tube in stomach, but the prison guards do it. They treat women like animals and pushed the tube into her lung. And then they push feed down the tube…'

She closed her eyes for a moment, then opened them again. 'McCarthy is Special Branch, Ellie. He is head of suffragette section. His agents watch our meetings. He saw you and Sylvia outside the Abbey and recognised you at Holland Park. If it was not for Vera, you would be in prison by now.'

'But you can't just go around shooting people, Anya,' Sylvia said, indignation in her voice.

'McCarthy is responsible for all suffragette arrests,' Anya replied. 'If we shoot him, we send a message that women cannot be treated like slaves.'

'This is ridiculous,' Elspeth said. 'You don't even have a gun.'

Anya suddenly stood up, lifted the hem of her skirt, and slipped a hand beneath the garment. When, a moment later, her hand reappeared it was holding a metallic object. And it took Elspeth only a second to register that the object was a pistol, the word 'Browning' stamped in the grey gunmetal. She gasped at the same time as Sylvia stood up, her chair skittering backwards as she stepped away from the table in shock.

Anya calmly placed the pistol on the table, the hilt towards Elspeth. 'Don't worry, Ellie. It is not loaded.'

'Where did you get it from?' Elspeth whispered, stunned at the pistol's appearance.

'If we want to be treated as equal, then we must be prepared to fight,' Anya calmly replied.

'This is madness,' Sylvia said, leaning against the wall of the kitchen, arms folded defensively across her chest.

A frown appeared on Anya's brow. 'I am surprised, Sylvie. I thought you would understand this.'

'Well, you don't know me very well then, do you,' Sylvia replied stridently. 'I could never envisage such a thing.'

'And neither could I,' Elspeth said, hearing the shock in her voice. 'Again: where did you get it from?'

Anya glanced at Vera before looking back at Elspeth.

'From someone I met at the gun range in Tottenham Court Road, where Vera and I have been practising.'

Vera? Elspeth, shocked, saw the look of uncertainty on Vera's face. 'Vee: is this true?' she asked.

Vera hesitated, then gave a confirmatory nod.

And now Elspeth felt truly torn: because as Anya had said, it *was* Vera who had saved them. She had recognised Inspector McCarthy and deliberately fallen into him, after which she had been arrested and taken to Paddington Green station. During questioning, McCarthy had demanded Elspeth's and Sylvia's real names and addresses in exchange for Vera's release. Otherwise, he said, Vera would be charged with assault. But Vera hadn't cracked, claiming she had unintentionally tripped into McCarthy and refusing to say anything more. Money from Sylvia's parents, and a sympathetic lawyer, had secured Vera's release on bail, but she was due to reappear in court in three weeks' time.

'Really, Vee?' Elspeth continued. 'You're part of this mad idea?

'We have a problem, Ellie,' Vera replied, 'because McCarthy must know that you and Sylvie planted the bomb at the Abbey. It's only a matter of time before he finds out your names. And when he does, you'll be arrested. You'll go to prison. Your careers will be over. But Anya's convinced me that if we shoot him—'

'You're talking about murder,' Elspeth interrupted.

Vera looked troubled, ran a hand quickly down her face, took a deep breath. 'Look, Ellie, you ought to know that a few years back, some of the sisters were planning to shoot Asquith, the prime minister.'

Elspeth's heart began to pound.

'With the constant suffragette picket outside parliament at the time it would have been easy,' Vera continued. 'But somebody warned the police and the plan was called off.' She paused for a moment. 'Don't forget that some of our sisters have died for the cause: Emily Davidson under the king's horse, Emmeline Pankhurst's sister Mary from police brutality, Grace and others from prison feed going into their lungs—'

'They put pneumonia on Grace's death certificate, but it was murder,' Anya interjected.

'And you think that shooting the prime minister or a Special Branch inspector is the answer?' Elspeth said, trying to suppress the panic in her voice.

'This is war,' Anya said. 'In war, blood is spilt. We fight an enemy that uses the police against us. We cannot get close to Asquith any more. But we can get close to McCarthy and his like.'

'I never for one minute imagined this,' Elspeth said, shaking her head in incredulity.

'I knew you'd find this difficult,' Vera continued. 'You and Sylvie did us proud with the Abbey bomb, and neither of you should feel bad if you decide not to involve yourselves with this—'

'*This*?' Elspeth said, standing up from the table. 'What you call "this", Vera, is killing somebody. And I'll have no part in it.'

'Me neither,' said Sylvia.

For a few seconds nobody moved, and then Anya took a step forwards picking up the pistol from the table and raising the hem of her skirt to slip it back inside her undergarments. 'Alright,' she said, brushing the front of her skirt flat. 'I'm going: there is no point in any more talk.' She strode past Elspeth, thrusting open the kitchen door and disappearing into the hallway beyond.

Vera stood up, her chair scraping the floor. 'Wait, Anya—' she called out, but the front door slamming told them that Anya had already left the house. Vera's shoulders sagged as she turned to Elspeth. 'I'm so sorry,' Vera whispered. 'I didn't… I…' She shook her head and hurried to the kitchen door, stopping briefly in the doorway to look back at Elspeth. 'She's upset… I'd better go after her.'

Elspeth watched Vera vanish through the doorway and a moment later the front door slammed once more. A sudden calm filled the kitchen as Elspeth looked across at Sylvia and shook her head in disbelief. 'I've always thought that Anya was eccentric,' she said, 'but this… it's madness.'

'I think she's mad with grief,' Sylvia replied, quite calmly, Elspeth was surprised to hear. 'When she spoke about her friend Grace… well I think she must have loved her very dearly, for she seemed quite deranged with sorrow.' She gave a short, sad smile. 'But she's very driven, Ellie. I think she's capable of anything. I think she'll shoot McCarthy if she gets the chance.'

'I think you're right.'

'So what are we going to do?'

***

Two days later Elspeth read the unsettling news that Britain had declared war on Germany. She was seeing a patient on the ward when excited shouts came from the corridor outside. A moment later, one of the porters burst through the ward doors, waving a copy of the *Evening Standard*. Elspeth was stunned, but also dismayed at the general excitement at the prospect of war. *Didn't people realise that fighting a war meant death and bloodshed?* Walking home along Praed Street that evening, she saw the Union Jacks, which hung like bunting in the shop windows, and the newspaper-stand banners that screamed 'WAR' in big, bold capitals. Her spirits fell further on seeing the happy grins of men she passed, seemingly eager for the fighting to begin, as if going over to Europe to thrash the Hun would be one big adventure.

But her mood lifted a week later when the Pankhursts announced an end to the militant strategy and pledged their support to the British war effort. Elspeth felt such relief that she would no longer have to decide whether or not to take part in the arson campaign. And in return for the WSPU ceasefire, the British government proclaimed an amnesty for all crimes committed by suffragettes – which meant Vera would no longer face criminal charges.

★★★

One morning in the middle of August, Elspeth arrived at St Mary's and was told by the head porter at the front entrance that a marconigram was waiting for her. She tore the envelope open and saw that it had been sent the previous evening from Dr Inglis, who was arriving in London that afternoon for an appointment at the War Office: would Elspeth come and meet her afterwards as she had a proposition to put to her? Elspeth was thrilled at the prospect and hurried up to the surgical ward to tell Sylvia the news. But on arriving at the ward she saw that Sylvia looked pale with worry. She hustled Elspeth into the ward sister's office, closed the door and then pulled a short blind down to cover the door's glass window.

'What's going on?' Elspeth asked her.

Sylvia slumped into a battered canvas chair. 'Anya's gone missing.'

'Missing?' Elspeth said, sitting in a chair opposite. 'What do you mean?'

'Just that,' Sylvia replied. 'She's disappeared.'

Elspeth frowned, blinked. 'How do you know?'

'Vera came over to see me last night. She said that Anya was upset about the WSPU decision to end the arson campaign, and that she and Vera had an argument about it yesterday morning. Then when Vera went round to Anya's lodgings in the evening to try to make up with her, her landlady said that Anya had left that same afternoon. She collected her deposit and simply vanished.'

'Does Vera have any idea why she's gone?'

'The last thing Anya said during their argument was that she would continue to work on her own.'

'Work on her own? You think that Anya plans to shoot McCarthy by herself?'

'That's what Vera's afraid of.'

A hollow feeling grew in the back of Elspeth's throat as she saw Sylvia gently bite her lower lip, a sign she recognised. 'There's more, isn't there, Sylvie?'

Sylvia hesitated, then nodded.

'Well, you'd do best to tell me,' Elspeth said.

Another hesitation was followed by a sigh, and then: 'According to Vera, Anya also said some things about us.'

'Us?' Elspeth felt a flicker of alarm. 'You mean you and me?'

'Yes.'

'What sort of things?'

'Paranoid things. That we might write to the police about her, have her deported, that sort of thing.'

Elspeth closed her eyes and pinched the bridge of her nose between a finger and thumb. She opened her eyes again. 'This is like a bad dream.'

'I know,' Sylvia said, a pained expression on her face. 'I feel bad I dragged you into all this. If I hadn't introduced you to Vera and Anya—'

Elspeth reached across to place a hand on the back of Sylvia's wrist. 'No, I've no regrets about anything we've done, Sylvie. The government wasn't listening to us; it hadn't listened to us for decades. I couldn't see any other choice but to do what we did.' She leant back in her chair. 'But now with the war… well, everything is different. This is an opportunity for us to do something decent, something constructive.' She paused. 'But this situation with Anya is worrying. Does Vera think she means to do us harm?'

Sylvia shrugged. 'It was difficult to know what Vera

was thinking last night. She was in a real state: tearful, unhappy. I've never seen her like that before, never seen her so upset.'

'Why?'

'Well, I can see that Vera has strong feelings for Anya. And I think she's torn between her affection and loyalty for her, and worry over the danger she might pose to McCarthy and possibly us. She knows Anya better than most, but even she doesn't know what she might do next.'

'I suppose the only person who does is Anya herself,' Elspeth said. 'But her behaviour is so odd that it's impossible to predict. And we still know so very little about her. We don't even know which country she's from.'

'So what do we do?'

Elspeth furrowed her brow. 'Seeing Anya handle that pistol made me realise she's quite capable of using it. If she finds the opportunity to get near McCarthy—'

'We can't allow that.' Sylvia took a deep breath. 'We have to warn him of the danger.'

Elspeth blinked and stared at her. 'You mean…'

'Write to him… anonymously… a warning.'

'But…' Elspeth began to say, then stopped as she realised the sense of Sylvia's suggestion. 'I never thought I'd ever contemplate such a thing,' she finally said, 'but Anya's behaviour is so worrying that warning McCarthy might be for the best.'

'I'd feel awful if something did happen to him…'

'I'll write the letter this evening,' Elspeth said.

'Good.' Sylvia sat forward in her chair. 'You know, Ellie, sometimes I wonder if Anya might be suffering from a mental illness, something like moral insanity.'

'You mean psychopathy?'

'Yes.'

Elspeth slowly nodded. 'You could be right, Sylvie. Psychopath's have no compunction about killing and Anya's quite casual about the idea of shooting McCarthy. But after that performance a few weeks ago, when she thought she was being followed, and now her paranoia about us… well, it's possible she might be suffering from a paranoid psychosis.' She paused. 'Which might be more dangerous.'

'Why?'

'Because when a psychopath kills it is usually for a logical reason, whereas when a paranoid psychotic kills, it is often for irrational, delusional reasons.'

'Like thinking that McCarthy is directly responsible for killing Grace?'

'Yes. Or that we might be about to tip off the police about her.'

'Well we *are* going to tip off the police about her.' A smile appeared on Sylvia's face. 'So strictly speaking that's not delusional.'

'This is serious, Sylvie.'

The smile faded. 'I know it is, Ellie.' She sighed. 'So what do we do after you've written to McCarthy? If Vera is right, maybe we should leave London?'

Elspeth suddenly remembered the marconigram. She reached inside her jacket pocket and gave it to Sylvia.

'Arrived this morning, from Dr Inglis, my mentor in Edinburgh.'

Sylvia quickly read the telegram. 'Why is she going to the War Office?'

Elspeth shrugged. 'She doesn't say. But I have a feeling it might have something to do with the fact she's the commandant of a Voluntary Aid Detachment in Edinburgh. I know she's trained over a thousand VADs and may be offering their services for the war effort. Anyway I'll go and meet her, find out what she's up to. It's just possible she might have something for us to do.'

8

London, August 1914

The black taxi sputtered along Horse Guards Avenue towards Whitehall. Sitting in the back seat, Elspeth peered through the side window and watched the white corner domes and ionic columns of the War Office hove into view. The driver pulled up at the kerb and Elspeth quickly paid the fare, then climbed out the cab and hurried past two khaki-clad soldiers standing guard outside the main entrance. Stepping through the double doors she found herself inside a spacious foyer, a large reception desk directly ahead of her, a uniformed porter wearing a peaked cap sitting behind the desk. A large bronze clock on the wall above his head showed half past five as Elspeth went up to him and told him she was there to meet Dr Inglis.

'—who had an appointment here this afternoon,' she continued. 'Is it possible to tell me whether she's finished or not?'

The porter lifted a clipboard and ran his finger down the page, 'She checked in at…' He moved his finger along the line. '… 3.57 p.m., but was only called in at… let me see… 5.23 p.m.' He glanced up at the clock above his head. 'She's had a long wait, ma'am, and only just gone in.'

'Oh thank goodness,' Elspeth said with relief. 'I thought I might have missed her.'

'No, she's only been in for five minutes – she might be some time yet.' He pointed to a row of chairs nearby. 'You can wait over there if you like.'

She thanked him and went to sit down. Leading away from both sides of the foyer, were two long corridors, the darkly polished wood floors extending the length of the building on either side, while at the back of the foyer a paisley-carpeted staircase led up to the first floor. Two army officers chatted as they walked up the stairs. She sighed and sank back into the chair, pleased she hadn't missed Dr Inglis. It had been a busy operating list at St Mary's and she had rushed to get here on time, worrying that she might be too late. Now she would just have to sit back and wait. She glanced down at the ochre-coloured marks on the back of her wrists, from the surgical iodine used to sterilise the skin, which she had failed to wash away during her hurried exit from the hospital—

'Elspeth!'

Startled at the call, Elspeth looked up to see a figure on the staircase, waving at her as she descended the steps. A slight woman, dressed in a brown skirt and jacket and holding a small leather holdall, Dr Inglis arrived at the bottom of the staircase and walked briskly towards the reception desk. The porter handed her the clipboard and pencil, and then pointed to a place on the page. As

Dr Inglis signed her name, he glanced up at the clock. 'Blimey,' he said. 'That didn't take long.'

'Well, there's no point in wasting time is there?' Dr Inglis replied; Elspeth was pleased to hear the familiar Scottish accent.

The porter grinned and nodded, and then doffed his cap to her as she walked past him to meet Elspeth.

'Elspeth, dear, I'm so pleased you could make it.' Dr Inglis leant forward to give her a hug.

'It's good to see you, too,' Elspeth said as they pulled apart. It had been almost a year since Elspeth had last seen her mentor and she looked older, her grey hair swept behind her head and held in place with an ivory clasp. 'I thought I'd missed you, but the porter told me you'd only just gone in.'

'Yes, it wasn't a very long meeting I'm afraid…' Her intelligent green eyes glanced up at the clock above the reception desk. 'Look, they kept me waiting much longer than I expected and I'm in a bit of a rush to get back to Edinburgh. Can you come to the station with me and we'll talk as we go?'

'Of course.' Elspeth led Dr Inglis back through the entrance, past the two soldiers on guard, and onto the pavement. A taxi was just pulling up at the kerb, and an army lieutenant stepped out of the vehicle, paid the driver his fare, and then held the door open for Elspeth and Dr Inglis.

'Kings Cross, please, driver,' Elspeth said and then sat back in the seat. As the taxi pulled away, she looked across at Dr Inglis. 'I'm sorry to hear your meeting didn't go well. Was it about your Voluntary Aid Detachment?'

Dr Inglis sighed. She looked tired, Elspeth thought, her brow furrowed with worry lines, shadows under her eyes. 'Yes, partly that. But as well as the volunteers we've trained, we've also established a Scottish Women's Hospital Unit and have raised enough money to send two hospitals overseas to care for wounded Allied soldiers: one to France and another to Serbia. Both hospitals will be staffed entirely by women. My meeting today was to let the War Office know of our plan.'

A hospital run entirely by women? Elspeth felt a sudden glow of excitement at the idea and its implications. However she knew how the male military hierarchy would have received such a radical proposal. 'They weren't interested, were they,' she said.

Dr Inglis shook her head, but then smiled philosophically 'The senior officer in charge of the medical services took a minute to read the proposal and then point-blank refused to accept it. He said – and I quote – "a casualty clearing hospital at the battle-front is not the safest place for those of a gentler, more sensible disposition"'.

Elspeth gently laughed at her mentor's attempt at an upper-class English accent. 'So he was condescending, with undertones of patronisation, and a hint of misogyny?'

'Exactly that. "Go back to Edinburgh and sit still" were his parting words to me.'

Elspeth shook her head. She was used to this sort of treatment from men – it was one of the reasons she'd joined the WSPU – but she still found it frustrating beyond belief. 'But you're going to go ahead with the plan anyway?' she said.

'Yes. This senior officer said the War Office will refuse to accept our hospitals, but I've already spoken to the French and Serbian governments via their London embassies, and they are more than happy to have us. You see, it's not just VAD volunteers that will go out with these hospitals. We also need experienced professional women, like surgeons, nurses, drivers... people like you, Elspeth.'

'So *that's* why you wanted to meet.'

'Yes. I'd really like you to come with us. With your surgical training and experience, you're just the sort of person we're looking for.'

Elspeth felt light-headed at the thought. 'I can't think of anything else I'd rather do right now.'

'We're also looking for experienced nurses, so if you know of anyone—'

'Yes! I do know someone who would be keen to join,' Elspeth said, thinking immediately of Sylvia. 'When do we go? We can leave immediately if you want.'

Dr Inglis laughed. 'Actually the French unit is already fully staffed and due to leave in a few weeks. It's the Serbian unit I'm recruiting for now, but because of the logistical difficulties of transporting staff and equipment, we won't be sailing until mid-December.'

That was three months away, thought Elspeth with disappointment. 'But we're both keen as mustard to help immediately. Do you know of anything else we could do before December?

Dr Inglis's brow furrowed. 'Well, there is one possibility. The Women's Hospital Corps left for Paris earlier this week. They're another women-only-staffed hospital led by a young surgeon, Dr Louisa Garrett Anderson. Her second in command is Dr Flora Murray, a physician I know well as we used to work together. I hear through the grapevine that one of their associate surgeons has just been diagnosed with tuberculosis and they're looking for a last-minute replacement. Their London contact is Dr Louisa Woodcock. She lives at number four Nottingham Place, here in London. I suggest you contact her to see if they'll let you join their unit and travel out with them.'

'That sounds perfect,' Elspeth said. 'If Dr Anderson will take us to Paris now, then we can come back to London in time to join you—'

'Just one slender note of caution, Elspeth,' Dr Inglis interrupted. 'You should be aware that Dr Anderson has a bit of a chequered past. She was at one time a member of the WSPU, and two years ago was imprisoned for militancy.'

'Oh,' Elspeth said, only just able to maintain her composure. 'I see. What exactly did she do?'

'She smashed the windows of a government minister's house in Knightsbridge,' Dr Inglis replied, with obvious distaste. 'A crime for which she received six weeks' hard labour in Holloway prison.'

'Well, thankfully, that sort of thing is now behind us,' Elspeth said.

'Yes, and by all accounts she's a very good surgeon. You'll recognise the surname of course.'

Elspeth frowned for a moment and then gave a slow nod. 'Of course: her mother is Elizabeth Garret Anderson, the first woman doctor in Britain?'

'Exactly. So you can see that she comes from a very good medical pedigree. If Dr Anderson's Paris Corp does have room for you, I'd strongly suggest you go with them. Some early experience of battlefield trauma before you join us in December would be very useful.'

Their taxi came to a halt outside King's Cross station. Dr Inglis opened the door and stepped outside.

'Please wait, driver,' Elspeth said, and then followed Dr Inglis onto the pavement. 'When exactly are you sailing for Serbia?'

'We're leaving from Southampton on the fifteenth of December, so you need to be back in London the week before.' She turned to look up at the station clock on the tower behind her. 'Well it was lovely seeing you, Elspeth, and I look forward to meeting you again in December. Do write to me at the Bruntsfield and let me know how you get on in Paris.'

'Of course.' Elspeth leant forward to give her a hug, and then watched her disappear inside the station. A moment later she climbed back inside the taxi and turned to the driver.

'Nottingham Place, please.'

9

Western Serbia, August–September 1914

Gabriel stood in the shade of a willow tree on the Serbian bank of the Drina, gazing down at a line of Austrian soldiers wading across from the Bosnian side. He had forded the river by horseback only a few minutes earlier, and after tethering the animal to the tree had stood watching the vanguard of the 6th Army follow him onto Serbian soil. Most of the soldiers were in pale blue uniforms, although some of the men were in the dark green of the elite Alpine regiments. However, all the troops were bare below the waist, having removed their trousers and boots, which hung – tied by their laces – around their necks as they waded through the thigh-deep water. Reconnaissance patrols had already scouted ahead, but no Serbian opposition – perhaps surprisingly – had yet been encountered. Just as well, thought Gabriel, as the men looked vulnerable, literally naked as they strode through the river, rifles and ammunition belts held high above their heads.

So far it had not gone well for Field Marshall Potiorek. It had taken not one, but three weeks for the 6th Army to finish their preparations for war, and Gabriel and his medical column had only left Visigrad – the last town before the Serbian border – earlier that morning. They were already two weeks behind schedule and Gabriel had heard that Potiorek was furious at the delay, his hope of a quick victory over Serbia as a birthday gift to the emperor now foregone. The troops had been told they would have to make quick progress in order to make up for lost time. Gabriel left the shade of the tree and trudged up the grassy slope to get a better view of the route they would soon take. A dried up water-track snaked uphill, a tributary along which water must once have gushed on its way down to join the river below. This defile meandered towards the hills of western Serbia, and beyond these were the mountains they would have to cross in order to reach the central Serbian plain and the town of Kragujevac on the far side.

Sudden laughter caught his attention and he turned to look back down at the riverbank. The soldiers who had just crossed were drying themselves in the sunshine, joking and sniggering at the sight of each other's river-cold shrivelled penises. The men were in good spirits, Gabriel thought as he watched them reassemble and begin to tramp up the slope.

He observed them for a little while longer, and then looked across to the Bosnian side of the Drina, where a line of ponies and mules – essential for moving supplies in this terrain – were waiting patiently at the water's edge. Beyond the animals a Red Cross flag marked the position of the Divisional Aid Station. A cluster of farm buildings had been identified near the riverbank, and after requisitioning them for military use, Gabriel had arranged for the walls and floors to be cleaned and disinfected so that they could be converted into a temporary hospital.

The last line of soldiers had finished crossing the river and Gabriel saw the first of the ponies being led into the water. From the red crosses on the animals' flanks he knew they were carrying the dressing station medical supplies. So he straightened the Red Cross armband on the sleeve of his captain's jacket – the only feature on his uniform that distinguished him from other officers of the same rank – and looked around to try and find the other staff from the medical column. Higher up the bank and a little further along, Lieutenant Peter Flieger was talking to Klaus, Gabriel's orderly, and the two new medical reservists, Berger and Schwann. The four men had serious expressions on their faces, their heads inclined together in a secretive huddle, and Gabriel was curious to know what they were discussing.

'Corporal Sparmacher,' he shouted up. Klaus quickly pulled away from the group – a guilty look on his face – and ambled down to Gabriel. Corporal Klaus Sparmacher had been with the Austrian army for many years, and during that time had been a faithful assistant to Gabriel, with a seemingly endless supply of good humour and a constant smile. However, some of Klaus's habits – a liking for idle gossip, a deep love of schnapps (his breath had smelt heavily of it this morning) and a natural inclination to laziness – were a source of continual irritation for Gabriel,

'Captain?'

'Come on, Klaus, we're under orders to make good time. Help get those ponies and medical supplies up here.'

'Yes, Captain.' Klaus replied with a salute and then began to saunter down the bank.

'And don't be all day about it,' Gabriel called after him and grinned as the old corporal started a slow rolling jog down the slope.

Flieger and the other two doctors arrived at Gabriel's side.

'Well, I'm relieved we're finally on Serbian soil,' Flieger said, and Gabriel couldn't tell whether his First Surgeon was genuinely pleased or not. Gabriel had grown to like Flieger, a loyal colleague and family man devoted to his wife and five children. He was also normally a plucky, hard-working surgeon, who relished a challenge, but today Gabriel saw lines of tension beneath his round, silver-rimmed spectacles.

'Well, Peter, I didn't realise you were so keen for the fighting to begin,' Gabriel said dryly, trying to keep a straight face.

Frown lines appeared on Flieger's brow. 'No, what I meant was, the quicker we start, the quicker...' He stopped as Gabriel could no longer hide the grin from his face. 'Oh,' he said, and then gave a short tight smile to allay his embarrassment.

'I know what you meant, Peter.' Gabriel glanced at the two men standing beside Flieger. Dr Thomas Berger and Dr Karl Schwann were reservists who had qualified from Vienna only one year earlier. Berger, a gangly youth with curly brown hair, had initially intended a career as a surgeon, but confessed to Gabriel he lacked the necessary dexterity for tying surgical knots and had thus developed an interest in anaesthesia. This was welcome news for Gabriel, because although anaesthesia had traditionally been a nurse's job, the chief now insisted that, wherever possible, trained doctors should take over this role. Dr Schwann, a reservist with short, sandy-coloured hair, had worked in a fever hospital in Vienna over the past year and was going to be the medical column's physician. Both men had appeared quietly confident during the two-week preparation for war, but Gabriel was surprised to see that – like Flieger – both men looked unsettled.

'Is everything all right?' Gabriel asked them with a puzzled frown.

'Oh yes, Captain,' Berger replied – a little too quickly for Gabriel's liking – and Schwann nodded his head.

'Are you sure?' Gabriel replied. 'There's nothing you are worried about, or want to ask?'

Both men shook their heads and Gabriel scratched his chin; something was obviously bothering them, he thought, as he turned back to Flieger. 'So, Peter,' he said, trying to lighten the mood. 'How's your little boy? Born the day the Archduke died, is that why you named him Franz?'

'No.' Flieger took his glasses off and wiped them on the sleeve of his jacket. 'It's nothing to do with the Archduke. Maria and I decided on names well before he was born. It was always going to be Francesca for a girl and

Franz for a boy.' He put the glasses back on and adjusted them on the bridge of his nose. 'Actually little Franz is driving his mother mad: he's not a good sleeper. Maria's often up with him during the night and during the day she has her hands full with the other four children.' He squinted through the lenses. 'Do you think this will be a long war, Gabriel? We heard the field marshal say it should all be over within a few weeks… but…'

'But what?' Gabriel asked.

Flieger hesitated. 'Well… there are rumours.'

Gabriel tensed. 'What have you heard?'

'I don't want to get anyone into trouble—'

'Just tell me,' Gabriel said, a note of impatience in his voice.

Flieger looked ill at ease as he spoke. 'Well, Kramer in supply division told me that the 5th Army's assault on the Cer plateau has been a disaster. He said that when the 2nd Army were transferred to Russia, it left the 5th Army flank exposed, and they've had twenty thousand men killed or taken prisoner. Apparently it turned into a rout.'

'Is this true?' Berger asked.

At last Gabriel understood their agitation. Well, he thought, it had only been a matter of time before the story leaked out. 'Yes, it's true,' he said. 'Chief Fischer told me about it yesterday. He learnt it from the 5th Army's chief surgeon when he asked for an urgent transfer of medical supplies. The news is unofficial at the moment and you're to keep quiet about it. High command is worried about the effect on morale.'

'Is it as bad as the rumour says?' Schwann asked.

'Yes, I'm afraid so.'

'What does this mean for us?' Flieger said.

All three men looked at Gabriel with concern. 'Well, it means we're on our own and that the Serbs can concentrate their forces against us. The chief had thought the field marshal might call our attack off, at least until the 5th Army has had time to recover. But for the time being, our orders are to carry on. Whether the field marshal will change his mind—'

A sudden harsh braying interrupted him, and all four men turned to look down at the river. The column of mules and ponies carrying the dressing station supplies was mid-way across the river, and Klaus was struggling with one of the mules, the animal whinnying with disapproval as the corporal hauled on the bridle, trying to coax it forwards. Suddenly the stubborn animal snapped its head back, jerking the reins in Klaus's hands and pulling him off-balance. With a splash he disappeared head first into the river and reappeared a moment later, much to the amusement of the men around him. Flieger and Berger burst out laughing, and even Gabriel could not help smiling as he saw Klaus flounder in the river, shaking water from his hair and cursing the animal, which mutely regarded him. The incident broke through the despondency that had descended over the group, and Gabriel glanced up the slope and saw that the last of the troops had disappeared into the defile. It was the perfect time to end the discussion.

'Look, Peter, there's no point in dwelling on these rumours. We have our orders and you know what we must do. So you'd better get moving: the lead units are well ahead.' He gave him a friendly pat on the shoulder and then turned to walk back down the slope towards his horse.

★★★

For the rest of that day, Gabriel and his medical column followed the soldiers of the Austrian 6th struggling through the thick brush and undergrowth on the hills of western Serbia. It was a hard physical slog, transporting men, animals and their supplies through the densely wooded countryside and up the forested inclines towards the mountains. For much of the way, Gabriel had to dismount and lead his horse, as it was too treacherous to ride along the slender tracks, with precipitous drops into streams and gullies that lay on either side.

It was nine o'clock and dusk was falling when they finally set up camp close to a small Serbian hamlet on the far side of the hills, the shadow of the western Serbian mountains looming only a few miles further east. The regiment had temporarily requisitioned the well in the centre of the village and several scruffily dressed, sullen-faced Serbian men, clad in the typical tubular woollen caps and oriental-style straw shoes, glowered at the Austrians as they refilled their canteens. A gaggle of small children and a few women in brightly coloured peasant clothes stood a little way behind them. Gabriel was uneasy for the civilians, worried that their obvious antagonism might incite the soldiers to acts of violence.

But the officers maintained good discipline among the troops, and after taking their fill of water the soldiers left the hamlet and erected their tents a few hundred metres away. It was a humid August night and Gabriel chose to sleep under the stars, chatting to Flieger and Klaus for a while before eventually falling asleep.

***

He woke before dawn and saw the first magenta tint of daybreak on the horizon. Then he closed his eyes again, and suddenly found himself standing on a station platform, dressed in civilian attire, waiting for a train to take him to Klagenfurt. A locomotive approached at speed, but did not stop: a blast of warm air and steam blew across his face, and the platform below his feet shook as the train screamed past him...

And then Gabriel realised that the screaming was not mechanical, but was like that of an injured animal... or person...

Waking from the dream, Gabriel heard the cries and shouts of men in pain. As he struggled to his feet he heard a strange whining sound: another artillery shell passed overhead and exploded twenty yards behind him, the rush of hot air and vibration from the shell burst knocking him off his feet.

He levered himself up again and saw that Flieger and Berger were already sprinting towards the screams of the wounded. Gabriel staggered up and stood in a crouch, squinting in the dawn half-light at the spot where the shell had landed. Other men were already hurrying towards the smouldering crater. Quickly he followed them, the ground beneath his feet littered with debris from the explosion. Scattered amongst these smoking chunks of earth he saw charred scraps of uniform, and a piece of gleaming white substance laced with red that he realised with shock was a segment of human femur. Then there was the sudden crack of a rifle shot, the report echoing from the mountain behind, and one of the soldiers by the edge of the crater slumped silently to the ground. Another crack, and this time Gabriel heard the bullet whine as it passed overhead, then heard someone a short distance away let out a strangled cry. Gabriel threw himself down, trying to hide, trying to grind himself into the hard summer-baked earth, unnerved that Serb snipers could find their targets so easily in the early-morning gloom. He waited a moment and then began to crawl forwards again. Smoke drifted across the ground, and, hoping it would hide him, Gabriel quickly got to his feet and ran, half-crouched, towards the smouldering depression in the ground and slithered into it.

The smoke was coming from burning uniforms on pieces of body lying in the bottom of the crater. No one was alive, and Berger and Flieger were already scrambling up the other side towards cries for help from further away. Sweet Jesus, Gabriel thought, as he looked at the fragments at his feet. There was a tent and four men sleeping here last night. Then another swishing sound came from above – like a curtain being drawn.

A mortar round sailed overhead and exploded near to where he had just crawled from, showering him with earth and stones. He crouched in the bottom of the crater, his hands over his head, his shirt clinging to his chest from the sweat pouring from his body. And then he heard a low moan. 'Help me.'

Gabriel raised his head above the edge of the depression; Flieger and Berger were peering back at him from the rim of another hollow nearby. In between the two craters was a soldier lying on his back, waving a bloodstained arm in the air.

This is my job, my destiny, thought Gabriel, as he clambered out and ran across to the soldier. He slipped his hands under the man's armpits and, ignoring his cries of pain, dragged him across to Flieger's depression. As he fell over the rim of the crater, another mortar explosion showered them all with clods of earth and gravel.

'Are you all right, Captain?' Flieger was saying, but Gabriel was already pulling at the wounded soldier's jacket sleeves.

'Help me get this off him,' Gabriel said.

Flieger and Berger helped him undress the man. Gabriel carefully examined him, and found a neat small bullet hole in the front of his thigh. Berger had a surgical pack with him, and as Gabriel applied a field dressing to the wound, he suddenly realised the gunfire and explosions had stopped.

'I think it's over,' said Flieger, who was peering over the lip of the depression. Cautiously Gabriel stood up and saw other soldiers picking themselves up from the ground, other heads emerging from nearby craters. He turned to Flieger.

'I want you to set up a temporary dressing station under the trees over there,' he said, pointing to a nearby copse. 'And send Schwann back to the hamlet to see if any civilians were injured.'

***

Schwann returned a short while later. 'The hamlet's deserted,' he said to Gabriel. 'Either the villagers were forewarned of the attack, or they fled when it started.'

'I see.' Gabriel was briefly troubled at this news, concerned that some among the Austrians might think the Serbian villagers had played a role in the ambush. But he was too busy to pay it much attention now: eleven men had been killed and seventeen wounded. 'Help Lieutenant Flieger stabilise the casualties, and find some stretcher bearers to carry the injured back to chief Fischer at the Aid Station on the Drina.'

***

The Austrians broke camp, and after making sure that all the casualties had been treated, Gabriel and the rest of the medical column followed the vanguard east towards the mountains. By early afternoon they had arrived at the lower slopes and stopped to set up another dressing station. With a small telescope, Gabriel watched as the Alpine troops continued up the gradient, moving like mountain goats as they climbed from boulder to boulder, crevice to crevice. He saw several orange flashes and puffs of smoke, and a moment later heard the echoes of a volley of rifle shots. A few seconds after that, another brighter, bigger flash of yellow within a bursting mushroom of dirty grey smoke appeared and he realised that a grenade had exploded on the slope. The air was filled with the dull ringing thud of explosions, as both sides threw more grenades up and down the mountainside.

Gabriel moved the telescope higher. In the bluffs and crags on the upper mountain heights he could see movement as enemy soldiers ran between the rocks. The sharp crack of rifle shots and the deep boom of exploding grenades reverberated between the peaks as Gabriel watched the Serbian snipers above and the Alpine troops below exchange fire.

'That fucking village we passed yesterday must have given our position away.'

Gabriel lowered the telescope. The young lieutenant who had just spoken the words was having his ankle bandaged by Klaus. 'Those villagers need to be taught a lesson,' he continued. 'Serbian bastards.'

'We don't know that for certain,' Gabriel said quietly. 'The enemy have spotters high on the mountain who would have seen us—'

'Pah.' The lieutenant waved a hand dismissively. 'It's the villagers. All the Serbs hate us Austrians—'

At another echoing volley of gunshots, Gabriel turned away and looked through the telescope again. A line of Alpine soldiers – a forward reconnaissance team – was making its way up the slope towards the Serbian positions. He saw more yellow flashes, heard the staccato rattle of rifle fire, then saw the men of both sides clash, grappling together on the slopes, man to man, bayonet to bayonet. He was sickened as he watched the melee: men sticking cold steel into each other, clubbing each other with rifle butts, strangling each other, killing each other. An awful sensation filled him and he lowered the telescope and turned away, partly in despair, partly in disgust that he was connected with such brutality.

The skirmish was quickly over, and from one of the wounded Austrians brought back to the dressing station, Gabriel learnt that a number of Serbian army observers, well hidden on the slopes above, had been found and killed. He was relieved at this news, which he hoped would dispel the rumours that any Serbian villagers had given their positions away. But then, just as the main assault by the rest of the regiment was about to begin, an order came up the line that they were to immediately disengage from the enemy and retreat to the Drina. The fight was over before it had even properly started.

Frustration showed on the faces of the men around Gabriel, angry about the enforced withdrawal as they cursed everybody and everything Serbian. He watched as the remainder of the casualties from the skirmish were carried down to the dressing station at the foot of the mountain, pleased to see that Flieger and the others had overcome their nerves and were managing the cases with skill. Several more pairs of stretcher-bearers were selected – strong country boys, with stamina and agility – who hoisted the stretchers up and began the long walk back towards the Drina.

***

By early evening the main body of troops was well on its way back towards Bosnia. At the back of the column, just ahead of the protective rear-guard, Gabriel rode alongside Flieger, with Schwann and Berger a little way behind. As they approached the hamlet they had passed on their way towards the mountains, Gabriel heard a faint wailing, which grew louder the closer they came to the village. By the time they reached the hamlet, the noise had increased to an anguished howling interspersed with screams and shouts of distress. As he rounded a corner and followed the dusty track into the centre of the village, Gabriel saw – with shock – the source of the problem.

Five bodies hung from a temporary gallows erected near the village well, gently swaying from side to side, one body spiralling to and fro. My God, thought Gabriel, his mouth falling open, revulsion in his gut as he realised that these were civilians. And then with horror he saw that two of the bodies were young women.

Clustered nearby, a group of older women and young children were weeping hysterically. In front of them was a line of Austrian soldiers, who held them back with rifles across their chests. Other soldiers were calmly watching the executions. Standing in front of the gallows was a sergeant smoking a cheroot, a rifle slung over his shoulders, an untroubled look on his stubbled face as he eyed the swaying bodies. Gabriel dug his heels into the horse's flank and galloped across, swung off the saddle and jumped to the ground.

'What the hell is going on? Those are women for God's sake!'

The sergeant removed the cheroot, spitting out a small piece of tobacco before lazily coming to attention.

'Just following orders, Captain.'

'What orders?' Gabriel shouted, angry at the sergeant's apparent indifference. 'To hang civilians?'

The sergeant's face was impassive and the soldiers standing to one side were eyeing the exchange with interest.

'My orders, Captain, were to take three men at random from this village and make an example of them. During the attack on our camp yesterday we found the village deserted, as if the villagers had been warned. Yet on our way back here today, we find it full again. The major believes someone in the village must have given our position away to the Serbs. That is spying, Captain, punishable by death. It cost the lives of a dozen of our boys.'

'And the women?' Gabriel said, his fists clenched tight by his sides.

'They assaulted my soldiers as we took the men away, and I am under instructions that no resistance is to be tolerated.' He flicked ash off the end of his cheroot. 'It may appear harsh, Captain, but the major has given clear instructions.'

'This is… this is…' The frustration Gabriel felt was tearing him inside, almost more than he could bear. His job was to save lives, not be part of something like this.

'May I remind you, Captain,' said the sergeant, 'that the Field Marshall's orders state that kindness to the Serbian population may endanger our troops.'

Gabriel watched the sobbing older women and children, their appalled, tear-streaked faces. One of the women gently spiralling on the end of her rope had glossy black hair, and hanging down her back were braids of brightly coloured ribbons, interwoven reds and yellows and blues. The contrast between the ugliness of the woman's death and the lustrous colours of her hair and ribbons was so shocking that Gabriel thought his knees would give way. This was so very wrong, a horrific deed that mocked his vocation. He was simultaneously sickened and conflicted – torn by his regard for the sanctity of life, yet the need to obey orders. He turned back to the sergeant.

'This is… inhuman,' he finally said, shaking his head again, his voice barely a whisper.

The sergeant shrugged. 'Only following orders, Captain. We're at war. Take it up with the major if you want.'

The sergeant's cheroot had almost burned down to his fingers. He lifted the stub to his lips and inhaled a last lungful of smoke, before turning to the soldiers standing behind him. 'Cut them down,' he said, flicking the cheroot away. He ground the smouldering stub with the heel of his boot and then walked away.

Later that day, as Gabriel rode back to Bosnia, he felt a new emotion, one he had never experienced before:

Shame.

10

Her nose pressed hard against the carriage window, Elspeth peered through the glass into the gathering twilight. The lights were only just coming on in the cottages and farmhouses of the Haute Normandie that slid past the train window. Sitting opposite Elspeth, Sylvia had her eyes closed, her head resting gently to one side: she had fallen asleep as soon as the train left Dieppe earlier that evening, exhausted after the long ferry crossing from Newhaven that morning. But Elspeth was too excited to sleep, thrilled that at last they were on their way to Paris.

The war had sped up the normally slow hospital bureaucracy and it had taken only a week to prepare for their departure. After Elspeth and Sylvia had been interviewed and accepted by the Women's Hospital Corp, they had handed in their notices to St Mary's, received their typhoid inoculations, and met with the St John's Ambulance Association, who organised passports, ferry tickets, and the necessary Red Cross travel permits to cross into France. With a suitcase each, and well stocked with Mothersils seasickness remedy, they had arrived at

Victoria railway station early that morning to catch the milk train for Newhaven.

The fields of Normandy quickly gave way to the Ile de France, and shortly before midnight the train entered the suburbs of Paris. Elspeth woke Sylvia as they pulled into the Gare du Nord. The two women collected their suitcases and stepped down onto the platform, where a tall girl in a white skirt and jacket, and a Red Cross armband, appeared to be waiting for them.

'Dr Stewart?'

'Yes?'

'Oh, excellent – I'm Rosemary, one of the VADs from the Women's Hospital Auxiliaire.' She shook Elspeth's hand and was then introduced to Sylvia. 'Welcome to Paris,' she said to them both, 'and apologies from Dr Anderson; she can't be here to meet you as she's still operating on a batch of casualties who arrived earlier today. But if you both follow me, there's a car waiting outside.'

As she and Sylvia shadowed Rosemary through the station concourse, Elspeth saw several hospital trains standing at other platforms. Pairs of white-coated male orderlies were stretchering casualties towards the station exit, and Rosemary followed them out into the station forecourt. There was no street lighting of any sort, and in the darkness Elspeth could only just make out the line of army ambulances standing by the kerb.

'I'm afraid there's a strict curfew and blackout in place,' she said, leading them past the ambulances and up to a parked car, where the driver, an older man with white hair, was asleep at the steering wheel. She tapped on the window but the man did not budge. 'Henri!' she shouted, and then rapped more strongly on the window with her knuckles. Still he did not rouse and so she opened the car door and shook him. Elspeth heard him jerk awake, and even in the gloom she could now see the whites of his eyes.

'*Je m'excuse*,' he said, sitting up and rubbing his face with both hands.

Rosemary turned to Elspeth. 'Henri's a bit hard of hearing,' she said, as the old man climbed out of the car and helped the women put their suitcases in the boot. And then with Rosemary sitting beside Henri, and Elspeth and Sylvia in the rear, they set off.

Driving slowly through the unlit streets, their headlights taped so that only a thin slit of light illuminated the cobbles, Elspeth saw a city vastly different from what she had expected. The rapid advance through France had taken the German army to within only thirty miles of Paris; the threat was considered so serious, Rosemary told her, that the government had fled the capital. All the shops, cafés and restaurants they passed were shuttered and padlocked, and the streets were deserted except for ambulances ferrying casualties to the hospitals. A flash of light suddenly appeared in the sky, and searchlights lit up the darkness, their brilliant white columns criss-crossing the night sky above the Eiffel Tower and spires on the Paris horizon.

'Look!' Sylvia said, suddenly alert as she pointed along the line of one of the searchlight beams. 'I think I can see an aeroplane.'

Elspeth pushed down the window of the car and leant out. Above her she saw a flash of silver and heard the panting throb of a plane's engine. She watched the searchlight pursue the craft, the plane's wings wobbling as it tried to escape the beam. And then the car swung into a narrow side street with tall buildings on either side and she lost sight of the chase.

The car rattled over bumpy cobbles before turning into the Champs-Élyseés, and after a short drive down the deserted avenue they arrived at the grand façade of Claridges Hotel. Even in the darkness Elspeth could see that the hotel was a gorgeous shell of marble and gilt. But carrying her suitcase through the revolving door and into the lobby, she was surprised at the lack of decor and furniture in the reception.

'The building was only finished two months ago,' Rosemary explained. 'When we arrived here last week there was no crockery or linen, and we only managed to get those by making a real nuisance of ourselves. The hotel's concierge says the military authorities would have had an easier time fighting the Germans than facing so many assertive Scottish ladies,' she said with a smirk, leading them across the lobby to the elevators.

'How much of the hotel do we have?' Elspeth asked as they waited for the lift to arrive.

'They've given us the top floor and we've converted several of the *de luxe* suites into small ward bays, each holding four beds, for the ordinary ranks. Some of the smaller suites have been converted into single rooms for the senior officers.'

A bell pinged and the lift arrived. 'Sorry, there's

no bellboy – they've all been called up,' Rosemary said, pulling the metal safety grill aside and leading the women into the lift cabin. She closed the grille and then pressed the button for the sixth floor.

'How many patients do we have?' Sylvia asked.

'We admitted our first casualties only eight days ago and yesterday there were forty-two patients on the wards. Then this afternoon we admitted another twelve. They're all British soldiers, from Mons and the Marne.'

They arrived at the sixth floor and Elspeth stepped out into a long white-painted corridor, a thick, plush turquois-and-gold carpet beneath her feet. Rosemary, however, waited inside the lift.

'The operating theatre is down there,' she said, pointing Elspeth towards the far end of the corridor. 'Dr Garrett Anderson said you should report to her as soon as you arrive.' She turned to Sylvia. 'I'll take you to our sleeping quarters; they're on the floor below.'

'Where *exactly* is the operating theatre?' Elspeth asked, looking along the corridor.

'In the suite at the far end. You'll find Dr Anderson in the bathroom.'

Elspeth raised an eyebrow. 'Bathroom?'

'You'll understand when you get there.' Rosemary said, with a cryptic smile as the lift doors shut.

A strong smell of new carpet, fresh paint and hospital disinfectant was in the air as Elspeth walked along the corridor, her shoes sinking into the thick pile. She passed a row of doors, came to the last one, turned the handle and entered.

A nurse was sitting at a desk in the middle of the room. In the dim light cast from a table lamp resting on the desk, Elspeth saw six trollies pushed up against the walls. On each trolley lay a wounded soldier: a second nurse was tending one of the soldiers, who had that dopey post-anaesthetic look that Elspeth recognised; fresh bloodstains on the dressed stumps of his amputated legs indicated recent surgery. Elspeth quietly introduced herself to the nurse at the desk.

'Ah, Dr Stewart,' the nurse replied. 'Dr Anderson is expecting you.'

'I'm told she's in the bathroom?' Elspeth inquired.

The nurse grinned. 'Yes, that's right. She and Dr Murray should be finishing soon. There's only one other case after this.'

Elspeth glanced at the patients around the room. 'This is your operating recovery area?'

'Yes, that's right.'

'So the bathroom must be…'

'Our operating theatre,' the nurse said, and then pointed to a door at the far end of the room.

Elspeth walked towards it and saw a piece of paper tacked to the frame.

Thursday, 25 September
Cpl E. Granger   L lung wound/drain
Pt. S. Davis   Abdomen debride
Pt. F. Smith   Bilateral leg BKA's
Pt. S. McCray   Skull Trephine

There were a further eight names on the list – twelve in total – ten of which had been scored through. Elspeth leant against the door, pressing her ear close to the wood, and heard an intermittent harsh rasping noise. Then she glanced at the eleventh name on the paper.

Pt. R. Perkins R Leg AKA

AKA, she knew, was shorthand for 'Above knee amputation'.

She pushed the door open – was briefly dazzled by the blaze from strip lights on the ceiling – and saw a large bathroom with floors and walls of glazed white tiles. Between the toilet and bath on one side, and two wash-hand basins on the other, stood a trestle table. And on this improvised operating table lay a young soldier. At his head sat a young woman in a white medical smock, dripping liquid from a brown bottle onto a gauze mask held over his face. Another woman, an orderly, Elspeth presumed, stood by her side. Elspeth slipped through the doorway.

Two surgeons were standing on either side of the patient, both dressed in the same white smocks as the anaesthetist but their gowns heavily bloodstained. Both wore white cotton surgical caps and muslin masks that covered the lower parts of their faces, leaving only their eyes visible above the veils. One of the surgeons was holding the patient's upper thigh, the bloodstained latex gloves gripping either side of a deep incision; the patient's knee, below the surgeon's hands, was a smashed mangle of grey bone and purplish muscle. The other surgeon was hunched over the leg, energetically sawing through the thighbone, deep within the wound. The harsh rasping sounds climbed in pitch as the saw cut through the outer cortex of the femur and then – with a shudder – the lower leg and knee separated from the thigh and rolled onto its side. The surgeon lifted the amputated limb, and, grunting with the effort, handed it to the orderly, who carried it away and dropped it into the bath. It struck the metal bottom with a thud, and even from where she was standing Elspeth could detect the unmistakable whiff of gangrene.

The surgeon holding the saw turned and placed it, with a clatter, onto a steel instrument tray by her side. Only now, as she picked up a steel bone file from the same tray, did she appear to notice Elspeth's presence.

'Ah.' she said, her voice muffled through the facemask. 'We have a visitor, Louisa.'

The surgeon standing opposite was adjusting the strap on a tourniquet as she looked up.

'Dr Stewart?'

Elspeth took a step closer. 'Yes.'

'Oh good.' She finished tightening the strap. 'We weren't sure your train would make it through. I'm sorry I couldn't greet you personally. I'm Louisa Garret Anderson and this,' she pointed at the woman holding the bone file, 'is Flora Murray.'

'Pleased to meet you, Dr Stewart,' said Dr Murray. She turned back to Dr Anderson. 'Alice can help me finish if you want to show Dr Stewart around, Louisa,' she said, nodding towards the orderly who had just dropped the leg in the bath.

'Good idea,' Dr Anderson replied and then walked over to the wash-hand basins. She rinsed her gloves under a tap at the first basin, then peeled them off and dropped them into the second basin. Arriving at her side, Elspeth saw that this basin was full of gloves floating in a faintly cloudy solution. Dr Anderson pulled her facemask down, and then picked up a large metal draining spoon. 'We've had quite a problem with supplies,' she said to Elspeth as she prodded the gloves below the surface, 'so we've had to improvise. This is dilute carbolic acid: we soak the gloves in it so they're ready to be used later.' She put the spoon down and dried her fingers on a towel. 'Well, we're very pleased to see you, Dr Stewart,' she said, shaking Elspeth's hand. 'We've been so busy. Even though Flora's primarily a physician, she's had to temporarily assist me with the surgical work.'

'I'm pleased to be here, too, Dr Ander—'

'Oh, please call me Louisa,' she interrupted, 'unless there's a man in the room. In which case I prefer us to use our formal titles.'

'Of course,' Elspeth replied. 'And similarly it's Elspeth – if you would prefer?'

Louisa fixed her with calm, clear eyes. 'Elspeth it is then.'

She removed the surgical cap, revealing short dark hair, then stripped off the bloodstained surgical smock and dropped it into a pannier next to the washbasins. She was dressed in a long grey skirt and linen blouse, and to

Elspeth's surprise the green-and-red WSPU badge was pinned to the front of her shirt. Pushing the door open, she led Elspeth back into the recovery area.

'There's one more case to do, but I'll take you on a quick tour before we start. By the way, what do you think of using a bathroom as an operating theatre?'

Elspeth grinned. 'I think it's a marvellous idea. Some might think it unhygienic, but I can see that the constant supply of hot and cold water, tiled surfaces and easy waste disposal make it the logical choice.'

Louisa smiled. 'I'm glad you approve. We've also got a sterilising room for the surgical equipment. We've installed some gas rings and fish kettles to boil the instruments. There's a dispensary and a mortuary chapel.' She looked a little sombre as she led Elspeth past the nurse at the desk and into the corridor outside. 'We've had two deaths so far, both French soldiers who came to us with untreatable wounds. They were buried with full military honours a few days ago. The French authorities provided a firing piquet of eight soldiers, two in front and three on either side of the coffins, and on the way to the church, everyone in the street saluted or crossed themselves.' Her face suddenly brightened. 'Mustn't get too maudlin' about it.'

She took Elspeth on a tour of the hotel suites, introducing her to the night orderlies on the way round. As they walked between the beds, Elspeth was quizzed on how she would have managed the wounded soldiers' injuries; Louisa seemed satisfied with her answers. Although most of the men they passed were asleep, one or two were awake. Elspeth could tell from their expressions that they were clearly in awe of Louisa.

'Some of the injuries are horrendous. It's quite shocking how brutal men can be towards each other. We've had to trephine skulls for bullets, explore open lung wounds, fix and plaster shattered compound fractures – actually the severely fractured thighs are the heaviest work as it can take the best part of an hour and four of our VADs to dress them. And of course there are a lot of abdominal and chest wounds. Come and look at this.'

They stopped beside the bed of a pale-faced young soldier, a red rubber tube from his chest draining into a bottle by the side of his bed, half-filled with bubbling bloodstained fluid. He coughed and flinched but still made the effort to smile as they arrived at his side.

'Breathing any easier, Corporal?' Louisa asked.

'Thanking you, ma'am,' he replied in a soft Welsh lilt. 'It's definitely easier now that tube's in place.'

She nodded. 'Good. We'll need to allow the lung time to re-expand. The bullet took a big chunk out of your pleura, so it might take a few days for the hole to seal. Are you sore?'

'A little, ma'am, and I feel like pukin' all the time.'

'That's the ether – does it to some people. It'll wash out in the next few hours.'

'All right, ma'am,' he replied. 'Thank you again.'

They left the room and started back towards the operating room.

'It's challenging work and long hours,' Louisa said

as they went, 'but a unique experience and fantastic opportunity to do some good, which is so rewarding. Personally I don't mind the hard work and feel refreshed by the complete change of life. Plus, after years of unpopularity over the suffrage, it's exhilarating to be on top of the wave, helped and approved of by everyone – except the English War Office.'

Elspeth laughed. 'Yes, Dr Inglis had difficulties with the War Office, too. They were not impressed by her proposal for a Scottish Women's Hospital.'

At the mention of Dr Inglis, Louisa pursed her lips. 'Ah yes, dear Elsie.' She briefly looked down at the WSPU brooch pinned to her blouse. 'She and Flora used to be good friends when they worked together in Edinburgh. But I know that Dr Inglis is not a keen supporter of the Pankhursts.' She looked at Elspeth in a curious way. 'You, I gather, have a different view on this issue?'

Elspeth tensed. 'Well, yes. I was... well, still am actually... a member of the WSPU.' She eyed the brooch before continuing. 'Not everybody agrees with some of their tactics, so I don't like to advertise my involvement until I know people's feelings.'

They had arrived outside the operating theatre again, but Louisa led Elspeth past it to another door. She pushed it open and silently signalled for Elspeth to follow her in. They were alone inside a large store cupboard full of linen sheets and wool blankets. Louisa lowered her voice.

'Actually, Elspeth, I already knew you were a WSPU member. And I suspect you know as much about my past.' Elspeth hesitated, but then nodded as Louisa continued.

'I have many contacts within the WSPU and had you checked out very thoroughly.' She dropped her voice to a whisper. 'And from what I've heard, and from what you are reported to have done' – she paused and Elspeth held her breath – 'well, let me just say that Flora and I are extremely pleased that an individual with the courage to execute such a deed has agreed to work alongside us.'

Elspeth gave a sigh of relief as Louisa continued.

'I know there are some – like Dr Inglis – who denigrate what the WSPU has done to further the cause of women's suffrage. But I am a firm believer that 'Deeds not Words' is the best credo for the advancement of our cause. In the past I undertook deeds that were viewed as criminal and was caught and punished. You, clever girl, were not caught. I don't regret my past deeds, and I don't think you should regret yours either. They were our only options at that time. I still believe in deeds not words, but the war has given us the opportunity to do *good* deeds, as we are here. It is still suffrage work, but in another form.'

'Thank you for that, Louisa,' Elspeth said with a mixture of pride and relief.

'Nobody apart from Flora and I know about this, and we won't discuss it with anybody else or bring it up again. Anyway, we'd better get back. You can help with the last case, let Flora get back to being a physician again.'

***

'Dr Stewart, please come quickly. Private Dalgliesh is having another seizure.'

Elspeth grimaced; I hope Flora returns quickly, she thought as she followed the VAD along the corridor and into the room where the young soldier was being nursed.

Six weeks had passed since Elspeth had arrived at Claridges, and in that time she had fully immersed herself in the work of the hospital, assisting Louisa in theatre and operating on a wide range of injuries: trephining holes in skulls, amputating limbs, debriding wounds, opening chests and abdomens, removing bullets and shrapnel, lancing abscesses, evacuating haematomas, stitching ears and noses and lips. The surgical work was much as she had imagined, but tetanus was not something she had seen before. Private Dalgliesh, a likeable Scotsman who seemed to be recovering from his wounds, had unexpectedly developed the fits and spasms of full-blown tetanus yesterday evening.

As Elspeth entered the room she saw his body arched on the bed, bent like a bow between his heels and the back of his head, his face drawn back into a ghastly grin with his teeth exposed. There was nothing she could do, and she and Rosemary waited until the convulsion passed and the young soldier fell back to the bed, pouring sweat, panting. He looked exhausted, but Elspeth could see that some of his muscles were still twitching: another seizure was only a few minutes away, and she knew he would not be able to cope with this for much longer.

They had already given the man all the anti-tetanus serum they had in the hospital – only fifteen hundred units – but the seizures had continued. However Elspeth knew of an experimental treatment. She remembered attending a teaching round at St Mary's where much higher doses of anti-tetanus serum injected directly into the spinal canal of a tetanus sufferer had saved the patient. She had told Flora about the case that morning, and Flora had immediately gone over to the British Military Hospital at Versailles to see if the Royal Army Medical Corps could give them more serum.

As Elspeth watched the exhausted soldier's spasms finally stop, the door to the room suddenly flew open and Sylvia appeared, wheeling a small procedure trolley in front of her. 'Dr Murray's just got back,' she said. 'She's got the serum and asked me to prepare for an immediate lumbar puncture.'

Before Elspeth could reply, Flora Murray entered the room holding a small canvas bag, a large smile on her face. 'They gave me ten bottles, Elspeth, each holding fifty thousand units,' she said breathlessly.

'Half a million units? Elspeth said, amazed.

Yes, isn't it wonderful? And apparently they've heard many good things about us. Did you know our survival rates are the highest of all the hospitals caring for British troops?' She opened the bag and removed a glass vial. 'Can you do the LP, Elspeth? I'll draw up the serum.'

Helped by Sylvia and Rosemary, Elspeth manoeuvred the young man into the foetal position. He did not resist their manhandling and appeared moribund, his eyes closed, his mouth slightly ajar. 'You'll feel a wee jag in the lower back,' Elspeth told the young man, but he gave no sign of awareness as she inserted the spinal needle through the skin between two of his lower backbones. She felt the pop as the needle entered the dural space: removing the end cap from the needle Elspeth was rewarded with several drops of glistening spinal fluid.

'You made that look easy,' Flora said, as she knelt beside Elspeth and connected the syringe to the end of the needle.

'He's a skinny wee thing, so it wasn't difficult,' Elspeth replied.

'You're too modest,' Flora said with a smile as she injected the contents of the syringe, and then pulled the needle out while Sylvia applied pressure over the puncture site. She stood up and looked down at Elspeth. 'Well, all we can do now is wait and see if it works.'

The following evening, after returning from an expedition to collect some casualties, Elspeth was pleased to hear that he'd had no further seizures. It was at the end of a busy day: she and Sylvia had accompanied Louisa by motor ambulance to Braisne, a small town only a few miles behind the fighting line. They had received a telegram that morning from the medical officer at the casualty clearing station asking if they could take some of the more seriously wounded back to Paris, and Henri had driven them there, a distance of nearly a hundred miles over roads cut up by the traffic of war.

The drive gave them the opportunity to witness at first hand the effects of the fighting: dead horses lying in the fields, bellies bloated, legs pointing in the air like a small child's crude cartoon of death; shell-splintered trees – stripped of bark and foliage – tilted at awkward angles from the effects of artillery fire; rows of abandoned houses, piles of rubble in the street, stray dogs sniffing amongst the debris for scraps of food. It was a terrible yet fascinating sight. They passed through this devastated landscape and eventually arrived in Braisne, where they found the wounded lying inside a church with no water or heating, the noise of nearby fighting rattling the stained-glass windows above their heads. They managed to find space in the ambulance for four of the more serious cases and then had to hurry back to Paris as the gates were rigidly closed for the eight o'clock curfew, passports and permits being of no use after that hour.

They arrived back just in time, and after helping unload the wounded and admitting them to the wards, Elspeth, Sylvia and Louisa retired to the mess kitchen for a late supper of cocoa and buttered toast.

'I don't think any other unit could have done better than we did today,' Louisa said with a satisfied smile. 'Our team performed superbly. And Flora says that Private Dalgliesh is doing very well, thanks to your suggestion.'

'Good teamwork is a result of good leadership,' Elspeth said.

'That's kind of you to say,' Louisa answered, 'but actually I think it's because women work better together than men. They're less competitive with each other and more willing to co-operate. I desperately wish the whole organisation for the care of the wounded – their transport, the disposition of base and field hospitals, their clothing and feeding – could be put into the hands of women. It is not military work, merely a matter of organisation, of common sense and attention to detail. Women could do it so much better than it is currently done.'

This is real suffrage work, Elspeth thought.

★★★

Eventually the fighting moved farther away from Paris and the number of wounded men arriving at the hospital began to diminish. By the end of October, there was even a rumour that the French president and his government might soon return to the capital. There were now periods during the day when little was happening on the wards, and Elspeth and Sylvia were encouraged to go out and enjoy the sights of Paris. Louisa and Flora led by example, taking a daily walk together to explore the narrow rues and alleyways of this part of the city. So one evening in early November, with the capital looking particularly beautiful on a moonlit night, Elspeth and Sylvia decided to go for a stroll.

It was an enchanting night. The streets in their quarter of the city were still deserted – most of the good houses in the area were still empty and shuttered – and the moon, suspended in the sky, bathed the cobblestones in a buttery light. For the first time since they had arrived in Paris, the magic of the city was revealed, and searchlights on the roof of the Madeleine and Eiffel Tower swept across the skyline to show the city in its true splendour. With the characteristic Paris architecture as a backdrop, Elspeth and Sylvia strolled contentedly across the cobbles and along the bank of the Seine, past the Grand Palais and the Chambre des Deputes.

At first they saw no other pedestrians, but as they walked past one of the bridges straddling the river, from a distance Elspeth spotted a couple silhouetted in the moonlight, standing close together as they leant over the parapet to peer at the water below. The affection between the pair was unmistakable as they stood with heads inclined towards each other, and as she walked past the entrance to the bridge Elspeth smiled at this typically tender Parisian scene.

She had already walked on a little farther, before she suddenly realised that Sylvia was no longer at her side, but had instead stopped at the bridge entrance to stare at the pair of lovers. Elspeth saw a curious expression on Sylvia's face; when she turned to look more closely at the couple on the bridge, she was startled to realise that she was looking at Louisa and Flora.

It was apparent that the couple did not know they had been seen: they slowly leant back and then – hands entwined – ambled to the far side of the bridge. Having witnessed this intimacy, Elspeth felt the heat rise to her cheeks.

Sylvia arrived at her side. 'Did you not realise?' she asked Elspeth, an amused look on her face. Elspeth's blush became deeper; how could she not have known this?

'Well… I knew they were close, but…'

Sylvia's eyes glinted like emeralds in the moonlight as she shook her head and laughed. 'Dear, Ellie: for someone so intelligent, sometimes you do amaze me.'

Elspeth gave a wry smile. 'Well that sort of thing doesn't much happen on the Isle of Skye.'

'Not that you'd notice if it did,' Sylvia said with a grin. 'It's not such a strange thing you know. It's only *l'amour*. We are in Paris, after all.'

★★★

One morning towards the end of November, as Elspeth and Sylvia were about to start their shift, the hotel concierge brought a letter up to their room. It was addressed to Sylvia and bore a London postmark.

'I think it might be from Vera,' Sylvia said, tearing the envelope open. 'It is,' she said excitedly and then began to read aloud.

"Dear Sylvie,
I hope this letter finds you and Elspeth both in good health and enjoying your work in Paris. As your hospital is at Claridges, I picture it being a very grand place, with gold-plated cutlery and silver service…"

Sylvia lowered the letter and looked up at Elspeth with a wry smile. 'I imagine a lot of people back home are wondering what a hospital inside Claridges must look like.'

'Keep reading, please,' Elspeth replied, impatient for news of home. Sylvie lifted the letter and again began to read.

"'The newspapers tell us that the Germans have now been pushed away from Paris, but I suspect you are still busy. The list of British casualties has shocked everybody here. My brother has been called up so I've been back to the farm to see him before he starts his training.'"

Sylvia fell silent while she read to herself, but then began to read aloud again. 'Then she writes about her parents… her father's emphysema… a bit about her mother…' She paused again. 'Ah, this is a bit more interesting:

"'And now for news of Anya. I spoke to Mrs Kingsbury, her landlady, last week and she said that the police had recently come round to ask her questions about Anya. They told Mrs Kingsbury that they'd checked the emigration records at all the ports and discovered that Anya had taken a ferry from Dover to Calais. Then the police checked with the French Railway authorities, and—'"

She stopped speaking and lowered the letter to her lap, and Elspeth saw the look of surprise on her face. 'What is it?'

Sylvia took a deep a breath and lifted the letter to read again. '"— checked with the French Railway authorities",' she repeated, '"and learnt that Anya caught a train to Paris."'

Paris? Elspeth sat bolt upright in her chair, but a look of relief had already returned to Sylvia's face.

'"From Paris, she was reported to have a bought a ticket for Marseille."' Sylvia continued, and then lowered the letter to her lap once more. 'How odd,' she said.

'Strange to think she might have been here in Paris, at much the same time as us,' Elspeth replied. 'I wonder why she's gone to Marseille… Perhaps she's trying to make her way back to wherever she came from originally?'

Sylvia nodded thoughtfully and lifted the letter again. She read silently for a moment and then suddenly her eyes opened wide. 'Vera's joined the Scottish Women's Unit!' she exclaimed, quickly turning the letter over, her eyes flicking to and fro as she hurriedly read the words. 'She's been accepted as a driver and is going to join us for the Serbian expedition!'

'Oh, let me see!' Elspeth said, snatching the letter away from Sylvia. She quickly read the relevant sentences. And then, as she moved on to the next paragraph, her face broke into a smile.

'What?' Sylvia asked, seeing the amused look on Elspeth's face.

'Vera goes on to write that everybody going to Serbia will have to wear a uniform.'

'*Uniforms*?' Sylvia said with obvious dismay. 'What sort of uniforms?'

'Tartan, apparently,' Elspeth said, trying not to laugh at the look of horror that appeared on Sylvia's face.

'*Tartan*?' Sylvia groaned, shook her head 'I can't *wait* to see what we look like in those.'

11

Central Serbia, December 1914 – January 1915

Klaus knelt beside the soldier's bed and peeled away the bandage covering the wounded soldier's abdomen. 'Nice job, Captain,' he said.

Gabriel looked down at the line of stitches, gently palpated the wound edge, and then bent forward to sniff: Good, he thought, no visible signs or smell of infection. He nodded, satisfied with his work. 'All right, dress the wound, Klaus, and see if you can find space on a wagon to take him back to Bosnia later today.' He stepped away from the patient and stretched the stiffness out of his spine. 'Any more to see?'

'No, Captain, that's everybody you operated on last night.'

Gabriel yawned. 'Good, I need some time to write up my notes.' A low growl – like thunder from a distant summer storm – came through the canvas wall of the post-operative tent. Gabriel exchanged an alarmed glance with Klaus, wrapped himself in his greatcoat and went outside.

The Divisional Aid Station was now situated in the middle of a farmer's paddock deep in Serbian territory.

They had arrived here three days ago, following in the footsteps of the Austrian vanguard that had launched another offensive two weeks earlier. Surprisingly the Serbians had put up very little resistance this time, and within ten days the Austrians had crossed the mountains deep into the central Serbian plain and taken Kragujevac, their objective since the war began. However, information gleaned from interrogated prisoners indicated that the reason for the Serbian retreat was that they had run out of ammunition for their fast-firing French howitzers. Field Marshall Potiorek increased the pace of advance, ordering his army even deeper into enemy territory. But the Austrian supply lines were already overstretched and vital supplies of food and ammunition failed to make it through to the front-line troops. The Field Marshall had been warned the lines were dangerously thin, but he insisted they press their advantage over the Serbs and push on.

The speed of advance meant that Gabriel's medical column struggled to keep up with the forward dressing stations. But keep up it did, and his wagons continued to trundle through the countryside, through shattered villages and towns. And in these devastated areas Gabriel saw the smoking ruins of buildings, the scattered possessions of fleeing civilians, the carcasses of cattle rotting in the fields, and the dead of both armies sprawled in the streets. Finally, at the end of the first week of December, the medical column had come to a halt at a farm only six kilometres west of Kragujevac.

The farmer's paddock was enclosed by hedgerows,

which sheltered the hospital tents from the wind. On the western side of the field there was a cluster of disused stables, which Gabriel had considered using, but the leaky roof and manure-soiled floors made them unsuitable for casualties. In the middle of the hedge on the opposite side of the field was a cattle gate, and Gabriel could see several of his orderlies standing by the gatepost, staring east towards the horizon, at clouds that flickered from the light of reflected shell bursts below. Even at this distance from the front Gabriel could feel the air hum and the earth tremble with each explosion. Christ, he thought – something big was happening. Klaus appeared at his shoulder.

'Doesn't sound good, Captain.'

'Is Trauber back yet?'

Klaus looked over Gabriel's shoulder, at a horse tethered outside the stables. 'That's his horse over there, Captain. He must have got back while you were doing your ward round. He'll be stabling his horse – I'll tell him to come and speak to you.'

As Klaus went off to fetch Trauber, Gabriel hugged his arms around himself for warmth and looked up at the sky; the ochre-tinged bellies of clouds drifted low overhead, pregnant with snow. There were a lot of things preying on his mind: as well as the dropping temperatures and impending snow there was also the re-supply problem. They had run out of paraffin, almost all food, and now were critically short of medical supplies, including basics like bandages and dressings. Yesterday a number of newly arrived casualties had brought rumours of a Serbian counteroffensive. There had been no formal communication from 6th Army command as to what exactly was happening, so Gabriel had sent Corporal Trauber, one of his orderlies, forward to find out what was going on.

'Sorry, Captain, I was just making sure my horse was secure.' Trauber looked tired, his eyes red-rimmed, his coat covered in a layer of dust, as he arrived at Gabriel's side, Klaus a little way behind him. 'I only got back a few minutes ago.'

'Did you find out what's happening?' Gabriel asked.

'There *is* a strong counteroffensive under way.' Trauber replied. 'The Serbs have been resupplied with shells for their French howitzers.'

'That's what I feared,' said Gabriel, glancing eastwards again and seeing another flash of light in the clouds on the horizon. He turned back to Trauber. 'How is Lieutenant Flieger getting on?'

'He's struggling to cope, Captain. They're sited on the eastern side of Kragujevac, where there's fierce fighting, and their dressing station is swamped with casualties. Some of the more seriously wounded have already started the journey back and should be arriving shortly. For the time being our lines appear to be holding, although there are rumours that some of our units have surrendered as they've run out of ammunition.'

'All right, thank you, Trauber. Get yourself cleaned up and try to find some breakfast – if you can.' He turned to Klaus. 'Tell the other orderlies to prepare for the imminent arrival of casualties.'

★★★

The wounded began to arrive later that morning, carried in the back of ox carts or in straw panniers strapped to the sides of mules. Working with Berger and Schwann in the resuscitation tent, Gabriel triaged the casualties to decide who should live and who should die. Those with untreatable wounds were sent to the comfort tent, where the dwindling supply of morphine was used to ease their passing, while those with a chance of survival were prepared for surgery. Then Gabriel went to work in the operating tent.

All afternoon and evening, Gabriel – with Berger anaesthetising the patients – struggled to deal with the tide of wrecked bodies. It was the surgery of the Napoleonic era: amputating limbs, ligating arteries, cauterising stumps, trepanning skulls, opening abdomens to stop bleeding and search for bullets or winkle out shards of shrapnel. But the wounded kept coming and so he worked on into the night, the operating tent illuminated by smoky candlelight as the paraffin for the oil lamps ran out. In the gloomy, sooty, sleep-deprived atmosphere of the tent, Gabriel toiled as if in a dream, in that state that occurs just before waking. His eyes were filled with images of broken bodies, his nose, with the sweet smell of chloroform and blood, his ears, with the sounds of men in pain. He worked through midnight and on into the early hours of the morning. Finally, shortly before dawn, he finished the last case.

Berger removed the ether mask from the patient's face and then supervised the orderlies, who hefted the patient off the operating table onto a stretcher and carried him out to the overfilled recovery tent. Gabriel peeled off his rubber gloves, dropped them into a bucket by the tent entrance, and walked outside. He felt completely spent, his body numb, his mind blank after such a period of continuous mental and physical activity.

Sweet Jesus, he thought; that was a night he would rather forget. To function amidst such carnage yesterday – to have been able to work effectively – he had suppressed his empathic nature and focussed only on the mechanics of saving lives. But now he thought about the poor young men whose legs and arms he had amputated and whose lives would be for ever changed. For a moment he felt their pain, and then immediately regretted it. Empathy would not help them now, and an effective surgeon must control his emotions and not allow it to interfere with his decision-making, a skill he knew was almost as important as controlling a scalpel.

He stretched his arms and sniffed the clean, cold air, and then walked over to the morgue tent to stare at the pile of amputated limbs stacked beside it, the result of yesterday's handiwork. He saw a rat nibbling at a bloody half-leg; angrily he picked up a clod of earth and threw it at the animal. As the rat scuttled away into the hedgerow, Gabriel made a mental note to tell Klaus and the other orderlies that all body parts must be placed inside the tent in future.

The fresh air was invigorating and the tension fell away from Gabriel's body. A powerful urge to sit down and close his eyes came upon him, but he dared not do so because there was a ward round to do on the post-op cases. Then his stomach growled and a cramp of hunger clutched his belly, and he suddenly remembered he hadn't eaten anything since yesterday morning. He sniffed the air again, and now could smell wood smoke, coffee, burnt toast. Squinting across the encampment he saw Klaus sitting on an upturned wooden crate outside the mess tent, a small campfire in front of him. As he walked towards him, Gabriel saw he was toasting a piece of bread over the fire whilst stirring a scorched pot of coffee that swung from a tripod in the flames.

'Where did you get the bread from?' Gabriel said as he sat on the edge of the crate next to Klaus.

'From the farmer.' Klaus nodded towards the farmhouse in the next field. 'Don't worry, Captain, I asked him very nicely,' he said with a reassuring smile.

Gabriel stared into the fire. It was extremely comforting to listen to the wood crackle and hiss, to feel the heat and watch the flames dance. The feeling of exhaustion was now overwhelming and for a moment he allowed his eyes to close… then he suddenly jerked awake as his head fell forward onto his chest and he almost slipped off the wooden crate. Klaus chuckled as Gabriel re-seated himself and took several deep breaths, forcing his eyes to stay open.

'You need coffee, Captain,' Klaus said, removing the pot from the flames and pouring some of the black liquid into a tin cup. Gabriel took the hot cup, holding it with the lower less-bloodstained part of his surgical gown. He took a sip and then smiled with surprise.

'Real coffee, Klaus. I'm impressed.'

'This is not a time for roast acorns, Captain. I'm sick of that ersatz stuff.'

'Where did you get it from?'

'Best not ask, Captain.'

Gabriel smiled, enjoying the heat of the cup on his hands and the bitter warmth of the coffee in his chest, the chance to let his mind idle. Then he realised how quiet it was: no gunfire, no explosions, no fighting. He tilted his head to one side, straining to listen.

'I noticed it, too,' Klaus said, watching Gabriel. 'I've been out here nearly an hour and heard no noise of battle. No more casualties have come in since midnight. Maybe the Serbs have run out of shells again? Maybe we've pushed them back, stabilised the line?'

'Or maybe our own front line has folded,' Gabriel replied, 'but wouldn't we have seen our men in retreat?'

Klaus shook his head. 'I haven't seen anybody coming back from the front.' He took a bite from the toasted bread and thoughtfully began to chew. 'I hope we have held the line. We badly need resupply.'

'How bad?'

'We have no oil and almost no food. And dressings and drugs are very low.'

'Let's hope they come today.'

'Phaw!' Klaus exclaimed. 'Forgive me for saying so, Captain, but our supply division is really bloody useless.'

Gabriel smiled. 'I think the problem is the lack of horses. We lost so many during the battle for the Cer heights.'

'Well they shouldn't have pushed us so deep, should they? We haven't been resupplied for days now. We can chop wood for heating, but food is another matter.' Klaus looked up at the sky. 'And I'm sure it'll snow today. If supplies don't arrive soon, we'll have no choice but to take it from the farms again.'

Gabriel scowled with frustration as he thought about his lot as an army surgeon. Operating on the wounded and putting his surgical skills to good use was one thing. But sitting in a muddy field with snow about to fall and no idea what was happening in front, or behind, was a completely different matter.

And he hated taking food from civilians. The Serbian peasant farmers had very little to spare, and killing their animals for meat and looting their winter stores felt wrong. In fact the whole war seemed wrong. Gabriel didn't normally bother himself with politics – surgery was his all-consuming passion – but now he questioned the invasion of Serbia. Was it really justified by the Archduke's killing? Did his murder also excuse the violent deaths and maiming of so many thousands of Austrian and Serbian soldiers, the slaying of civilians? Gabriel was supposed to have pride in the Austrian army, and he still felt a strong sense of duty towards his comrades. But having witnessed the execution of the Serbian villagers, he was ashamed at the way the war was being conducted, and now he realised he had also lost his conviction that this was a just fight…

'Damn this stupid war,' he said, and then without thinking swallowed the rest of the coffee, wincing as the hot liquid burned his gullet. He grimaced; served him right – he needed to stay composed whatever the circumstances.

A wry smile played on Klaus's face. 'More coffee, Captain? There's no milk to take the heat out of it, but some schnapps might cool it a little.'

'A drop of schnapps would be wonderful,' Gabriel said, stretching the mug over to Klaus, who refilled it with coffee and a generous slug from a small hipflask he produced from his greatcoat. Gabriel pulled the mug back, took another sip and sighed. He felt calmer now, more relaxed, the caffeine finally waking him. His mind was active again. Why was it so quiet? What was it that Corporal Trauber had said yesterday? That some of the advance units had run out of ammunition and surrendered? So what should he do – stay or break camp? And if he did re-deploy, which way should he go? Forwards? To the rear?

'I'd better send someone forward again to find out what's going on,' he said, thinking out loud.

'Good idea,' Klaus replied. 'But Trauber's exhausted: he's been up all night. I'll go if you want.'

Gabriel thought for a moment. 'All right. We can manage without you for a while but don't take any chances. As soon as you know what the situation is, report back to me. I'll get one of the other orderlies to accompany me on the round this morning.'

Klaus nodded and, still finishing his toast, trailed off towards the stables.

Gabriel sipped the remainder of his coffee and chewed

on a piece of toast as he watched Klaus saddle a horse and lead it towards the gate on the eastern hedgerow. The warmth of the coffee in Gabriel's stomach and the heat of the fire on his face were so comforting that the urge to sleep washed through him again. He really should go to the recovery tent and start the round of the post-ops, but the feeling of heaviness over his eyes was back and the desire to let them close for an instant was irresistible. He shouldn't really, but he couldn't stop himself giving in to the urge. He would only shut them for a few moments… Just one or two minutes of delicious rest…

***

Some sixth sense, or noise, or subconscious awareness roused him, and Gabriel awoke with a jolt. In the confusion of his post-sleep stupor he was uncertain whether he was dreaming or not, because standing in front of him was a young soldier dressed in grey Serbian uniform, his rifle held at hip height, the barrel pointed directly at Gabriel's chest.

'*Ustati, ustati,*' the soldier said, motioning upwards with the rifle barrel, but Gabriel – sleepily bewildered – remained frozen to the spot.

'*Aufstehen!*' the soldier shouted, and then stepped forward and jabbed Gabriel with the rifle barrel. There was no doubting the painful reality of the hard metal tip on his chest and Gabriel finally understood he was not dreaming. Behind the youth he could see a dozen other Serbian soldiers with rifles. Dear God – what had happened? He rose to his feet – teetering slightly – and the soldier took a step back; he pointed the rifle at Gabriel's hands and then motioned skywards.

'*Hande hoch!*'

Gabriel obeyed and lifted both arms into the air. Over the head of the soldier he saw Berger and Schwann and the rest of the orderlies being marched out of the tents at rifle-point and made to stand in the middle of the field with their hands raised. Klaus was standing by the wooden cattle gate next to his horse, his greatcoat on the ground and arms above his head as two Serbian soldiers searched through his clothes. Gabriel realised he must have dozed off for only a minute or so, as it appeared that Klaus was leaving the paddock just as the Serbs arrived. Why had they had no warning? Why in God's name hadn't they received orders to evacuate?

The young soldier moved behind Gabriel and with a thrust of his chin indicated that he should walk over to join the other captives sitting in the middle of the field. Gabriel did as instructed. As he arrived at the group, one of the guards surrounding the prisoners motioned to Gabriel that he should sit down. The ground was muddy and Gabriel squatted on his haunches with his arms raised, trying to keep his balance. Klaus was marched across to join the circle of prisoners and sat down on the tails of his greatcoat next to Gabriel.

'Those bastards took my hipflask,' he whispered.

'I think that's the least of our problems, Klaus.'

'I can't believe this is happening, Captain.'

'How far did you manage to get?'

'I was just leaving the field when I collided with this group of Serbs. They took my horse and ordered me back into the field. I think they must be an advance patrol, because in the distance I could see a large column of enemy coming towards us. I couldn't see any sign of our own soldiers. It looks like a disaster, Captain. They must have completely overrun all our forward positions.'

'Any sign of Flieger or anybody else from the forward dressing station?'

'No, all I could see was Serbs.'

'No talking!' one of the guards shouted in German, glowering at Klaus, who cast his eyes down submissively.

Gabriel shifted uncomfortably as he observed the Serbian captors surrounding them. The guards were grinning confidently as they looked down at their prisoners, and a feeling of utter hopelessness grew in Gabriel's chest and throat; for the Serbs to have captured his hospital so easily, told him that the entire Austrian front must have collapsed during the night. The magnitude of this insight was so shocking, so humiliating, that he was almost incapacitated with frustration, angry that incompetent leadership had resulted in this catastrophe. After several minutes of squatting in the mud, the feeling of helplessness became so unbearable that he decided he must do something.

He slowly began to stand; Klaus's eyes widened as he watched him. 'Captain, what are you doing?' he hissed. 'They'll shoot you if you're not careful!'

Gabriel – ignoring him – was now standing

completely upright, his arms still above his head. Two of the guards saw him and suddenly unslung their rifles. '*Hirurga*,' Gabriel shouted. He had picked up a few basic Serbian phrases and words, and the Serbian for 'surgeon' was one of them.

Now all the guards had their rifles raised and pointed at Gabriel's chest. His heart was pounding furiously and he knew he was taking a chance, but it was better than the feeling of vulnerability he had squatting on the ground.

'*Hirurga*,' he shouted again and then – hands still raised – he lifted an index finger and bent his wrist to point at the Red Cross armband on his greatcoat.

An irate-looking Serbian lieutenant, hand on the butt of his holstered revolver, walked through the circle of guards.

'You are prisoner of Serbian army,' he said angrily in pidgin German. 'You must sit down, obey orders, or will be shot.'

'I am a surgeon,' Gabriel replied in German. 'There are Serbian and Austrian wounded in my tents.'

'*Serbian*?' The officer frowned and then turned to look at the hospital tents. 'Serbian soldiers in there?'

'Yes, Lieutenant. Under the Geneva Convention, medical staff should not be made prisoner—'

'Psshht.' The Serbian lieutenant held his index finger to his lips and Gabriel stopped talking as the officer thought for a moment. 'Who chief here?' he asked.

'I am the senior surgeon,' Gabriel replied. The officer turned to speak to two of the guards standing nearby, who stepped towards Gabriel. The lieutenant spoke again.

'You will follow. Bring one other.'

Gabriel looked down at Klaus, who nodded and then stood. The lieutenant motioned that they should lower their hands: with relief Gabriel obeyed, feeling the blood rush back to his fingertips. With Klaus beside him, Gabriel followed the officer towards the tents; the two guards trailed behind. The lieutenant lifted the entrance flap to the recovery tent and ducked inside, and Gabriel and the others followed him in. Inside the tent the officer quickly scanned the rows of cots and lines of bandaged men, then barked a few words of Serbian.

Three soldiers slowly raised their hands and the lieutenant walked over to the nearest. The man – a huge, bushy bearded Chetnik called Luka, wearing an eye-patch over his left eye – had arrived at the aid station four days earlier, blinded by grenade fragments from his own, very-short-fused, Serbian grenade. Angry at being taken prisoner, the surly guerrilla fighter had initially refused treatment from the Austrian medical staff. But eventually he had let Gabriel examine him: after anaesthetising the Chetnik's eyes with cocaine and using a magnifying glass and tweezers, Gabriel had managed to pick out several fragments of grenade casing imbedded in the man's cornea. Klaus had regularly irrigated his eyes with saline, and within a few days his sight had returned – completely in his right eye and partially in his left – for which the Chetnik appeared very grateful.

With his curly black beard and eye-patch the

grinning Serb resembled a medieval pirate, and Gabriel watched anxiously as he spoke with the lieutenant. But the Serbian officer seemed satisfied and after a moment he walked back to Gabriel.

'He says you make good care,' the lieutenant said to Gabriel. 'But all Serbian patients will be transferred to military hospital in Kragujevac. Maybe is today, maybe is tomorrow. Until they go, you will look after, will make good care.' He pointed at Gabriel and Klaus. 'You two will look after everybody here.'

'I need the other doctors and orderlies—' Gabriel began to say, but the lieutenant shook his head, his hand moving assertively to the handle of his revolver.

'No. Just you two,' he repeated and then, leaving no time for further discussion, turned to speak to the two guards before leaving the tent.

The guards were clearly under instructions to watch Gabriel carefully. They sat on upturned wooden supply boxes just inside the entrance-flap to the tent, watching as Gabriel and Klaus began the post-op round of the casualties. Most of the Austrian casualties were terrified at the double uncertainty of their predicament – of being wounded, and of being taken prisoner by a bitter foe – and the only happy faces were those of the three Serbian patients. Luka grinned as Gabriel peeled away the dressings on his arms and then looked underneath the eye patch, noting with a degree of professional pride that all the wounds were healing without infection. He told Luka – using a mixture of pidgin German and Serbian – that in time the sight in his left eye might improve further, but that he should wear the eye patch for the next few weeks. Luka extended his hand and even though the Chetnik's arm had several wounds in it, Gabriel's hand was crushed from the strength of the other man's grip.

'Good luck, Luka. Stay out of trouble,' Gabriel said in German.

'*I* no need luck,' Luka deep voice boomed back at him. '*You* need luck, *Hirurga*: Austria finished now.' He drew a finger across his neck in a throat-cutting gesture and then laughed, a low-pitched rumble from his chest, white teeth gleaming through the thick tangle of his beard.

The Austrian soldiers were more difficult to comfort, although Gabriel did his best to assure them he would do everything in his power to help. For the next few hours he and Klaus continued their round, inspecting wounds, removing dirty dressings, putting on new bandages and providing the injured with what little food and water was available.

As he worked, Gabriel could hear increasingly frenetic activity through the canvas of the tent: the tramp of feet on wet earth, the clank of buckles and buttons on field webbing and straps, the noises and voices of growing numbers of men. In spite of the wood-burning brazier in the tent it grew steadily colder as the morning progressed, and, looking upwards, Gabriel could see a gently spreading shadow on the sagging canvas roof as snow settled onto the tent. By early afternoon they had run out of water, so Gabriel picked up a small steel basin and empty water can and walked over to the guards at the entrance-flap. Both soldiers stood as he approached, warily gripping their rifles tighter as Gabriel tipped the basin upside down to show it was empty. He put the basin on the ground and pointed outside the tent, and then waggled his fingers to mime snow falling. The two guards looked at each other for a moment; then one of them stood and opened the entrance-flap, indicating that Gabriel should follow him outside.

After being inside the tent all day, the brightness of the freshly fallen snow – even in the low December light – was dazzling, and Gabriel was forced to shield his eyes from the glare. Although it had already stopped snowing, several centimetres lay on the ground, and, squinting against the brightness, Gabriel was astonished to see that the field was now full of Austrian prisoners, either huddled under the awnings of the stables, or standing in groups in the central part of the field. Pairs of Serbian guards patrolled the periphery of the paddock just inside the hedgerow, their rifles pointed inwards as they walked. In the cold air, clouds of steam rose from the prisoners' mouths as they clustered together for warmth, like penguins in an arctic storm. Gabriel guessed there must now be three or four hundred men standing in the paddock, with a further unknown number inside the stables.

The guard appeared impatient, jabbing the rifle barrel into the small of Gabriel's back. Gabriel walked forward and chose an area where the ground looked undisturbed. He bent to scoop handfuls of clean snow into the steel bowl, compressing it until it was full of compacted ice.

As he did this he discreetly scanned the men standing in the centre of the field: amongst the uniformly grey and blue coats he quickly spotted a flash of red; a Red Cross armband. The man looked towards Gabriel at the same time and began to wave his arms, and as Gabriel squinted back at him he realised with relief that it was Flieger.

Gabriel stood and turned to the guard, pointing first at his own Red Cross armband and then at Flieger, who was walking quickly towards him. The guard looked uneasy as Flieger approached but allowed him to walk up to Gabriel. Flieger's nose was red from the cold and his lips and ear lobes were blue, but he appeared otherwise unharmed.

'Thank goodness you made it back, Peter,' Gabriel said. 'What's happened?'

Flieger's breath was a cloud of white in the freezing air. 'Our frontline troops ran out of ammunition and entire regiments surrendered en masse. It's a disaster.'

Gabriel heard the guard stamp his feet and turned to see him gesture with his rifle that Gabriel should pick the snow-filled basin up. Gabriel lifted the basin, but before starting back to the tent he turned to Flieger again.

'Find the senior-ranking Austrian officer and ask him to talk to the Serbian commander. It looks as though they are turning this field into a holding camp and we'll need to dig latrines and find shelter for the men.' He looked up at the sky. 'In this weather and with little food or shelter, we can expect a lot of medical problems.'

Flieger nodded and Gabriel started back towards the recovery tent. But he stopped just before the entrance flap and looked back to see Flieger, a forlorn figure, still standing on his own, hugging himself for warmth. And then Gabriel remembered: today was 4 December, the Austrian feast of St Nicklaus. Back in Sarajevo, Flieger's children would be writing wish lists for their Christmas presents. This year, thought Gabriel, Christmas would be unlike anything they had experienced before.

12

London to Kragujevac,
December 1914–February 1915

Salonika port: the gateway to the Balkans.

Elspeth stood with twenty other women on the harbour front, her suitcase by her side, a strong smell of fish and sea-salt in the air, watching the ten remaining VADs rowed ashore. The oarsmen – good-looking, sun-tanned Greek boys with well-muscled forearms – skilfully steered the rowing skiffs through the crowded waters and deposited the VADs and their baggage on the harbour wall. While the boats were unloaded, Elspeth looked back out to sea, at the *Nile* – the French passenger ship they had just arrived in – which was anchored nearby. Beyond the *Nile* was a line of dirty black colliers with green electric lights slung between their funnels, and beyond them a white hospital ship with a red cross on its flanks.

'Why is everybody looking at us?' someone asked, and Elspeth turned to Dr Frances Wakefield, the Serbian unit's physician, who had spoken the words. Dr Wakefield was staring at the mix of people on the quayside: khaki-clad British and French troops; traditionally clothed

Arabs, Greeks, Spaniards and Turks; tall, deeply black French Senegalese soldiers, red fezzes perched on top of their heads. All of these men were gazing back at the women with interest.

'Well, I don't suppose they've seen many women in uniform before,' Elspeth replied with a smile. She liked Dr Wakefield, who was a small but determinedly cheerful woman with straggly light brown hair and merry eyes.

'Aye, they've probably never seen a Scotswoman either,' added Dr Lillian Chesney curtly. She was the unit's senior surgeon, a gruff but well-meaning woman with a sharp-featured face, short black hair and a piercing gaze.

'Well, they could hardly miss us in all this tartan,' joked Sylvia, and Sister Louisa Jordan – a dark haired, plump-faced girl standing beside her – burst out laughing, but then stopped when she realised that Dr Chesney was giving her 'a look'. All of the women were dressed identically in scots-grey skirts and jackets – the collars and epaulettes trimmed with tartan – a broad tartan sash and rainproof poncho, and a grey, wide-brimmed, tartan-ribboned hat. It was certainly an eye-catching uniform, thought Elspeth, although not a particularly elegant one.

'Nothing wrong with tartan, Sister Jordan,' Dr Chesney said, and Elspeth saw the young ward sister squirm under the intense gaze of the unit's senior surgeon.

'I think that's everyone ashore now,' said Dr Eleanor Soltau. A tall figure with curly dark hair and blue eyes, she was the last of the unit's four doctors and would be the hospital's chief medical officer until Dr Inglis was able to travel out to Serbia in a few months' time. As well as Elspeth and the other three doctors, there were twenty-six other staff: eleven trained nurses, including Sylvia; two cooks; two drivers, one of whom was Vera; a laundress; and ten VADs, the last of whom were climbing out of the skiffs and onto the harbour wall.

'I've asked the harbour master to organise some porters to take our luggage and medical supplies straight to the railway station,' Dr Soltau said. 'But as it's only a short distance from here, I thought we could follow them on foot; it'll be nice to find our land legs again.'

It did indeed feel good to be to be on solid earth, Elspeth thought, as she strolled through the cobbled streets with Sylvia and Vera by her side. The ten-day sea voyage from Southampton had not been without risk. They'd travelled in a Royal Navy transporter, HMS *Ceramic*, which did not fly the Red Cross flag from her mast, and had explosives and ammunition in her holds. This made them a legitimate target for the enemy, so immediately land was cleared the lifeboats were swung over the sides and Elspeth and the others were summoned to lifeboat drill. They'd even been tracked by a German submarine through the Bay of Biscay, Elspeth learnt from one of the ship's crew. It had been a relief to arrive safely in Malta, where they'd transferred to the *Nile* for the final stage of their journey.

As Dr Soltau led the women towards the station, Elspeth looked at the exotic shapes and vibrant colours that surrounded her. Between the rows of high whitewashed stone buildings, she saw the blue-green of the surrounding hills and the icy grey of snow-capped mountains; within the city itself the red-tiled roofs of turreted houses and minarets contrasted against the green of cypress trees and palm fronds waving in the breeze. It all looked breathtakingly wonderful.

They were met at the station by a tall, black-moustached Serbian army major, dressed in field-grey uniform. He spoke good English and introduced himself as Dr Curcin, their designated Medical Liaison Officer, who would look after them during their stay in Serbia.

The Serbian government's original plan had been for the women to set up their hospital in Skopje in the south of the country. 'But circumstances have changed,' Dr Curcin announced. 'The good news is that the enemy have been comprehensively defeated and the war is temporarily over in Serbia. But there are hundreds of casualties, and several thousand Austrian soldiers are being held prisoner. They are all in the north of the country, near the town of Kragujevac. That is where the fighting has been particularly fierce and the military hospital in Kragujevac is struggling to cope with all the wounded. There are also worrying reports of fever.'

'Fever?' Dr Soltau asked, a troubled look on her face. 'What sort of fever?'

'It is not yet clear,' he replied. 'But a number of hospital staff have fallen ill with it and some have already died.'

'It'll probably be typhoid, or maybe typhus,' Dr Wakefield interjected.

'*Typhus?*' Dr Soltau repeated, looking alarmed.

'Yes, that is our fear,' said Dr Curcin, 'that it might be the beginning of a typhus epidemic. There are also reports of fever breaking out in the prison camps surrounding Kragujevac, which hold thousands of Austrian captives. That is where medical assistance is most urgently required.' He hesitated before continuing. 'So my question to you, dear ladies, is: would you be willing to go to Kragujevac?'

Dr Soltau conferred with the rest of the unit. The women had already been vaccinated against cholera and typhoid, but there was no vaccine for typhus. Therefore, travelling up to Kragujevac presented a significant risk to everyone. Nevertheless every last woman agreed that if this was where they were most needed, this was where they should go.

Dr Curcin appeared very pleased with their decision as he escorted them to the northbound platform, where a train was waiting. Most of the carriages were already filled with civilian refugees who were returning north now that the fighting was over. But Dr Curcin had reserved one carriage for the women. Their medical supplies and equipment were loaded into the baggage compartment and the women climbed aboard.

Once inside the carriage Elspeth sat on a three-seater bench next to Frances Wakefield. Sylvia, sitting directly opposite, was her usual cheery self, chattering away quite happily to Louisa Jordan in the aisle seat beside her. But Vera, in the window seat on the other side of Sylvia, seemed unusually quiet. As the train pulled out of the station and headed north, Elspeth saw Vera staring pensively through the window at the passing Serbian countryside.

'Penny for them?' Elspeth asked Vera, when she finally turned her head away from the window.

'Oh. Well, I know it's a stupid question,' she said, an embarrassed expression on her face, 'but I don't understand the difference between typhus and typhoid. I thought we'd been vaccinated against both?'

'It's not a stupid question at all,' Elspeth replied. She turned to Dr Wakefield. 'You know more about this, Frances; perhaps you could explain?'

Dr Wakefield nodded, her eyes bright as she spoke to Vera.

'Typhoid is an infection caused by swallowing typhoid bacteria, usually from contaminated food or spoiled drinking water. It causes fever with diarrhoea or constipation, and stomach pains. But as long as the food we eat is properly cooked, and our drinking water boiled, we probably won't catch it. Also, we've all been vaccinated against typhoid, so even if you did swallow the bacteria, the vaccine will either protect you from getting infected, or at least make the illness less severe.'

'And typhus?' asked Vera

Dr Wakefield glanced at Elspeth before she replied. 'Well, that's more of a problem. It was only discovered three years ago that lice carry the typhus bacteria inside their guts. It is believed that lice in your clothes defecate onto the skin, and bacteria in the faeces pass directly through the skin into the body. So it's different from typhoid in that it's not caught from eating or drinking, but through skin contact with lice. The illness is different as well: there is fever and a rash, a very high temperature, headache and muscle pains. But the main symptom is confusion; in fact, the name typhus comes from the Greek *typhos*, which means stupor.'

'And we haven't been vaccinated against typhus?'

'No. A certain Dr Plotz in New York claims to have isolated a bacterium from infected patients and says he can produce a vaccine from it. But his work has not yet been proven.'

'Is there any treatment?'

'No. There is little we can do, apart from make the correct diagnosis. You just have to let the infection take its course. After five to ten days of fever, there is usually a crisis with high temperatures. Then the fever breaks and most people recover.'

'Most?'

'With good nursing care and decent food, two-thirds of patients should survive. However, for a wounded soldier, badly fed and dirty, the chances are much less.'

Sylvia nudged Vera in the ribs with an elbow. 'Don't worry, Vera; you're as strong as an ox. You'll be fine. Just don't let those beastly lice get under your corsets.' She slid a hand into Vera's sides and began to tickle her, eliciting a yelp of laughter. Watching her two friends fooling around, Elspeth smiled and shook her head. Let's hope, she thought, that Dr Curcin's fear of an epidemic did not materialise.

★★★

Kragujevac, eighty miles south of the capital, Belgrade, was the site of Serbia's main military arsenal, and Elspeth remembered Dr Curcin saying that the battle for this strategically important town had been particularly fierce. However, the first stage of their train journey was up through northern Greece and then across the border into southern Serbia, neither of which had been affected by the war. The train stopped briefly at Skopje station, where Elspeth had her first glimpse of the enemy: at the far end of the platform she saw a small group of Austrian prisoners standing in a circle; tired-looking men, in frayed pale-blue uniforms which hung off skeletal frames, their eyes compliantly downcast. A detachment of Serbian soldiers dressed in grey, with bright yellow straw moccasins on their feet and red-woollen hats on their heads, stood guard, rifles pointed towards the prisoners, bayonets fixed, eyes focussed on their captives.

The next stage of their journey was across the central plain of the Kosovo region. It appeared that the war had not yet touched this area either, and through the carriage window Elspeth saw ploughed fields, straw thatched cottages and red-tiled farm buildings with herons nesting on the chimney tops. But as the train climbed up into the Serbian highlands – with snow on the hills and eagles soaring high above the rocky crags

– the scars of battle began to appear: the broken stumps of shell-blasted trees, dead cattle lying in shell-cratered fields, the ruins of burnt-out barns and farmhouses. Eventually they neared Kragujevac and the train slowed as it passed through the fire-scorched outer suburbs of the town. The carriage fell silent as the women pressed their faces up against the window, squinting through the evening gloom at piles of broken cobblestones on the streets, fallen telegraph poles, and houses and shops with windows smashed and roof tiles missing.

A small, grey-bearded man – almost gnome-like – with darkly shadowed, red-rimmed eyes was waiting for them on the station platform.

'I am Dr Dmitri Anitch, from the First Reserve Military Hospital,' he said to them.

'You speak good English, Dr Anitch,' said Dr Soltau.

'I visited the London teaching hospitals some years ago,' he explained as he led Elspeth and the others out of the station.

'How is the fever situation?' Elspeth asked.

'Very bad. I am now sure it is typhus. The situation in my hospital is desperate; three of my medical colleagues have died this week and I am the only surgeon well enough to operate.'

'Can we visit your hospital tonight?' Elspeth asked.

Anitch shook his head as he led them to a row of ox-wagons waiting outside the station. 'There is no street lighting and it is unsafe to travel in the dark. I'll take you there tomorrow morning after we've found a suitable location for your hospital.'

Elspeth watched a number of Serbian guards load their hospital equipment, luggage and other supplies into the wagons. Then she and the other women climbed on board and the small convoy set off through the rubble-strewn streets. After a twenty-minute journey they arrived at a large ivy-covered, whitewashed villa on the outskirts of the town. Anitch explained that the villa had previously been used as a private medical clinic and had ten rooms, each holding three beds, which could be used as the women's sleeping quarters. The villa had some minor exterior damage from the fighting – a few bullet holes in the walls – but the inside of the building was undamaged and the rooms clean and recently decorated. Dr Anitch and Dr Curcin left for the First Reserve Hospital, promising to return early the next morning, and then Cook fired up the oven in the kitchen to prepare a late supper of toast, tinned meat and cocoa. Finally, the women went to their bedrooms, and Elspeth, Sylvia and Vera – sharing a room together – climbed, exhausted, into their beds.

The next morning Dr Anitch and Dr Curcin reappeared. Dr Soltau suggested that Elspeth, Dr Chesney and Dr Wakefield should accompany her, and so the party of six left the villa and began to walk towards the centre of town. After walking only a few hundred yards along the debris-littered streets, side-stepping piles of broken paving stones as they went, they came across two ox wagons pushed up against the pavement. Dr Curcin pulled back a thin tarpaulin sheet covering the first wagon, and Elspeth was shocked to see five wounded Serbian soldiers lying on the wooden floor. In the next wagon they found a similar number of injured Austrians, still in their bloodstained, mud-soiled uniforms. All the men looked malnourished and cold, so Dr Soltau sent Dr Wakefield back to the villa to tell the VADs to bring them food and warm clothing.

Elspeth and the others carried on walking and arrived in the centre of town, where they saw that some of the shops – even some of the restaurants – contained casualties. Walking inside the nearest building, a butcher's shop, they found eight Serbian wounded lying on the sawdust floor, their wounds covered with dirty field dressings. The rancid smell of decay was in the air, and Elspeth watched as Dr Curcin knelt to speak to one of the soldiers. After a few words the soldier removed his jacket and shirt, and Elspeth was shocked to see sores on his buttocks and shoulder blades, a result of lying too long on the hard floor. Another soldier had a gangrenous foot. Elspeth felt torn: her instinct was to stay and help the poor men. Dr Soltau, however, insisted that their first priority was to find a building they could use as a hospital. So it was with great difficulty that Elspeth finally left the building and followed the others away.

Ten minutes later they arrived at some wrought-iron gates, behind which Elspeth saw a two-storey brick building, fronted by a square concrete courtyard. Anitch told them that this was the town's high school, but as most families had fled Kragujevac it was no longer in use. Dr Soltau pushed the gate open and Elspeth followed her into the yard. The school appeared to have been abandoned in a hurry, as the main entrance door, approached by a short flight of stone steps, was unlocked. Inside the building on the ground floor they found a number of empty classrooms, but also a canteen, a good-sized kitchen, proper toilets and running water. More classrooms, a library and offices for teachers were on the first floor.

'Aye, we can clear the classrooms of desks and they can be converted into ward bays and an operating suite,' said Dr Chesney.

A smile appeared on Dr Soltau's face. 'Yes. I think this will do very nicely as our hospital,' she announced.

'Excellent,' Dr Curcin said with a beaming smile. 'I will go and arrange for a detail of Austrian prisoners to come here and clear the classrooms. They can also bring over your medical equipment and help erect the beds.' He paused. 'There are a number of well-trained nursing orderlies amongst the Austrians. If you wish, you may keep a few in the hospital to assist with the heavier manual work.'

'That would be a great help,' Dr Soltau replied.

'I will also organise a permanent detachment of Serbian guards to watch over them.'

Dr Soltau nodded her agreement and then turned to Dr Chesney. 'Lillian, can you go back with Dr Curcin, and fetch our nurses and VADs? We should make an immediate start on disinfecting the floors and walls of the school buildings.'

Dr Chesney agreed and followed Dr Curcin out of the building.

Dr Soltau turned towards Dr Anitch. 'Would it be possible for Dr Stewart and I to be shown round your hospital?'

He looked embarrassed. 'The conditions in my hospital are very poor. We are badly overcrowded and the wards are dirty as the cleaners have fled from fear of infection—.

'We understand the situation is challenging,' Dr Soltau interrupted. 'But seeing your difficulties will help us understand how we might defeat them.'

Reluctantly Anitch agreed, and after another walk through streets sprinkled with more broken paving and fallen roof tiles, Elspeth and Dr Soltau finally arrived at a large red-bricked building: the First Reserve Military Hospital.

There had clearly been heavy fighting in this area, and the exterior walls of the hospital were heavily pockmarked with bullet holes; many of the windows were patched with boards and pieces of packing case. But the conditions inside the building were far worse: Anitch told them that although the hospital had been built to accommodate two hundred patients, there were now four hundred men packed within its walls. As she walked onto the surgical ward, Elspeth was shocked to see the crammed rows of patients lying on straw mattresses, the lucky ones on top of the mattresses, the unlucky ones on the floor between or even underneath the beds. She could see only one, exhausted-looking orderly, dressed in a dirty white gown, carrying a chamber pot and ignoring the pleas of men as he walked by them.

Elspeth felt queasy at the sight, but turning towards Dr Soltau, she was impressed to see that the chief medical officer's face was impassive.

'I see your difficulties,' Dr Soltau said in a calm voice. 'Can we see the fever ward please?'

In the next ward they encountered the same overcrowding of beds; the smell of the place was dreadful, a mousy, musty, feculent odour.

'And your laundry?' Dr Soltau asked, holding a handkerchief to her nose.

They followed him out – Elspeth was relieved to be away from the fetid stench – and along a corridor to another large room. Four large iron steamer units were on one side of the room. A large pile of dirty uniforms lay on the floor on the other. The air was hot and steamy and carried the smell of washing and soap. A Serbian soldier sat on a chair in the far corner of the room with a rifle across his lap, watching three Austrian prisoners load the dirty clothes into the steamers. They were using two long pieces of wood like chopsticks to lift and carry the uniforms, but, seeing Dr Anitch, they stopped their work to bow their heads to him. He waved at them to continue, and after smiling and bowing their heads to Elspeth and Dr Soltau, the men returned to their task.

'The Austrian prisoners are happy to work here,' Dr Anitch said, 'even if it is a dirty and dangerous business. They tell me it is better here than the prison camps.'

Good Lord, Elspeth thought. What must the prison camps be like if they would rather be here than there?

'Come and see this,' he said and led them towards a pile of dirty clothes. 'But don't get too close.'

Elspeth bent forward and squinted at the rags on the floor, and then focussed on the sleeve of an Austrian officer's jacket. 'Oh my goodness,' she said, seeing the tiny dark bodies of lice outlined against the pale blue of the uniform. Beside her Dr Soltau jerked back with surprise.

'They're active now because they don't like being separated from the warmth of the body,' he said. 'It is a plague of lice. Every soldier – Serbian or Austrian – has them.'

'Can't you just burn the uniforms?' Elspeth asked.

'No. This is all they have to wear. There is no spare clothing.'

'I think we've seen enough, Dr Anitch,' Soltau said. 'We must get back. The quicker we convert the school to a hospital, the quicker we can help you.'

'Your arrival in Kragujevac is a blessing,' he replied. 'You can see how badly you are needed.'

***

'Are you sure about this?' Elspeth asked Sylvia as the two women walked towards the triage room.

'Yes, absolutely certain,' Sylvia replied. 'I'm going to help Dr Wakefield run the new typhus hospital.'

Six weeks had elapsed since the women had arrived in Kragujevac. Six long, challenging weeks, during which Elspeth had worked harder than ever before, helping the other women to turn the school into a fully functioning surgical hospital, and operating on the large number of Austrian and Serbian wounded who had lain for so long without proper medical help. Dr Soltau had originally brought beds and medicines to equip a one-hundred-bed hospital, but there were so many casualties that she eventually found space in the school's ten classrooms for one hundred and seventy patients. The work was arduous, and seeing so many young men permanently disabled by the misfortunes of war was heart breaking. But eventually the backlog of surgery was almost done.

And then typhus had struck.

Dr Soltau had always emphasised that her major concern was to protect the women from infection. Everyone in direct contact with patients had been given typhus uniforms, consisting of long white high-collared calico gowns, which were to be tucked into their boots and rubber gloves. For those women attending patients with proven fever, hair was compulsorily cropped to one inch and fully enclosed in a white cap. And for every arriving casualty a strict admission policy was enforced: the patient was placed on a rubber sheet and stripped of all clothes – which were sent for steam disinfection – the head and body were shaved, and finally the patient was rubbed from head to foot with paraffin.

However, in spite of this, the number of cases of typhus rose.

Dr Soltau responded by opening a fever ward in the hospital, but as the number of cases climbed even higher, she decided to establish a separate typhus hospital in a disused tobacco warehouse on the outskirts of town. Dr Wakefield was to be the only doctor working in this hospital, and she would be accompanied by eight of the VADs and five trained nurses. And to Elspeth's surprise, Sylvia – who had so far only ever worked on surgical wards – had volunteered to be one of the two sisters working there.

'What patients with typhus need most is good nursing care,' Sylvia said. 'The backlog of surgical cases is mostly finished here, so I'll be more useful organising nursing care in the new hospital.'

'You do realise you'll have to chop off most of your lovely hair, don't you?' said Elspeth.

'I'd been thinking it needed a bit of a cut anyway,' Sylvia replied, picking at her blonde fringe. 'In any case, it'll grow back quickly once all this is over.'

'Who else volunteered to go with you?'

'Louisa Jordan will be the other senior nurse.'

'And Vera?'

'Dr Soltau wants all patients with typhus to be taken up to the new hospital. So Vera will drive them there.' Dr Curcin had managed to find the women an old Serbian army ambulance, and Vera was to drive it when required.

'Well I'm staying here,' Elspeth said. 'There's still a steady stream of surgical work coming in from the surrounding towns and villages.' She paused for a moment. 'You will be careful, Sylvie, won't you? Those calico gowns are not fail-safe.'

'Don't worry, Ellie – I do know what I'm doing…'

She stopped talking as they arrived at the triage

room, a small space that had originally been the school caretaker's storage cupboard, but had been converted into an area to assess and disinfect all potential admissions to the hospital. Two injured soldiers – one Serbian in grey uniform, one Austrian in pale blue – lay on rubber sheets on the floor. Standing above them were two of the Austrian prison orderlies, holding heavy scissors and shaving equipment, waiting for instructions.

'Gut mornink, Dr Stewart, Sister Calthorpe,' the prison orderlies chimed, almost in unison. Dr Soltau had selected six Austrian prisoners to help with the heavier work in the hospital, and the men were pathetically grateful to have been chosen, bowing their heads and smiling deferentially every time Elspeth walked past. They had happily complied with having their heads and bodies shaved to the skin and then disinfected with paraffin. Once sanitised and re-dressed in their steam-sterilised uniforms, the Austrians had helped to clear the classrooms; had washed the floors and walls, and moved the beds into the designated ward areas. They were now responsible for shaving and disinfecting all new admissions to the hospital.

Elspeth acknowledged their greeting with a brief nod of her head and watched the two orderlies remove the bandages from the soldiers lying on the floor. Then, with Sylvia by her side, she looked down at the exposed wounds.

The Serbian soldier had a relatively simple bullet wound to the calf; that could wait until tomorrow, Elspeth thought. But the Austrian soldier, a grizzled-looking veteran with a badly smallpox-scarred face and a bushy moustache, looked very unwell. Elspeth did a quick inspection and saw a neat bullet hole with surrounding bruising and reddened skin over the right kidney area. The soldier managed to raise a smile at her through his tobacco-stained teeth. 'I have blood in my urine,' he said to her in heavily accented English.

'You speak English?' Elspeth asked.

He nodded. '*Ja*. A little. I am a trained orderly.'

'You worked in a field hospital?'

'*Ja*. With the Austrian 5th Army medical column.'

'Then you know that blood in the urine—'

'*Ja, ja,*' He nodded his head. 'I know – is very bad sign. The bullet is in my kidney.'

'Yes, you need surgery. Have you eaten today?'

'Not for several days.'

'Good. We'll operate right away.'

'My surgeons would say there is no point. A kidney shot is usually a fatal wound.'

Elspeth smiled at the calm acceptance of his fate. 'We'll see about that. What's your name?'

'Sergeant Huber.'

'Well, have faith, Sergeant Huber.' She looked across at Sylvia and nodded.

Sylvia turned to the two orderlies. 'Shave and disinfect him please, and then take him straight up to theatre.'

★★★

It was a dismal wintry Sunday afternoon in late February.

The funeral of one of their own.

Elspeth fought to hold back her tears as she watched a young altar boy carrying an iconic gold orthodox cross, followed by a Serbian priest dressed in funereal robes, leading the procession of Scottish women, Austrian prison orderlies, and Serbian soldiers out of the school and towards a nearby church. Immediately behind the priest came the coffin, carried by four of the prison orderlies, the slim pine box swaying as the pallbearers found their feet on the uneven ground. Behind Elspeth, at the rear of the column, a small band of musicians played a mournful death march, the slow thump of a drum and the sombre notes of a tuba emphasising the sadness of the occasion. The music was so melancholy that Elspeth struggled to keep her composure as she looked up at the coffin and tried to comprehend that a dear friend and talented ward sister was lying inside it: cold, lifeless, killed by the typhus. She could hardly believe that this vibrant young woman was no longer alive.

Standing beside her, Vera sniffed loudly, and Elspeth turned and saw her watery, red-rimmed eyes; she realised that almost everyone in the procession – including the Austrians – was weeping, or trying to blink back tears at this first loss of life amongst the Scottish women.

But surprisingly, at the sight of the prison orderlies' grief, Elspeth felt her spirits rise; she had come to like the Austrians, with their jokes and light-hearted manner. She saw the tender care they gave the wounded Serbian soldiers. To think that only a few weeks ago these men had been trying to kill and maim each other. It seemed absurd, and the futility of war made her angry. Good, she thought – better angry than depressed.

The funeral cortege passed through a wooden archway and the gate of the churchyard. The coffin was laid on a trestle beside the open grave, and Elspeth listened as the priest incanted the Serbian funeral rites in a gloomy monotone. Dr Soltau gave a brief eulogy before Dr Curcin stepped forward.

'Dear Scottish ladies, I know I speak for all the people of Serbia when I say that our hearts are broken at the loss of your sister, who died as valiantly as any soldier sent into battle. You have travelled here from your homeland to help save the lives of our countrymen and women. Your sacrifice, and the ultimate sacrifice of your beloved sister, will not go unrecognised.'

He stepped back from the graveside and nodded at the four prison orderlies. They lifted the coffin from the trestle and, using tapes to support its weight, began to lower it into the grave. As the pine casket disappeared from view, the band began to play another melancholy lament, and the emotion of the moment brought a lump of sorrow to Elspeth's throat. She looked across at Vera – saw her swallowing hard, also trying to control her grief – then turned back to see the tapes pulled up as the coffin reached the bottom. The priest picked up a handful of earth and scattered it into the grave; and then an orderly line of soldiers, prisoners and nurses formed and began to pass by the burial hole, each person bending to pick up some soil and drop it on the coffin. Elspeth joined the queue and released her handful of black earth into the grave, and heard the dull, hollow sound as it struck the lid of the coffin.

As she walked away from the grave, she felt a hand touch her elbow and turned around.

'I still can't believe that Louisa's dead,' whispered Sylvia, her voice quavering, her eyes bloodshot and puffy.

Elspeth knew that Sylvia had been strongly affected by the loss – the pair had worked closely together for the past month – and as they left the churchyard, she simply put an arm around Sylvia's shoulder, pulled her close, nodded her understanding. 'I was upset about it at first,' Sylvia continued. 'Now I'm just angry.'

'But we mustn't forget that Louisa helped save Frances Wakefield's life,' Elspeth replied. In spite of wearing the calico uniforms and gloves, several of the women at the typhus hospital had caught the infection, including Dr Wakefield. However, she had survived, thanks to Louisa's and Sylvia's nursing skills. 'You must look at the good that Louisa did during her life.'

'I know, but still… it's hard to accept she's gone.'

Elspeth gave Sylvia's shoulder a squeeze. 'Let's get back to work. I've found that it's the best thing for clearing one's mind of grief or anger.'

13

'Lieutenant Schwann requests that you come to the stables immediately, Captain.'

'What's the problem, Klaus?'

'The lieutenant thinks we may have a case of typhus, sir.'

Gabriel, sitting on an upturned wooden box inside the surgical tent, sat bolt upright and then quickly put down his pen and closed the ledger he had been updating. As Klaus led him outside and across the paddock towards the stable block, Gabriel felt a steel finger of fear pierce his stomach; he had been worried about the possibility of typhus for some time now.

As he had predicted, their Serbian captors had turned the paddock and former aid station into a prisoner of war camp; rolls of barbed wire had been placed inside the hedgerow and watch towers were erected, while Serb guards patrolled the camp borders. As senior surgeon in the camp, Gabriel had organised the digging of latrines and then tried to find a covered sleeping spot for every man, either in the stables or one of the hospital tents;

no easy task as there were now more than five hundred prisoners in the camp.

Gabriel had been summoned to meet with Major Dragas, the Serbian officer in command. Due to the atrocities committed by some Austrians during the invasions, there was a fear of retribution, that prisoners might be tortured or worse. But Gabriel had found Dragas to be a reasonable man. Food was scarce for everybody – Serbians included – yet the prisoners' rations were no worse than those they had received from their own unreliable Supply Division. However, Dragas had removed all the aid station's surgical instruments – they could be used as weapons to aid escape, he had told Gabriel. Dragas was also unable to provide the camp with any medical supplies or cleaning materials, like soap or bleach.

Very soon, as Gabriel had feared, the lack of proper washing facilities meant that everybody was afflicted with lice.

And with lice came the possibility of typhus.

As he arrived at the stable block, Gabriel saw a large group of Austrian soldiers standing outside, while Peter Flieger lingered in the doorway, a worried expression on his bespectacled face. 'I've evacuated the stables, but Lord knows where we're going to put all these men,' he said.

'Where's Karl?' Gabriel asked.

'He and Thomas are with the soldier in the stall at the far end.' He pointed along the length of the wooden building.

Inside the darkness of the stables, a musty smell of old hay and horses lingered in the air as Gabriel walked towards the last stall. Berger and Schwann were standing over a soldier lying in a lozenge of daylight that fell through the stall window onto the straw-covered floor. Schwann said nothing, but simply bent down and pulled away the thin blanket covering the soldier's body. The man was in the throes of a rigor – teeth clenched, body shaking, skin gleaming with sweat – but it was the sight of the rash that was like a slap in the face to Gabriel. He'd seen this distinctive mottling before, in cases of isolated, sporadic typhus in peasants from the poorer parts of Bosnia. But now, in the squalid conditions inside the camp, he knew that a case like this might herald the start of an outbreak of epidemic typhus.

Gabriel looked across at Schwann and gave a sombre nod. 'Yes,' he said. 'I'm afraid that's typhus.'

***

Two weeks later, in the camp of almost five hundred men, more than three hundred had caught the infection and over two hundred of them had died.

Gabriel had tried hard to prevent the epidemic. He had ordered the first patient to be nursed in isolation in a tent in one corner of the field. However, the next day a further three prisoners who had slept in the same stall presented with fever and skin rash, and again typhus was diagnosed.

The sick men were placed in the same isolation

tent as the first case and a panicked Gabriel requested an urgent meeting with Dragas. But the major was unable to provide assistance – no lime or bleach or other disinfecting materials were available – and all that Gabriel could do was quarantine the stable block and arrange for the straw to be burnt. The following day a further seven men who had slept in the stables fell ill, as well as two others who had helped burn the straw. The day after that, another nineteen men presented with symptoms, among them some who had been sleeping in the tents, suggesting the disease had spread outside the stables. And then the men began to die: the first case, and then another seven of the next ten infected men. Gabriel established a second typhus tent, then a third, quarantining them to one corner of the field, an area that grew bigger every day. But the outbreak continued and every day more cases were diagnosed. Every day more men died. Gabriel was almost overwhelmed by the feeling of fear and helplessness, of being unable to do anything to stop the horror of the epidemic.

Initially they dug separate graves in a field outside the camp but the number of men dying rose, such that every morning they had to dig a fresh pit to bury the bodies of men who had died overnight. The death rate was particularly high among the medical orderlies: eight caught the infection and all of them perished. Gabriel had insisted that the remaining orderlies inspect their clothes twice daily for lice and kill them using a candle flame run along the seams. Schwann had also heard that a mixture of Vaseline and paraffin rubbed onto the skin might deter the lice, so every day they smeared the pungent mixture onto their bodies before starting their rounds.

However, these measures did not work and the doctors began to fall ill. The first was Thomas Berger.

Gabriel felt numb as he watched the young doctor struggle with the infection, unable to help except to administer what little aspirin they had left. After a week of rigors Berger fell into a coma. Gabriel was at his side, powerless to do anything as Berger sank deeper into a void from which he could not be retrieved. Of the thirteen original medical staff in the camp, only Gabriel, Schwann, Flieger and Klaus were still alive. Dear Lord, thought Gabriel, are we all going to die?

By the end of February – after eight harrowing weeks of the epidemic – Gabriel began to develop a curiously fatalistic attitude to the infection. He found that he had lost his fear of falling ill and instead had become intrigued to know whether – if he were to catch typhus – he could survive it or not. His rational brain told him this was a stupid notion, as every medical worker so far infected had died. But he did not fight the idea, because in some way it comforted him. Before the war started he had never considered he might die young, had always had a strong sense of destiny about his life, which did not include dying from fever in a remote, muddy Serbian field. Yet now, with death a strong possibility, he realised that there were many more unpleasant ways to die than slipping into a fever-induced coma and drifting away in your sleep.

And then that morning, Schwann had presented with a fever. Initially there was no sign of a skin rash and Gabriel had hoped it might be some other infection. But during the afternoon a blotchy eruption appeared on Schwann's neck and chest, and Flieger agreed it was likely to be early-stage typhus. Schwann had insisted he be isolated with the other sufferers in one of the typhus tents.

It was just after midnight as Gabriel approached the tent where Schwann had been taken. The glimmer of a candle was dimly visible through the canvas and Gabriel ducked his head through the entrance-flap to see Flieger asleep at a table, his head resting on the table-top, wax from a candle dripping perilously close to his hair.

'Peter, wake up,' Gabriel said as he shook him. 'You'll set yourself on fire.'

Flieger lifted his head with a start. 'Oh, sorry, Gabriel,' he said, removing mud-stained glasses with one hand, rubbing his eyes with the other. 'I must have drifted off.'

'How's Karl?'

Flieger yawned as he put his glasses back on. 'I examined him a few minutes ago. The rash is all over his torso now – it's definitely typhus.'

'His temperature?'

'Forty degrees an hour ago.'

'Have we anything to bring it down?'

'No. There's no aspirin or camphorated phenol left.'

Gabriel chewed his lower lip. 'Where is he?'

Two lines of sleeping men lay on the floor of the

tent, and Flieger pointed along the length of one of the rows. 'That's him at the back – with Sparmacher.'

Following Flieger's finger, Gabriel saw Klaus kneeling by a man at the far end of the tent. He walked towards them, treading cautiously between the rows of sleeping men, careful to avoid stepping on a splayed arm or leg. Arriving at Schwann's side, Gabriel saw that the young physician was in the throes of a rigor, his body in spasms, his face a rictus grin as Klaus mopped his brow with a cloth. The tremors gradually settled and Schwann looked up at Gabriel, blinking several times before he recognised him.

'Oh… Gabriel… I'm s-sorry,' Schwann said through teeth that still chattered from the rigor. 'Peter and I th-th-think it's definitely t-typhus.'

Gabriel smiled encouragingly at him. 'Don't worry, Karl. We'll get you something for the fever. You're going to be all right.' Schwann tried to smile back at Gabriel, a faint-hearted effort and more of a grimace as he was overtaken by the residua of the tremors. His face was taut, like a bed-sheet pulled tight, and there was a sallow look around his eyes that Gabriel had seen before – in Thomas Berger. He simply *had* to get some drugs for the fever or Karl would also die.

As he walked back to his own tent, Gabriel decided he would go and speak to Major Dragas at first light. But as that was several hours away, he would first try and catch a few hours' sleep.

★★★

A gentle breeze caressed the side of Gabriel's face and the heat of the sun on his back was strong as he stood on the shoreline of Worthersee Lake. The aromatic smell of pine resin was heavenly, and on the far side of the shimmering turquoise lake Gabriel recognised the forests near his hometown of Klagenfurt. He knew this place so well – had spent many a happy day here as a youth – and felt wonderfully warm and relaxed. On a floating wooden platform ahead of him a group of young men and women were sunbathing, some diving into the water with a splash and then laughing as they swam back to the shoreline.

He heard his name called, and, turning to look along the thin shingle strip by the edge of the lake, saw two figures sitting at a small café table. Facing him was chief Fischer, smoking his pipe. Sitting opposite the chief was a woman in a long white dress, her head hidden by a summer parasol. On the table was a tiered wedding cake from which, with her free hand, the woman picked pieces of icing sugar and marzipan. The chief removed the stem of the pipe from his mouth and called again.

'I said hello, young Gabriel,' he shouted. 'Come and greet your bride.'

A café table on the shoreline? This made no sense…

'Hurry, Gabriel,' the chief said. 'Time waits for no man.'

Gabriel strode towards the figures, the shingle beneath his boots crunching with each footfall, his heart pounding as he approached. The woman slowly turned around and Gabriel saw with a shock that instead of a face, there was a bony skull: the grinning, empty face of death.

He woke from the dream with a jolt, breathing fast, his forehead damp with perspiration, the sensation of warmth already gone, replaced by cold discomfort in his back and legs. He levered himself off the hard ground and tried to confront the images from the nightmare, which – like water sieving through a colander – were already fading from his brain.

The dream had quite obviously been about death, that much was clear. So far, Gabriel had managed to suppress his fears – he would not have been able to function as a doctor if he hadn't. But the nightmare told him that fear still lurked inside him. The chief had wanted Gabriel's destiny to be marriage, but was it to be death instead?

The icy ground below his body disrupted his thoughts. He had taken to sleeping on the floor of the operating tent, as the doctor's sleeping tent was now filled with typhus cases, but even with a groundsheet underneath him, he was still chilled to the marrow. He stood and stretched – trying to ease the ache from his back and legs – then stepped carefully towards the entrance flap and went outside.

Dawn must have broken only a few minutes earlier, and in the early morning gloom he could just see the entrance gate on the eastern edge of the camp. Two guards were on duty, the smoke from their cigarettes intermingled with steam from their breath as they stood by the gate. It was devilishly cold, Gabriel thought, shivering as he drew the collar of his greatcoat tight underneath his chin and carefully made his way over the icily rutted ground towards the gate. In the early half-light it was difficult to see the undulations, and he trod cautiously, testing each step for firmness underfoot, his boots occasionally crunching through ice-filled puddles. The guards eyed him as he approached.

He told them he needed to speak to Major Dragas urgently, and watched as one of them walked to the farmhouse that had been requisitioned as the commandant's office. Gabriel waited, stamping his feet to keep warm, flexing his fingers and toes as he strove to drive away the cold that seemed lodged deep inside his bones. After a while the guard returned, accompanied by two other soldiers. The gate was opened and Gabriel motioned through. Walking him towards the farmhouse, the two escorting soldiers keep their distance from Gabriel, their rifle barrels pointed towards him in case he might accidently brush against them. The Serbs had stopped patrolling inside the camp several weeks ago and it was obvious to Gabriel that they were terrified of a disease that was a far more serious threat to them than the Austrian army had ever been.

His previous meetings with Dragas had always taken place indoors, but on this occasion Gabriel was asked to wait in the courtyard between the farmhouse and barn. Several minutes later the major came down the steps of the house, buttoning his greatcoat as he stopped two metres away from Gabriel.

'Thank you for seeing me, Major.' Gabriel spoke

in German; Dragas cocked his head as he listened. 'The epidemic is out of control and more than half the prisoners have died,' Gabriel continued. 'We have run out of all medical supplies and I urgently need soap, aspirin, opiates, camphorated phenol, bandages and disinfectants like lime, naphthalene and sulphur.'

A look of concern passed across Dragas's face, but he did not reply.

'The situation is desperate,' Gabriel continued. 'Please, Major – as a matter of humanity you must help us.'

Dragas took his cap off and ran a hand across the short stubble of his hair. Then he replaced the cap. 'Very difficult,' he said in faltering, pidgin German. 'Typhus not only in camp. Now in civilians. In Valjevo, in Kragujevac, in many place. Many peoples die. Babies, womens.' He shook his head. 'Everywhere very bad.'

Gabriel's heart sank: as prisoners he knew they were a lower priority for resources.

Dragas looked solemnly grave for a moment. Suddenly he lifted his head and frowned, and then his face broke into a smile. 'I have idea,' he said, his look unexpectedly animated. 'In Kragujevac is new hospital. *Skotski damé.* You go speak. Ask them. Maybe help?'

Gabriel blinked. Dragas's German was difficult to follow. Skotski meant Scottish and damé meant women. By *Skotski damé* did Dragas mean there were Scottish women? In Kragujevac?

As Gabriel tried to work out what Dragas was saying, the major seemed to have already made a decision and barked orders at one of the guards, who tramped off towards the barn. Listening to Dragas's excited pidgin German, Gabriel gathered that he was to go back to the camp and fetch an orderly, and they would both be taken to Kragujevac to visit these Scottish women. As if to confirm this understanding, an uncovered wagon rolled out of the barn with two oxen straining at the yoke, the soldier on the driving platform prodding them with a stick.

Dragas disappeared up the steps into the farmhouse while Gabriel waited for the cart and then climbed up and sat on the wooden floor. The other guard clambered up to sit beside the driver, who jabbed the oxen with the stick, setting the wagon into motion again.

Arriving back at the camp entrance, Gabriel gave Sparmacher's name to the guard on duty and waited while Klaus was summoned. A few minutes later Klaus appeared, looking bemused as the guards let him through the gate. He climbed up and sat next to Gabriel, both men leaning against the hard wooden back of the wagon. A third guard climbed into the cart and sat underneath the driving platform, facing backwards, the rifle on his lap pointed at Gabriel. The driver prodded the oxen with his stick once more, and with a lurch the wagon rolled forwards.

For the first half-hour of their journey the wagon lumbered along a bumpy unmarked trail, and although it was exciting to be away from the squalid conditions inside the camp, Gabriel still felt the cold deep in his bones and the discomfort from the jarringly hard wooden floor beneath his back and legs. But after a while the wagon joined an asphalted road with ditches on both sides, and the going was faster and smoother as the oxen pulled the wagon more easily. In the snow-filled fields on either side of the road, Gabriel saw the rude evidence of war – unburied cattle with crows pecking at their flanks, abandoned artillery pieces, the corpses of Austrian soldiers in their faded pale blue uniforms. He also noticed triangular black flags hanging over the doorframes of cottages and farmhouses that they passed. Making eye contact with the guard sitting in front of him, Gabriel pointed at one of the flags and made a shrugging gesture. The soldier looked at the flag and then turned back to Gabriel.

'Typhoose,' he said, morosely.

Eventually they reached Kragujevac, the metal-rimmed wooden wheels of the wagon clattering noisily over the stone-cobbled streets. Apart from small groups of Austrian prisoners clearing the debris into wheelbarrows – cigarette smoking Serbian guards watching them at work – the streets and alleyways appeared mostly deserted. As the driver weaved the wagon between craters and piles of cobblestones, a three-legged dog suddenly appeared in front of them and then loped away down an alley. Gabriel saw more black flags on the fronts of the houses they passed, and then saw a Red Cross flag hanging outside a battle-scarred building; the sign above the entrance told him it was the First Reserve Military Hospital. The wagon passed an old church, a stack of coffins leaning against its outer wall, a group of bedraggled Austrian prisoners digging graves in the cemetery.

Finally they arrived at a low stone wall and came to a stop outside a wrought-iron double entrance gate. Through the iron struts Gabriel could see a double-storey brick building fronted by a courtyard. A Red Cross sign was tied to one side of the gate. On the other side was another sign – *"Skotski Damé Bolnica"* – with the words "Scottish Women's Hospital" written in English underneath.

A Serbian guard with a rifle slung over his shoulder was standing outside. After speaking with the driver, he opened the gate and the wagon rolled into the courtyard and came to a halt outside the building. Gabriel stood up and shivered with cold. The ache in his back and legs had worsened after the long journey on the hard floor of the wagon. He felt strangely lightheaded as he looked around and saw an old army ambulance stood in one corner of the courtyard. The vehicle's bonnet was open, and a tall, broad-shouldered, short-haired woman with her shirt sleeves rolled up to the elbow was doing something to the engine with a spanner. Several Austrian prisoners were at work sweeping the floor of the courtyard, and they stopped to lean on their brooms and stare at Gabriel as he clambered over the side of the wagon. The prisoners appeared alert and well nourished, their heads and faces clean-shaven, their uniforms faded but spotlessly clean. As they gazed at him, Gabriel realised how scruffy he must seem to them: unshaven, dirty clothes, unwashed hair flopping over his forehead. He stood self-consciously next to Klaus as one of the Serbian guards jogged up a short flight of stone steps and disappeared inside the building.

As he waited, one of the Austrian prisoners in the yard strolled over to Gabriel. From the insignia on his uniform Gabriel saw that he was a medical orderly, a sergeant, a grizzled-looking veteran with a badly smallpox-scarred face. His head was clean-shaven and from the lack of tan on his upper lip Gabriel could tell that at one time he had sported a generous moustache. The soldier smiled – his parted lips revealing only a few broken, tobacco-stained teeth – as he glanced at the silver stars on Gabriel's jacket collar.

'Where are you from, Captain?' he asked.

'A prisoners' laager about six kilometres west of here,' Gabriel replied, rubbing the back of his neck, which was also now aching. 'And you, Sergeant?'

'I was with the 5th Army Medical Column, sir.' He turned to indicate the other prisoners. 'We were captured more than two months ago and I was sent here for surgery on a bullet wound. After I recovered, the women kept me on to help with their work.'

'What sort of work, Sergeant? What is this place?'

The soldier leant on his broom and sucked air through the gaps in his teeth. 'Well, it's a hospital, sir, run entirely by women, sir.'

'Women?'

'Yes, sir. From Scotland.'

Gabriel looked across at the tall woman, who had closed the ambulance's bonnet and was rolling her shirtsleeves down. 'And what are they doing here in Serbia?' he asked the Sergeant.

'They're here to care for the wounded, sir.'

Gabriel frowned. 'And these women surgeons, sergeant: are they any good?'

'Oh yes, sir, very good indeed,' the sergeant said, turning to look at the other Austrians behind him, several of whom were nodding in solemn agreement. He turned back to Gabriel. 'They are technically the equal of any surgeon I ever worked with in the 5th Medical Column. But they are more...' He paused, '... more thoughtful about their work and gentler with their patients.'

Gabriel was surprised to hear the veteran soldier speak with such obvious affection for these women.

'And we respect them, sir,' the sergeant continued. 'They saved my life, and the lives of many other men, both Serbian and Austrian.' A wistful look appeared on his face. 'They're angels, sir, true angels—'

The sound of a throat being cleared interrupted him, and Gabriel turned to see two women dressed in long grey skirts and jackets standing at the top of the stone steps outside the building: a taller, older woman with curly hair, looking down at Gabriel with interest, and a younger dark-haired woman with clear blue eyes who was smiling at the sergeant. The sergeant smiled back at her with obvious devotion and then stepped forward to position himself between Gabriel and the two women in an overtly protective gesture.

'With all due respect, Captain,' he said. 'I must ask you not to come too close. We have a strict shaving and delousing policy to prevent the spread of typhus. Until then you must keep your distance.'

Gabriel nodded. 'I understand, Sergeant.'

'Good day,' the older woman said in hesitant German. 'Your guard tells me you are from a nearby prison camp?'

'That is correct,' Gabriel replied in good English. 'I am Surgeon Captain Gabriel Bayer of the Austrian 6th Army, and this,' he pointed at Klaus, 'is Corporal Sparmacher, my orderly.'

Klaus clicked his heels and bowed his head.

'We are currently held in a prison camp a few kilometres west of here,' Gabriel continued. 'The camp commandant suggested I speak to you as we have typhus in the camp, and have run out of all basic sanitary supplies and medicines.'

The older woman tilted her head slightly and narrowed her eyes. 'I see.' She took several steps closer, at which point the sergeant moved to reposition himself directly between her and Gabriel.

'That's quite all right, Huber,' she said. 'I'm sure Captain Bayer will be careful.'

The sergeant gave Gabriel a severe look before stepping aside.

'Don't mind Huber,' the older woman said to Gabriel with a smile. 'He means well.'

Gabriel tried to return the smile, but the cold and stiffness in his back and neck had become worse and he shivered as the woman continued.

'I'm Dr Soltau, the chief medical officer for the hospital. And this,' she turned to indicate the younger woman, 'is Dr Stewart, one of our surgeons.'

With an effort Gabriel clicked his heels and bowed his head in succession to both women. Now, having appeared almost indifferent to him, the younger woman suddenly locked eyes on his face and began to stare at him as Dr Soltau continued speaking.

'You speak good English, Captain Bayer – much better than my German.'

Gabriel half-smiled at the compliment, although uncomfortably aware of the intense scrutiny he was now under from the younger woman. 'I learnt English as a visiting surgical trainee in New York and London,' he quietly replied.

Dr Soltau's eyebrows lifted slightly. 'Really? Who did you work with?'

The chill in Gabriel's bones disappeared and a wave of heat coursed through his body. His brain was fogged, his thoughts clumsy as he tried to find the words…

'Um… Frank Billings… at Mount Sinai,' he mumbled. 'And… Lockhart-Mummery at St Mark's.'

'Ah.' Dr Soltau nodded. 'Both world-class surgeons from first-rate hospitals. But you have some eminent surgeons in Vienna, like Professor Billroth…'

But now her voice faded away. Gabriel could still see her lips moving, but a buzzing in his ears prevented him from understanding what she was saying. The younger woman was still staring at him in a strange manner, and when he glanced across at Klaus, he saw that he was also looking at Gabriel in an odd way. Gabriel felt suddenly lightheaded and the muscles in his legs felt weak; he swayed and knew he would not be able to stay on his feet for much longer. He would have to tell this woman what he needed as quickly as possible.

'Forgive me for interrupting,' Gabriel said before she could finish, 'but my camp has been decimated by typhus.' He was now aware that everybody was staring at him as he continued. 'Three hundred men in my camp have contracted typhus and more than two hundred have already died,' – he paused as another wave of dizziness swept through him – 'a mortality rate of seventy per cent. We lack soap, aspirin, disinfectant, food—'

'Captain Bayer.'

They were the first words the younger woman had spoken, and they stopped him mid-sentence. She walked down the steps and stood level with Dr Soltau.

'Before you say anything else,' she said. 'I can see you are not well, and there is a rash on the side of your neck.'

Gabriel reached up and touched the skin below his jaw – which felt hot and itchy – and realised that something was very wrong inside his body. He had spent the last few hours attributing the growing aches and pains to a combination of cold weather, lack of food and the uncomfortable ride in the ox wagon. Now, however, the symptoms were worse and he could no longer ignore them. The buzzing in his ears became higher-pitched and his vision began to dim. He swayed again and knew he was about to fall, but then Klaus stepped towards him and put an arm around his shoulder, keeping him upright. Dear Klaus, thought Gabriel; not frightened to put his life on the line for me.

And now Gabriel experienced an intense feeling of regret: that at the very moment of his arrival it should become apparent to these women that he was ill –

certainly with typhus. It was the last thought to enter his mind, as his vision began to spin, and a black veil descended over his eyes…

★★★

Gabriel regained consciousness when he felt strong hands take a grip of his shoulders and ankles and lift him off the ground. He opened his eyes, but was too weak to protest as Huber and another of the Austrian prison orderlies carried him across the courtyard to the rear of the ambulance and placed him on the floor inside. He briefly saw the tall woman who had been working on the engine grinning down at him as she closed the door to the vehicle, and then he heard the engine start and felt the ambulance begin to move. He felt a moment of panic: he had failed, he was being taken back to the camp without the supplies he so urgently needed. He tried to lift his head, to insist on the supplies that he needed to save the men in his camp. But there was no strength left in his body and all he could do was lift his skull a few pitiful inches off the vehicle floor before it fell back again with a painful thump. Then once more the veil of darkness descended.

He regained consciousness again as he was lowered onto a thin rubber sheet on the floor of a room somewhere. Where had they taken him? What was going to happen? There were black spots before his eyes, and as he tried to blink them away he dimly saw two figures in white loom over him. Gloved hands gripped him again, this time pulling the boots from his feet and the clothes from his body; he had neither the energy nor will to resist while they stripped him naked and left him shivering on the floor. He focussed his vision and saw that the figures in white were two male orderlies. But standing to one side was another white-gowned individual; a figure with fair eyelashes and soft green eyes. Then he glimpsed a strand of blonde hair under her white cap and with a jolt realised it was a young woman. Despite his illness, his nakedness shamed him and he clutched his hands in front of his groin and rolled onto his side away from her. One of the orderlies laughed and then spoke in Austrian-accented German.

'He's shy, this one!'

He pulled Gabriel's hands away from his groin, and then, helped by the second orderly, rolled him onto his back. Then, while one orderly held his head steady, the other cut Gabriel's hair with a pair of scissors. When finished, the first orderly foamed soap onto his head, chest, and groin while the other sharpened a cut-throat razor on a leather strap. Again Gabriel was held as his scalp, face and torso were expertly shaved. As the razor moved nearer his groin, Gabriel made another feeble attempt to cover himself, but the orderly laughed as he easily pulled Gabriel's hands away.

'Keep still now or we might cut off something important!'

Gabriel's head lolled to one side. Again his eyes met those of the woman who silently observed him. The orderlies rolled him onto his front and soaped him again, and then shaved the hairs from his back and legs. Cold liquid was poured onto his skin – paraffin, from the smell of it – and the orderlies massaged it into his back, legs and arms. Where his skin was raw from the razor the paraffin burned and he winced, but they ignored his discomfort, rolling him onto his back and rubbing more of it into his face, chest and groin. His humiliation almost over, they lifted him onto a stretcher, dressed him in a surgical gown and covered him with a blanket.

The young woman stepped forward. She gazed down at him for a moment and then nodded at the orderlies, apparently satisfied with their handiwork. Then all three left the room. Underneath the blanket Gabriel had stopped shivering and for a few moments the chill sensation in his bones vanished, replaced instead by a heat that steadily rose in his limbs and torso. He began to shiver again; gently at first and then more fiercely as the rigor took hold of him, seizing him, shaking him, making him shudder like a rat in the jaws of a terrier. His body shook so much that he was almost overcome by its violence. Then as quickly as it had started it passed. Temporarily relieved but drained, all he was aware of was the hard floor below his back.

Two more shaven-headed Austrian orderlies appeared, this time dressed in standard-issue army uniforms. They grunted as they lifted the stretcher and carried Gabriel out of the room. Swaying gently on the canvas, Gabriel stared up at the ceiling, the white-washed ceiling joists, cobwebs in the corners. He heard the footsteps of the stretcher-bearers on the stone floor and smelt the familiar odour of hospital disinfectant overlaid with… what? Tobacco? They entered a wide-spaced, high-ceilinged room filled with beds – proper sleeping cots, not straw mattresses or blankets on the floor – and Gabriel was lowered onto an empty bed next to a wall. The stretcher was removed from under him and two white-capped and -gowned female nurses appeared. They smiled at him and tucked him under real sheets and blankets and – wonder of wonders – placed a real pillow beneath his head.

Then one of the women held a tablet in front of his lips. 'Aspirin,' she said.

He opened his mouth and she placed the tablet on his tongue, then held a mug to his lips. He managed to take a sip of water to wash it down, and then his head was lowered onto the pillow. The other nurse gently wiped Gabriel's face with a flannel, dabbing at the sore areas where the razor had scraped him.

'It won't sting for long,' she said with a smile. 'Sleep if you can. We'll try you with some soup in a little while.'

He nodded, closed his eyes and sank into an uneasy sleep filled with troubled voices and vivid colours, and haunting images of the pits where the bodies in his camp had been buried.

14

Kragujevac, February – March 1915

That same evening Elspeth finally decided to have her hair cut. She did this partly as a gesture of support for Vera and Sylvia, but also because the number of Scottish women affected with typhus had risen. As her clinical role was primarily as a surgeon, it was not intended that Elspeth should look after patients suffering from typhus. However, several of her patients had unexpectedly developed the disease while recovering on the surgical wards, and last week another of the surgical nurses, Sister Minishull, had died from it. So Elspeth sat in her nightgown in their bedroom, and, with Sylvia looking on, Vera cut her hair down to an even inch all over.

After she had finished, Vera brushed a few stray hairs from Elspeth's shoulders and then stepped back to admire her handiwork. Looking at her reflection in a small hand mirror, Elspeth saw an angular, youthful face looking back at her, almost like a pageboy, she thought. Sylvia's face appeared in the mirror as she peered over Elspeth's shoulder.

'Nice work, Vee,' she said with a smirk. 'All you need do is paint a mascara moustache above her lip and Ellie could get a job as a male impersonator at the London Palladium.'

'Lord knows what they'd say about us back in London if they could see us now,' Elspeth said, running her fingers over the unfamiliar stubble on her scalp. 'Probably accuse us of trying to look like men, as well as steal their jobs.'

Vera laughed and walked towards the door. 'I'll get the broom from the kitchen and sweep up the mess,' she said as she left the room.

As Elspeth continued to study her reflection in the mirror, Sylvia yawned and lay down on her bed, hands clasped behind her head.

'Busy day?' Elspeth asked.

'Very.' Sylvia yawned again. 'We admitted another seventeen patients, which means we've got nearly a hundred and fifty typhus cases. They're doing pretty well mostly, although three more died this afternoon.'

Elspeth turned away from the mirror to look at Sylvia. 'An Austrian surgeon was transferred to you this afternoon; he wasn't one of the deaths, was he?'

Sylvia frowned. 'No, I don't think so. The ones that died this afternoon were all Serbian.' Then she suddenly sat up on the bed. 'Why do you ask?'

'Oh, nothing important,' Elspeth replied, just as Vera re-entered the room, carrying a brush and pan. 'It's just that earlier this afternoon a young Austrian surgeon and his orderly arrived from a nearby prison camp that had been badly affected by typhus. The surgeon was asking whether we could spare some aspirin, disinfectant, and so forth. But before he could finish, he collapsed. Turned out he was coming down with typhus himself.'

Sylvia furrowed her brow. 'We had so many admissions today, Ellie, I'm not sure… '

'Oh, I remember him,' interrupted Vera. 'I'd just finished fixing the magneto on the ambulance when I saw him go down like a stack of cards. I drove him up to the typhus hospital. Don't you recall, Sylvie? Huber helped me get him out.'

'Ah, Huber,' Sylvia said with a mischievous grin. 'Your faithful devotee, Ellie.'

Elspeth had saved Huber's life by deftly extracting the bullet imbedded near his kidney and draining the surrounding abscess. Due to a mixture of Elspeth's skill and the old soldier's resilience he had survived the operation, only to fall ill with typhus a week later. Amazingly, he had survived this as well – due entirely to the nursing care he had received – and it was obvious that he now worshipped all the women in the hospital, and Elspeth in particular.

Elspeth, ignoring Sylvia's teasing, stayed silent.

'I think you should marry him,' Sylvia continued. 'You'd become Mrs Huber, with your husband, Fritz, and five little Huberettes in tow – all dressed in lederhosen. Think of the scandal back in London.'

Elspeth smiled at the image. 'You seem to be determined to marry me off, Sylvie. Can't you do any better than a gap-toothed sixty-year-old?'

'If you don't mind, Ellie, Sergeant Huber is not a day over fifty-nine, and although I agree some of his teeth are missing, the rest of them are the most magnificent shade of mahogany.'

'Yes, very funny.'

'Anyway, what did your Austrian surgeon look like?' Sylvia – still grinning – continued.

Elspeth shrugged, and then looked across at Vera.

'About six foot,' said Vera, 'and slim; straight black hair.'

'And grey eyes,' added Elspeth. She ran her fingers over her head again, the sensation of short bristles unfamiliar on her fingertips. 'He spoke quite good English actually.'

A light of recognition appeared in Sylvia's face. 'I think I know who you mean. In fact, I'm pretty sure I saw him being de-loused at admission. Poor man, I felt quite sorry for him: although he was delirious, he seemed aware enough to know a woman was watching. Anyway, he's on the ward now.' A sly smile appeared on her face. 'Why are you so interested in him?'

'Oh please Sylvie, I'm not *interested* in him,' Elspeth said, mildly irritated at Sylvia's insinuation. 'It's just that he had an orderly with him, who seemed most distressed when the surgeon collapsed. Dr Soltau agreed to give the orderly the supplies that the surgeon asked for, and he was escorted back to his camp with them. But the surgeon was unconscious when all this was decided, so I don't think he knows. If he's still alive, you might tell him. I think it would put his mind at rest.' She crossed to her own bed and sat on the edge, plumping her pillow.

Sylvia nodded. 'Of course, Ellie. I'll keep an eye out,'

she paused, 'for this *special* Austrian of yours.' Elspeth gave her a sharp look, which was ignored. 'After all,' Sylvia continued, 'it sounds as if he's younger than Huber *and* has all his own teeth!'

★★★

At the fever hospital, Gabriel fought his battle against the typhus bacillus. His body, weakened by the hardships of the past months, was ill-prepared for such a ruthless enemy and for the first two days he lay in a fever-induced stupor, only awake for short periods of time, during which his muscles ached, his brain throbbed with every heartbeat, and his skin felt as if it were on fire. In the evenings his temperature soared, causing body-wracking rigors that left him exhausted, weakening him still further. He was delirious during these attacks, with a loud buzzing in his ears and his mind filled with images of monstrous creatures, bear-like animals with bloody claws and teeth that tore at his body.

He was nursed by a mix of Austrian prison orderlies – who spoke soothing words of German – and the Scottish women, whose accents he couldn't always understand. Dressed in their white caps and long anti-typhus gowns they looked to him like ghosts, and featured heavily in his dreams as ethereal spirits who drove away the bloody-pawed bears. They were always around him; taking his temperature and pulse, helping him when he needed to pass water, sponging the sweat from his face and body. They also tried to feed him, but initially he could take only water and a little broth. The uniformity of their clothing made it hard to distinguish one from another, but on the morning of the third day he woke feeling that his fever had diminished slightly and able to think clearly for the first time since he had arrived. Two of the ghosts arrived at his bedside to change his bedding. Under the white cap of one of them he saw fair eyelashes and bright green eyes, and suddenly realised that this was the woman who had been watching him when he had first arrived at the hospital. As she skilfully removed the sheet he was lying on, she smiled down at him.

'I can see you're a bit more with us today,' she said, rolling Gabriel towards her while her colleague slipped a clean sheet into the space his body had vacated. 'Your temperature is down and your pulse is lower.' They rolled him back again, snapped another sheet taut above the bed and lowered it over him. 'We'll try you with some breakfast in a moment. You need to eat if you're to beat this.'

Gabriel wanted to respond, but he hadn't spoken for so long that his cheeks and tongue felt numb. He tried to speak, but the words came out as an indistinct mumble. The woman cocked her head as she listened to him; then she gave a disappointed frown.

'I'm sorry... I can't understand what you're saying.' She walked to the end of the bed and lifted the observation chart, looking at the name inscribed across the top. 'You are the Austrian surgeon, Captain Bayer, aren't you? You do speak English, don't you?'

Gabriel slowly nodded, and then – with an effort – began again, forcing his brain to find the correct words, and commanding his tongue to work correctly.

'Yes… I…' He stopped to lick his lips once more. 'I can… speak English.' His throat felt so parched that he thought it might crack. A moment later – as if she knew what he was feeling – she was holding a tin cup in front of him. He lifted his head and drank from it, feeling the cold water soothe his throat. Then she removed the cup and stood by his side, patiently waiting for him to speak again. As he looked up at her, he wondered if she was one of the Scottish women surgeons he remembered the veteran Austrian sergeant telling him about.

'Thank you, Doctor,' Gabriel said in clear English.

'Oh, I'm no doctor,' she answered cheerfully. 'I'm the ward sister. Actually we've only one doctor for more than a hundred and fifty patients here, so you only get to meet her if you're *very* ill.' She gave him an impish smile. 'So you really don't want to meet her if you can avoid it. In any case, all you need is good nursing to recover from typhus. My name is Sister Calthorpe, by the way.'

He nodded at her and then looked around the ward, taking in his surroundings for the first time since he had arrived. 'How long have I been here?' he asked.

'Three days. This is the fever hospital. You were moved up from the surgical hospital when they saw you had typhus.'

Three days? Gabriel levered himself up onto his elbows.

'I must get back to my camp, Sister. My men... they need supplies and—'

She leant forward, placing a gloved hand on his forearm. 'Don't worry, Captain. I am told your orderly was sent back to the camp with a wagonload of supplies, including food and medicines. Now you must forget about them and focus your energies on fighting this infection.'

Gabriel sank back onto the bed, exhausted but relieved. 'Thank you.' She curled her fingers around his wrist and he felt her gloved fingertips on his radial pulse. After a moment she removed her hand and placed it on his forehead.

'Your pulse is down but your temperature is still high.' She leant forward to undo the top button of his gown, pulling the collars aside to inspect his neck. 'And you still have a rash. This is only day three and the fevers are likely to continue.' She re-buttoned his gown and leant back. 'You'll need every ounce of your strength to see this thing through, so it's important you try to eat something.'

It took him a moment to nod his understanding. In order to survive he would to have to accept this unfamiliar feeling of being dependent on others. But it felt strange to be on the receiving end of medical care. It was normally his job to stand at a patient's bedside and tell them about their illness and how they were going to be treated. Once again she seemed able to read his thoughts.

'And another thing, Captain Bayer,' she said with

a serious look. 'You doctors make the worst patients because you think you know it all. But I'm going to treat you just like all the other patients here and you will follow my orders like all the rest. Do you understand?'

Gabriel, despite his weakness, smiled. 'Just like my nurses back in Sarajevo,' he said.

'Just like good nurses everywhere,' she said sternly, but he saw a glimmer of amusement in her eye as she turned away to help the nurse at the next bed.

★★★

As she had predicted, his temperature rose again that evening and the delirium returned. Over the next three days the fevers came and went, but at times he was able to eat a little maize bread and soup. The pyrexia was worse at night – the monstrous phantoms still haunted his dreams – but during the day he felt slightly better and even tried to speak to the patients on either side of him. The man in the bed on Gabriel's left was confused and spoke in ramblingly incoherent Serbian. The fellow on Gabriel's right did not appear confused, although he looked very unwell: breathless, bluish lips, a harsh rasping cough. One of the Austrian orderlies looking after the fellow exchanged a few words with him in German and when the same orderly arrived at his bedside, Gabriel asked him who the man was.

'He's General Appel, the commanding officer of the Austrian 6th Army. He was admitted with typhus a few days before you were.'

Of course, thought Gabriel: General Appel. He had last seen him at the briefing that Field Marshall Potiorek had given just before the war began, back in August. It was hard to believe that the shaven-headed, gasping figure in the next bed was the same man. After the orderly left his bedside Gabriel tried to speak to Appel, but the General's bouts of coughing and breathlessness prevented him from replying. As the evening wore on Appel developed violent, bed-frame-rattling rigors and became deliriously confused. Shortly before midnight a woman that Gabriel hadn't seen before was brought to the General's bedside. The nurses addressed her as "Dr Wakefield" and Gabriel watched as she tried to keep him alive, administering injections for the fever and pummelling his chest to get him to cough up the pus and mucus that was blocking his lungs. In spite of these efforts, the General's breathing became more laboured, and Gabriel heard his agonal gasps in the early hours. Ten minutes later two orderlies came and wrapped his body in a sheet and took the linen-shrouded corpse away. Ten minutes after that another man – this time a Serbian officer – was placed in the same bed.

Gabriel's fever fluctuated over the next few days. Sister Calthorpe appeared to take a special interest in him, perhaps, he thought, because he was one of the few Austrians who could speak decent English. She asked him many questions: about the prison camp, his life as a surgeon, where he'd worked before the war. But his replies were listless because he felt so dopey, so discouraged by the fever and aching in his joints that he found it hard to concentrate on conversation for very long. And then on the afternoon of the eighth day, his temperature soared once more.

Now his body became a furnace as the rigors swept through him with renewed intensity. He knew this was the critical time and had witnessed it in the prison camp; patients appeared to improve over the first few days, only to die during their crisis a week later. The intense heat of the fever prevented his brain from functioning properly and he was only vaguely aware Sister Calthorpe was by his bedside. He felt a sharp stab in his buttock and heard her tell him that he had been given an injection of camphorated ether to lower the fever. Throughout the afternoon and early evening she was by his side, sponging sweat from his face and forcing him to drink the broth and water she brought him. The delirium worsened – bringing with it the bloody-clawed bears – and then Dr Wakefield appeared. Even in his confusion, he knew his life lay in the balance, but the ache in his muscles and joints and the terror of his delirium were so unbearable that a part of him gave himself permission to let go, to allow himself to slip away, to be free of the pain and torment.

He made an effort to banish these negative thoughts, to hold on and resist the urge to give up and sink into the blissful peace of oblivion. When Dr Wakefield went off duty, the Austrian night orderlies were by his bedside. He closed his eyes and tried to sleep, but the monsters in his nightmares did not allow him to. But eventually even the monsters disappeared, leaving his mind a blank screen.

And he knew he could not hold on for much longer.

But somehow he did.

Somehow he endured.

And then, in the early pre-dawn hour and after a long night of drenching sweats and pain and nightmares, the fever finally broke.

★★★

It was quiet in the ward as he lay on his back, damp with perspiration, looking up at the ceiling. He was exhausted and it felt as if his body was a piece of rubber tubing that had been stretched out of shape. But the buzzing in his head had gone and he could think clearly for the first time in days. He swept his legs back and forth under the sheets, enjoying the simple pleasure of pain-free movement, then managed to sit up and swing his legs over the side of the bed.

The ward was softly illuminated by a hooded oil lamp on the wall at the far end, and he lifted the damp surgical gown and peered at his abdomen: even in the dim light he could see that the rash had faded and lost its angry red look. He felt an urgent need to pass water and so he carefully stood – his legs trembling like those of a newly born foal – and took a few steps towards the end of the bed. But he felt dizzy and was grateful when one of the orderlies materialised by his side and helped him to the latrine. Back in bed he fell asleep again, but this time it was deep and dreamless; when he woke it was daylight and he had no fever, no pain, no headache.

Utter bliss flooded through him because he knew he had won his battle. He had survived.

He watched as the day shift of nurses arrived on the ward, saw them putting on their calico typhus uniforms before they began their rounds. He sought Sister Calthorpe's face amongst them and when he did find her, could see she was trying to suppress a smile. He could not help himself from grinning at her as she crossed towards him.

'Good morning, Sister.'

'Good morning, Captain Bayer,' she replied, pursing her lips, her face professionally neutral. 'You're looking much better this morning. We were a little worried about you last night.' She picked up his observation chart, nodding her head as she studied the numbers, before allowing him a satisfied smile. 'I was very pleased to hear from the night orderly that your crisis seems to have passed. Pulse down, temperature normal: I think you may be over the worst.'

'Thank you, Sister. I feel so much better today. I'm very grateful for all you've done.'

'You did it largely by yourself, Captain. We only provided the right conditions for your body to heal itself.'

'I'm still grateful. I don't think I would have survived if I'd been in the prison camp.'

Her face became sombre. 'I hear the mortality from typhus in your camp is almost seventy percent?'

He nodded again. 'More than ninety percent amongst the medical staff.'

245

'I'm sorry to hear that,' she said. And then – very matter-of-factly – added, 'Our mortality is only sixteen percent.'

Gabriel looked surprised.

'You don't believe me?' she said.

'No, I do,' he replied quickly. 'I've seen at first hand the good work you do here.'

'Well,' she said, with a gleam in her eyes. 'That's what's possible when women are allowed to take charge of a hospital.'

He smiled. 'I have never before come upon the concept of an all-woman hospital before. But I am grateful for it, because it saved my life.'

'Do you have any female doctors in Austria?'

He shook his head.

'A pity,' she said. 'They have much to offer.'

Gabriel considered her comment and was instantly intrigued. Why not women doctors? He'd seen the dexterity in the fingers of his mother and other women when doing needlework, preparing food, cleaning – he could think of no rational reason why they could not be trained as well as men to become surgeons. Maybe better than some men: after all it was Thomas Berger's lack of dexterity that made him take up anaesthesia instead of surgery...

Oh, sweet Jesus, he'd almost forgotten. Thomas was dead. Now he remembered the reason he'd left the camp: Schwann was unwell. Had he survived? The smile on his face vanished as he sat forward.

'Sister, I have to get back to my camp as soon as

possible—' But she was already wagging a finger in front of his face.

'Now, I don't want any nonsense from you about discharging yourself. You've only just passed the crisis,' she said with a stern look. 'It's far too early to even *think* about discharge yet.'

'But, Sister—'

'No buts. I've told you before, Captain. You're not allowed to argue with me.'

He sank down again, frustrated. 'But when do you think I will be well enough to return to my camp?'

Her eyebrows came together as she considered his question. 'Although you are over the worst, you'll continue to feel quite tired for several days yet. You've lost quite a bit of weight and you'll need at least a day or two of proper feeding. We'll review you tomorrow and if your temperature is still normal, we can talk about it then.'

He didn't fight her, but simply nodded his head and lay back into his pillow. Although a strong sense of duty to the men in his camp pricked his conscience, he still felt exhausted. So he was partly relieved – albeit guiltily – to hear her say he must stay another day to rebuild his strength.

She returned the chart to the end of his bed. 'Now if you'll excuse me, Captain, I've other patients to attend to.'

★★★

In their bedroom in the villa that evening, shortly before lights-out, Sylvia, Vera and Elspeth prepared for bed.

'Your Captain Bayer has done very well,' Sylvia said. She was sitting on her bed, filing her fingernails with an emery board while Elspeth sat at a table in one corner of the room, penning a letter to Dr Inglis. Vera, sitting on the bed beside Sylvia, was cleaning the electrodes on a dirty sparkplug with a toothbrush.

'He's not *my* Captain Bayer,' replied Elspeth without looking up, as she continued to write.

'Well, you know what I mean: it was you that had him sent up from the surgical hospital and told me to look out for him. Anyway, I really thought he wasn't going to make it yesterday evening; even Dr Wakefield was doubtful. But he pulled through during the night and this morning was even asking when he could be discharged.'

Elspeth looked up at Sylvia. 'So he's made a full recovery?'

'Mm,' said Sylvia, a faint rasping coming from the sandpaper on her nails. 'He'll be well enough to be discharged tomorrow I should think.' She held her fingers up to the light and inspected the cuticles for a moment, then lowered them and carried on filing. 'I suppose he'll be sent back to his camp,' she said, almost wistfully.

Elspeth continued to stare at Sylvia for several seconds. 'That's the third time this week you've mentioned Captain Bayer,' she finally said. 'I do believe, Sylvia Calthorpe, that you've developed a bit of a soft spot for him.'

Vera stopped brushing the sparkplug and looked

across at Sylvia. 'Oh no; don't tell me you've gone and fallen for a Hun?'

Sylvia smiled at her teasing, but carried on filing her nails.

'No, of course not, Vee,' she said. 'I'm a professional, he's my patient, and a good nurse doesn't do that sort of thing. Besides, he's not a Hun: the Austrians seem to dislike the Germans almost as much as we do.'

'Hm,' Vera said, eyebrows raised, a sceptical look on her face as she resumed cleaning the plug.

Sylvia stopped her filing. 'Look, I'm not romantically interested in Captain Bayer. It's just that I think he's a decent sort of chap.'

Vera made a face as if to say she didn't believe her, and Elspeth was intrigued. At St Mary's Hospital, Sylvia had the pick of London's finest young doctors; handsome, intelligent men, every last one with good career prospects. Yet Elspeth had watched Sylvia deflect all their advances. Now – for the first time that Elspeth could recall – Sylvia seemed genuinely interested in a man, and she would like to know why.

'Well you could keep him on as an orderly,' Elspeth said. 'I remember him telling Dr Soltau that he's worked at St Mark's and Mount Sinai before, so he's clinically experienced. I don't know whether he could handle taking orders from a woman, but if he could, I'm sure he could be used in some capacity on the wards.'

Sylvia looked down at her fingers again as she resumed her filing. 'It's a good idea, but I'm not sure he'll agree. He seems quite concerned about the men in his camp, says it's his duty to get back to them. But I'll suggest it to him tomorrow and see what he says.'

★★★

Gabriel slept well that night, and when he woke the next morning his pulse and temperature were still normal and he felt hungry for the first time in more than a week. Guilt and a sense of loyalty to his men still prompted him to think of returning to the prison camp, even though the same thought filled him with dread. But he was also keen to know what had happened since his absence. Had Schwann survived his bout of typhus? Had Peter and Klaus coped while he was away? Then he saw Sister Calthorpe arrive on the ward. She walked towards him, stood at the end of the bed, lifted his observation chart.

'Your pulse and temperature are still normal. You are officially cured of typhus, Captain.'

He nodded. 'I know you said I should not rush to leave, Sister. However, I have a duty to my men and still feel I should return to my camp as soon as possible.'

'You'll have to see Dr Wakefield first,' she folded her arms across her chest, 'but if you still insist you're fully recovered... Well, I'm sure Dr Wakefield won't stop you from going back to your camp.'

He nodded again. He was uneasy at the thought of returning, but it felt like the right decision.

There was a momentary silence as she watched his face. Then she sighed and unfolded her arms. 'Look, Captain, I do understand you feel it is your duty to return to your camp. But would it not be better to stay a while longer, to build up your strength before you go?'

He would have preferred that, but couldn't bring himself to say so. She was still studying his face. 'Might I make a suggestion?' she said.

'Of course.'

'Dr Soltau sent the supplies you requested back to the camp with your orderly, and you told me that there are two other doctors – a physician and a surgeon – still working there.'

'That is correct.'

'Well it strikes me that you don't need to be back in the camp with any degree of urgency. I think you told me that you don't have any surgical instruments, so it's not as if you could perform any surgery, could you?'

'No…' He frowned; what was she trying to say?

'Well, Captain, typhus is ravaging Serbia and has already killed many doctors and nurses. We've lost several of our own to it, and even Dr Wakefield shouldn't be back on duty: she's only just recovered and far from fully fit, which is why you've hardly seen her on the wards.'

Gabriel suddenly knew what she was about to propose.

'So there will always be room for a prisoner with your background and training, whose skills would be much better utilised here in Kragujevac, than in the camp where you have no proper equipment or facilities. You would of course only be working as an orderly and would have to accept orders from our doctors and nurses.' She paused. 'And they are all women.'

He continued to listen to her in silence.

'If you think you could stomach the idea of taking orders from a woman, then I'm sure we could use you. You'd be much better off here than in the camp, and your excellent spoken English would help with translation. There may even be the opportunity to work in the operating theatre – only as an assistant of course.' She refolded her arms as she waited for him to respond.

He thought for several seconds before replying. 'Your offer is very appealing, but I feel a responsibility to the men in my camp. I would be failing in my duty if I did not return to them—'

'And what about a responsibility to the people of Serbia?' she retorted, her voice unexpectedly raised, her eyes filled with sudden indignation. 'They who have suffered so much since *your* country took them to war? Don't you think you would be repaying them an obligation, staying here, using your skills to help them at this difficult time?'

He was stunned by the passion of her outburst, her words stinging him with their truth. He *was* thinking only of his own position; his country *had* invaded Serbia. Potiorek's strategy *had* resulted in death and misery for the Serbian people. She had presented him with a strong moral argument in favour of staying. And she was right, there was very little he could do in the camp. For a moment he felt ashamed, but when he looked back at her but saw that already her anger had gone, that her gaze had softened.

'I'm sorry. I shouldn't have lost my temper,' she said.

'But I can't bear to see waste. And it would be a waste, you, languishing ineffectively in that camp.'

He shook his head. 'You have no need to apologise, Sister.' He paused and then came to a quick decision. 'If anything it should be me apologising to you, because you are absolutely right, both from a moral and practical point-of-view. If you will have me, I would happily work here as an orderly. I would have no problem accepting orders from your doctors or nurses – women or otherwise.'

'Excellent decision, Captain Bayer.'

'I've learned it's best not to argue with you, Sister.'

'Very wise,' she answered as she turned away with a smile.

***

The next day Gabriel began work as an orderly in the fever hospital. As he was now immune to typhus he did not wear the calico typhus clothing, but instead found his old uniform – shirt, trousers, and even his jacket with three silver stars still attached – clean and freshly steamed in a neatly folded pile in the laundry.

It was good to be out of bed, he thought, as he accompanied the nurses on his first ward round. However, it was not easy adjusting to this new role. Not that he considered nursing duties unimportant – indeed, he now knew from personal experience how vital it was for a patient's recovery – but it was strange to watch others make decisions on patients and then have to carry out their instructions. The other Austrian orderlies knew of his rank and offered to do the more menial tasks, but Gabriel declined, telling them he wanted no special treatment, that he would do his share of the work no matter how trivial. But after a whole afternoon spent emptying and rinsing out piss-pots, he realised it would take him some time to get used to his new position.

The prison orderlies had been allocated their own room. Although they were locked in at night, it was warm and dry and they received two good meals a day – heaven compared to the conditions in the prison camp. And it was wonderful to be working with patients again, discussing their symptoms and problems and complications. On the first ward round that morning, Gabriel diagnosed a missed septic arthritis, and by the next day Sylvia and the other nurses were already asking for his opinion whenever Dr Wakefield was unavailable.

On the third morning, as usual, the guard unlocked the door of the prisoners' sleeping quarters. But as Gabriel left the room, he was surprised to find Sylvia waiting for him.

'I have some good news for you, Captain,' she said. 'Two of the surgeons at the school hospital have gone down with fever, leaving only one surgeon well enough to operate. Dr Stewart has a full list of cases and needs an experienced assistant. Would you be willing to help?'

'Help?'

'Yes.'

'You mean… in the operating theatre?'

She nodded.

A grin spread across his face. 'I should be delighted.'

'Excellent. I've cleared it with the guards. They will escort you there immediately.'

'Thank you very much, Sister.'

'Don't let me down,' she replied. 'It was me who suggested your name.'

15

Early morning at the school hospital, and Elspeth was
already inside one of the converted classroom wards,
about to examine a patient due for surgery later that
day.

But she was feeling ill at ease.

The previous morning, both Dr Soltau and Dr
Chesney had presented with fever and taken to their
beds. Later the same day, two ox wagons loaded with
eight urgent surgical transfers from the nearby town
of Valjevo had rolled into the hospital courtyard.
Examining the casualties, Elspeth had seen that several
of the transfers were complex and would require
the skills of two surgeons. But she was now the only
surgeon fit enough to operate. She had gone to the First
Reserve Hospital to ask for help from Dr Anitch, but
he could spare her no one and had told her she would
have to do the best she could and not worry about the
outcome. But Elspeth was unhappy with risking lives
in this way, and had discussed her problem with Sylvia
that evening.

'But if the cases are complex and you need a trained surgeon,' Sylvia had replied, 'why not use Captain Bayer? I've watched him on the wards over the past few days; he's hard working and perceptive. He speaks good English as well as German, and he has a smattering of Serbian. What do you have to lose by giving him a try?'

Elspeth had agreed; it seemed like the only sensible choice, although now she wondered if she had made the right decision. Well, she told herself, she would know soon enough.

She heard the door to the ward open and looking up from the patient saw two Serbian guards appear in the doorway, followed a moment later by Gabriel.

It was the first time she had seen him since he had collapsed so spectacularly in the school courtyard almost a month ago. Now, as she watched him walk towards her, Elspeth studied his appearance: a little thinner, perhaps, in his pale blue uniform, his black hair much shorter, of course, but a warm intelligence still perceptible in the silver of his eyes.

'Captain Bayer,' she said, nodding her head in greeting.

'Dr Stewart,' he said, bowing in return. 'It is a pleasure to see you again. The last time we met, I was unfortunately not at my best.'

She smiled. 'I'm glad to see you've recovered. Has Sister Calthorpe explained my problem?'

'She has, and I am very sorry to hear about Dr Soltau. I met her only briefly as you know, but she struck me as being extremely nice. How is she doing, may I ask?'

'She still has a high fever. But there is no rash and this morning she developed a sore throat. There is an exudate covering the back of the pharynx—'

'Diphtheria, you think?'

'Yes,' she replied, reassured he had arrived at the same provisional diagnosis she had. 'It is easy to assume every new case of fever is typhus, but in these conditions it's important to keep an open mind.'

'I agree. As well as typhus, I saw diphtheria, pneumonia, even meningitis in my camp. Well, I truly hope she recovers.'

His empathy for Dr Soltau was unexpected and warmed her to him. She could see why Sylvia was drawn to him: a confident yet kind manner, the look of someone you could trust. 'Our lead surgeon, Dr Chesney, has also gone down with bronchitis.'

'I see.' He nodded. 'Well, I am honoured to be asked to help and excited at the prospect of operating—'

She saw him flinch as an ear-splitting roar of a motor engine from the courtyard cut off his words.

'Oh don't worry,' she said, trying to suppress a smile at the startled expression on his face. 'It's only our electricity generator.'

He straightened up, grinning sheepishly at her. 'Sorry for being a... how you say... scaredy-cat. Yes?'

She gently laughed and then realised she was looking forward to being in theatre with him. 'Dr Soltau brought it with us from England. It's a noisy beast, but invaluable for guaranteeing a steady electricity supply for the theatre lights and X-ray machine.'

His eyebrows rose. 'You *brought* an X-ray machine with you?'

'Oh yes,' she said pertly. 'One of our women studied physics and radiology at Cambridge and brought a small device with her. It's been invaluable.'

'How we could have done with an X-ray machine in our field hospital,' he said, and she saw him shake his head in wonder. For a moment there was a silence as they looked at each other, and then she broke the awkwardness of the moment by pulling her pocket watch out of her jacket and flipping open the lid. 'Well, they'll be waiting for us in theatre,' she said, closing the lid with a snap. 'I just need to see one more case. It's the first on our list today and probably the most challenging.'

They crossed to one of the beds and Elspeth began to examine the patient; a Serbian corporal who became breathless with even the gentle effort of sitting forward to remove the top of his gown. His lips and fingers were purple with cyanosis, the skin of his chest scarred and puckered, and via Aurelia, the translator, Elspeth told the soldier there was a collection of pus – an empyema – surrounding his left lung, caused by a shrapnel injury received a few months ago. The X-ray showed a fragment of metal lodged close to his heart she told him. The pus needed to be drained and the shrapnel removed to prevent a recurrence of the empyema.

★★★

As she explained all of this to the soldier, Gabriel stood by Elspeth's side and studied her with a growing sense of fascination. He had never met a female surgeon before. Now he was spellbound at her confident assessment and correctly proposed solution to the problem. She finished her examination and then led him out of the ward and along a corridor to a main staircase, then up one flight of stairs towards the first floor. As they reached the landing, she started to tell him about another patient on the list.

And as he listened to her enthusiastic analysis of this case, a smile of wonder spread across his face. He felt nothing but admiration for her, and her colleagues. To have travelled all the way to a war zone at such a dangerous time, showed a selfless dedication he had never witnessed before. So he was startled when – as they arrived outside the operating theatre – Elspeth stopped talking mid-sentence and suddenly turned towards him.

'You appear amused, Captain Bayer,' she said, her voice sharp, her hands on her hips, the diamond blue of her eyes alight. 'Have I said something comical, something you don't agree with?'

'Oh,' Gabriel said with dismay. 'No, not at all. Please do not take offence, Dr Stewart. I'm just amazed… amazed that—'

'Amazed?' He saw that her eyes were now ablaze. 'And why is that, may I ask?'

Gabriel blinked, then opened and closed his mouth without speaking, eventually finding his tongue. 'I am sorry, Dr Stewart… my English… is a little rusty. What I wanted to say is that I am amazed at the competence and commitment of all the women in your unit. We have no women doctors in Austria. Yet having been nursed back to health by Sister Calthorpe, and now watching you at work, makes me realise what a valuable asset has been wasted all these years.'

At first she seemed surprised at his reply, and then he saw two spots of scarlet slowly appear on her cheeks. She looked down at her shoes for a moment, then looked up at him from under partly lowered eyelids.

'I must apologise for my outburst,' she replied. 'In my country, the majority of men do not respect the abilities of female surgeons. So when I hear the word "amazed", I am apt to assume it is being used in much the same way as when describing a talking pig, or a cow walking on its hind legs.'

Gabriel gently laughed at the images, relieved she had already forgiven him. 'You have no need to apologise. I know that what you say is true about the majority of male doctors. But I am not one of them. I can see you understand surgical method.'

'That's kind of you to say, Captain Bayer, but you haven't actually seen me operate yet.'

'Well then,' he said with a smile, pushing the theatre door open for her. 'Show me.'

He followed her inside, into a classroom that had been converted into an operating theatre, the centre of the room dominated by an improvised operating table overhung by several lights mounted on a stand. Elspeth introduced him to three other nurses already in the room: Monica, a fresh-faced scrub nurse, preparing the sutures, scalpels, and other tools of surgery; Aurelia, a VAD, a cheery girl who spoke fluent Serbian and would act as a translator; and Lydia, a pretty but quiet nurse who Gabriel was told would administer the anaesthetic.

As they waited for the patient to be brought in, Elspeth held a roentogram plate up to the light and showed Gabriel the shadow of a large empyema – pus in the cavity surrounding the left lung. She also pointed out a small triangular density, the piece of shrapnel that had caused the empyema. Although the shard of metal was close to the heart, her plan, she told him, was to open the chest, wash out the pus, remove the shrapnel, and leave a drainage tube in place.

'You mean Bulau drainage?' he said and she nodded. His eyebrows rose. 'That surprises me. We use Bulau's method in Austria, of course, but I thought the British method for empyema was to resect a portion of the ribs and allow free drainage of the pus?'

She smiled. 'In Paris we tried Bulau's method of an underwater seal and chest drain and found it much less traumatic. So we are happy to adopt Germanic practice if it's better for our patients—'

She was interrupted by the clatter of the theatre door swinging open. Two orderlies appeared with the Serbian corporal lying on a stretcher, which they hoisted onto the operating table. The soldier's face was tense, his breathing rapid, his eyes wide as he scanned the unfamiliar surroundings. But Gabriel saw the man relax as Elspeth walked over to him and placed her hand on his wrist. She smiled reassuringly at him, and then looked across at Lydia and gave a subtle nod of her head.

As Gabriel washed his hands, Lydia took a gauze

mask and held it an inch above the soldier's face, dripping liquid from a bottle labelled 'Chloroform' onto the mask, while Aurelia – sitting at the soldier's head – whispered gently soothing words of Serbian. Gabriel put on a white cotton gown, a cap, and a muslin veil that covered the lower part of his face. Then he squeezed his hands inside the largest pair of rubber gloves he could find, realising that the women must have smaller hands as even the largest gloves were a tight fit. He heard a change in breathing from the patient as the chloroform took effect and saw Lydia lower the mask tightly over the man's nose and mouth. Now she took another bottle – labelled ether – and dripped liquid from this onto the mask. Gabriel heard the breathing become deeper, slower, more regular. After another minute Lydia pinched the soldier's ear; there was no response. She turned to Elspeth and Gabriel.

'He's under. You can begin.'

Gabriel stood beside Elspeth as she pulled away the surgical gown to expose the soldier's torso, the scars on the chest wall puckered and red. With Gabriel's help she rolled the man onto his right side and slid a wooden wedge underneath his body; then rolled him back so that his left flank was elevated and exposed. Monica handed Elspeth a small pastry brush and a jar containing a brown liquid.

'Iodine,' Elspeth said to Gabriel, her voice slightly muffled by the face veil as she painted the chest wall with the solution. 'Dr Alexander Fleming, one of our microbiologists at St Mary's, has undertaken studies that suggest it is a more effective sterilising agent than carbolic acid.'

She stepped back as Monica covered the wedge and torso with sterile drapes, leaving only the iodine-coated chest wall uncovered. Then Elspeth stepped forward again and pressed her gloved fingers over the scar tissue. She palpated a gap between the ribs. Keeping her fingers in place she looked expectantly up at Gabriel, who had already been given a scalpel by Monica; he placed its handle in Elspeth's free hand. Without hesitation she made an incision, a stripe of red appearing as the skin parted beneath the blade's razor edge and tiny hoses of blood began to spurt in the air.

They worked together quickly, efficiently and wordlessly: he clipping the spraying vessels with artery forceps and tying them off with catgut, while she dissected down through the skin and muscle between the ribs. He saw her push a gloved index finger through the chest wall into the pleural cavity: a spout of foul-smelling yellow fluid erupted from the hole. She waited for the flow of pus to stop and then widened the hole with the scalpel. Then she turned to Monica.

'Tuffier, please.'

Monica handed her a metal device consisting of two wide steel blades separated by a serrated rod, a contraption Gabriel had not seen before. Without explanation Elspeth inserted the blades into the incision and then – using a ratchet which gripped the serrations on the rod – she levered the blades apart, causing the gap between the two ribs to spring open, widening the space into the lung. Gabriel was astonished. It was a novel type of rib separator, a hands-free device the like of which he had never seen before. Now he could see deep inside the lung cavity. He saw Elspeth lock the blades apart using a thumb screw on the rod. She glanced up at him and even though the lower part of her face was obscured by muslin, he could tell from the wrinkles around her eyes that she was smiling at him.

'You haven't seen one of these before, have you?' she said.

'No.'

'It was invented by Theodore Tuffier in Paris only last year. Monsieur Tuffier was kind enough to lend us one and it proved so invaluable that I knew I had to bring it out here. It's extremely useful, almost like having a second pair of hands.'

His initial surprise at the competency of these women was now surpassed by a feeling of inadequacy, as he realised that many of their innovations – first the iodine, now the Tuffier – were ahead of his own. And he could see that Elspeth was in her element: slipping her slender wrist between the blades of the Tuffier and into the man's chest; pushing the lung aside with her fingertips; squinting along the back of her forearm.

'Ah. I think I see it.' She dropped her head, rotated her wrist, strained for position. 'Damn, it's wedged against the pericardium… must have passed through the cardiac notch in the pleura.'

He saw her wrist bob in time with the soldier's heart-beat and knew her hand was touching the outer lining of the heart. This, he realised, was the critical moment of the operation. He saw Monica's head jerk forward slightly, saw furrows appear on Lydia's forehead. Aurelia stood motionless beside him. Everybody seemed to be holding their breath. Everyone that is, except for Elspeth, who by contrast appeared calmly absorbed in the procedure, still dipping her head, still scrunching her eyelids, still twisting her arm.

'Oh... wait a minute... I think...' She slowly removed her hand from the wound, and Gabriel saw a black, jagged, triangular piece of iron, the size of an arrow head, held delicately between her thumb and index finger.

'Och, will you look at that,' Lydia said, and Aurelia and Monica burst out laughing, causing the tension in the room to dissipate in an instant.

'*Very* well done,' he said with emphasis, studying the wrinkles around her eyes, which told him she was smiling with satisfaction.

An elbow nudged his side and he turned to see Monica holding a large metal syringe. 'Sterile saline,' she told him. He grinned behind the mask as he took it from her and flushed the pleural space, washing out as much pus and debris as he could. Then he peered into the hole.

'The lung and pericardium seem undamaged. That piece of shrapnel must have ricocheted off a rib and lain undisturbed for months before declaring as an abscess.'

She was also looking inside the cavity. 'Yes, I think we're done,' she said, placing a rubber tube into the wound and then unclipping the thumb screw on the Tuffier to allow the ribs to spring back into place around the drain. After removing the Tuffier, Gabriel began to stitch the wound, securing the tube in place with a purse-string suture. Elspeth placed the other end of the drain through a hole in the lid of a half-filled glass jar on the floor by her feet. Gabriel recognised it as a standard underwater seal for chest drainage, and the bottom of the tube began to bubble as the re-expanding lung displaced air from the soldier's pleural space. Glancing at the clock on the wall, Gabriel saw that the operation had taken only thirty minutes. It had been fast, skilled work. This team, this woman; they knew their stuff.

There were another eleven cases on the list to be done that day. Five of the cases were minor procedures – draining abscesses, closing fistulas, debriding wounds – but the remaining six were more challenging: skull wounds, amputations, abdominal and chest explorations. They stopped briefly for bread and soup at lunchtime but continued to work through the afternoon and into the early evening. And suddenly they were on the final case.

'This last patient will be interesting,' Elspeth said. 'He's a bit of a brigand, a member of a Cheta, one of the irregular units supporting the Serbian army. We've treated a number of Chetniks; they're a hardy lot and pride themselves on their resilience, but this poor chap's got a bullet in his liver. Unless we get it out there's a real chance he won't pull through, although when I saw him first thing this morning he wasn't at all keen on an operation.'

'That doesn't surprise me,' Gabriel said. 'We treated a few Chetniks in my field hospital. They hate us Austrians and it took a great deal of persuasion before they would let us even touch them.'

Elspeth nodded. 'This one's a rather large man and the roentogram shows a bullet in the upper right abdomen, possibly in his liver. He was shot by another member of his Cheta in an accidental discharge two weeks ago, and in Valjevo they tried conservative management without improvement. He has a swinging fever and probably has an abscess between the liver and diaphragm.'

Gabriel furrowed his brow. 'I would normally leave a bullet embedded in the liver alone. This type of surgery can be very high risk you know.'

'Well, of course I know, and I'm not keen on operating on him either,' she replied. 'But after two weeks of doing nothing, he is going downhill. I think an operation may be his best chance, but I'd be interested to hear your opinion.'

At that moment the door opened and Gabriel stepped back as two more stretcher-bearers – grunting and gasping with effort – slowly backed into the room. The man on the stretcher was huge and both orderlies strained to lift him and deposit him on the operating table. As they walked away, Gabriel stepped forward and the man turned his head towards him. It was a large head, the pallor of his face offset by a heavy growth of black beard, but Gabriel immediately recognised the eye-patch across the man's left eye.

'Luka,' he said with surprise and quickly turned to

Elspeth. 'What an odd coincidence,' he said to her. 'I know this fellow. I've treated him before.'

The big bearded Chetnik had also recognised Gabriel and was waving his right hand at him. Gabriel stepped forward and saw that Luka looked ill, a grey pallor underneath his good right eye and a light sheen of sweat across his broad forehead. 'I thought I told you to stay away from trouble,' Gabriel said to him in German.

Luka grinned, then flinched and clutched the right side of his abdomen. 'I pleased see you, *Hirurga*,' he replied in pidgin German. 'Not Austrian bullet. Stupid boy in Cheta… his rifle shoot by accident.'

'First a Serbian grenade, now a Serbian bullet.' Gabriel said, then tutted, shook his head, smiled.

Luka fixed his gaze on Gabriel. 'You operate me?' he asked.

But Gabriel didn't immediately reply. Instead he pulled back the surgical gown and placed a hand on Luka's grossly distended abdomen. He saw the blood-encrusted bullet hole, glanced at the Chetnik's anaemic complexion, and then felt the heat of fever in the man's brow. After two weeks like this, he knew that an operation was the Serbian's best chance of survival. Elspeth's opinion was good and he looked across at her and nodded. He turned back to Luka. 'Yes,' he said in German. 'Dr Stewart is right. You need an operation.'

Luka looked at Elspeth first and then at Gabriel. '*Skotski damé*: she operate me also?'

'Yes. Dr Stewart is a good surgeon and you're a two-man job.'

'But she no man – she *damé*.' Luka paused. '*Damé* is good *hirurga*?'

'Yes, Luka. The lady is a very good surgeon.'

Luka looked doubtful. '*Damé* should be home, have babies…' Then he paused and Gabriel saw a look of comprehension came over his face. 'Ah.' He nodded his head sagely, as if he only now understood. '*Skotski damé* is *Virginesh*.'

Virginesh? Gabriel frowned, but then heard Aurelia stifle a giggle and turned to see a look of amusement on her lips. Elspeth, like him, appeared puzzled at the word. 'What does he mean by that?' she asked Aurelia.

'He thinks you're a *Virginesh*, Dr Stewart,' Aurelia replied.

'A *what*?'

'A sworn virgin.'

Elspeth blushed, but Aurelia quickly smiled. 'Oh, it's not what you think. A sworn virgin is a woman who has taken a vow of chastity and chosen to live her life as a man. It's a well-known tradition in all the Balkan countries.'

Elspeth looked across at Gabriel. He shrugged at her. 'Maybe he thinks you Scots have a similar tradition?' he said.

Elspeth turned to Aurelia. 'Is that what he thinks…? That I'm one of these… people?'

Aurelia spoke to Luka and after a rapid exchange of words with him, she turned back to Elspeth 'Yes, Dr Stewart. There are no women doctors in Serbia, let alone any women surgeons, and with your short hair, and manner—'

'Yes, all right, Aurelia,' Elspeth interjected sharply and Gabriel saw her look of irritation. 'Just tell him no, I am not one of these creatures. I am a woman through and through and have no need to pretend to be a man.'

While Aurelia spoke to Luka, Gabriel turned to Elspeth. 'You're not offended by his assumption, are you?' he asked her.

She shrugged. 'It is frustrating to know that he thinks in order to practice surgery, a woman has to adopt the garb and manner of a man. But at least he acknowledges that some women are capable of doing all the things men can do—'

'I think,' Aurelia interrupted, 'that whatever I say to him, in his own mind he still sees you as a sworn virgin. It's the only way he can understand the concept of a woman behaving like a man. But I think he's beginning to come round to the idea of letting you operate on him. He says there is a sworn virgin fighting in his Cheta that he would trust his life with.'

Gabriel looked down at Luka but could still see a shadow of doubt on the bearded Chetnik's face. 'Dr Stewart is a very good surgeon, Luka,' he said. 'You're lucky to have her operating on you. Trust me.'

'Trust?' The look on Luka's face was scornful. 'I no trust Austrians.' Then his face relaxed. 'But you, *Hirurga*... you I trust.' He looked at Elspeth and then back at Gabriel again. 'Is good. You and *Virginesh* operate me.'

Gabriel turned to Elspeth. 'He's agreed to have the operation.'

'Oh good; what did you say to him?'

271

'That he is lucky to have you operating on him.'

'Well, let's hope I don't let him down.'

'I know you won't.'

***

The operation was difficult because of his immense girth. But with Gabriel's help, Elspeth made an incision over the entry wound in his abdomen. He watched her as she dissected down and found a bullet wedged between the ribs and capsule of the liver. Then as Elspeth had predicted, she found a sub-phrenic abscess tucked up high between his liver and diaphragm. He helped her drain the pus from it and then began to close the wound. It would have been a tricky operation under ordinary circumstances, made more difficult by his size. But he saw how confidently and expertly she had dealt with the problem and all had gone smoothly. Finally, after inserting the last stitch, they were finished.

It was late now, but the day had gone well, Gabriel thought, as he stripped off his gown and gloves, then thanked the three nurses for their help. From the genuine warmth in their smiles as they congratulated him on his work, he knew that they shared in the same sense of accomplishment as he and Elspeth had.

'It's been a real pleasure working with you today,' Elspeth said as they left the theatre and stood in the corridor. 'If you don't mind, I'd like you to stay with us until Dr Soltau and Dr Chesney have recovered.'

'I am happy to help for as long as you need me.'

'You'll have to sleep in the same room as the other Austrian orderlies.'

'I expect no special treatment.'

She nodded and walked him past the top of the staircase and a little further along the corridor until they came to another classroom. A number of hospital beds were arranged around the walls. In the middle of the room, several school desks and chairs had been pushed together to make an improvised dining table. Four Austrian prisoner orderlies were sitting there, smoking and chatting. One of the men looked vaguely familiar to Gabriel; this orderly looked up at him with surprise, and then quickly stood to salute him.

'Captain Bayer,' Sergeant Huber said. 'I'm very glad to see you've made a full recovery.'

'Ah, Huber,' Gabriel replied, recalling the sergeant's smallpox-scarred face and gap-toothed grin.

'I heard Dr Stewart was being assisted by an Austrian doctor,' Huber continued, 'but I didn't realise it was you, sir. So now you know what a wonderful surgeon she is.'

'Yes, she certainly is,' Gabriel replied, and saw the pink in Elspeth's cheeks as she smiled shyly to allay her embarrassment.

'Well, I can see you're among friends here, Captain,' she said. 'I'm sure Huber will get you some supper before you turn in. I'd like to see how the post-ops are doing first thing, so perhaps you might join me for an early-morning ward round before we start in theatre.'

'Of course. Good night, Dr Stewart.'

'Good night, Captain Bayer.'

***

As she left the school hospital and walked back to the women's villa later that evening, Elspeth reflected on a busy day's work. After operating on eleven complex cases, she would normally have expected to feel tired, possibly exhausted. But she was exhilarated: she had learnt most of her surgery by assisting experienced male surgeons in Edinburgh and London, and previously had always been required to follow their lead, in much the same way that a female dancer would follow the lead of her male partner.

But with Gabriel it had felt very different.

She had set the pace of their work in such a way that it had taken on a definite rhythm – almost like a surgical tango – dictated by her. She had felt remarkably relaxed and confident working with him, and it was strange to see how their hands seemed to instinctively know where to position themselves as they carried out their work, their fingers occasionally touching. She could tell from the deft handling of the instruments that his skills were no less than her own, and after only a short while, and without having to ask him, his movements began to anticipate hers in such a way that it almost felt as if his hands were controlled by her thoughts. It had felt strangely intimate in a way she had never experienced before. And it wasn't just the fact that their surgical minds seemed so attuned; she had felt respected by him as an individual. Without being obsequious. He had supported her in a quietly assured manner, allowing her to perform at her best. Behind the sharply intelligent eyes she sensed a considerate and warm individual; he had been a real pleasure to be with. She could well understand why Sylvia had taken to him.

Arriving back at the villa, she collected a mug of cocoa and plate of toast from the kitchen and then went to her bedroom. Opening the door, she saw Vera and Sylvia sitting at the table in the corner, the latter with an expectant look on her face.

'Well?' Sylvia asked eagerly. 'How did it go, Ellie? I'm dying to know.'

Elspeth sat down next to her, placing the toast on the table between them. 'Oh, it was fine,' she said nonchalantly. She lifted the mug to her lips.

'*Fine?*' Sylvia said, as Vera leant past her to pinch a piece of toast from the plate. 'Is that all you've got to say?'

Elspeth took a drink of cocoa before replying. 'Well, yes: it went well.' She picked up a piece of toast and took a bite.

'Oh come on, Ellie,' said Sylvia. 'Monica was saying that the quality of your and Captain Bayer's surgery was the best she had ever seen.'

Elspeth took her time to chew, swallow and take another sip of cocoa before replying, holding the warmth of the mug to her chest. 'It did go *very* well. And of course you were right about him, Sylvie. He's a very competent surgeon, but also a nice man and a delight to work with.'

'More specifics; please: what was it like to operate with him?'

Elspeth paused to think about the question before she

answered. 'Well, when I've operated with men before, I've always felt slightly patronised in that by simple virtue of being a man, they must somehow be better than me, even if they have less clinical experience.' Sylvia nodded as she continued. 'You know the sort of thing: an eyebrow raised here, a pout of the mouth there, giving their colleagues a knowing look whenever you come up with an interesting clinical observation. But there was none of that from Captain Bayer today; no arrogance or superiority, no hint of competition. It's the first time I've ever operated with a man who supported me in every way, a way that indicated respect and admiration for my abilities.'

'Ugh,' Vera said, shaking her head in disgust. 'Don't tell me that *you've* gone and fallen for him as well, Ellie?'

Elspeth smiled as Sylvia raised her eyebrows as if to say, 'Well, have you?'

Elspeth sighed and then shook her head. 'Don't be ridiculous, both of you.'

'But there is something about him, isn't there?' said Sylvia.

Elspeth yawned, stretched her arms and stood up from the table. 'I'm off to bed. The day is catching up with me and I have an early start tomorrow.'

***

The next morning Gabriel rose early and went to the ward to find Elspeth already waiting for him. Accompanied by Aurelia and two of the VADs, they began a round on the post-op patients. The Serbian sergeant with the empyema was now breathing easily, and upon inspecting the water bottle by his bed, Gabriel saw that the end of the rubber tube had stopped bubbling, indicating that his lung had fully re-expanded. He carefully loosened the purse-string stitch around the drain – freeing both ends – while Elspeth took a firm grip of the tube. Then catching his eye she gave him a nod and yanked the tube out. Gabriel quickly pulled the ends of the purse-string suture tight around the defect and tied a surgical knot, while she leant over him with a pair of scissors to snip off the loose ends. Then Gabriel heard her give the VADs instructions to redress the wound and ask Aurelia to tell the soldier to begin mobilising.

A few beds further along, Luka was also in good spirits, flashing a grin at Gabriel from within the tangle of his beard. The wound on his abdomen looked healthy and dry, and Elspeth asked Gabriel to tell Luka that the operation was a success, saying the stitches would be removed in seven days, and that he should be well enough to leave hospital shortly after that. Then Gabriel pointed at Luka's eye-patch and motioned for him to lift it.

Luka raised the patch with one hand – his eye blinking at the unfamiliar brightness – and Gabriel leant forward to gently separate the eyelids.

'Hm – looks much better.' He turned to Elspeth. 'Perhaps you could ask one of the VADs to bathe the eye with warm dilute saline.' He turned back to Luka again. 'You can keep the patch off from now on.'

The Chetnik appeared pleased and reached out to shake Gabriel's hand. Then he grinned at Elspeth before turning to Aurelia and exchanging words with her.

'What did he say?' Elspeth asked her when they had finished speaking.

'He thanks you for what you have done,' Aurelia replied. 'And he again mentioned the sworn virgin he knows from his Cheta. He said she's one of the bravest Chetnik fighters he knows, but that you're one of the best surgeons he's met.'

Gabriel saw Elspeth flush with pride as Luka extended his hand to her. 'Good luck, *Virginesh*,' Luka said to her in pidgin German.

Gabriel smiled when he saw Elspeth wince from the firmness of the big Serbian's grip, and as they left Luka's bedside he turned to her. 'Congratulations. I think you've just convinced a Chetnik that a woman can be as good a surgeon as a man.'

'Hm,' Elspeth said with a wry smile as she shook her cramped fingers. 'I think if I'd shaken his hand for much longer, I might never practise surgery again.'

★★★

After their round finished, they went upstairs to the operating theatre to begin the day's list. There were fewer patients – most of the work on the Valjevo transfers had been done yesterday – so their last case was finished by early afternoon. However, Huber told them that three more cases were expected later, and Elspeth told Gabriel to have a break. 'I'll come for you when they arrive,' she told him.

As Gabriel walked back to the Austrian orderlies'

quarters, he decided he ought to familiarise himself with the layout of the hospital. It was only now, as he strolled along the corridor, that he realised that the building must have once been a high school. And then he stumbled upon the library.

The room was no bigger than any of the other classrooms, one side piled from floor to ceiling with empty desks and chairs, the other side full of books; some stacked on their original shelving while others lay in a scattered heap on the floor. Many of the books had their covers ripped away, their pages shredded like large pieces of confetti, torn apart, he supposed, for use as kindling. It had been a while since he had seen a book and he had an urge to read something.

He wandered into the room and started to look at the intact books on the shelves, tilting his head as he scanned through the titles on their spines. But disappointingly all the words were in Serbian; so he began to rummage through the books strewn on the floor. With mounting excitement he realised they must be a collection of foreign texts, because the first book he picked up was in Greek, and the next was in Russian. He dug deeper into the pile and with a thrill saw Goethe's *Faust*, but half its pages were torn or missing. Then he saw *Hamlet* and next to it *Titus Andronicus*; with delight he realised he had found a collection of Shakespeare's plays.

After checking through more than twenty books, he found to his disappointment that most were so damaged as to render them undecipherable. But delving further into the pile he discovered two undamaged copies:

Macbeth and *Romeo and Juliet*. If he was going to be here for some time, he thought, it would do him good to practise his English. As they were both slim volumes he slipped one tome into each pocket of his jacket and then went back to the orderlies' quarters. The room was empty and so he stretched out on his bed and began to read.

He had been reading for no more than an hour when he heard a noise and lowered the book to see Elspeth standing in the doorway watching him. He swung his legs over the side of the bed, sat up and smiled at her.

'What are you reading?' she said, pointing at the volume in his hands as she walked into the room.

He looked down. 'This? Oh, it's *Macbeth*.' He stood and gave her the book. 'I found it in the school library. I need to practise my English. I hope it is permitted?'

She flipped through the pages. 'I don't see why not.' Then she shrugged her shoulders and handed it back to him. 'Actually you might as well, because we're so short of fuel for the braziers that the VADs have been using some of the books as firelighters.'

'I thought as much. Well, in that case, I'm pleased I saved it from the flames.'

'You have a liking for Shakespeare?'

'Doesn't everybody? Even we Austrians appreciate him.'

'I would have thought that you'd be more interested in the German playwrights, like Schiller and Goethe.'

'There are some Austrian playwrights as well, you know.'

'Oh? I don't know any.'

'Our most famous is Franz Grillparzer.' She frowned, and then shook her head as he continued. 'He wrote *Sappho*, about the poetess of ancient Greece who threw herself from the high cliffs of Lesbos when she found out her love for the youth Phaon was unrequited, and that he preferred her maid Melitta, instead of her.'

'Sappho? As in Sapphic love?'

'Yes. Why?'

'I would have thought she would have been more interested in her maid than the youth.'

He smiled. 'Well either way she was unhappy about it. And like all good tragedies it finishes with her coming to a grisly end – same as this.' He waved the copy of Macbeth in front of her.

She looked past him and he turned to see her staring at the copy of *Romeo and Juliet*, which lay at the foot of his bed. He reached down to pick it up. It was a slim book, cloth-bound in grey moleskin, the title and author in gold lettering on the front cover. As he handed it to her he saw an expression of amusement appear on her face.

'I see you have a liking for tragedy *and* romance,' she said, rubbing her fingertips over the velvety surface.

He grinned. 'You mustn't read any significance into the title: that and the *Macbeth* were the only two undamaged books I could find. But yes, I do like Shakespeare's romantic plays.'

'Hm,' she said, making a face as she leafed through the pages. 'I've always thought the plot absurd: he kills himself because he believes her dead, and then she kills herself too.' She closed the book and gave it back to him.

'In real life, Romeo would quickly have gotten over his grief and married Juliet's best friend.'

He laughed. 'Well, that tells me what an emotionally controlled person you are, Dr Stewart. The point of the story being that the depth of their passion overcomes their instincts to survive.'

'Well I prefer my women characters stronger, more rational.'

'Do any particular ones come to mind?'

She furrowed her brow. 'Well, I suppose Wanda from *Venus in Furs* would be one.'

Gabriel was astonished. 'Sacher-Masoch's heroine? I'm surprised you've read his book.'

'It was required reading as a medical student for our psychiatry lectures on deviancy,' she said with another smile. 'Masoch's Austrian, isn't he?' He nodded as she carried on. 'Well, everybody thinks the book is about Masoch's sexual predilections – his masochism – but at the end of the book he writes that the real moral of the story is that a woman can only become a man's true companion when she has the same rights as he, and is his equal in education and work.'

Ah, Gabriel thought: women's equality. It's interesting what you can learn about a person from the books they read. 'If I'm honest,' he said, 'I haven't thought much about women's rights before—'

'Why would you?' she interrupted. He saw her slight frame tense with passion. 'Most men haven't, because it doesn't impact on them. That's why British women have taken to public protest, even risking imprisonment so that men *do* think about the issues.'

'I was going to say, that although I had not thought about it before, seeing the quality of your work has convinced me that equality for women is a right and proper end.' He saw her relax. 'So in Scotland, do your women receive the same educational rights as men?'

'Some. A few universities will permit women to attend lectures, but many still do not allow us to sit for a degree.'

'It's no different in Austria, maybe even worse: it was only seven years ago that all males in Austria became entitled to a vote. Even now, without the right social connections it's difficult for a man to progress in his chosen career. The only way I could train as a surgeon was to win a place at medical school on a military scholarship. And of course I knew that one day I might be called upon to go to war, that I might witness battle injuries and death, but...' He paused as a sudden flashback of the young Serbian woman with braided ribbons swinging from a gallows appeared in his mind. He turned away for a moment to shake his head and try to clear the image. When he turned back to her again he saw that she was looking at him with concern.

'You've seen some bad things?'

The unexpectedly gentle tenor of her words took him by surprise. He didn't want to talk about the things he'd seen and so he said nothing, but gave a slow nod. For several seconds a comfortable silence stretched between them. After a while, as if she knew what he was feeling, her voice suddenly brightened.

'Oh, I almost forgot,' she said cheerfully. 'We need to go down to triage. Huber says the patients have arrived.'

'Of course,' Gabriel said, trying to muster enthusiasm although secretly disappointed that their private time together had come to an end. 'Please lead the way.'

She led him downstairs to the triage room, where Gabriel saw three patients lying on stretchers on the floor. Two of the wounded wore Serbian grey, but the third was in the pale blue of an Austrian private. Two orderlies stood waiting with razors and a jug of paraffin; one of them was Huber and he looked pleased at Gabriel's appearance.

'I was just coming to see you, Captain,' he said. 'I remember you saying you came from a prison camp a little west of here?'

'That's right. Why do you ask?'

Huber pointed at the Austrian soldier. 'Because that boy was transferred from a prison camp from the same area.'

Gabriel turned to Elspeth and she nodded at him to go over. The soldier – a young boy only sixteen, or possibly seventeen, years old – looked up as Gabriel approached: his eyes opened wide.

'Captain Bayer!'

Gabriel squatted down next to the stretcher. The youth was grinning with recognition, but at first Gabriel could not remember him. He saw that the boy's left hand had been amputated – the sleeve of his jacket was pinned back to cover the stump – and there was a long scar in the side of his neck, but try as he might Gabriel could not recall his case.

'It's Private Arbus, sir,' the youth said, sitting up and removing his jacket with his good arm. 'You operated on me in the field hospital before it became the prison laager?' He waved the stump of his left arm in the air.

As he studied the young man's face and stump, fragments of memory begin to re-assemble in Gabriel's brain: a frightened-looking youth; a shattered hand and forearm with the brilliant white of bone protruding through purplish skin; the smell of decay. The details were vague, the memories blurry.

'Um...'

'You do remember me, sir, don't you?' the youth implored. 'They all said it was a miracle I survived.'

And now the details flooded back: a young private hit by machine gun fire in the neck and hand; a tourniquet applied for too long; gas gangrene of the hand and forearm; the orderlies saying, 'Leave him, he won't live.' But Gabriel had stitched the neck wound and amputated at the forearm and the boy had survived.

'Of course: Private Arbus.'

The young soldier looked relieved. 'I'm very glad to see you, Captain. It's good to know you're alive.'

Several thoughts quickly flashed through Gabriel's mind. 'Have you come from the camp?' he asked.

'Yes, sir. I developed an abscess in the stump, and Lieutenant Schwann arranged for me to be transferred—'

'Schwann? Karl Schwann is alive, you say?'

'Yes, Captain; alive and well. Dr Schwann had typhus several weeks ago and he survived. But we didn't know what had happened to you, sir. When Corporal

Sparmacher returned and told us you had collapsed with typhus—'

'Klaus is well?'

Arbus grinned. 'Oh yes, sir; Corporal Sparmacher is very well. It would take more than typhus to finish that old dog off.'

Gabriel got to his feet and for a moment felt dizzy – whether from standing up too quickly or from relief he couldn't tell and didn't care. He turned towards Elspeth and saw from her expression that she had not understood their conversation. 'He's just given me some very good news,' he explained, a grin on his face. 'Our physician, who was very ill with typhus, has survived.'

'Oh, I'm very pleased for you, Captain,' she said, and he could see from the shine in her eyes that she really was. Then he glanced down at Arbus again and saw that the smile on the young soldier's face had disappeared, replaced by a darker, more serious look. Straightaway Gabriel knew the significance of the look and he squatted beside Arbus again.

'Tell me,' he ordered.

Arbus hesitated. Then; 'It's Lieutenant Flieger, sir.'

Gabriel felt the air leave his lungs. He knew what Arbus was about to say, and, wanting to delay the news, he bowed his head and closed his eyes for a moment. Then finally he lifted his head and opened his eyes again.

'Typhus?'

Arbus nodded. 'I'm sorry, sir.'

Gabriel stood up and covered his face with his hands. After hearing such good news about Schwann, it seemed so cruel, so unfair. Poor Peter, his wife, his children—

'Bad news as well, Captain?' Elspeth said, breaking through his thoughts.

She had walked forward and he could feel her standing beside him. His hands fell by his sides, but he kept his face turned away from her as he gave a simple nod.

'One of your colleagues?'

He was still looking away from her as he replied. 'Lieutenant Flieger is… was… my First Surgeon. He wasn't yet thirty. Married. Five children…'

His voice petered out as he felt her hand touch his shoulder, her fingers resting lightly on the epaulette of his jacket. The tenderness of this gesture so moved him that finally he turned to look at her, into the clear blue of her eyes, which seemed to shimmer with understanding. She held his gaze for only an instant, but in that moment he felt something pass between them: the euphoria at the report of Karl's survival, followed so quickly by the news of Peter's death… it was as if his whole view of life had been flipped upside down. Previously he had been solely obsessed with progressing his career as a surgeon, but now it felt as if a veil had been lifted from his eyes. Never before had he been so aware of the precious nature of time, the importance of friendship, of family, of love. He felt engulfed by this flash of insight. And now he had a strong sense of destiny about being here, in this place, at this time, with her.

But she was already looking away from him, inspecting the stump of Arbus's arm. Then, avoiding his gaze, she turned to Huber.

'It's a stump abscess and can wait until tomorrow's list,' she said. Then as an aside to Gabriel, and still without looking at him: 'We'd better examine these other two.'

He stepped past her towards the first Serbian soldier, who had a full-length bandage on his lower leg. 'He may be lousy, so it's safer if I do it,' Gabriel said. He knelt beside the man and un-wrapped the bandage, all the while aware of Elspeth's presence behind him.

'That can also wait until tomorrow's list,' she said, peering over his shoulder.

'I agree,' he said, but she had already turned towards the last soldier. Gabriel stood and walked past her, then knelt beside the man who had a bloodstained turban bandage wrapped around his hand. He carefully peeled it away to reveal the last three fingers of the soldier's hand, which were twisted and dry, blackened like scorched twigs on the end of a fire-burnt tree branch.

'It's dry gangrene,' she said. 'It can also wait until tomorrow's list.'

He nodded and stood up. She was still evading his gaze, and suddenly he realised that she, like him, must have felt something pass between them. He saw her turn to Huber.

'You can shave and delouse them, then have them taken straight up to the surgical ward.' She paused for a moment. 'I think we're done for the day,' she announced to the room. Gabriel's pulse quickened as she walked towards the door. 'I'll see you tomorrow morning, Captain Bayer,' she said without turning to look at him, before slipping into the corridor.

★★★

'I need to speak with Captain Bayer,' Huber said to Elspeth.

It was a lunchtime in early April, three weeks since Gabriel had begun working at the school hospital, and Elspeth was just leaving the operating theatre after another full morning of surgery. Gabriel was still changing out of his surgical gown inside the converted classroom behind her when Huber, accompanied by one of the Serbian guards, had caught her in the corridor outside.

'What do you want him for?' Elspeth asked Huber.

'We're to take Captain Bayer to Dr Chesney,' Huber replied, glancing at the guard standing beside him. 'She says she wants to speak to him immediately.'

At that moment Gabriel appeared in the doorway, still buttoning his uniform jacket. Elspeth knew he must have heard Huber's words as she saw him frown at the sight of the guard before turning towards her.

'Do you know why she wants to see me?' he asked her.

'No,' Elspeth replied. She felt mystified at the presence of the guard. 'She never mentioned it to me this morning.' She turned back to Huber. 'Did Dr Chesney say what it was about?'

'*Nein*,' Huber replied with a shake of his head. 'Just that we must bring Captain Bayer to her office right away.'

'Oh well,' Gabriel said, an accepting smile on his face. 'Dr Chesney's the chief, so I'd better go see what she wants.'

Elspeth shrugged. 'I'll see you back in theatre after lunch.' Gabriel nodded, then followed Huber and the guard along the corridor towards the chief medical officer's room.

I wonder what she wants to speak to him about, Elspeth mused as she descended the staircase and walked towards the canteen. Dr Chesney – who had just recovered from bronchitis – had temporarily taken over the post of chief medical officer from Dr Soltau, who had returned to England to convalesce after a nasty bout of diphtheria. Dr Elsie Inglis would be coming out to take over the role of chief medical officer next month, but until then Dr Chesney would be in charge.

However, Elspeth knew that Dr Chesney was unhappy about the fact that Gabriel – as a man, and an Austrian one at that – had been assisting her in theatre. Well too bad, thought Elspeth. Gabriel had been a great help to her over the past three weeks.

But during those weeks, Elspeth had often thought about the incident in the triage room when Gabriel had looked at her with such intensity that she had felt something melt inside her. It was her compassionate nature that had prompted her to go up to Gabriel, when she had seen his distress upon learning the news of his colleague's death. But the intense emotion she had felt with him at that moment had been unsettling, and whenever she relived the experience she realised that her feelings for him might be more than simple empathy for the pain of a fellow human being. She told herself not to be foolish: she hardly knew him, had only worked with him for a short time. But there was something engaging about him, an intelligent sensitivity in his eyes that – once she gazed at him – made it difficult for her to look away. She knew it was ridiculous to consider that anything could happen between them; he was, after all, an enemy of her country – a 'Hun', as Vera had called him – even if he wasn't actually German. He was also a prisoner. She needed to get a grip and would do so. She had always been strong-willed and would simply banish these thoughts and feelings from her mind.

So the morning after that incident she had met him on the ward as usual, and during their round of the post-op patients her behaviour towards him had been civil but formal, her conversation polite, professional, to the point. In the operating theatre everything was as it had been before: smoothly efficient, fast, the theatre nurses praising the quality of their work. She was relieved that he made no subsequent attempt to re-kindle the emotion of that earlier moment, appearing solely focussed on the work, apparently interested only in helping her with the cases.

And that is how it had continued right up until today, although it had been a constant battle, trying to control her feelings whenever he looked at her, or – as would invariably happen – their gloved fingers touched during surgery.

She arrived in the canteen and took a light lunch

with some of the VADs, before making her way back to the staircase. And then, just as she reached the top of the landing, she saw Dr Chesney advancing towards her.

'Ah, there you are, Elspeth. I'll be working in theatre with you this afternoon.'

Elspeth clutched the bannister rail. 'But Captain Bayer—'

'I've arranged for the guards to escort Captain Bayer over to the First Reserve Hospital this afternoon. He's going to help Dr Anitch with his cases from now on.'

'Oh.' A feeling of emptiness rose from the pit of her stomach.

'Yes. To be honest with you, Elspeth, I was surprised to learn that an Austrian officer has been assisting you these past weeks. We are a Scottish Women's Hospital, and the surgery in our hospital must be seen to be performed by Scottish women, not Austrian men.'

'But you and Eleanor were both ill, Lillian. The cases were complex and I needed a trained surgeon, not a nurse or physician. What *else* was I supposed to do?'

'You could have spoken to Dr Anitch at the Reserve Hospital. I'm sure he could have spared you somebody.'

'Of course I spoke to Dr Anitch,' Elspeth replied brusquely. 'But he had nobody to spare. He was even using a medical student to assist him with his work.'

'Well, that's exactly why I'm sending him there. Anitch has more need of him then we do now I'm recovered.'

'But it seems so rushed, sending him away at such short notice after all the assistance he's given us—'

'That can't be helped. Dr Anitch needs help right away,

and I'm ready to return to work. Or do you have a problem with that?' She fixed Elspeth with a long, hard look.

'I…' Elspeth hesitated and then sighed. 'I understand.'

'Good. Now, let's get back to work.'

She walked past Elspeth, and with a heavy heart Elspeth began to follow her back towards the operating theatre. Part of her was relieved – Gabriel's presence was a distraction – but another part of her was bereft at the thought of his leaving. And suddenly she knew she had to say goodbye to him. She stopped walking. 'I'll join you in a minute, Lillian,' she said, turning back towards the staircase. 'I've left my pocket watch in the canteen.'

'Aye, I'll see you inside,' Dr Chesney replied, and then disappeared into the operating room.

But Elspeth hurried past the top of the staircase and carried on towards the orderlies' room farther along the corridor. She stuck her head inside the room: nobody was in sight and Gabriel's bed, pushed up against the wall, was empty. She realised that she must have missed him and her heart sank even further as she turned back towards the operating room. But just as she was walking past the top of the staircase, she heard Gabriel's voice.

'Dr Stewart!'

Elspeth stopped, peered over the bannister, and was pleased to see Gabriel hurrying up the stairs, a look of relief on his face.

'I'm glad I found you,' he said as he arrived on the landing, breathing hard, as if he had been running. 'Dr Chesney is sending me over to the First Reserve Hospital.'

'Yes, she's only just told me,' Elspeth replied tersely. She was suddenly aware that her fingers were trembling and the only way she could control them was by clenching her fists. 'I'm sorry it's come at such short notice. I really had no idea that she was going to say this to you—'

'No need to apologise.' Gabriel smiled, as if to say he could feel her frustration. 'I don't blame Dr Chesney. I can see how it looks: an Austrian prisoner performing surgery on Serbian soldiers.'

His quiet, dignified acceptance of the situation helped calm her anger. 'Well, I am very grateful to for your help over these past weeks, Captain Bayer.'

'It was a pleasure for me.' He smiled at her again. 'I just wanted to say goodbye to you, and thank you for trusting me. I've really enjoyed working with you, Dr Stewart.'

'And I've enjoyed working with you too,' she said, trying to ignore the feeling of emptiness growing inside her. 'I hope you understand that with Dr Chesney's recovery and the imminent arrival of Dr Inglis we're fully staffed again. You'll be much better off at the Reserve Hospital, where they're desperate for good surgeons like you.'

'I was going to say much the same about you, Dr Stewart. You are a very talented surgeon and your patients are lucky to have you as their doctor.'

She smiled. 'We sound like a mutual admiration society.'

He laughed. 'I sincerely hope we may meet again some day.'

'I do too.' She had said the words very calmly, very matter-of-factly, but there was a desperate desire to say something stronger to him, to reach out and touch his hand. She hoped he might say something more to her, and for an instant her hopes rose as she saw him lift his chin and his lips parted; she waited for him to speak, and a moment – a long moment – elapsed. Then his lips closed and he softly smiled.

'I must go. The guards are waiting for me in the courtyard.'

She nodded. 'I must go too. Dr Chesney does not like to be kept waiting.'

'Of course. Goodbye. And good luck, Dr Stewart.'

'Good luck to you too, Captain Bayer.'

He gave her one last smile and then turned away. And she watched him walk along the corridor and onto the staircase, finally disappearing from her sight as he descended the stairs.

16

Kragujevac, August 1915

Gabriel stood on the platform at Kragujevac railway station, the heat of the afternoon sun on his back, the soft calling of cuckoos coming from the trees adjoining the railway track. Beside him was the squat figure of Dr Anitch, and standing behind them both was a Serbian guard, rifle slung casually over his shoulder and hands in pockets as he stood watch over Gabriel.

Anitch seemed oddly restless, thought Gabriel, as he watched the diminutive surgeon look at his pocket watch for the third time in as many minutes. 'Dr Plotz's train is late,' Anitch said edgily, just as the distant shriek of a steam whistle cut through the warm air. Gabriel walked up to the edge of the platform, and gazing through the haze of heat shimmering over the rail track, saw a locomotive and carriages appear through a cutting between two hills north of the station.

'I think this must be him, Dmitri,' Gabriel said. Although they had been working together for only a few months, he and Anitch had struck up a cautious friendship, their shared vocation as surgeons gradually overcoming their national differences. Having got to know Anitch, Gabriel could tell that he was nervous at the prospect of meeting the internationally renowned microbiologist. But Gabriel was excited, curious to know what the man who claimed to have isolated the typhus bacillus would be like. Anitch had told Gabriel that Dr Harry Plotz from Mount Sinai Hospital in New York had arrived in Belgrade only a few days earlier, invited by the Serbian authorities to try to produce a vaccine against the infection. Plotz had brought with him all the incubators, culture media and other essential paraphernalia necessary to manufacture a vaccine, but had first decided to re-culture the typhus bacillus from infected patients in the region. As the epidemic was centred on Kragujevac, Anitch had been telephoned yesterday with instructions to find suitable patients for Plotz and offer him every possible assistance.

'Why don't you come and meet him with me?' Anitch had asked Gabriel the previous evening. 'You told me you've previously visited Mount Sinai where Dr Plotz works, and as you're now immune to typhus, you can more safely collect the blood samples for him.'

Gabriel had happily agreed to Anitch's request, and now he watched the train stop at the platform in a cloud of steam and smoke. Several carriage doors clattered open, and from behind one of them a surprisingly young man emerged. Of short height and stocky build, and with a round, soft, baby face, he was wearing a crumpled linen suit and red bowtie and had a pair of gold-rimmed spectacles jammed over his nose. He was holding a large black leather holdall as he stood and peered along the platform, looking momentarily lost as he shielded his eyes from the glare of the sun with his free hand. Gabriel knew at once that this must be the famous American.

'Good to meet you,' Plotz replied, after Gabriel had introduced himself. 'And you too, Dmitri. Please call me Harry,' he said after being presented to Anitch. 'I'm sure glad you fellows can speak English, because I know only a little German and even less Serbian.'

As they left the station and walked towards the waiting car, Plotz chattered enthusiastically to Gabriel about the prospect of permanently eradicating typhus through the use of his vaccine. And as he listened to the young American's grandiose conversation, Gabriel felt uneasy; although he liked Plotz's extrovert manner, there was a brash confidence that he found unsettling in one so young. Then again, Gabriel thought, as he climbed into the back of the car and sat beside Plotz, maybe he really was a genius, a veritable Mozart of the microbiological arts? One thing that was certain about him was his sharp eye.

'I'm interested to see you fellows are on opposite sides of the conflict,' Plotz said, the black leather holdall resting on his knees as he eyed Gabriel's uniform. 'I don't have a problem with that, and I would like to make it clear I have no allegiance to any particular country. I'm a neutral only here as a scientist to isolate this damn typhus bacterium and produce a vaccine. I'll happily work with anybody, in any government, in any country – Serbian, Austrian, I don't care – as long as I can get on with my work.'

Anitch, sitting beside the driver in the front of the car, turned around. 'Dr Plotz—'

'Harry,' Plotz reminded him.

'Sorry… Harry. Yes, I agree. As doctors, our duty is to mankind, to men, women and children everywhere, regardless of nationality.'

'Good,' Plotz said, nodding in approval. Then he turned to Gabriel. 'So: you're on the losing side, Gabriel; what's it like being a prisoner, huh?'

Anitch appeared shocked at the bluntness of the question, but Gabriel saw the grin on Plotz's face and laughed. 'Well, Harry, I'm sure Dmitri could arrange for you to spend a few hours behind barbed wire so you can find out,' he said, winking at Anitch, who visibly relaxed.

'I think I'll pass on that offer,' Plotz said, chuckling as the car pulled away from the kerb. 'Besides, I'm on a pretty tight schedule. The train left much later than it should, and I need to collect the samples and catch the next train back to Belgrade so I can set up the cultures.'

'Yes, I'm puzzled about that,' Gabriel said. 'Dmitri tells me you want blood samples from infected patients, but Nicolle's experiments from five years ago showed that lice spread the infection. So I would have thought that looking inside lice would be the best method for finding the bacillus?'

Plotz grinned confidently. 'But you don't know for certain that every louse carries the bacillus, whereas a patient with fever and other features of typhus *will* have the organism inside them. That's the beauty of my method, Gabriel: it doesn't rely on the louse.

Over the past two years New York has seen an influx of immigrants from the Balkans who've arrived at Ellis Island with fever and other symptoms consistent with typhus. I've cultured blood samples from some and managed to isolate a bacterium which I'm pretty certain is the cause of typhus.'

Gabriel raised an eyebrow. 'So you're not *completely* certain?

Plotz clutched the holdall to his chest as he laughed, clearly thinking Gabriel's question inane. 'Oh it's the typhus bacillus all right.' Then he swiftly changed the subject: 'By the way, you guys, your English is pretty good. Where did you learn?'

'I spent some time in London,' Anitch replied, rather too quickly, Gabriel noted, possibly because he thought Gabriel's questioning of Plotz's methods disrespectful.

'And you, Gabriel?' Plotz asked.

'I also spent time in London, and I was a visiting surgical fellow at Mount Sinai.'

'That's my hospital.' Plotz looked surprised and impressed at the same time. 'Who'd you work with?'

'Frank Billings.'

'Frank? Sure Frank's a colleague, and a great surgeon.' He paused. 'Either of you doing any research?'

Anitch shook his head, but Gabriel nodded. 'Yes. Before the war I was researching sepsis in bullet wounds.'

'Tell me more,' Plotz said, clearly intrigued.

Gabriel briefly outlined his research, and then; 'I had hoped to present my results at the London Surgical Infection conference last October, but...' He shrugged.

'Sure,' Plotz nodded. 'The war has disrupted a lot of things.' He paused. 'You ever think about moving to America?'

'No.' Gabriel frowned. 'Why?'

'Well, the Balkans… in fact the whole of Europe… is such a mess at the moment.'

Gabriel smiled but saw Anitch flinch at the unsubtle nature of the comment.

Plotz also appeared to notice Anitch's reaction. 'I don't mean to offend you, Dmitri, but you got to admit it. The whole continent is in flames and this war could go on for some time.' He looked across at Gabriel again. 'So America's the place to be if you're interested in research.'

'There is much to be done here first,' Gabriel said.

'Sure: whatever. But you should think about it. By the way,' he added, again changing the subject, 'where are the typhus patients managed?'

'They're all quarantined in the Scottish Women's Fever Hospital,' Gabriel replied.

'Scottish women? What's that all about?'

'A group of women surgeons from Scotland have set up several hospitals to care for the casualties,' Gabriel said. 'They run Kragujevac's typhus hospital—'

'Actually,' Anitch interjected, 'we have to go to the school hospital first, as I need to ask Dr Inglis for permission.' He turned to Plotz. 'She's the chief medical officer for all the Scottish Women's Hospitals in Kragujevac,' he explained.

'Sure, Dmitri – whatever,' said Plotz. 'As long as we don't miss the next train back to Belgrade.'

As Plotz told Anitch about the types of patient he was interested in sampling, Gabriel fell silent at the thought that he might see Elspeth again, a scenario he hadn't expected. Several months had passed since their farewell outside the operating theatre, when he had been so close to telling her how he felt about her, but had held back, mostly out of fear of making a fool of himself. And it *was* a foolhardy notion to think that anything could happen between them; he was her country's enemy – a prisoner of her country's allies – and they came from cultures a thousand miles apart.

So he had said nothing about his feelings. But since then, barely a day had gone by when he hadn't thought of her, the recollection of their time together having a comfortingly uplifting effect on his mood. He realised that the chance he might see her today was slight, nevertheless he felt his pulse quicken at the mere possibility.

They drove through the gates of the school and parked in the centre of the courtyard, the three men leaving the vehicle to walk into the school building. As they entered the surgical ward on the ground floor, the sights and smells triggered a flood of pleasant memories for Gabriel. The nurses, VADs and orderlies on the ward were all familiar and he received numerous smiles and nods of recognition. Anitch spoke to the ward sister. Dr Inglis and the other surgeons were in theatre, she said, but she would be informed of their arrival immediately.

As the three men waited in the middle of the ward, Gabriel was disconcerted at how jittery he felt. Was it because he might see Elspeth again? How absurd; he must regain control of his emotions. He consciously made himself relax, but after several minutes the ward door swung open and his heart began to pound as several figures entered the room.

The first was a slightly built older woman he didn't recognise. The second was Monica, the theatre nurse, and when she saw him she gave him a friendly wave; he smiled back at her. And then a third woman appeared… but he felt his smile slip when he saw it was not Elspeth, but Dr Chesney, who fixed him with her beady eyes, frowned and then pouted her lips, but eventually gave him a brief nod of acknowledgment.

The three women walked up to Anitch and the older woman was introduced to Gabriel as Dr Elsie Inglis.

'Dr Bayer, of course,' Dr Inglis said to him with a smile. 'I've heard many good things about you from Dr Stewart and Monica. We're very grateful for the help you gave when so many of our staff were ill.'

'It was my pleasure,' Gabriel replied.

He watched as Anitch introduced Plotz to Dr Inglis, who listened to the young American's enthusiastic explanation of his visit. And Gabriel was so focussed on their discussion that he it took him a moment to realise that a fourth person had quietly slipped into the room behind Dr Chesney, and was peering over Chesney's shoulder at him, a shy smile on her lips, her sapphire eyes locked on his face. Suddenly he realised that Dr Inglis was speaking to her.

'… Elspeth: Dr Chesney and I can finish the last case,

so why don't you escort Dr Plotz to the fever hospital and help him identify some suitable patients.'

'Of course,' Elspeth replied and then turned towards Plotz. 'I'll just get my jacket and meet you in the courtyard in a moment,' she said to him, her smile lighting up her face before she hurried out of the ward.

As they left the hospital and walked back to the waiting car, Plotz spoke to Gabriel. 'That Dr Stewart is one happy-looking gal.'

'She's also a very competent surgeon,' Gabriel replied.

'Well, she sure is one heck of a pretty thing.'

She did indeed look beautiful, Gabriel thought. Her hair had grown back since he had last seen her, and there was an aura about her that made it difficult to look away. He suddenly realised how much he had missed her and became aware that he had a stupid grin on his face, obviously, he realised, at the thought of spending time with her, no matter how brief.

Plotz was already sitting in the middle of the back seat of the car with the black bag resting on his knees when Elspeth reappeared, dressed simply in her grey uniform skirt and jacket over a white blouse. Gabriel held the door open for her, a melting feeling inside his chest as she slid past him with a smile and sat next to Plotz.

On the short journey up to the fever hospital, it was apparent that Plotz was greatly taken with Elspeth, quizzing her about her experiences in Serbia. Sitting on the other side of Plotz, Gabriel periodically glanced over the young American's head and saw that Elspeth looked happy, her eyes shining, the white of her teeth visible as she smiled or laughed at a witty aside made by Plotz. After a while Plotz ran out of questions and turned back to Gabriel.

'So, Gabriel: Dmitri tells me you caught typhus earlier this year. What does that feel like?'

Out of the corner of his eye Gabriel saw Elspeth fight to keep a straight face as she turned away, the back of her hand at her mouth as she tried to stifle her amusement.

Gabriel shook his head and gently laughed. 'Well, it was not a lot of fun, Harry.'

'It's a serious question, Gabriel,' Plotz said, attempting a look of sincerity. 'I've taken my own vaccine, so I'm confident I'll never catch it.'

'But you haven't tested the vaccine's efficiency yet, have you?' Gabriel said, surprised to hear that Plotz had already used it – on himself.

'We'll do the studies soon, and I'm in no doubt they'll show the vaccine's effectiveness…' He broke off as the car came to a stop outside the fever hospital. 'This it?' Plotz asked, peering doubtfully through the window. 'It looks more like a factory.'

'It was a tobacco warehouse before we converted it into the fever hospital,' Elspeth said.

Plotz shrugged and opened his pocket watch. 'Anyway I'm glad we're here. I need to get these samples quickly so I can make that train.'

They hurried into the hospital and as they entered the ward Gabriel saw Sylvia's eyes widen at the sight of him. Introductions quickly made, Elspeth informed her of the urgent purpose of the visit. Dr Wakefield was busy with an emergency chest drain, Sylvia told them as she began to pull notes from a trolley beside the nursing desk and directed one of the VADs to collect the temperature charts from all the recent admissions with typhus. She gave the notes to Plotz, who flicked through the pages while Elspeth scanned the temperature charts. Between them, they chose five subjects.

The first patient was an Austrian soldier, and after Gabriel explained the purpose of the procedure the soldier agreed to provide a sample and held out an arm. Gabriel rolled his shirtsleeves back, then cleaned the skin of the soldier's arm with ethanol. Plotz handed him a glass syringe and needle: Gabriel took the blood sample, injected it into a glass bottle filled with culture broth, and handed it to Plotz. The same procedure was used to take samples from a further three patients.

But during the sampling on the last patient, several drops of blood splashed onto the back of Gabriel's right hand and wrist. After injecting this sample into the last bottle, Gabriel stepped aside. He held his blood-contaminated arm away from his body while Plotz secured the samples inside his bag before looking at his pocket watch again.

'Aw, jeepers, look at the time,' he said. 'Dmitri, I really *have* to get back to the station now. The next train for Belgrade is due and I must catch it if these are to be of any use.'

'Of course: we'll go right away,' Anitch replied, but then he looked at Gabriel – still holding his blood-tainted hand to one side – and frowned. 'Perhaps you should stay and clean yourself up, Gabriel,' he said, 'and I'll collect you after I've dropped Harry off at the station.'

Gabriel nodded and automatically extended his hand towards Plotz, before remembering it was soiled with blood and withdrawing it. 'Better not shake,' he said with a dry look. 'We don't know yet how effective that vaccine of yours is, Harry.'

Plotz, who had extended his hand at the same time, laughed. 'Oh, don't you worry, Gabriel: it's effective all right,' he said with a chuckle. 'Anyway, it's been a pleasure. If you ever want to work in New York again, be sure to let me know – I'd be happy to write a recommendation.' He nodded at Elspeth and Sylvia. 'Dr Stewart, Sister Calthorpe, also a pleasure.' Then with Anitch at his side, he hurried out of the ward.

The urgency of Plotz's departure over, Gabriel looked at Elspeth and saw her smiling at him. Suddenly Sylvia's voice broke his thoughts.

'Tut tut, Captain Bayer,' Sylvia said, arms folded in mock severity as she studied the flecks of blood on his wrist. 'That last sampling was not your tidiest effort, was it? It's just as well you're immune to typhus. I hope you haven't forgotten where the wash basins are?'

'No, Sister, I remember everything,' Gabriel said. 'In particular that it is best not to argue with you.' He heard Elspeth gently laugh as he bowed his head to Sylvia, then spun on his heel and walked towards the washroom.

★★★

'Hm,' Sylvia said to Elspeth when Gabriel was out of earshot. She was frowning thoughtfully as she spoke. 'I haven't seen you looking this jolly in ages, Elspeth.'

Elspeth didn't reply, but instead felt the heat rise to her cheeks as she recalled the moment she had gone down from theatre to meet the famous American. The last person she had expected to see was Gabriel. But at the sight of him, she had felt such a thrill that even now she could not stop herself from smiling at the memory. As she had entered the ward she had seen he hadn't noticed her, and it had pleased her to stand quietly behind Lillian Chesney, watching Gabriel as he listened to Dr Inglis and Dr Plotz's conversation. For some minutes she had studied him, thinking he looked well, although she could read some sadness in his eyes. But eventually he had glanced in her direction, and with delight she had seen his sombre look vanish, replaced in an instant by a smile that filled his face…

She suddenly realised that Sylvia was speaking to her; she might, in fact, have been speaking to Elspeth for some time…

'*Well*, *well*, Dr Stewart.' Sylvia now said, her hands on her hips, a look of understanding on her face. 'I hadn't realised—'

'There's nothing to realise, Sylvie. Yes, I am happy to see him, but—'

'You don't have to explain, Ellie. Look, I have to help Dr Wakefield with the chest drain. There should still be some hot water left in the nurses' room samovar to make tea for yourself and Captain Bayer while you wait for Dr Anitch to return.'

'Yes Sylvie, but—'

However, before Elspeth could finish, Sylvia had already turned away with a mischievous smile on her face, and Gabriel was walking towards her, rolling down his shirtsleeves, his jacket slung casually over his shoulder.

'Sister Calthorpe had to leave?' he asked.

'Um…Yes… Dr Wakefield needs help with that chest drain.'

'Ah. I see.' There was a moment's silence as they smiled diffidently at each other. Then, 'That Dr Plotz is quite a fellow isn't he?' Gabriel said as he re-buttoned his shirt cuffs.

Elspeth shrugged. 'I don't know him well enough to draw any definite conclusions. But he must have a good reputation, if the Serbians asked him to come all the way over from America.'

'In Austria we would call him a "Wunderkind": I think in English you say "prodigy"?' She nodded as he continued. 'He has accomplished a great deal at a very young age. But I'm surprised he's chosen to use blood to culture the typhus bacillus. It's proven that lice spread the disease, so the bacillus must be inside the gut of the louse. That's where I would be looking.'

'Well, I think it's because in America he only had access to patients with typhus, and not to lice. Anyway he's found a bacillus in the blood of patients with acute typhus, so…' She shrugged.

'But is it the cause of typhus?' Gabriel looked doubtful. 'I do believe he's found a bacillus, but is it the cause of the infection?'

'Why wouldn't it be?'

'There are many bacteria that live inside man, so how do we know the bacillus he has isolated – this Plotz bacillus of his – is the cause of typhus?'

She looked into his eyes. 'You're referring to Koch's Postulates, aren't you?'

The slightest of smiles appeared on his lips. 'I am indeed.'

'I think I see what you're getting at,' she said, pleased to be temporarily distracted from her feelings by thinking about the science of the problem. 'So far Plotz has only fulfilled the first two of Koch's postulates: finding an organism in infected patients and then growing it in pure culture. But he also needs to show that his bacterium will cause typhus when introduced into a healthy host.'

'Exactly – otherwise he could end up looking very foolish.'

She nodded. 'I do feel a little sorry for him. There must be a great weight of expectation on him to produce a vaccine quickly. It would be quite easy to make a mistake. Ideally, he should have more time to test his bacillus in the same way that Koch did for tuberculosis…' She faltered as she saw him trying not to grin. 'What?' she said, when he finally could not help but smile at her.

'It's just… so rare to meet a surgeon, with such a good knowledge of microbiology.'

For a moment she looked thrown, but then her face

relaxed. 'As you know from before, I would normally be offended at hearing such a comment from a man. But this time I'll take it in the spirit I hope it was meant, as a genuine compliment—'

'As a genuine compliment to a surgeon,' he interjected, 'who just happens to be a woman.'

Her face broke into a smile. 'My microbiology training in Edinburgh was very good. Anyway, would you like some refreshment? Dr Anitch may be a while before he returns and Sister Calthorpe has said we might find some tea in the ward office.'

'If it's not too much trouble, that would be very nice.'

She led him to the nurses' room, which had previously been the warehouse supervisor's office. Opposite the door was a window with a vista of leafy tobacco fields, and underneath the window was a table, upon which sat a copper samovar, wisps of steam leaking from a tap, a teapot, cups and tea-box stacked beside it. Apart from a desk and two chairs to one side, the room was otherwise empty. Gabriel took a seat at the desk while Elspeth half-filled the teapot with hot water and swirled, then emptied it. As she carefully measured tea leaves into the pot and refilled it with fresh hot water, she could sense his fascination with her total absorption in the task.

'I've long known about the English obsession with tea,' he finally said. 'But I see you Scots are just the same.'

She placed the teapot and two cups on the desk, and then sat opposite him. 'It's a tradition of the British Empire,' she said, 'from the great tea-estates in Ceylon and India.' She lifted the pot lid and looked inside as she swirled the contents. 'It's even in our language now. We have tea dances, tea gardens, tea rooms – it's all part of our nation's identity.'

'And in Austria, we identify with the coffee bean,' he said, and Elspeth smiled as he continued. 'When the Austrians saved Western Civilisation by defeating the Turks at the Battle of Vienna in 1683, they found sacks filled with strange dark beans. And so began our love affair with all things coffee. The Viennese cafés are famed for their varieties of coffee – fiaker coffee, rum coffee, iced coffee – so for us Austrians, coffee is as much a part of our culture as tea is in yours.'

'Well, I'm sorry, Captain Bayer, but we have no coffee. So you'll have to make do with tea for now,' she said with mock seriousness. He dropped his head slightly and pouted with feigned sadness, and looked so ridiculous that she couldn't help but gently laugh.

'You are a cruel woman to torment an Austrian about his lack of coffee,' he said. 'I can stand the lice, the dirt, the cold. But the lack of coffee is almost unbearable.'

She laughed once more and he grinned back at her; for a moment they held each other's gaze. Then she looked down at the teapot and swirled the contents again. After a while she placed it on the table and looked up at him.

'Is there anything else from Austria you miss?'

He furrowed his brow. 'I was born and brought up in Klagenfurt.' He looked at her, but she shook her head. 'It's a small town in the Austrian Tyrol,' he explained, 'in the mountainous region between Austria and Italy. It's a beautiful place, surrounded by lakes and mountains. My mother – she was a nurse – died a few years ago, but my father still lives there.' She saw a wistful expression appear on his face. 'He is a retired pastry chef, but still makes wonderful strudels and tortes.'

'I've eaten apple strudel before,' she said.

'That's the most well known, although my favourite is cherry strudel. And he makes the most fabulous Sachertorte,' he said, and she frowned; 'It's a very rich and moist chocolate cake,' he explained.

'Like a chocolate gateau?'

'Yes, but less cream, more chocolate.'

'Sounds delicious.'

'It is.' He paused before continuing. 'And what do you miss most about Scotland?' he asked her.

'Well...' She lifted the teapot lid for one final inspection. 'You might expect I'd be missing the Scottish countryside. But the rolling hills and trees of Serbia – especially the pines – remind me so much of the Isle of Skye that I don't miss it at all. And we are very lucky to find so many of our home comforts here: tea, of course, Colman's mustard, Peak Frean biscuits, Dundee marmalade – I have most of the things I'm used to at home.' She began to pour tea into one of the cups. 'I'm really content helping our Serbian allies, using my training as a surgeon to serve my king and my country.'

He smiled and nodded, and a comfortable silence developed as she filled the second cup. 'I've not asked you before, but is there a Mrs Bayer?' she suddenly found herself asking as she pushed the cup towards him.

The question seemed to take him – as well as her – by surprise. 'Oh…' He paused.

She could feel herself beginning to blush. 'I'm sorry Captain… it was impertinent of me—'

'No no, it's quite all right,' he said, already waving a hand dismissively. 'I'm happy to answer.' He paused and took a deep breath. 'My career has always been the most important thing in my life. I never really had the time… surgery is hard. It can be a very…'

'Demanding vocation?' Elspeth said, finishing his sentence for him. He nodded. 'I know that well,' she continued. 'Sometimes, think I'm married to my career as a surgeon.'

He picked up the cup, and holding it in both hands took a drink of tea. 'And do you have a…' –He hesitated before he found the right word – 'a "sweetheart", I think you say?'

She felt flustered at the question, disconcerted that it made her face feel hot. And then she felt foolish because – after all – she had asked him almost the same thing.

'No,' she said, avoiding his gaze. 'Like you, I've been too busy to look for romance. Besides, most women doctors I know are unmarried, for much the same reason.' She felt him looking at her, but picked her cup up and kept her eyes on the rim as she took a sip of the brew.

'You love being a surgeon, don't you,' he said, a statement rather than a question. She looked up at him again and smiled.

'Oh yes. It's the most important thing in my life. I've wanted to be a surgeon for as long as I can remember. It's all I've ever wanted.'

'It's most unusual: a woman, so passionate about being a surgeon.'

'Actually I remember the exact moment I knew it was the career for me.'

'Really?'

She nodded, holding the cup to her chest, staring out of the window at the tobacco fields and smiling as she recalled the memory. 'My father was a general practitioner on Skye. One day I was playing with my dolls on the front lawn of the practice – I must have been about six or seven years old, I think – when I saw a young boy carried into the waiting room by his parents. I didn't know it at the time of course, but he was very ill with diphtheria, choking and gasping from swollen glands in his neck. Then I heard the mother shout in anguish, and out of curiosity I followed them into the waiting room and saw the boy had stopped breathing.' She lowered the cup to the desk and Gabriel nodded for her to continue.

'Then my father hurried out from his office and performed an emergency tracheotomy on the boy, right there and then, on the floor of the waiting room. And I watched it all unfold in front of me because, in the chaos of the moment, I had been forgotten about and slipped quietly into a corner of the room and stood there, amazed by what I was seeing. I saw my father calmly slice through the tracheal rings in the front of the neck with a scalpel – I can still hear the hiss of escaping air even now – and then the gratitude in the eyes of the parents when the boy began to breathe again. The incident hadn't frightened me at all: not the blood, nor the parental panic, not even the sight of the scalpel parting the tissues in the neck. On the contrary, it had been a fascinating thing to watch.'

'I can see it made quite an impression on you.'

She nodded. 'At one point Morag, our receptionist, noticed me. She ran across and took my hand, tried to lead me away. But I struggled free and pushed her aside: she was getting in my way and I didn't want to miss a second of it.'

Gabriel gently chuckled. 'I have a picture of it in my mind,' he said. 'You, a wide-eyed little girl with pigtails, standing silently in the shadows, pushing an older woman aside—'

'Reasonably accurate, except I had plaits.'

He laughed again as she continued. 'And what about you, Captain: what made you decide to become a surgeon?' she asked.

He lowered his cup to the table. 'Well, it was not an event as dramatic as yours.' He paused. 'I can't even remember the precise moment as you do. But my mother was a nurse, so I had always considered a career as a doctor. My parents were not rich, so it was only through a scholarship with the army that I was able to train as a surgeon.' He paused. 'I always knew that I might one day be called upon to fight a war… I expected that.' He sighed. 'But I never expected to see some of the awful things I've seen.'

She nodded; he fell silent and she smiled in sympathy with him. 'It must have been a shock being taken prisoner.'

'It was. I hadn't expected that either.'

'Well, you may not be prisoner for much longer. Dr Curcin told us that German and Bulgarian forces are reported to be massing at the Serbian borders. Another invasion is expected any day now.'

He nodded. 'Yes. Dmitri told me about the rumour.' He gave a wry smile. 'It doesn't surprise me. Three times we Austrians failed to overcome the Serbs, so the Germans will have lost patience and decided to do it themselves. And it's an opportunity for Bulgaria to take revenge for their defeat at the hands of the Serbs during the last Balkan war.'

'If it happened, you might be freed.'

'I suppose so.' He hadn't spent any time thinking about the possibility of freedom. Now his first thought was about her. 'But what would your hospital do if the invasion comes?'

'Dr Curcin has told Dr Inglis that we should evacuate south to Greece, but she is most reluctant to leave and says we should stay and continue to look after the wounded.'

A worried frown came over his face. 'I agree with Dr Curcin. You really must leave if another invasion comes.'

She smiled at his obvious concern for her. 'We'll see.' And then, concerned at the gloominess of their conversation, she quickly changed the subject. 'You studied medicine in Vienna I gather.'

Yes,' he said. 'I qualified nine years ago.'

'I've heard the training there is excellent, a legacy of your Professor Billroth. Even Dr Inglis spent time studying in Vienna and she highly recommends it, saying it helped broaden her experience. She also studied in America.' She gave him a curious look. 'I was just thinking about Dr Plotz's suggestion before he departed. Would you ever consider moving to America?'

Gabriel frowned. 'I haven't thought about it before,' he said, scratching the short stubble on his head. 'But I never intended staying in the army permanently. Before my posting to Sarajevo, I worked in Vienna and always thought that one day I might return to work there as a civilian surgeon.' She saw a sadness cloud his eyes. 'But the war has changed how I feel about my country. I don't like what I have seen done in the name of the Austrian people.'

He paused; she stayed silent.

'So yes,' he continued, 'there have been times I thought it might be good to make a fresh start. However, I cannot foresee what will happen to me, whether I will survive the war or not or what the future of Austria will be. The war has been a terrible thing for my country.' He saw a flare of surprise in her eyes and realised the tactlessness of his last remark.

'Of course I realise that the Serbian people have suffered worse,' he quickly added, 'much worse. But I've seen a whole generation of Austrian youth – their finest young men – die on the battlefield or of diseases in the prison camps. And that our local dispute with Serbia should have expanded into a war that involves Russia, France, Germany – even your own country…' He shook his head in disbelief. 'It's the terrible waste of life that shocks me more than anything.'

She stayed silent while he paused.

'It was after the Battle of Vienna that the reign of the Hapsburg Empire began,' he said. 'And I think that this war – this Great War – may well mark the end of that empire. Our losses of men and materiel, our poor leadership…' He shook his head unhappily. 'I could be accused of treason for saying this, but the Austro-Hungarian Empire will not survive.' He gave a sad smile. 'The coffee beans will go on, but the Hapsburgs won't.'

She smiled again and another comfortable silence developed. After a moment, Gabriel spoke again. 'And what would your friends and family think if they could see you sitting here, drinking tea with one of your country's enemies?'

She knew there was a serious side to the question and so she frowned as she considered it. 'Well, you are a fellow doctor and not a combatant, so I think that would give you special exemption—'

'That's avoiding the question,' Gabriel said teasingly.

She feigned indignation. 'No, it's not… don't you feel that the brotherhood… the sisterhood even… of medicine extends beyond national boundaries?'

'Of course I do. I feel that very strongly.'

'Well then.'

He smiled at her as she continued. 'And I don't care what anyone else might think. It's my business who I drink tea with, or talk to.'

He tapped the table with the flat of his hand to mime applause. 'Bravo, Dr Stewart. But you still haven't answered my question, which is what *they* would think about it.'

She sighed. 'Honestly?'

He nodded and her face became serious.

'Well, I'm afraid your allies have been thoroughly demonised back in England. Dr Inglis brought some English newspapers with her, which tell of the German excesses towards the French and Belgians. So the Huns, as they are called in Britain, are hated. And unfortunately you Austrians are stigmatised by association. So no, I don't suppose my friends would approve of my drinking tea with a captain in the Austrian Imperial Army.'

'It's to be expected, I suppose.'

She gave him a sad smile and again their eyes met. The intensity of his gaze was unsettling and she looked away, and then lifted the cup and finished the tea. 'And if your friends and family saw you here,' she said, 'drinking tea, fraternising with a member of the enemy, what would they think?'

'Well.' He placed his empty cup on the table in front of him before continuing. 'If they knew you as I do,' he said, holding her gaze, 'they would realise that I am the luckiest man in the world.'

Surprised at such an overt compliment, her heart began to race as she looked away from him and then down at the empty cup held tightly to her breast. How should she respond…?

But sudden footsteps startled her, and looking up she saw Anitch striding through the door.

'I am *so* sorry for the delay,' he said breathlessly. 'Dr Plotz's train was running late…' He paused, frowned, blinked. 'Is everything all right?' he said, giving Elspeth a curious look.

Elspeth felt as if her face was on fire. 'Yes, everything is fine, Dr Anitch, except that it's rather hot in here.' She fanned her cheeks with her hands. 'I should have had a cool drink,' she said, smiling as she stood up from the desk. 'Anyway, I really should get back to the hospital.'

'My driver will give you a lift—'

'No,' she said curtly, but then saw the look of surprise on Anitch's face. 'I mean thank you, but no, Dr Anitch. I would much rather walk if you don't mind – the fresh air will do me good.'

Anitch bowed his head. 'As you wish, Dr Stewart.'

She walked around the table to shake his hand and then turned to Gabriel. 'It was good seeing you again, Captain Bayer.'

'Yes, and thank you for the lesson in tea-making, Dr Stewart,' he said, as they shook hands. 'I sincerely hope we meet again.'

'So do I,' she said with a smile, then turned and left the room.

PART TWO

1915–1916

1

Kragujevac, October 1915

Shortly after dawn, one morning in the first week of October, and Gabriel was asleep in the Austrian orderlies' room inside the First Reserve Hospital when the low rumble of distant artillery fire roused him from his slumber. As he lifted his head from the pillow, the other prisoners in the room began to wake.

'I think that's from the north,' whispered one.

'Maybe it's Belgrade?' murmured another.

'They sound like Austrian guns – big ones.'

'It must be the offensive.'

Gabriel got out of bed and walked to the metal-barred, west-facing windows. He pulled the sackcloth aside, pressed his face against the cold bars, and, squinting northwards, saw flashes of light low on the horizon. The other orderlies were already clustering around him.

'It *is* from the north!'

'We could be free soon!'

He could feel the other orderlies' excitement as they pressed around him and he backed away to allow them access to the window. It *was* the next offensive – he was certain of that – but unlike others in the room he was not so sure it heralded freedom: it might instead mean danger.

Arriving on the ward later that morning, Gabriel met a worried looking Anitch who told him that the German invasion had indeed begun, and that they were about to hold an emergency meeting of all hospital staff to discuss the evacuation plan. And he also had a favour to ask of Gabriel.

'If, as seems likely, the town is about to be captured,' Anitch said, 'all the Serbian medical staff will evacuate the hospital. But I'm asking if you would be willing to stay behind and look after any casualties who are too sick to move.'

'Of course,' Gabriel replied, pleased to be entrusted with the care of the Serbian soldiers he and Anitch had operated on over the past few months.

'Good. The other Austrian orderlies will also stay here under your command. As senior medical officer you'll be in charge, at least until the German medical columns arrive to take over formal responsibility for the care of the wounded.'

The emergency meeting took place in the dining area near the hospital kitchen, and Gabriel arrived and took a seat unobtrusively at the back of the room. He could see that almost all the Serbian staff – orderlies, porters, cooks, hospital carpenters and engineers – looked worried and were muttering surreptitiously to each other as they sat at tables nearer the front. Anitch arrived a few minutes later, accompanied by a uniformed officer who Gabriel didn't recognise, and who was introduced to the room as Dr Curcin.

'As many of you will have gathered,' Curcin began, 'early this morning Belgrade came under attack from Austrian and German assault troops.'

The news of German involvement did not surprise Gabriel. After three failed Austrian attempts, it seemed inevitable that Germany would take command of the offensive.

'We have reports that there are two armies involved,' Curcin continued. 'The German 11th, with support from the Austrian 3rd. Reports indicate that units from the German 11th have crossed the Danube and entered Belgrade, where there is heavy fighting in the streets.'

Interesting, thought Gabriel: if the 3rd Austrian Army was in the assault, it meant his own 6th Army must have been so badly mauled during the last offensive that it was no longer capable of taking part in the fighting. What, he wondered, had happened to Field Marshal Potiorek?

'There are also reports that Bulgaria has mobilised along our eastern border and is expected to attack within the next few days.'

Although it did not surprise Gabriel to hear that Bulgaria had mobilised, he still saw the shock on the faces of the other men in the room. Serbia would not be able to withstand an offensive from three nations: they would be trapped between the Germans and Austrians in the north, and the Bulgarians in the east and south, with nowhere to retreat to. Well, almost nowhere: one possible route of escape was west across the mountains of Montenegro into Albania, although those icy peaks were rumoured to be impassable in winter.

'We must be ready to receive casualties from the Belgrade front,' Curcin said, 'but we also need an evacuation plan for the possibility that Kragujevac may be overrun.'

Gabriel saw the anxious looks from several of the Serbian hospital staff.

'If it appears inevitable that the town is about to fall,' Curcin continued, 'all walking wounded will be discharged and given railway permits and discharge papers which will allow them to travel home without accusations of desertion.'

There were nods of understanding.

'Then it will be the turn of the medical staff to evacuate the hospital.' He looked at Anitch, who stepped forward, clearing his throat.

'Once the walking wounded have gone,' Anitch said to the hospital staff, 'you will all go straight to Kragujevac railway station, where specially reserved trains will be waiting to take you south to the Czar Lazar Military Hospital in Krusevac. Those patients who are too sick to move will stay behind. They will be under the care of Dr Bayer until the arrival of the German and Austrian medical columns.'

Several men sitting in front of Gabriel turned and smiled approvingly at him, and Gabriel felt a warm glow of pleasure at the trust that Anitch had placed in him.

'Those of you who have worked with Dr Bayer,' Anitch said, 'know him to be a capable and conscientious surgeon. I have every confidence that our wounded will be well looked after by him.' He paused and looked at Dr

Curcin, who shook his head as if to say he had nothing further to add. 'That's all for now,' Anitch continued. 'We will let you know of any new developments. Now, please go back to work.'

The hospital staff rose and trooped out of the dining room, but Gabriel – the last to leave – was stopped by Anitch on the way out and introduced to Curcin.

'I'm very pleased to meet you, Dr Bayer,' Curcin said to him in English. 'Dmitri and the Scottish women speak very highly of you.'

'I've enjoyed helping Dmitri,' Gabriel said, looking at Anitch with a smile, 'and it was an honour to work at the Scottish hospital. They are an amazing group of women.'

'Amazing... yes,' Curcin said with a wry smile, 'but also stubborn. When rumours of this invasion first began, I tried to persuade Dr Inglis that she needed to prepare for a possible evacuation. But she didn't even want to discuss it, so committed is she to staying with her patients.'

'But the women *must* be evacuated if the town is likely to fall to the Germans,' Gabriel said. 'Their safety cannot be assured during an invasion of the town. Can't you just order them to leave?'

'Unfortunately not. It is entirely Dr Inglis's decision. I can make a recommendation, but that's all. In fact, I am about to drive over to the school hospital and inform Dr Inglis of the latest development.' He sighed. 'Knowing her as I do, however, I suspect that even if the capture of Kragujevac is imminent, she will insist on staying.'

'Would it help if I came with you?' Gabriel asked.

'As an Austrian officer, my knowledge of the likely behaviour of my allies might just convince her.'

'I hoped you would say that,' Curcin said with a smile. 'But I'm not optimistic: Dr Inglis will need a lot of persuasion.'

***

Gabriel stood beside Dr Curcin in the middle of the school hospital surgical ward, waiting for Dr Inglis, who had had been summoned out of theatre to speak with them. She entered the ward – ungloved, but in a bloodstained surgical smock – and stood with arms folded resolutely across her chest as she listened to Curcin's plea to prepare for evacuation.

'Absolutely not,' she said, when he had finished speaking. 'Under no circumstances will I abandon my patients. It would be morally wrong and I would be reneging on my duty as a doctor.' She lifted her chin and folded her arms tighter across her chest. 'May I remind you that we are working under the remit of the International Red Cross, and the Geneva Convention exempts medical personnel from imprisonment?'

'I know that,' Curcin replied. 'But we have no guarantee the Germans will adhere to the Conventions. You have been assisting an enemy. They may be very hostile.'

'We'll just have to take our chances. The answer is still no.'

'You have much valuable hospital equipment here,'

Curcin persisted. 'Electrical generators, X-ray machines, surgical instruments. You will lose all of it when the Germans arrive.'

'Then we will manage without it.'

A look of frustration passed over Curcin's face. 'But, Dr Inglis—'

'I've stated my position, Dr Curcin, so there's no point in any further discussion.' She moved as if to turn away. 'Now as you can see, I'm very busy—'

'Dr Inglis,' Gabriel assertively interrupted. 'You should know that I will be staying in Kragujevac until the Austrian and German medical teams arrive. If you did agree to evacuate, I would personally ensure that every patient in your hospital is treated in accordance with the Geneva protocols.'

She had paused at his interruption and now she sighed. 'Look, I'm sorry, Dr Bayer, but the answer remains no. Not that I don't trust you; indeed, I have heard many good things about you. But I cannot bring myself to abandon my patients to whatever fate—'

'I don't mean to be impertinent, Dr Inglis,' Gabriel interrupted again, 'but perhaps you are only thinking of yourself and not your staff.' Her eyes flared with surprise and then a flicker of indignation as he continued. 'I believe there may be a real risk to the women in your group.'

Her indignation faded in in instant. 'What do you mean?'

'You must have heard the rumours of atrocities committed against some women in Belgium and France?' Although she made no reply, her expression told Gabriel that she knew of the reports. 'I believe there is a real possibility that your women might attract unwanted advances from some of the Germans.'

'You surely don't mean—'

'Unfortunately I mean exactly that,' said Gabriel, and saw a look of shock pass across her face.

'There is also the Nurse Cavell situation to consider,' added Curcin.

She still looked shaken as she swung towards him.

'As you no doubt remember,' Curcin continued. 'Edith Cavell, a senior nurse in a hospital in Belgium, has been tried and found guilty of helping prisoners escape. We have just learnt that she is due to be executed by the Germans within the next few days. The International Red Cross and Geneva Conventions have been of little use in protecting her.'

'For your staff, if nothing else,' Gabriel added, 'it would be safest if you were to relocate to Krusevac.'

She looked away and was silent for a time: Gabriel knew she was wrestling with the dilemma. 'So if I were to agree to evacuate, you would promise to come here and take charge of my patients?'

'Yes. Of course.'

Her face slackened and she exhaled heavily. 'All right, if it comes to it, and the town is about to fall, then we will evacuate to Krusevac.'

'Very good,' a visibly relieved Curcin said. 'I'll keep you informed about the military situation.'

★★★

One week later: Elspeth – operating on a patient in the school hospital theatre – heard a roaring noise like a giant oak tree crashing to earth. The floor below her feet shuddered slightly and the surgical lamp hanging above the patient on the table began to dim and flicker.

Oh no, prayed Elspeth, gripping the suture forceps more tightly as she looked up at the wavering light. *Please don't go out on me.*

She stepped back from the operating table and cocked her head to listen: that last explosion had sounded even closer, she thought. Standing on the opposite side of the table, Aurelia and Monica stood stock still, their brows above their surgical veils furrowed with anxiety as they looked up at the ceiling. A few shards of plaster released by the tremor from the shell burst had begun to float down and all three women stepped forward to cover the exposed, semi-sutured wound of the soldier on the table with their upper bodies. Elspeth waited for the falling debris to stop and then straightened up again.

'Thank goodness we're almost finished,' she said to Lydia, who was sitting at the soldier's head. 'We need to get him downstairs quickly, so you'd better wake him.'

Lydia nodded, then removed the gauze mask from the soldier's face and began to pinch his ear as Elspeth inserted the last stitch.

'Cut please,' Elspeth said, and Monica leant past her to snip the suture with scissors. Satisfied with her work, Elspeth stepped back and looked across at the two Austrian orderlies waiting patiently in the corner of the room. 'You can take him down to the ward. Be sure to ask Captain Bayer to see him as soon as he arrives—'

Suddenly, the door to the operating room swung open and a frantic-looking Serbian guard appeared and shouted something unintelligible at her.

'What did he say?' Elspeth asked Aurelia.

'He said it's now seven o'clock, and that if we're to make the last train we have to go with him right away,' replied Aurelia,

'Well, we're done,' Elspeth said, stripping her gloves off and loosening the surgical mask. 'So you can tell him that all three of you will be going with him now.'

'What about you, Dr Stewart?' Monica asked.

'I'm going to say goodbye to Sister Calthorpe first, so I'll meet you at the station later.'

Monica nodded, and then helped by Aurelia and Lydia began to quickly throw the surgical instruments into a large holdall. Still dressed in her surgical gown, Elspeth hurried through the door, out along the corridor and down the staircase to the ground floor.

The order to evacuate had come late that afternoon, when Dr Curcin had arrived to tell Elspeth and the other women that German patrols had been sighted on the outskirts of town. The fall of Kragujevac was imminent, he said, and it was not clear how much longer the railway line could be kept open. The women should go straight to the station, he added, as the last train south to Krusevac would leave at nine o'clock that evening.

Dr Inglis had immediately called an emergency meeting and sent most of the women straight to the station under the protection of a detachment of Serbian guards. She had then instructed Huber to load the ambulance with medical supplies and told Vera to drive it down to the Czar Lazar Hospital in Krusevac: Sylvia was to go with her as an escort. Elspeth had also overheard Dr Inglis instruct one of the Serbian guards to go to the First Reserve Hospital with a message for Captain Bayer, asking him to come over as soon as possible to take over the care of the patients who were too sick to be moved.

As Elspeth ran through the entrance and stood for a moment on the steps leading down to the courtyard, she saw that dusk had already fallen. There was a strong odour of burnt explosive in the air – similar to the smell of fireworks on Guy Fawkes night – and even in the gloom she could see several columns of white smoke on the horizon. Further smoke-trails were scudding past the outline of a three-quarter moon above her head. There was steam on her breath and the evening air felt cold as she hugged the surgical gown tighter around her body and walked down into the courtyard.

Bathed in soft moonlight ahead of her was the hospital's ambulance, the outline of Vera in the driver's seat dimly visible through the cab window. Huber was crouched in front of the radiator, energetically cranking the vehicle's starting handle: the engine of the ambulance suddenly came to life with a throaty roar. Smoke sputtered from the exhaust and the headlights flooded the courtyard with light.

And now Elspeth saw Sylvia at the back of the ambulance, pushing with both hands at doors that did not seem to want to close. Elspeth hurried towards her, and, adding her own weight against the doors, forced them shut and allowed Sylvia to fasten and lock them together.

'Thanks,' Sylvia shouted above the noise of the vehicle's broken exhaust. 'It's like trying to close a jack-in-the-box.'

'How much stuff have you got in there?' Elspeth shouted back.

'As much medical equipment and supplies as we could squeeze in.' Sylvia rattled the handle to make certain it was locked and then walked Elspeth around the side of the ambulance, where it was less noisy. 'But there's still space in the driver's cab. Come with us, Ellie. It'll be fun, all of us together.'

'I hardly think a night drive with the German army on your heels could be described as "fun".'

'How about "exciting" then?'

Elspeth gave a wry smile. 'I think I'll take the train. Dr Inglis is still uneasy about leaving our patients, so I want to make sure she gets to the station on time.'

'Well, just make sure you do,' Sylvia said, opening the door.

'We will, and probably get to Krusevac before you.' Elspeth said, glancing through the school gates into the street outside, where a column of refugees and wagons were trundling past. 'I think you'll find it slow going on the roads. I'll get the samovar going and have hot cocoa waiting for when you arrive.'

Sylvia smiled, leant forward to give Elspeth a hug

and climbed into the cab. Elspeth walked around to the driver's side and, leaning through the window, gave Vera a farewell peck on her cheek. Huber held the gates to the schoolyard open as the heavily laden vehicle began to move forward, belching exhaust fumes as it rolled and swayed out into the street. With blasts of the motor-horn the ambulance cleared a space in the column of refugees and Elspeth waved at it; Sylvia's head appeared through the passenger-side window to wave back at her before the vehicle was lost to view in the mass of evacuees.

'Maybe you should have gone with them?' Huber said, a concerned look on his face as they both walked back towards the school building.

'Don't worry; I'm going with Dr Inglis—' She was interrupted by a volley of nearby rifle-fire that echoed through the courtyard.

Huber's expression became even more troubled. 'Then you must please hurry. It is not safe on the streets.'

As she ran up the steps to the entrance, she almost collided with Dr Inglis, who was coming out.

'Ah there you are, Elspeth. Lillian's gone over to the villa to fetch our bags. All the VADs and nurses have gone to the station. As soon as Lillian's back we'll join them—'

At that moment the sudden clatter of metal-rimmed wheels on cobblestones swamped her words, and Elspeth turned to see an ox wagon trundle through the schoolyard gate and stop beside Huber. The driver, a small boy wearing a uniform several sizes bigger than him, was pointing in the back of the wagon and Elspeth hurried back down the steps: lying on the floor of the cart – the wood planking awash with blood – were three badly wounded soldiers. The men were alive, but all three were pale and semi-conscious.

'Dear Lord,' said Dr Inglis, who had followed Elspeth across the courtyard and was gripping the edge of the wagon, a look of anguished concern on her face as she studied the casualties. 'Look, I'm sorry, Elspeth, but I just can't leave them to suffer. You and Lillian should go, but I'm staying. Huber can anaesthetise for me—'

But Elspeth was already looking at her pocket watch. 'And I'm staying as well,' she said, closing the lid with a snap. 'If we're quick, we can still get to the station in time.' Before Dr Inglis could answer, Elspeth was already halfway up the steps. 'Have them taken straight up to theatre, Huber,' she shouted as she dashed through the entrance door.

★★★

The casualties were carried up to the operating theatre. Once they were there Huber administered the ether and Elspeth and Dr Inglis began to operate. By eight o'clock they had finished the first two cases: a soldier with a sucking chest wound, and another requiring an emergency amputation. But just as they were about to start the last case, the door to the theatre swung open and Lillian Chesney appeared, accompanied by the last two remaining Serbian guards and one of the Austrian orderlies.

'I can't believe you're still here, Elsie,' she said,

a shocked expression on her face. 'We must leave immediately. The guards won't wait any longer and German patrols have been seen only a few streets away.'

'I have to finish this last case, Lillian,' Dr Inglis replied as she retied her surgical mask. 'Dr Bayer hasn't appeared yet and I can't just go—'

'But you are the hospital's chief medical officer, Elsie.' Elspeth could hear the exasperation in Dr Chesney's voice. 'What is needed now is your skill as a leader, not as a surgeon.'

Dr Inglis hesitated, but then lowered the surgical mask. 'But, Lillian—'

'Our priority must be the safety of our volunteers.' Dr Chesney persisted. 'And as the head of the unit, you *must* be with it at this critical time.'

'But—'

'There are no "buts" about it, Elsie: we have a duty to the women of this hospital, as well as the patients we serve.'

'I agree with Lillian.' Elspeth now found herself saying.

'Thank goodness one of you is thinking clearly,' said Dr Chesney.

'You must go, Elsie,' Elspeth continued and then turned to Dr Chesney 'In fact you should both go and lead the evacuation to Krusevac. I'll stay and finish this last case and then meet you at the station.'

As she said the words, Elspeth knew she would be taking a risk, but it felt like the right decision for the group. Plus, it was the only way Dr Inglis might be persuaded to leave.

'Anyway, Captain Bayer will probably arrive at any moment,' Elspeth continued, 'and I'll join you as soon as he gets here.'

'And what if he's late and you miss the train?' Dr Inglis said.

'If we stand here debating, then it's certain all three of us will miss it,' Elspeth replied. 'And the unit cannot function without you or Lillian as its leader, Elsie.'

There was a moment's silence. Then Dr Inglis stepped away from the table and peeled off her gloves. 'You're right, I'll do as you suggest.' She untied her gown and followed Dr Chesney and the Serbian guards to the door. The Austrian orderly stepped aside to let them pass, but Dr Inglis paused in the doorway. 'Huber should administer the anaesthetic, and this orderly can help with the instruments—'

'I'll be fine, Elsie,' Elspeth interrupted. 'Just go. I'll see you at the station.' Dr Inglis hesitated, nodded, and quickly left the room, the Austrian orderly closing the door behind her.

The operating theatre was quiet again as Elspeth – pushing all thoughts of the last train from her mind – focussed on the final patient, a Serbian major with a depressed fracture of the back of his skull. Pressing on the boggy, broken skin of his scalp, she could see a large piece of skull bone had been pushed into the occipital lobes – the rear part of the brain, which controlled vision – and by waving her fingers in front of his face she quickly determined that he was blind. In order to save his eyesight she would need to lift the depressed bone. But that was not the priority, because when she unwrapped a bloodstained dressing tied underneath his jaw, a jet of blood spurted from a large wound in the left side of his neck. She looked at Huber.

'Right: we'll use chloroform this time.' She turned to the other orderly. 'And you,' she said, 'put some gloves on, apply pressure here, and hand me those instruments when I ask for them…'

★★★

A short distance away in the First Reserve Hospital, Gabriel finally finished operating and checked the time. *Damn!* It was eight o'clock and he knew from the messenger who had arrived earlier on that Dr Inglis was relying on him to provide cover for her patients. Quickly he stripped off his surgical gown, threw his army greatcoat over his jacket, and hurried towards the main entrance.

The hospital corridors were deserted, as Dmitri and the rest of the Serbian staff had left for the railway station two hours earlier while Gabriel, assisted by the other Austrian orderlies, had finished off the remaining surgical work for the day. Hurrying outside, Gabriel saw that the night sky was peppered with sharp points of luminosity, the soft radiance from the low moon insufficient to hide the light of the stars. As he carefully picked his way along the rubble-strewn pavement towards the women's hospital, a rifle shot made him flinch and the flash of a flare shell lit up the street. He ducked into an alleyway and waited for the artificial daylight to fade; then waited a moment longer for his night vision to return. From a nearby street he heard shouting, the crack of a gunshot, a scream, an answering volley of rifle shots, then silence. He waited a moment longer and finally, cautiously, slipped back into the street.

The darkness made him more reliant on his hearing and as he was about to climb over a low brick wall he heard the crunch of a boot on broken glass, followed by a soft cursing in a language he could not determine. He hid behind the wall and held his breath. A few seconds later he heard the slow careful footsteps of people trying not to make any noise. He waited for the footsteps to pass and then raised his head to cautiously peer over the wall.

Four soldiers, each man wearing a spiked khaki-covered steel helmet, were moving away from him along the street. He watched them disappear from view and then moved on again.

A few streets later he heard more noise and hid in another alleyway. From within the alley's shadow he saw several rifle-wielding Chetniks, sheepskin jerkins and ammunition bandoliers slung across their chest, the flash of reflected moonlight on a knife in a belt. He knew they would kill him without hesitation if they saw him, so he waited until they had passed, then carried on in this fashion, hurrying from street to street, dodging from building to building, hiding until he was certain it was safe to continue. His back and legs ached with the tension of running and crouching, but finally the outer wall of the Scottish Women's Hospital came into view and he sprinted the last few metres and arrived, breathing heavily, at the gates.

He slid into the central courtyard. It was deserted apart from an empty wagon, the floorboards stained with blood, two exhausted oxen gazing at him with sad brown eyes. He ran up the steps and through the door. At first he didn't see anybody. Good, he thought, the women must all be at the station by now. But as he reached the staircase to the first floor he heard a cheery Austrian drinking song. Looking up the stairs, Gabriel saw two swaying Austrian orderlies, arms around each other's shoulders, one of them holding a bottle of surgical spirits in his hands while the other held onto the bannister.

'It's Captain Bayer!' the one holding the bottle said; then he pulled away from his comrade and raised his arms in welcome. 'Have a drink – celebrate our freedom!'

Gabriel took a deep breath, struggling to contain his anger at the sight of these drunkards. 'Have all the women left for the station?' he asked, ignoring the bottle waved in front of his face

'Yes, Captain…' the man tried to stifle a giggle, 'they've all gone.' He rocked from side to side. 'The Serb guards have gone… and the women have gone… except for—' He toppled back onto the staircase and burst into laughter.

'Except for who?' Gabriel demanded, but the man was unable to reply through laughing. The other orderly pointed up the staircase, towards the operating theatre.

'Dr Stewart…' he said, and then also collapsed into laughter.

Elspeth? Gabriel hurried up the staircase and along the corridor. As he arrived at the door to the theatre it swung open and an Austrian orderly wearing gloves and a bloodstained white smock appeared.

'Thank God you're here, Captain,' he said. 'We've told Dr Stewart to go or she'll miss her train—'

But Gabriel was already pushing past him. Entering the room he saw Elspeth stooped over the operating table, carefully placing a stitch in a deep gash in the patient's neck. Huber was at the patient's head, holding a mask over the man's face, tilting the man's neck to one side to allow Elspeth better access to the wound. Sweet Jesus, thought Gabriel, what on earth was she still doing here? Feeling a strong urge to go up to her, grip her by the arms and shake some sense into her, he nevertheless managed to control himself and went up to the table, dropped his head to her eye level, and waited for her to notice him. After a moment she lifted her head and her gaze latched onto him. She looked at him for a moment and then her brow furrowed with concentration as she dipped her head and began to insert another stitch. Gabriel turned and glared at Huber, who had an expression of pained resignation on his face.

'I'm sorry, sir,' he whispered to Gabriel. 'I've tried to make her go, but you know how stubborn she can be—'

'Careful, Huber,' Elspeth said, without lifting her head as she placed the final suture. 'My German may not be perfect, but it's good enough for me to understand most of what you say.'

Gabriel watched Elspeth tie the suture and snip the

ends off. Then she straightened up and pulled down her surgical mask

'Well, hello, Dr Bayer,' she said, as if she had only just noticed him. 'I must say we were expecting you to arrive a little earlier—'

'Elspeth, please.' His voice was gentle but urging. 'If you're to catch the train, you must leave now' – and then, remembering the danger of the journey he had just undertaken, he added – 'or maybe you should stay and accept being taken prisoner—'

'It's fine, Gabriel.' Her voice was calm. 'I know what I must do. I'm going to finish this as quickly as I can, then I'll hurry across to the station to try and make the train. And if I miss it… well then, I'll accept my fate and hand myself over to the Germans when they arrive.'

'But—'

'No.' She help up a gloved hand in front of his face, a pair of suture forceps poised delicately between thumb and forefinger. 'I've made my decision. Now, you can either help me, or delay me further by arguing. Which is it going to be?'

He sighed. Then he quickly slipped out of his greatcoat, walked across to the scrub bench at the side of the room, and pulled on a pair of rubber gloves. And as he walked back to the operating table, Huber looked at him and shrugged his shoulders as if to say: see what I mean?

★★★

It took them ten minutes to finish. Gabriel watched Elspeth dissect the skin wound over the skull fracture, and then with his help she peeled back a flap of scalp to reveal the underlying bone. A piece of metal shell casing was lodged in the depressed skull fragment, and grasping it with a forceps she used it as a shrapnel handle to lever the bone upwards. Underneath the bone there was a blood clot, which Gabriel washed out with saline to reveal the membranes surrounding the brain. Excellent, he thought; they did not appear to have been breached. The contours and grooves of the brain looked healthily pink and shiny, with only one area of redness where the depressed bone had caused a minor contusion. Elspeth prised the piece of shrapnel out of the bone fragment and then – like fitting a last piece of jigsaw – she anchored the fragment in place, level with the surrounding skull. Huber had used up the last of the chloroform and the soldier began to wake as they placed the final stitches. It was satisfying for Gabriel to hear the soldier accurately count the number of fingers that he held up in front of his eyes.

As Gabriel peeled off his gloves, he saw Elspeth hurry over to Huber. The old Austrian sergeant put his hand out for her to shake, but she ignored it and instead put her arms around him and pulled him forward into a hug. As they parted, Gabriel saw tears in the eyes of the veteran soldier.

'Please be careful, Dr Stewart,' Huber said, 'you are like a daughter to me.'

She nodded and then went to fetch her coat and

cape. Watching her, Gabriel felt a knot of tension build in his stomach.

'Elspeth, I think it's too dangerous—'

'I'd rather not fall into German hands if I can,' she interuppted, fastening her cape as she waited by the door. 'But you don't have to come with me if you don't want to.'

He put his greatcoat back on and crossed to her. 'How could you even *think* I would let you go out there on your own?'

'I hoped you would say that,' she replied with a smile.

★★★

Elspeth's sense of duty to her patients was so strong, that when she made her decision to stay and operate on the last case she hadn't worried whether she would make the train or not, hadn't fully considered all the consequences of her decision. But now, as she and Gabriel ran through the gates and out into the street, she felt the first stirrings of worry at the position she had placed them both in, because the sounds of fighting were now very loud. A nearby volley of gun-fire echoed through the darkness and she began to feel guilty that Gabriel had felt obliged to accompany her. At the same time she was glad he was by her side, holding her hand as they hurried through the unlit streets towards the station.

He suddenly pulled her into a side alley, where it was even darker, although the moonlight cast enough light for him to guide her through the narrow, winding passageway. At the end of the alley he crouched down and she did the same, watching as he peered cautiously into the street beyond. Suddenly he pulled back into the shadow, and turning round he silently touched a finger to her lips to indicate she should stay quiet.

She nodded, and a moment later heard hooves clopping slowly on the cobblestones. Leaning her face slightly out of the shadow, she peered past his shoulder into the street beyond where two horses and their riders were silhouetted against the night sky. Steam rose from the horses' nostrils and moonlight glimmered on the burnished spikes of the German cavalrymen's helmets as the two riders, carbines held above the heads of their animals, twisted in their saddles and scanned the street ahead. The ears of the horses swivelled, but the animals were mostly silent apart from a gentle snort or the clop of a hoof being repositioned on the cobbles.

Elspeth slowly – so very slowly – pulled her face back into the shadow but kept the cavalrymen in view, holding her breath as she watched them scrutinise the street ahead. Then she saw the spurs on the boot of the nearest rider dig into the flank of his animal, and both men and horses continued their slow walk forward, eventually breaking into a trot, and then cantering down the street. She heard Gabriel exhale – he must have been holding his breath as well, she thought – before he turned to her.

'They've gone,' he whispered. He took hold of her hand and gently gave her fingers a reassuring squeeze.

She squeezed back to let him know she was fine. Then he led her out into the street again.

After several tense minutes of hiding and running, they arrived at an intersection with the avenue she knew led directly to the railway station. A strong smell of burning timber filled her nostrils. Elspeth crouched behind an overturned cart on the street corner, Gabriel beside her as they peered between the spokes on one of the cartwheels. Halfway along the left side of the avenue she saw a house ablaze: coils of smoke were spiralling up in the gentle night breeze, orange flames licking out from under the exposed roof timbers, the buildings on the opposite side of the avenue brightly lit by the fire.

Elspeth could hear a faintly distant hiss of steam and looking towards the far end of the avenue saw the outline of the station building, less than a hundred yards away. Silhouetted faintly against the night sky above the building was a drifting plume of smoke, which she knew must be from the train waiting at the platform below.

But for how much longer? She knew there was very little time left and was filled with the desperate urge to run there as quickly as possible, to join Dr Inglis and the others and not be left behind. But the stretch of avenue leading up to the station was brightly illuminated by the fire, and anybody hiding in the pockets of shadow on the left side of the street would spot them immediately.

And then the blast of a steam whistle pierced the air and Elspeth knew that the train's departure was imminent.

Gabriel turned to her, his cheekbones darkly under shadowed by the flickering light from the flames. 'I'm worried at how exposed we'll be,' he whispered, 'but we've no choice if you're to make the train. You go first; I'll be close behind. Stay tight to the houses on the right and move as fast as you can.'

She needed no further bidding and slid out from behind the upturned cart. And then, holding the hem of her skirt, she began to run up the pavement on the right side of the avenue, sensing Gabriel close behind her as they hurried towards the station.

They were half way along the avenue and level with the burning house when from across the street Elspeth heard a cry – 'Halt!' – followed an instant later by the flash and roar of a gun. She felt the wind of the bullet pass a few inches in front of her nose and slam into the wall of a house to her right, the shock of it causing her to skid to a halt and drop to the pavement. The strength seemed to leave her legs as she squatted in a doorway, her eyes closed, praying that whoever had shot at her would not shoot again…

***

Gabriel's heart hammered in his chest. He had almost fallen over Elspeth when the shot had been fired and she had ducked into the doorway. As he stood and regained his balance, he looked across the street and saw four men emerge from shadow beside the burning house. All wore German army steel helmets and three had rifles pointed at him, while the fourth – an officer, Gabriel presumed – held a handgun.

Slowly, Gabriel straightened up. '*Nicht Schiessen, Nicht Schiessen, Nemoj Pucanje,*' he shouted, pointing at the Red Cross armband on the sleeve of his greatcoat. '*Doktor, Arzt, Hirurga.*'

Another flash, another crack of gunfire, and this time the bullet passed slightly above Gabriel and into the wall behind his head, showering him with plaster dust as he ducked down again. He heard laughter and looked up to see the man who had fired the rifle, a smirking young private, pull the bolt back on his rifle and eject the spent cartridge, the brass glinting in the firelight and tinkling as it fell onto the cobbles below.

'That's enough, Schneider!' The officer barked angrily in German. 'You'll bring every damned Chetnik down on our heads!'

A ribbon of smoke wafted from the rifle's nozzle as the private scowled at the officer, snapping the bolt forward to chamber another round before returning his attention to Gabriel.

The four soldiers formed a semi-circle around Gabriel as he crouched in the doorway beside Elspeth. From the insignia on their uniforms Gabriel could see they were German infantry: two privates and a sergeant carrying rifles, the officer – a lieutenant – holding a luger. There was a cold-eyed indifference about all four as they stared at him, but it was the look in the eyes of the private who had fired the rifle that was most frightening. His manner towards the officer had been insolent, almost defiant, and he was looking at Gabriel with undisguised hostility. The lieutenant waved his pistol at Gabriel.

'Get up.'

Gabriel slowly began to stand, but Elspeth seemed shocked and was slow to move.

'I said get up!'

Gabriel gently held Elspeth's upper arm and helped her to her feet, brushing plaster dust from the shoulders of her cape as they stood.

'Well, well: a *Fraulein*,' the lieutenant said as Elspeth stood straight and looked him in the eye. He holstered the luger, then folded his arms across his chest and smiled at the sergeant standing beside him. Then he turned back to Gabriel.

'Who are you? Do you have identity papers or—'

'They're spies, Lieutenant,' the glowering private interrupted, 'sneaking around out here in the dark.'

'I said that's enough, Schneider,' the lieutenant said. He looked back at Gabriel. 'I repeat: who are you?'

Gabriel looked him directly in the eyes. 'Lieutenant, I'm very relieved to see you. My name is Captain Bayer and I'm a military surgeon in the 6th Austrian Army. I was captured last December and have been a prisoner here since then.'

The lieutenant made no reply, his arms still folded.

'This,' Gabriel nodded to Elspeth, 'is Dr Stewart, a Scottish surgeon who has been working under the auspices of the International Red Cross, caring for casualties from both sides. As a non-combatant she is entitled to your protection—'

'If you're an Austrian prisoner, why are you out on the streets?' The lieutenant's eyes were cold and hard, unwaveringly fixed on Gabriel's face. 'Why aren't you in a prison camp?'

'I was escorting her to—'

'This is a waste of time, Lieutenant.' Gabriel heard the impatience in Schneider's voice. 'If he's Austrian like he says he is, why he is creeping around with her, out here, in the dark? She's working for the British army—'

'No,' said Gabriel with an assertive shake of his head. 'No. She's a Scottish doctor working for the Red Cross, not the British army—'

'You shut your mouth, spy,' Schneider said, stepping forward to point the rifle directly at Gabriel, the tip of the barrel only inches from his forehead.

The lieutenant unfolded his arms and looked pointedly at the sergeant, who quickly stepped forward to push the barrel of Schneider's rifle towards the ground. 'Get back in line,' the sergeant said, 'or I'll have you on a charge when we get back.'

Schneider glowered at the sergeant but took a step back. Gabriel had not flinched in the face of his hostility but knew the situation was on a knife-edge. He could see the tension in Schneider's hands, his forefinger still in the trigger-guard, his eyes desperate for any excuse to shoot. The lieutenant nodded at the sergeant, then turned back to Gabriel and folded his arms again.

'So you're an Austrian… you say. Have you proof of your identity?'

Gabriel slowly lifted a hand and pulled the upper part of his greatcoat aside to reveal his faded blue uniform, then twisted the collar forward to show the three silver stars.

'That doesn't prove anything,' the lieutenant said. 'You could have taken those off a dead Austrian. Do you have your identity card or pay-book?'

'I lost my identity documents when I was captured.'

'How inconvenient.'

Gabriel ignored the sarcasm. 'I'm a surgeon. I was transferred from my prison camp to work in the military hospital. If we go there now—'

'So you have no proof of your identity—'

'—if we go there now,' Gabriel persisted, 'the hospital staff will confirm my identity.'

In the silence that followed, broken only by the snap of burning timbers from the house opposite, the lieutenant lifted a hand to massage his chin between thumb and fingers. As he pondered their fate, Gabriel saw the sergeant lean towards him.

'I think he's lying, Lieutenant—'

'I'm not lying,' Gabriel said, trying to keep the desperation out of his voice. 'I'm an Austrian military surgeon.'

'He speaks German with a strange accent,' the sergeant continued, ignoring Gabriel's plea. 'He has no papers and we caught him red-handed helping a member of the enemy escape.' His eyes flicked towards Elspeth. 'Or he could be trying to desert. Either way, it's a capital offence.' Then he turned towards Elspeth again and this time his eyes did not leave her face. Gabriel saw the look and knew what he intended. Their only hope was for the lieutenant to remain in control of his men.

'Lieutenant, my accent is Austrian. *Please*. We're on the same side. We're Allies, for heaven's sake. If we go to the hospital—'

Another blast of a steam whistle pierced the night, followed a moment later by a loud hiss, and a moment after that by the rhythmic sound of a train beginning to move.

Gabriel glanced across at Elspeth, who was looking towards the station with dismay. He knew she had picked up enough German to follow most of the conversation, and he could tell from the ashen look on her face that she fully understood what the sergeant – possibly all of them – had planned for her.

The lieutenant cleared his throat. 'Under the regulations of the emergency powers invested in me,' he said to Gabriel, 'I find you either guilty of desertion, or of helping a member of the enemy to escape. For both these offences the punishment is death.'

Gabriel blinked in disbelief as the lieutenant turned to the still scowling private. 'Use the bayonet, Schneider. No more shooting. You've made enough noise as it is.'

An evil smile appeared on Schneider's face, and looking at the malevolence in the private's eyes Gabriel felt a wave of fear run through his body. But his fear vanished in an instant when the lieutenant moved towards Elspeth; instinctively Gabriel stepped in front of her and stood between them. But there was a movement to his side, and as he turned towards it he saw a rifle butt approach his face: with a flash of light and an excruciating pain in the left side of his head, Gabriel found himself lying on his back on the hard cobbles, Schneider standing over him.

Trying to refocus his vision, he turned his head to see the sergeant kick at the door to the house behind him, which swung inward with a crack of splintering wood. And then – each man gripping her by an elbow –the lieutenant and the sergeant took hold of Elspeth and threw her through the shattered doorframe. In the light of the flames from the burning house, Gabriel saw the interior of the hallway with Elspeth sprawled on the floor, the lieutenant and the sergeant standing over her.

Gabriel tried to lever himself up off the cobbles, but the strength in his arms had gone and his vision was fading just as he heard the distinctive metallic click of a bayonet being fixed to a rifle. He looked up, and the last thing he saw before his vision faded completely was Schneider grinning as he pressed the tip of the bayonet into the notch at the base of Gabriel's throat…

★★★

Elspeth – dazed, panicked – lay on her back on the floorboards, looking up at the lieutenant, who towered over her, straddling her body with his feet. She managed to roll over onto her front and tried to crawl away, but he sat down on her waist and grabbed hold of her arms, and then turned her onto her back. She tried to wriggle free, but he leant forward and, gripping her wrists, pinioned her arms to the floor above her head. His face was close to hers; his breath rank. She turned her face away from his, but then felt another weight on her legs as the sergeant sat on her knees. Again she tried to twist and arch her body, but try as she might she could not move, was powerless under their combined mass and strength. When she felt the sergeant lift her skirt she closed her eyes and turned her head away, realising there was nothing more she could do. This surely could not be happening…

★★★

A sudden burst of light and noise exploded into the confined darkness of the tiny hallway as a rifle was fired from the doorway…

★★★

Up until this point Elspeth had managed to resist crying out. But at the deafening sound of the gunshot, and the shock of the lieutenant falling on top of her, she screamed at the top of her lungs, then arched her back to try to push him away again… and now she was able to free her herself and push him aside, sliding out from underneath him, gasping for breath as she sat up against the sidewall of the hallway.

She saw that both men were lying beside her, the lieutenant obviously dead – pieces of skull and brain fragments hung from a gaping hole in the back of his head – while the sergeant writhed on the floor behind him, clutching at the front of his neck, trying to hold back a torrent of blood, which spurted between his fingers.

Too shocked to do anything but stare, Elspeth watched him jerk and spasm, his movements weakening until eventually his hands fell away from his throat. He twitched once and then stopped moving completely. She could see that the bullet which had killed him must have passed all the way through his neck and out into the back of the lieutenant's head. But who had fired the shot? Squinting against the glare of the flames, she saw the outline of a huge, bear-like figure framed in the doorway. The figure stepped into the hallway, boots crunching on broken glass, and after a moment of silence Elspeth heard a deep, booming, bass voice.

'Ah: *Virginesh*.'

***

Gabriel felt as if he was at the bottom of a deep ocean, struggling to reach the surface against the weight of water pushing him down. And then reality broke through as he became aware of a painful throbbing in the side of his head, hard cobblestones beneath his body and someone calling his name.

'Gabriel. Wake up, Gabriel.'

He recognised Elspeth's voice before opening his eyes, and, when he finally managed to focus, saw her kneeling beside him.

'Elspeth,' he croaked, suddenly remembering what had happened. 'Are you all right?'

'Yes, I'm unharmed,' Elspeth said, cupping his chin with one hand as she inspected a cut on his forehead. 'But you took a bit of a knock.' She wiped a streak of blood away with her thumb.

'I'm fine,' he said. Behind her he could see three other figures outlined against the flames: chetniks, each man dressed in a sheepskin jacket, long leather boots, and tubular woollen hats. They stood over the body of Schneider, who lay in a widening pool of blood, staring open-eyed at the sky, his throat cut from ear to ear. The body of the other private lay nearby, his throat also cut.

Another Chetnik appeared behind Elspeth and stood over her, and Gabriel looked up in astonishment. 'Luka?'

The big Chetnik grinned as he pointed at his left eye and spoke to Gabriel in pidgin German. 'I see *very* well now, *Hirurga*. I see you creeping through streets and we follow you here. Then we hear shots and see German patrol. I see they will kill you and so...' He glanced at the body of Schneider, made a throat slitting gesture with his finger, and then turned back to Gabriel. 'You helped me, *Hirurga*, so now I help you.' He turned to Elspeth. 'And you too, *Virginesh*.' And then he laughed, clearly delighted at the turn of affairs.

Gabriel recalled seeing the chetnik patrol on his way to the women's hospital, not for one moment suspecting that Luka might be amongst them. Luka was still grinning as he extended a hand and pulled Gabriel to his feet, then clapped him gleefully on the shoulder. But a moment later, when another gunshot echoed from nearby, the grin vanished. 'German patrols everywhere,' Luka muttered. 'We must go.'

'Can you take Dr Stewart with you?' Gabriel asked Luka. 'She was meant to take the train to Krusevac but missed it.'

Luka frowned, then sagely nodded his shaggy head. 'Yes. The rest of my Cheta waits near the station. We must leave now. Too dangerous, too many Germans. *Virginesh* cannot stay here. If Germans find, they rape, then kill. We walk south on railway line.'

'To Krusevac?' Gabriel said. 'To where the other Scottish women have gone?'

'Yes.' He turned to Elspeth and placed a hand on her shoulder. '*Virginesh*, you come with Cheta?' he said in Serbian, pointing towards the station.

Gabriel saw that Elspeth did not understand. 'Luka will take you with him, Elspeth. It's your best chance of getting to safety—'

'But you no come with us, *Hirurga*,' Luka interrupted. 'Chetniks no take prisoners. They kill all Austrians. You must go back to hospital.'

'Yes, I understand,' Gabriel replied. 'But Dr Stewart will be safe with you? Women are safe in your Cheta?'

Luka grinned. 'Yes, *Virginesh* will be safe. Another *Virginesh* in Cheta speaks good English.'

'But Dr Stewart is not a *Virginesh*—' Gabriel began to say, but then flinched as two more gunshots were heard, sounding even closer than before. The other Chetniks looked uneasy and had already started to move towards the station, and Luka looked at Elspeth and motioned urgently to her that she should follow him.

She nodded her understanding, but as Luka hurried after the others Elspeth waited a moment and then lifted her hand to wipe away another streak of blood which had trickled from the wound on Gabriel's head. 'You'll need a stitch in that when you get back to the hospital,' she said. 'You will be careful going back, won't you?'

'Don't worry about me,' he said. Despite the throbbing in his head he felt euphoric that Elspeth was going to be taken away from here. And the touch of her hand on the side of his face felt wonderful. 'Just make sure you get safely to Krusevac.'

'I will.'

He felt a strong urge to lean forward and kiss her goodbye, when Luka shouted from further up the avenue. 'Must come now!'

I'd better go,' she said, giving him a last smile before she turned away to hurry after Luka.

And as he watched her vanish into the smoke and darkness, Gabriel wondered if he would ever see her again.

2

Road to Krusevac, October–November 1915

As she ran towards the station, Elspeth glanced back and for a moment could still see Gabriel standing in the middle of the avenue, shrouded in the smoky orange glow from the burning house. But then Luka shouted to her, urging her to run faster, and she was forced to look forwards once more. By the time she arrived at the station and glanced back again, Gabriel had disappeared completely from view.

The station was cloaked in darkness and Elspeth crouched against a wall in the shadows outside while Luka disappeared through the station entrance with the other chetniks. A moment later he reappeared, accompanied by another figure only dimly visible in the moonlight. Luka motioned Elspeth forward. '*Virginesh*,' he quietly said as Elspeth went towards him. He turned to introduce the person standing behind him. '*Govori Dobro Engleski.*'

Elspeth knew enough Serbian to understand Luka's meaning: this was the sworn virgin he had mentioned, and that she spoke good English. But because of the dark it took Elspeth several seconds to take in the young chetnik standing before her: the leather boots, the bandolier of ammunition slung across the sheepskin-jerkin-covered chest, the cradled rifle. But instead of the usual tubular woollen hat that most Chetniks wore, this one wore a red beret. And the hair beneath the beret was a glossy jet black; the angular facial features distinctly familiar…

'Anya?' Elspeth said, her voice raised in querying disbelief.

The figure frowned, brown eyes wide in astonishment as she leant towards Elspeth.

'Ellie?'

They looked at each other for several long seconds, Elspeth aware of Luka staring at them both with a look of puzzled bemusement. And then Anya was leaning her rifle against the station building wall and stepping forward, throwing her arms around Elspeth and drawing her into a hug, and Elspeth was reeling with shock at the realisation that the person who was hugging her, this other sworn virgin that Luka had been so keen for her to meet, was actually Anya.

Her chin resting on Anya's shoulder, Elspeth saw Luka frown and then grin as he watched their embrace. Anya pulled away, her hands still on Elspeth's shoulders, shaking her head in incredulity. 'I can't believe… what you doing here, Ellie?' she whispered, and even in the dark Elspeth could see the whites of Anya's eyes shining with joy and surprise.

But then another gunshot reverberated down the avenue and Anya quickly pulled away. She picked up her rifle and silently motioned Elspeth to follow her and Luka through the station entrance. He led them both through the deserted station building and out onto the platform, where Elspeth saw a dozen chetniks crouching in the shadows. The platform was dimly illuminated by two flickering oil lamps, and littered with the debris of retreat: abandoned clothes and suitcases, empty cardboard boxes, children's toys. Elspeth crouched beside Anya as Luka dropped off the edge of the platform and down onto the railway line, presumably, Elspeth thought, to scout ahead and make certain it was safe. While they waited, Anya turned to her.

'I can't believe it, Ellie,' she whispered. 'What are you doing in Serbia?'

But Elspeth was still lost for words, her mind spinning as she tried to come to terms with Anya's unexpected presence.

'Are you working as a doctor?' Anya persisted. 'We have heard good things about a women's hospital here in Kragujevac. Is that you?'

'Y-yes...' Elspeth finally stuttered. 'I've been working... in a hospital here.' She paused. 'But with the Germans about to capture the town... we've been evacuated to Krusevac.' She was finding it difficult to speak coherently, could still hardly believe she was talking with Anya.

Anya frowned. 'The train that left here a few minutes ago: I saw many women on it—'

'Those are the women from the Scottish hospital,' Elspeth whispered, finally collecting her thoughts. 'Vera and Sylvia would have been with them, except they drove down earlier—'

'*Vera and…*' Anya began to say, before clapping a hand over her own mouth when she realised she had spoken aloud, 'Vera and Sylvia?' she whispered.

'Yes. Sylvia's a ward sister and Vera's an ambulance driver,' Elspeth continued. 'They've driven ahead to Krusevac—'

'They're here? In Serbia?'

'Yes – truly.' Elspeth grinned at the amazed look on Anya's face. 'I would've gone with them, but I was delayed.'

Now it was Anya's turn to remain silently open-mouthed as Elspeth continued. 'But if they'd come to the station, I doubt they would have recognised you,' she said, pointing at Anya's trousers. 'You're dressed just like a man.'

Anya glanced down at her legs and then looked up and smiled. 'There are many women in the Serbian army,' she said, 'but I am the only woman fighter in a Cheta. The other Chetniks treat me like a man as long as I dress like them, fight like them, kill like them. We eat the same food. We live and die together.'

'I still can't believe we've found each other,' Elspeth whispered. 'But why didn't you tell us you're—'

A scuffling noise interrupted her, and Luka's head suddenly reappeared above the lip of the platform. He motioned for them to follow him, and Elspeth, Anya and the other Chetniks slipped off the platform edge and joined him on the railway line.

Luka led them a short distance along the track until they arrived at a signal box a little way outside the station. The interior of the box was lit from within, the light shining through the window illuminating another group of chetniks crouching on the embankment below. One of these men – a wiry fellow carrying a carbine and with a revolver tucked in his waistband – stood up and shook hands with Luka. Anya whispered to Elspeth that the man was Marco, the overall commander of the Cheta. He appeared surprised to see Elspeth, but Luka whispered in his ear and a moment later a smile appeared on Marco's face.

'Ah. *Skotski damé Hirurga,*' he said, nodding to indicate he already knew of the Scottish women. Then, placing a hand on Elspeth's shoulder, he pointed down the embankment. In the dim light from the signal box Elspeth saw a figure lying on the grassy incline. She quickly scrambled down the bank, where she found a Chetnik – a youth of about eighteen – lying on the slope. The grass was slippery with blood and there was a perfectly round hole in the lower part of his left trouser leg. Marco and Anya were already by her side as she slid both index fingers inside the hole and ripped the material apart. There was a small entry wound in one side of his calf and a much wider exit hole opposite, which still oozed blood. She used a knife that Anya gave her to cut the trouser leg away, and then into strips, which she wrapped around the wound and tied in place. She saw the youth flinch at the pressure of the bandage, but it stopped the bleeding; it would do for the time being. With her support, he was able to stand and use his rifle as a crutch to hobble up the embankment. Marco whispered an order to the other chetniks and quietly the group began to march along the railway track.

It was a cold, clear night, the stars shining overhead, the trees sharply outlined by the moon on the horizon. However, at ground level it remained pitch black and now Elspeth understood why they were on the railway: it would have been impossible to travel on the road in the dark, but as long as they stayed within the metal rail tracks it would lead them south. Marco set a fast-paced march, which was undertaken in strict silence, Elspeth following the outline of Anya as best she could, her boots occasionally scuffing the rail to one side. It was disorienting trying to judge the distance between the sleepers and at times she stumbled and almost fell on the uneven surface. But she kept her balance and managed to keep pace with the others, although after more than an hour of hard walking and in spite of the cold she was perspiring from the exertion. Then Marco stopped and knelt on the track, and like the others she did the same, silently waiting, holding her breath, her ears alert for any sound.

A minute later she heard an owl hooting, and Marco responded by cupping his hands and replying twice with the same sound. A light appeared on the line ahead and swung to and fro for a moment before vanishing again. Marco stood up, and as the group moved forward Elspeth saw a figure holding an oil lamp shrouded with a hood, a faint orange glow faintly visible beneath the cover. Marco greeted the figure who silently led them down the embankment and into an adjoining field.

It was even darker down here and without the railway track to guide her Elspeth knew even less of what lay below her feet. But her lack of vision had heightened her other senses, and now she could hear and feel the crunch of maize stalks below her boots that told her they were in a field of corn. They came to a hedgerow and the guide let them through a gap into another field. Ahead of her the stars suddenly disappeared as a high shadow loomed against the night sky. She heard a hinge creak as a door was opened and then felt herself swept forward into a warm dark interior with the pungent smell of animals and hay. The hinge creaked again as the door was closed and the hood covering the oil lamp was pulled away, flooding the room with light, and revealing they were inside a barn.

The tension of the past hour lifted in an instant, and Elspeth saw the Chetniks smiling with relief as they removed their bandoliers of ammunition and slumped onto bales of straw. Marco ordered two of the men on guard duty and gave instructions for sacking to be placed underneath the doors to prevent light from spilling outside. Elspeth flopped against a hay bale, removed her boots and stretched her legs out in front of her. She could see that most of the other Chetniks were also in various states of relaxation: taking food from their knapsacks, talking quietly amongst themselves, cleaning their weapons. But then she saw the young soldier with the calf wound lying on top of a hay bale opposite her and she padded across to him in her stockinged feet to untie the bandage around his leg.

The bleeding had stopped but the calf was badly swollen, the skin a dusky purple colour and firm to the touch, like cooked steak. She was troubled at how quickly infection had set in, but gave him a smile of encouragement and asked Anya if any of the men had surgical spirit or alcohol with them. One of the chetniks pulled a bottle of cognac from his knapsack, and even though she knew it would hurt him Elspeth poured some of the spirit directly into the wound, washing out as much dirt and debris as she could; the soldier flinched but made no sound. Then, with Anya and Marco watching her, she re-bound the leg with a scarf that another of the Chetniks gave her.

'What you think?' Anya asked, after Elspeth had finished dressing the wound.

'There's already infection. It might even be early gangrene.'

'Gangrene?' Anya's eyes grew wide.

'I'm afraid so. And there's not much I can do to stop it progressing. You should tell Marco he won't be able to walk tomorrow, so he must find him a wagon or some other transport.'

Anya translated for Marco, who nodded and then walked away to confer with Luka.

'Every Chetnik has two hours of guard duty,' Anya said. 'I must do mine at midnight, but now we have time to rest. We must be quiet, Ellie, but we can talk.'

She led Elspeth back to where she had left her boots

and they sat beside each other, resting their backs against the hay bale behind them. Elspeth's mind was still racing from all that had happened to her that evening; fleeing the hospital with Gabriel, encountering the German patrol, their rescue by Luka. But the realisation that it was actually Anya sitting beside her gave her the most surreal feeling of all. 'I still can't believe it's you, Anya,' Elspeth said. 'Why, when we were in London, could you not tell us you were from this region?'

Anya gave a rueful shrug. 'I am sorry I couldn't tell you.' She smiled. 'But now we have time for me to explain everything.'

As they sat beside each other, bathed in the soft glow from the oil lamp, Anya told Elspeth her story: of how she had been born Anya Zerajic in a small village outside Sarajevo, one of three daughters to the village schoolteacher; and of how her cousin Bogdan Zerajic – a law student at the University of Belgrade and member of the nationalist organisation Young Bosnia – wanted to rid the country of their Austro-Hungarian occupiers.

'Bogdan was very brave,' Anya told Elspeth. 'Two years ago he tried to assassinate the Governor of Bosnia, General Varesanin, and when he failed he turned the pistol on himself rather than risk capture. The police burned his body, but kept his head on display in a museum.'

'Oh, how awful,' said Elspeth, shocked at the barbarity.

'And then Varesanin's successor, Oskar Potiorek, turned his skull into an ink pot.'

Elspeth's hands flew to her mouth in horror as Anya continued.

'The Austrian Secret Service, the OSS, arrested and tortured several members of Bogdan's family. I was also at the University of Belgrade, studying English. I had also been a member of Young Bosnia, and the OSS wanted to bring me in for questioning. So I was forced to flee my country.'

'I can imagine how difficult that must have been.'

Anya nodded. 'So I fled: first to Paris and then London. In London I met Grace and joined the WSPU. But I knew the WSPU were watched by Special Branch and I was scared that if they find out I am Bosnian, they may tell OSS agents in the Austro-Hungarian embassy.'

Then she told Elspeth about the day she heard that Gavrilo Princip – an admirer of Bogdan and fellow member of Young Bosnia – had assassinated Franz Ferdinand.

'The happiest day of my life, Ellie, because we avenge Bogdan. Now I think war will come. But I say nothing. I keep quiet. And when war begins I decide to go home because I want to fight for my country.'

'So that's why you disappeared,' Elspeth whispered with dawning realisation. 'It wasn't anything to do with the WSPU stopping the arson campaign?'

'No. It was only because of the war.'

'So you weren't angry with us for not wanting to kill McCarthy?'

Anya sighed. 'I was angry at how police oppress women, but inside my heart, I know you are a doctor and cannot kill.'

'Is that why you decided to become a sworn virgin…
I think you call it *Virginesh*?'

'You know of this tradition?'

'Luka tried to explain it to me, but I'm not sure I
fully understand.'

'It is a tradition in the Balkans. A woman must
swear a vow of chastity, and then is allowed to live and
dress as a man, to carry a gun, to do all the things that
men do.'

'But why would you choose to become a man?'

'For many reasons,' Anya replied. 'After Bogdan's
death there were no sons in my family, and a family
considers itself cursed without male heirs. Also I want to
fight in the war, but I cannot join the Serbian army as I
was born in Bosnia. So I decided to join a Cheta. But the
Chetniks do not take women, so…' She shrugged. 'And
also… I am happy as a man.'

Elspeth raised an eyebrow. 'You're happy to live your
life as a man?'

Anya smiled. 'Yes, I am very happy. Before – when I
was young – I did not feel like a girl. I wanted to play like
a boy, to run, to fight, to climb trees, to do everything
like a boy. For me now, being a man is good. From now
on, my life will be as a man.'

Anya had always been an enigma, Elspeth thought:
her look and dress sense, her hatred of McCarthy, her
love for Grace. But with her explanation as to why she
had become a sworn virgin, she finally made sense.
Elspeth sat forward and clasped her knees to her chest.
'When you disappeared without telling anyone,' she

said, 'Vera was most worried. She thought you might try to harm McCarthy, or maybe even us…'

'Harm *you*?' Anya shook her head. 'No, I would never harm you, Ellie.'

'Then we heard you'd gone back to Paris and taken a train for Marseille.'

'Yes. And from Marseille I took a boat to Salonika.' A grin spread across her face as she leant forwards so her eyes were level with Elspeth's. She hugged her knees to her chest and rocked back and forth with amusement. 'You thought I was a fanatic, and that I might hurt you? And then you go to Serbia,' – she began to laugh – 'where I have gone!' She pressed her face into her knees and snorted, trying to stifle her laughter as the other Chetniks stared at her. Then she lifted her head again. 'Shh, must keep quiet,' she whispered.

'Well, you were acting strangely,' Elspeth whispered back, feeling a mixture of stupidity and annoyance. 'What else were we supposed to think?'

'I would never harm you, Ellie. You are my sisters, you and Vera and Sylvia…' Anya hesitated and sighed. 'I would like very much to see Vera again.'

'Well, she and Sylvie should be in Krusevac by now. If we go there, you can see them both.'

Anya grimaced. 'I don't know, Ellie. This attack is too much: the Germans in the north, the Bulgars in the east and south…' She shook her head. 'My Cheta will travel south to the Kosovan plain, where we make last stand. Probably we die. If we be lucky, maybe we live…'

'Oh you'll live, Anya,' Elspeth said cheerfully.

Anya gave a sad smile that told Elspeth she didn't believe this, but then her face brightened. 'Maybe. But first we go to Krusevac – is on way to Kosovo – and I will see Vera again.' She shook her head and turned her face away. 'Vera in Krusevac,' she said quietly to herself as if she could not believe the news. Then she blinked several times, and Elspeth was fairly certain she could see moisture in Anya' eyes.

★★★

Anya was called away to do her guard duty and Elspeth lay down and wrapped herself in straw, closing her eyes and immediately falling into the deep, dreamless slumber of the exhausted. When she was shaken awake by one of the Chetniks the next morning, it seemed as if she had only been asleep for a few minutes. But from the light coming through the slats of the barn she could see that dawn had already broken, and so she put her boots back on and went over to the wounded Chetnik. As she had feared, his condition had deteriorated overnight; his forehead was hot to the touch, his eyes glazed, his leg more swollen than the previous evening. When she gently pressed the skin of his calf, a trickle of malodorous grey pus oozed through the scarf bandage: it did not look good.

She went outside the barn and saw it had turned cold, a freezing rain falling from the sky. Luka and Marco had already spoken to the farmer who owned the barn, and a small four-wheeled canvas-covered wagon, pulled by two yoked oxen, was standing outside the door. The wounded soldier was carefully lifted into the back of the wagon, and Marco asked Elspeth to sit alongside the youth so she could attend to him during the journey. Then, with one of the Chetniks leading the oxen and the others walking alongside them, their small convoy set off.

They made reasonable progress that morning, the wind whipping the rain into the wagon sides, causing the canvas to snap and flutter as they trundled along a muddy dirt track. Elspeth was glad to shelter inside the wagon and did her best to care for the youth, but he steadily deteriorated, becoming more restless and confused, finally slipping into a coma.

The small track broadened into a wider road that ran alongside a fast-flowing river. Anya told Elspeth that they were now in the Sumadija Valley, which would lead them all the way to Krusevac. They were passing close to the town of Cuprija – more than half-way to Krusevac, Anya said – when the road left the riverside and climbed higher up the side of the valley. The muddy track dipped and rose, but by the afternoon they had managed to find a level place to stop and rest the oxen while Luka, Marco and the others watched Elspeth remove the scarf from the boy's leg. The purple discolouration on his calf had spread to his thigh, and Elspeth could smell the distinctive odour of necrotic tissue. Underneath her fingertips she felt the crackle of tiny pockets of gas and knew the youth had fulminating gas gangrene; even if she had the instruments to amputate the leg, he would not survive. Marco looked particularly upset as Anya translated Elspeth's opinion and he nodded, then squeezed Elspeth's wrist, giving her a look that told her she should keep trying.

They started up again, the road climbing even higher on the valley side as it followed the river upstream. The rain became heavier and Elspeth saw the slope of the valley rising above her head, with rivulets of water streaming down from the rain-sodden ground, trees tilted at outlandish angles from earlier landslips. Fifty yards below her, the river was a churning cauldron, but as they followed the road upstream she suddenly saw a solid wall of water and realised it was a waterfall, a rainbow arcing majestically in the spray mist suspended over the rocks beneath.

Standing out colourfully against the drab, muddy-grey surroundings it was the first inspiring thing she had seen for days, and it immediately lifted her spirits, giving her hope that everything would work out for the best. As they drew level with the waterfall, across the far side of the river, in the distance beyond, she saw a small stone cottage with wisps of smoke spiralling from the chimney. Looking like a goat- or sheep-herder's dwelling, it reminded her so strongly of Scotland that for a moment she felt a twinge of homesickness as she recalled similar cottages from her village on the Isle of Skye.

The oxen continued to pull the wagon up the valley and now their small convoy encountered increasing numbers of refugees. Most of the civilians were on foot, all looking cold and wet and depressed, but a few luckier ones were riding in wagons, their bedraggled oxen pulling carts overloaded with bundles of clothes and furniture. Elspeth peered through the canvas opening at the front of her wagon, and over the heads of the oxen and the Chetnik leading them, she saw the long column of refugees stretch ahead of her, dipping into the hollows on the road, then reappearing on the crests, like some prehistoric reptile slithering across the hills.

It was raining hard now, and the procession of wagons had to stop and skirt landslides on the road caused by rainwater gushing off the hills above. A short while before dusk the wounded soldier became even less responsive, his breathing an intermittent gasping, his pulse thready and irregular. Elspeth knew he was near to death, and as his face and hands were icy cold she took off her coat and cape and wrapped him in them. It was the least she could do, to keep him warm for his final moments.

The convoy was forced to stop as they came upon another narrow point on the road, caused by a further landslip, and dusk was falling as Elspeth watched the refugees ahead of her filter around the obstruction. She looked up at the slope of the valley rising above the wagon and saw rainwater gushing down onto the road, the only noise the thundering of the river below and the young soldier's stertorous gasps. Then the noise of his breathing fell away, and when she reached for the young soldier's pulse she could no longer find one.

The dead Chetnik's eyes were half open, and as Elspeth leant forward to close them she felt the wagon shudder, then heard a sudden loud rushing noise and several cries of alarm. Looking through the canvas opening, she saw a wall of earth and trees sliding downhill towards her, and a split second later the wagon shook as a wave of mud slammed into its side. Wood splintered as the yoke snapped and she saw the oxen scramble free of their wooden harness. Then she was knocked off her feet as the landslide pushed the wagon off the road and onto the slope below; a moment later the wagon started to trundle downhill towards the river. She had only just managed to struggle to her feet when, like a boat being launched down a slipway, the wagon splashed into the river in a plume of spray, and Elspeth was thrown face forward into the water that had flooded over the floor of the wagon, gasping with shock at the icy coldness of it.

Scrambling to her feet again she realised – with relief – that although she was shin-deep in water, the wagon was still afloat. But it was already drifting quickly downstream, the broken yoke dragging behind like a floating anchor. She managed to get to the canvas opening, and looking back she saw Anya and Marco sprinting frantically downhill and then along the riverbank as they tried to keep pace with her. However, the current was strong, and the wagon accelerated so quickly that within a few seconds they were lost from sight.

Something touched her shin: she looked down and saw the body of the dead Chetnik – still entangled in her coat and cape – bobbing in the water by her knees, and realised that the wagon had not sunk any lower: it was floating like a raft. So she tried to stay calm, tried to think, tried to work out what she should do. She would have to leave the wagon soon – she had not forgotten the waterfall they had passed earlier – but the current was strong and she knew that if she were to jump into the river and try to swim to safety she would be swept away.

But then she realised that as well as drifting downstream, the wagon was also drifting towards the far riverbank. And after another minute – and knowing she was now very near to the waterfall – there was a sudden judder, and the wagon slowed as its wheels scraped the riverbed. Thank goodness; shallow water, she thought, as she stepped out and felt the riverbed below her feet, gasping again as cold water reached up to her thighs. The current was still strong, but, holding her arms out for balance, she managed to push against the weight of water and wade ashore.

She paused for a moment on the bank, shaking the water from her skirt and watching as the current caught hold of the wagon again, dragging it downstream. Dusk had almost fallen and with it the temperature. She began to shiver violently as she stood in the semi-darkness, her sodden skirt clinging to her legs. She looked back across the river; it was too far to swim back safely, so she would have to find shelter on this side for the night. A sudden crashing sound echoed towards her and she knew that the wagon must have gone over the waterfall onto the rocks below.

And then she remembered the cottage she had seen earlier, when they had drawn level with the waterfall on the way up the valley.

She scrambled up the bank onto dry land and hurried downstream as quickly as she could. Her boots squelched with every step and her wet skirt clung to her legs, but she dared not stop as there was so very little daylight left. Coming across a dirt track running parallel to the river, she decided to follow this downstream, then rounded a curve in the road and, with relief, saw the cottage come into view. A light was shining through the window and smoke was spiralling from the chimney.

A dog began to bark; the door to the cottage opened and an old man and young boy suddenly appeared. The boy was holding a shaggy-haired dog on a leash, which was barking and straining towards her, while the old man – grey beard and hair – had an ancient shotgun in his arms. Elspeth, hugging her arms to her chest, could barely speak for the chattering of her teeth, but managed to say the words she had heard from so many wounded Serbian soldiers when they first arrived at her hospital.

'*Po… mozi… m-m-mi.*'

The old man listened to her plea for help and lowered his gun while the young boy shouted at the dog, which promptly stopped barking and sat back on its haunches. Looking carefully at Elspeth for a moment, the old man held a hand out to her and motioned for her to come forward. She was shivering too much to do or say anything but follow him as he led her inside.

It was a small, single-storey stone dwelling, little more than one room. A fire in the hearth on the wall in front of her with a cooking pot suspended from a metal bar. It took her several minutes to stop shaking and recover her composure as she stood in front of the fire, feeling the blissful heat of the flames. Eventually she was able to speak, and, using a mixture of her limited Serbian and hand signs to explain her situation to the pair, she eventually managed to establish that the old man was called Stefan, and the boy – his grandson – was called Milo and was eight years old. After a while, the old man produced a blanket, which he held between himself and Elspeth, and she was grateful for the modesty this provided as she removed her sodden boots and skirt and then wrapped herself in several goatskins that Milo pushed underneath the blanket. Sitting on the floor by the fire, wrapped in the animal skins, she watched as Milo put a ladle into the pot over the fire and handed her a small bowl of goat stew. The warmth of the stew – the first hot food she had eaten for two days – was like a tonic, and she felt the heat return to her fingers and toes. As she ate, the boy watched, smiling shyly as he sat beside her on a straw mattress, stroking the dog, which lay at his feet.

Completely spent, Elspeth could feel her eyes closing from fatigue. The old man sat in a chair on the other side of the hearth, puffing contentedly on a pipe, periodically looking at her or into the flames of the fire. An oil lamp hanging from the low rafter threw out a soft yellow glow, and the only sounds were an occasional whimper from the sleeping dog and the intermittent sucking noises made as the old man drew on his pipe. As the boy put another log on the fire, sparks jumped off the embers and Elspeth arranged her damp clothes and boots in front of the hearth. Then, overcome by tiredness, she curled up on the floor, closed her eyes, and fell asleep.

She woke briefly in the middle of the night to find the dog nestled against her flank. Rain was hammering on the cottage roof and the fire had gone out, but she was warm inside the goatskins and as it was still dark outside the window she fell asleep again. The next time she woke, daylight was streaming into the cottage, and the man, the boy and the dog were nowhere to be seen. However, the fire had been rekindled and when she reached out and touched her clothes she found they had almost fully dried.

She quickly dressed. Going outside, she saw that it had stopped raining, but a drop in temperature had caused ice to form on the puddles. A tinkling of bells alerted her and she found the old man and the boy tending a herd of goats at the back of the cottage. She walked across to them, and by pointing at the river and miming walking, she tried to indicate that she wished to cross back to the other side. The old man seemed to understand her and spoke to the boy, who disappeared inside the cottage and reappeared a little while later with a small parcel. From the smell Elspeth could tell that it contained goats cheese and bread, which she was very happy to take. She gathered that Milo was going to show her the way, and so she smiled at the old man, then stretched out her free hand and touched him gently on the forearm.

'*Hvala puno*,' she said, and the old man smiled and nodded at her Serbian attempt at "Thank you".

Taking the dog with him, Milo led her back upstream. Across the opposite side of the river and higher up on the road, Elspeth could see the congested column of refugees as they continued to flee southwards. They passed the point where the landslide had thrown her into the river and after another mile came upon a primitive footbridge – boards of wood slung between two ropes, a third rope above as a handrail – which stretched across the water. It looked very flimsy to her, but Milo tied the dog to a nearby tree and she followed him as he stepped onto the first plank. In her still slightly damp skirt it was not easy going and Elspeth dared not look down at the torrent rushing below. However, she kept her nerve and soon was across the bridge and on the far bank of the river.

She shook Milo's hand and then watched as he walked back across the bridge, untied the dog, and, with a wave, started back the way he had come.

Elspeth scrambled up the muddy incline and finally arrived just below the surface of the road. One of the refugees walking past – a young man leading a mule piled with clothes – leant over the edge and extended a hand to her. She thanked him in Serbian as he pulled her onto the road, and he smiled at her before moving on. She brushed the mud from her skirt and then stood for a moment to catch her breath, watching the faces of the people walking past.

Now she felt truly lost: on her own and inadequately dressed, in a country she barely knew, trying to get to a place she had never been to before. There were no familiar faces in the masses that were walking by, and there was nobody to help her but herself. And then she thought of what Sylvia and Vera and Gabriel would do.

'Come on, Elspeth,' she told herself. 'Stop moaning and get on with it.'

And so she slipped back into the column of refugees.

3

Klagenfurt, November 1915

It was a crisp and clear autumnal morning, the mist above the buildings bordering Klagenfurt Central Square having lifted some hours ago to reveal a sky that was now an iridescent blue. Gabriel sat at a table outside Café Fruehauf on the square, the sunlight flickering through the leaves of a nearby beech tree as he waited for the chief to arrive. He closed his eyes and tilted his face towards the weak November sun, the light glimmering pinkly through the skin of his eyelids. It was wonderful to be home again, he thought, sitting outdoors, warm and comfortable in his army greatcoat, with nothing to do except relax. As he waited for the chief to appear, his mind drifted back to the events of the past few days, and in particular to Elspeth.

The last time he had seen her was more than a week ago, when they had run into the German patrol: thank God Luka had spotted them. He had watched the Chetniks lead Elspeth away towards the station and then lost sight of her in the smoke and darkness. He dared not think she hadn't made it safely to Krusevac, but that night had been very dangerous. Gabriel had only just managed to make it back to the First Reserve Hospital unscathed. The following morning the German 11th Army had marched into Kragujevac to take formal possession of the town and Gabriel had met their medical team. They were particularly interested to hear how the typhus epidemic had been contained, but Gabriel had detected the usual German disdain towards all things Austrian. Nevertheless he had answered them as best he could and had to admire their efficiency as, by the end of that first day, a full team of German army surgeons were in place in both the First Reserve and Scottish Women's hospitals.

A day later the Austrian 3rd Army medical column arrived and Gabriel was formally relieved of all medical duties and ordered to report to the Prisoner Repatriation Section – PRS – which had set up its offices in an empty warehouse near the railway station.

Inside the hanger-like space of the warehouse, a long line of recently released prisoners were waiting to be registered, and after a long wait, Gabriel had eventually been seen by a staff sergeant, who informed him that the Austrian 6th had redeployed to the Italian border in southern Austria, not far from his home town of Klagenfurt. But before Gabriel could re-join the 6th, he would have to be examined by one of the PRS physicians.

He had queued again in front of another desk, and after a while was seen by a fresh-faced doctor who looked as though he had only just come out of medical school. The young man was respectfully friendly as he weighed Gabriel, asked him to strip to the waist and listened carefully to his chest. But when he removed the stethoscope and told Gabriel to get dressed, there had been a serious look in his eyes.

'I'm afraid you're not fit to return to duty at the moment,' he'd told Gabriel. 'You've lost a good deal of weight and there are some crackles in your right lung apex. It could be nothing, but it might be TB. Have you any other symptoms – cough, night sweats, bloodstained phlegm in the morning – that sort of thing?'

Gabriel had shaken his head. 'No. I feel quite well really, only rather tired, as you might expect.'

'Ideally you need a chest roentogram, but the Serbs have destroyed all their X-ray equipment.' He had produced a sheet of paper, written on it in pen, dried the ink by blowing on the letter and then given it to Gabriel.

'I've signed you off for a month,' he'd said. 'I think you should go home to Klagenfurt and have the roentogram taken there. If it's all clear, then report to the Army Medical Board in Vienna at the end of the month: they will decide if you're fit enough to re-join your unit. And if the roentogram shows a shadow… Well, you don't need me to tell you what that means.'

Gabriel nodded, and although he tried to look concerned he felt a weight lift from his shoulders. He knew he didn't have TB – he had seen enough patients to know the symptoms and signs – but a month's leave from the army was just what he needed.

He had arrived in Klagenfurt the previous morning and gone straight to the hospital to have his chest roentogram taken. It was, as he had suspected, completely normal. He'd spent the first night at his father's small apartment near the square, and then, after waking early, had quietly dressed and gone out for a stroll to remind himself of the splendour of the city. After his walk he had taken a seat outside the café, enjoying a leisurely breakfast as he waited for the chief to arrive.

He lowered his face from the sun and opened his eyes. Klagenfurt was closer to Venice than Vienna, and many of the shops, cafés, and government buildings bordering the town's central square were of a baroque Italian design, with vivid pink and yellow renaissance decoration. Gabriel studied the faces of the people walking past his table. Conspicuous in his uniform he attracted numerous glances, and through the smiles and nods of acknowledgments he could tell that the citizens of Klagenfurt were still proud of the Austrian soldier. However Gabriel also saw a despondency in the eyes of these ordinary people, undoubtedly due to the terrible losses their army had suffered in Serbia and Russia.

And now Italy had declared war on Austria. Klagenfurt was close to the Italian border, and on his walk that morning Gabriel had seen several convalescing soldiers, pale-faced men with arms or legs in plaster, sitting on their own at a café table, a half-empty bottle of schnapps or wine in front of them.

The 6th Army were transferring their wounded to hospitals in Klagenfurt, and Gabriel had been delighted to learn that chief Fischer was temporarily based in the town. Gazing distractedly at the people strolling by his table, Gabriel suddenly noticed a tall, grey-bearded man in uniform striding through the square towards the café entrance. It had been a while since he last saw him, but the straight-backed profile of the chief was unmistakable. Gabriel called across, and the chief stopped for a moment – even at this distance, Gabriel could see the smile that creased his mentor's face – then walked briskly towards him.

'My dear boy,' the chief said, arriving at Gabriel's table. 'I'm so pleased to see you.'

'It's good to see you, too,' Gabriel replied, grinning at the chief's enthusiastic double-handed handshake. 'I can't believe it's more than a year since we last met.'

'I'm very relieved you're alive. We lost so many men you know.' Gabriel nodded as the two men sat down, the chief scanning Gabriel's face as he sat opposite him. 'You're very gaunt. I can see you've lost quite a bit of weight. Nothing serious I hope?'

'They thought it might be TB. But the roentogram is all clear.'

'So you just need a bit of feeding up – that it?'

'Yes. A year as a prisoner does wonders for one's figure.'

The chief laughed. 'Well, let's see if we can't do something about that.' He snapped his fingers at a waiter loitering in the heat of the café entrance. 'Two coffees, please,' he said when the waiter arrived, 'and a large portion of strudel with extra cream.'

For the next hour the two men sat in the weak autumn sunlight, drinking coffee, the chief smoking his pipe, Gabriel describing his experiences as a prisoner, the horror of the typhus epidemic, falling ill with typhus, being nursed back to health by the Scottish women, and of course Harry Plotz and his typhus vaccine.

In return, the chief told Gabriel how the battered remnants of the 6th Army had been transferred to the mountains on the Austrian-Italian border. Gabriel listened to the hellish tale of mountain fighting; hand-to-hand combat on ice-covered rock, no trees or bushes for cover, no trenches for protection. However, the Austrians were fighting a purely defensive battle, the chief said, and so far had been able to hold their positions.

And it was while Gabriel was listening to the chief's story, that he became aware of a stranger in the square – an older-looking man who at first had been walking past their table – who had suddenly stopped, turned around, and begun to stare at Gabriel. At first Gabriel thought it was the typical civilian veneration for anyone in a soldier's uniform. But the stranger's eyes flicked between Gabriel and the chief, almost as if he recognised them both. Indeed the man looked vaguely familiar to Gabriel: dressed in typical hill-walking clothes – boots, gaiters, leather cap and eagle's feather – and carrying a knapsack and an antler-handled walking stick. There was something about him – an air, a manner – which stirred a memory in Gabriel's mind. Then the man lifted a hand to remove his leather cap.

'Good Lord,' Gabriel exclaimed, sitting bolt upright in his chair, jaw sagging in astonishment.

The chief swivelled to follow Gabriel's open-mouthed gaze as the stranger stepped forward. Gabriel saw his mentor's eyes initially widen in surprise, followed by the briefest flicker of contempt, which had vanished by the time he stood to greet the visitor.

'Field Marshall Potiorek,' the chief said, extending a hand. 'What an unexpected pleasure.'

To Gabriel the moment was surreal. The last time he'd seen Potiorek had been more than a year ago, when Potiorek had been in full uniform, standing in front of a roomful of officers, ordering the invasion of Serbia. But the figure standing in front of Gabriel now was almost unrecognisable as the man who had once governed the whole of Bosnia and started this great European war. Without his uniform, Potiorek could so easily have been mistaken for any other ordinary citizen returning from a morning walk in the mountains. Except for the look of intensity in those eyes; two cold black pebbles now fixed on the chief's face.

'I'm no longer a Field Marshall,' Potiorek replied. 'I'm retired. Although even in retirement, I am still entitled to use my former non-combat rank.'

It was a moment before the chief understood. 'Oh. Of course, General Potiorek.'

'I would prefer that. I'm not unhappy to be out of the limelight. My days of service to the Emperor are over.'

The chief motioned towards Gabriel. 'You do remember Captain Bayer, General?'

Potiorek made a quarter turn towards him. 'Of

course.' He bowed his head. 'How could I forget? I recognised you as I walked by just now, Captain.'

'General.' Gabriel gave a brief formal nod of his head in return. Potiorek was looking at him strangely, as if he had something to say.

'Actually, Captain, I'm pleased to have met you again.' Potiorek blinked, then exhaled deeply. 'I never properly thanked you, for what you tried to do that terrible day. The Archduke was mortally wounded, but you did your best. For that, I give you my gratitude.'

Gabriel – surprised that the topic of conversation had so quickly turned to that awful day – opened his mouth to respond but could not find any words. It was the chief who finally broke the awkward silence. 'Please General, won't you join us for a drink?'

Potiorek hesitated and then glanced around. Although only one other outside table was occupied, the older couple sitting at it were regarding him with undisguised curiosity. 'Forgive me, good doctor, but I'd rather not,' Potiorek replied. 'I don't like to be seen in public. I normally avoid the city centre; I was only passing through from my morning walk in the mountains—'

'Please, General,' the chief said, 'we would consider it a great honour if you would join us, even for one drink.'

'No,' Potiorek said, looking uncomfortable at the chief's persistence. By now, other passers-by in the square were staring at him as they walked by. 'Thank you for the invitation, but—'

'Please, Herr General,' Gabriel said, finally finding

his voice. 'I would also like you to sit and share a drink with us.'

'I'm sorry, Captain.' Potiorek began to back away.

'It would help me if you could stay and talk,' Gabriel said. 'Because I was captured last December.'

Potiorek stopped. 'Oh. I see.' He straightened his shoulders. 'You were taken prisoner?'

'Yes.'

'And released when the Germans broke through last month?'

'Yes.' Gabriel stared into Potiorek's eyes 'I would very much like to understand what happened.'

Potiorek nodded thoughtfully. 'Very well, Captain. I'll stay for one drink.' He glanced at the couple sitting nearby, still watching him with interest. 'But we're in the shade now' – he motioned towards the entrance to the café – 'so perhaps we should go inside?'

The chief nodded and led Potiorek towards the door. A blast of steamy warmth greeted Gabriel as he followed them into the café, which was full of people eating lunch. Almost immediately, Gabriel was aware of a lull in conversations as customers looked up from their tables to take in the newcomers. From the glowering glances and whispering-behind-hands, Gabriel gleaned that Potiorek was well known in Klagenfurt, but not well liked.

Ignoring the almost-palpable antipathy in the room, the chief confidently led them towards a small table near the back of the café. While Gabriel and Potiorek removed their coats, the chief snapped his fingers at a waiter standing by the bar and ordered a bottle of Zweigelt red and three glasses. As the waiter went to fetch the wine, Gabriel saw that most of the other customers in the café were still silently watching them.

'So, Herr General: why have you moved to Klagenfurt?' the chief asked, cheerily ignoring the hostile atmosphere in the room as he settled himself into his chair.

'When I relinquished the Governorship of Bosnia,' Potiorek quietly replied, 'I lost my grace-and-favour apartment in the Konak. Then I resigned from the army...' he paused, as if the memory gave him pain. 'Anyway, I decided to move back to Austria. Vienna is too public a place for me, but my brother has a house on the outskirts of Klagenfurt. We are just two old men, two old bachelors, living a simple life. I read, write a bit, take a walk most days in the mountains or by the lakes. I chop wood, attend to the garden. The house is comfortable and has everything we need. The only item I took with me from the Konak is the chaise longue from my bedroom.'

Gabriel suddenly recalled the patterned Ottoman couch in Potiorek's dressing room. Lying – dying – on the couch he could clearly see the Archduke in his bloodstained tunic, calling out for his wife...

'Why of all things,' Gabriel asked, 'did you take that with you?'

'As a permanent reminder,' Potiorek quickly replied, as if he had always expected to be asked the question, 'of the Archduke's final moments.'

There was silence as Gabriel absorbed Potiorek's reply, but before he could think of a suitable response, the waiter returned with the bottle of Zweigelt and three glasses.

'Good health, gentlemen,' the chief said, raising his glass in the air once the wine had been poured.

'*Prost*,' replied Gabriel. Potiorek nodded, then lifted his glass. There was the gentle clink of crystal as the three men toasted their meeting. Gabriel drank some of the heavy red wine, which was pleasantly warm and smooth on his tongue. Potiorek drained half of his glass in one quick swallow, before replacing it on the table and turning towards Gabriel again.

'You see, Captain, I carry a heavy burden over the Archduke's death. I still feel that fate dealt me a harsh hand, and that it was an unlikely set of circumstances that led to his assassination. Ultimately, however, I must accept that final responsibility lay with me: I invited him to Sarajevo and he was under my protection. That protection failed, and I will have to live with the consequences of that for the rest of my life. And believe me, Captain, when I say that living with that knowledge is like a life sentence.'

Potiorek's openness was surprising, thought Gabriel. He had expected the general to be more defensive. This should be a good opportunity to ask some hard questions. He glanced across at the chief and saw his mentor lean back in his chair, giving Gabriel a subtle nod as if to say, "go ahead and ask".

'And what about the failure of the invasion of Serbia,'

Gabriel continued. 'Do you accept responsibility for that, too?'

A thin smile appeared. 'We now know that our plans had been given away by Colonel Redl. The Russians knew all our troop dispositions and logistics, where we would strike, in what strength and order. They passed all this information to the Serbs. Should I be blamed for such a disadvantage?'

'But we had known about Redl's treason for some time, so why weren't the plans for war changed?'

'Because there was not enough time. Once it was clear that Russia would support Serbia, our best hope of victory lay in a fast pre-emptive strike against the Serbs.'

'Maybe *too* fast,' Gabriel said. 'You pushed our troops forward so quickly that we badly over-extended our supply lines. Then, when our exhausted soldiers were attacked, they had insufficient ammunition to defend themselves.'

Potiorek shifted uncomfortably in his chair. 'The Serbs appeared to be on the verge of total collapse and my judgement was that one final push would finish them off. But then – as luck would have it – the French resupplied them with ammunition and… well, you know the rest.'

'I saw General Appel die from typhus,' Gabriel said quietly. 'He was in the bed next to me when I was in hospital.'

Potiorek nodded. 'Poor Michael.'

'Many others died from typhus.'

'You cannot blame me for those deaths, Captain.' Gabriel heard an edge in Potiorek's voice.

'But what about the atrocities on the Serbian population? I saw civilians executed, women hanged like... like...' Gabriel could not find the words to describe what he had seen.

For several seconds Potiorek said nothing. 'There were a number of unfortunate incidents where the actions of Serbian civilians caused the deaths of Austrian soldiers,' Potiorek said, a steely tone to his voice. 'Incidents where Serbs were found hiding arms and ammunition, or supplying food to the Chetniks, or giving away our positions. And where there was proof of such infractions,' he shrugged, 'well, Captain, military law is harsh, but that has long been the nature of warfare.'

'And the orders you issued prior to the first offensive, that no mercy or kindness was to be extended to the Serbian population? Was that not an incitement to the men to commit the brutalities and excesses I witnessed?'

'I knew well before this war began that this would be a total war, one country against another, one people against another,' Potiorek replied. 'It was always going to be bloody and brutal. The assassination of the Archduke was designed to goad us into a war. The Serbs are responsible for that. My orders were appropriate for the nature of the conflict—'

'Appropriate?' Gabriel said, feeling his shoulders tighten in anger. He suddenly realised he had raised his voice and the room had grown deathly quiet. Glancing away from Potiorek, he saw the other patrons staring at him. He turned back to the General, trying to keep his voice level as he spoke. 'How can it be appropriate to hang a woman, to allow her children to watch their mother strangle on the end of a rope—'

'The issue is not as simple as you might think.' Potiorek's voice was soft again, but his eyes remained cold and hard. 'Both of you' – he glanced across at the chief – 'are medical men, guided by your Hippocratic oath, which behoves you to behave with kindness and compassion. But the job of a soldier is to win at all costs, and too strong a sense of compassion can be fatal. If you take your foot off your opponent's throat, he will come back at you and kill you. No, Captain, my orders were consistent with the compassion of war.'

He paused, waiting for a response, but Gabriel – frustrated by his fluent justification – could not think of a suitable reply.

'It is easy to assume, Captain,' Potiorek continued, his fingertips steepled below his chin, 'that I am some sort of demon, or madman, or incompetent. But I assure you I am none of these. I have been told that there will be a military commission when the war is over – whenever that will be – and that this commission will examine the reasons for our military failures. I have been told that I will have to give an account of all my actions, which will then be made part of a public record. The Viennese newspapers have speculated over my mental health since the Archduke's death. I have read reports that either I must be mad – in which case I ought to be in an asylum –

or if sane, then I am criminally culpable and should face the hangman.'

He said these last words very matter-of-factly, his face betraying no emotion as he paused for a moment before continuing. 'Well, I believe that I deserve neither course of action. When the time comes, however, I will happily face that commission, and I will tell them exactly what I've told you today. And I will leave it in the hands of my peers, and my God, and will accept whatever they find, whatever they decide.'

The entire café appeared to be watching their table. Potiorek glanced about the room and took in the sea of hostile faces, then reached for his half-empty glass and drained it in one long swallow. He set the glass back down on the table with a thud. 'Gentlemen, I have said as much as I am prepared to say.' He stood up quickly, pushing his chair back – which scraped noisily on the tiled café floor – and putting a hand inside his jacket pocket to pull out a fifty krone note.

The chief was also standing, his hand on Potiorek's forearm. 'No, please, Herr General, we invited you—'

Potiorek shrugged the hand away. 'No. I insist.' He placed the note underneath the wine bottle, then turned to Gabriel. 'I apologise for what you must have suffered, Captain. I hope you come through the rest of the war unscathed.' With a click of his heels he quickly bowed his head to both men, before turning away and weaving between the tables towards the front of the café. The eyes of the entire room followed him as the entrance door swung open for a moment – allowing in a blast of cool autumn air – and closed with a clatter. Then, like a slow wave gently breaking over a shingle beach, the noise of whispering grew as the citizens of Klagenfurt put their heads conspiratorially together again, and began an excited gossiping about Potiorek's unexpected appearance.

'Sweet mercy,' Gabriel said. 'He was the last person I ever expected to see.'

'You did well in getting him to admit his mistakes.' The chief sat down again. 'He is finished now, of course, a sad shell of what he used to be.'

'I almost didn't recognise him,' Gabriel said, settling himself into his chair.

'Chopping wood. And *gardening*!' The chief shook his head in disbelief. 'Who would have thought it?'

'And in Klagenfurt of all places.'

'Actually, that I *can* understand.'

Gabriel frowned. 'What do you mean?'

'His desire to return to his hometown, to where his brother lives.' The chief smiled. 'My family come from Graz, and I intend to retire there after all this is over.'

'I can't imagine you retiring, chief.'

'Oh I won't give up work completely. In fact I've been promised an emeritus teaching position at the university hospital in Graz. You'll have to come and visit me there, after the war has ended – assuming we both survive it of course.'

Gabriel grew thoughtful at the chief's last comment. When he had been ill with typhus he had accepted the possibility of his death. But as he thought of Elspeth again, he suddenly realised he very much wanted to stay alive.

'Chief, before you leave I must tell you about the most amazing woman I met during my time in Serbia…'

4

Plains of Kosovo, November 1915

After re-joining the column of refugees, Elspeth continued walking on the valley road towards Krusevac. She knew that she looked different from everybody else – a lone woman, dressed in a damp, mud-stained uniform jacket and skirt, tartan patches on her sleeves – and she attracted curious stares from some of the refugees; a few even tried to talk to her. But finding their Serbian dialect almost impossible to follow, all she could do was shrug her shoulders, smile apologetically, and shake her head to let them know she could not understand them.

And so she carried on walking, continuing to scan the column for a familiar face, for somebody – anybody – that she might know. But there was nobody in the crowd of refugees that she recognised, and an emptiness rose within her as the wrench of separation from her comrades brought on the first pangs of loneliness. However she knew better than to let herself wallow in self-pity, and so she pushed the feeling away and steeled herself to focus only on her goal: getting to Krusevac.

A sudden low rumble rolled along the valley road and, along with everyone else in the column, Elspeth stopped and turned. On the distant northern horizon the grey hulls of clouds flickered with the light of shell bursts reflected from the ground below. The explosions were louder than yesterday, telling her the pursuing German troops were close on their heels, trying to stop the fleeing Serb army from escaping south. A child started to cry and the mother hushed the frightened infant as the line of refugees began to move again, a little more urgently now, a little more desperately.

By mid-morning the ice on the road had melted and it was muddy underfoot as Elspeth plodded along, placing one booted foot after another into the mush, trying to work out how far she had yet to go. She knew it was a distance of fifty miles from Kragujevac to Krusevac, and yesterday they had passed Cuprija, which was about halfway between the two. If she could walk three miles each hour, she thought, she should be able to get to Krusevac in eight hours – hopefully before darkness fell. This thought spurred her on, and so she pushed herself to walk faster, continuing at this pace to ensure she reached Krusevac in good time. In the early afternoon she stopped for a few minutes to eat the bread and goats cheese that Milo had given her. But sitting by herself at the side of the road, she quickly felt a chill breeze cut through her thin jacket and so she finished her meal and began to walk again. Now she really missed her rain-cape and coat as the wind increased, whistling along the valley and whipping her skirt about her legs. She held the collar of her jacket closed at the throat and tried not to think too far ahead, but with no food left and dressed as she was, she knew she would be in trouble if she did not reach Krusevac before nightfall.

The road began to descend from the hills, dropping from the higher slopes onto flatter terrain near the valley floor. It was still muddy from all the previous days' heavy rain, but it was also wider and straighter, which allowed her to make faster headway. But she was feeling really tired now, and in the late afternoon – and still with no sign they were anywhere near Krusevac – she saw that the light had begun to fade, and many of the refugees were stopping to set up overnight camps. The smoky yellow glow of campfires began to spring up by the roadside and soon she could smell roast maize and meat – probably horsemeat, she knew, but any meat was better than none. She was exhausted and would have loved nothing better than to stop and rest, maybe try to beg some food from the other refugees. But already it was colder – she could see the breath in front of her face – and, knowing that the temperature would drop even faster as darkness fell, she ignored the ache in her legs and forced herself to keep moving, to use the emptier roads to make faster progress.

And then several rectangular dark shapes appeared on the distant road ahead. As she carried on walking the objects grew larger and she saw that they were vehicles, four drab-green army lorries parked on either side of the road. She stopped for a moment and squinted through the deepening gloom: were they Serbian? German? Austrian? Bulgarian? It was impossible to tell at this distance and so she walked forward again, more slowly now, more cautiously. The sides of the vehicles were covered in mud-splatter, but on one of the cab doors she saw two brighter colours; a stripe of red and one of white. For a split second her heart hammered in her throat: that was the Austrian flag wasn't it? But looking more closely between the red and white stripes she saw a strip of dark blue overlaid with a double-headed eagle and sighed with relief; it was the Serbian emblem – thank goodness!

Hurrying forward once again, she saw that the vehicles were positioned on either side of a junction between the main route south, and a smaller spur road that led away in an easterly direction. There were two signposts at this junction: one on the main route which read 'Pristina 102 km', and another on the smaller spur which read 'Krusevac 1 km'.

Only one kilometre to go! Her heart soared at the thought of Sylvia and the others waiting for her in Krusevac. As she arrived at the junction, she saw four artillery pieces dug into shallow depressions on either side of the road, and counted about a dozen Serbian soldiers working on the guns. A Serbian officer – a captain dressed in a heavy greatcoat – stood prominently amongst them. He looked cold, the collar of his coat raised beneath his officer's cap, his breath a veil of white mist in the chill air as he barked orders to the soldiers who were man-hauling the artillery pieces up onto the road. Then he appeared to realise he was being watched and scrambled up the side of the depression towards her.

'*Ko ste vi?*' he asked.

'*Skotski Hirurg,*' Elspeth replied.

'*Ah. Skotska dama.*' He smiled and nodded at the tartan epaulettes on her jacket. '*Iz Kragujevacke bolnice?*' he asked her: from the hospital in Kragujevac?

'*Da,*' she nodded her head. '*Idem u Krusevac.*' I go to Krusevac. '*Idem u bolnicu Czar Lazar.*' To the Czar Lazar Hospital.

But he frowned and shook his head.

'*Ne.*' He shook his head again. '*Nemci su zauzeli Krusevac.*'

She flinched, knowing enough Serbian to understand his meaning: that the Germans had captured Krusevac.

'*Krusevac je evakuisan,*' he continued.

Krusevac evacuated? Her pulse quickened. '*Gde su evakuisani?*' Evacuated to where? she asked

'*U Pristinu.*'

Pristina? Dear Lord – that was a hundred kilometres south of here.

'*Svi su evakuisani u Pristinu,*' he continued: everybody has been evacuated to Pristina. '*Skotske damé su isto evakuisane u Pristinu.*' The Scottish women have also been evacuated to Pristina.

She had missed them again, and for the first time that day she felt herself slump with exhaustion, the hot prickle of tears at the corners of her eyes. She blinked – just managing to hold the tears back – and saw him look at her with concern as he placed a hand on her shoulder. '*Ne brini te,*' he said gently: don't worry. '*Mi idemo u Pristinu. Mozete ici s nama.*' We are going to Pristina. We can take you with us.

***

The captain's name was Babov, and as his squad of men continued their work of hauling the artillery pieces one-by-one up onto the road, he told Elspeth that they were part of the Serbian rear-guard, tasked with keeping the road open for the evacuation from Krusevac. It had begun the day before, when it was obvious that the Germans were about to take the city, and that morning he had personally seen an ambulance and two ox wagons containing women dressed in the same uniform as Elspeth pass through the junction on their way south to Pristina. Krusevac had fallen only that afternoon, and now his orders were to dismantle his guns and follow the evacuees south to the plains of Kosovo, where he would receive further instructions. He told her that she was lucky to have found him, as they planned to leave within the hour and would drive to Pristina throughout the night.

It had grown considerably colder since dusk had fallen, and as Elspeth watched the soldiers finish coupling the cannons to the backs of the lorries, she began to shiver. Babov must have noticed because he climbed inside one of the vehicles, and after rummaging around he clambered out again holding an army greatcoat. There was a small hole in the chest pocket and obvious bloodstaining on the lining, but Elspeth quickly overcame her squeamishness and put the coat on; it was either that or freeze. As soon as the last gun had been coupled to the lorry, Babov called his squad to attention and announced Elspeth's presence, saying she was one of the famed Scottish women surgeons from Kragujevac and would be travelling with them to Pristina. From the smiles of respect the soldiers gave Elspeth it was obvious to her that they had heard good things about the women's hospital. She asked if anyone needed her medical attention, but all the men shook their heads. Babov told her that apart from the previous owner of the greatcoat, everyone had managed to avoid injury.

Babov barked a final order to the soldiers, who clambered inside the lorries, and then he pointed Elspeth towards the cab of the lead vehicle. She climbed up and sat next to the driver, watching as starting handles were cranked, engines fired into life, and headlights threw beams of yellowy light onto the road ahead. The captain climbed in next to Elspeth and then the driver pushed the accelerator and the lorry lurched forward.

It was very slow going on the unlit track, which was rutted with potholes and strewn with debris; broken or abandoned carts and wagons, discarded clothes or furniture, an occasional dead ox or horse. For much of the time the convoy travelled only a little faster than walking pace, but sitting between the driver and Babov, luxuriating in the warm fug of the cab, Elspeth was relieved to be with this group of men, happy to be out of the cold and able to rest her weary legs. Behind her was a canvas partition, and through this she could hear the camaraderie of the soldiers in the rear of the vehicle: their conversation, their laughter, the smell of tobacco smoke from their pipes and cheroots. A hand holding a hunk of maize bread suddenly appeared through the canvas and Babov reached up to take the loaf. He broke it into three portions, giving one to the driver, another to Elspeth, and keeping the third for himself. Only now did Elspeth realise how famished she was, and with water from a canteen she savoured the bread, its sour-bitter flavour. She chewed thoughtfully as she stared at the contours of the road ahead, which were revealed in the dancing headlights as the lorry swayed and rolled on the uneven surface.

After this frugal meal, and now comfortably warm and safe in the company of the soldiers, Elspeth rested her head back against the seat. And as soon as she did so, an irresistible urge to close her eyes came over her and she immediately fell asleep, only vaguely aware when the hard-sprung vehicle jolted as it swerved to avoid obstacles on the road. She woke only once during the night – when the lorries stopped to change drivers and refuel the tanks from jerry cans – but she was fully awake as the dawn broke, the early-morning sunlight dazzling through the side window of the cab, the road ahead a shimmer of white from sunlight reflected over the frost.

With daylight they made much quicker progress, but within an hour the sun had disappeared behind a gathering bank of red-tinged snow clouds. By now they had left the hills and mountains of Serbia well behind and were in more open territory. Babov told her that they were on the plains of Kosovo, not far from Pristina. Another hour later and cottages and farms began to appear on either side of the road, and then, like a mirage in the desert, on the horizon Elspeth saw a jumble of grey and white shapes. She quickly realised it was a vast encampment, a landscape composed of army bivouacs and marquees, and also green-coloured civilian tents and temporary shelters made from blue tarpaulins and white canvas sheeting. As their lorry drew nearer and the encampment grew larger, Elspeth peered through the grime-stained window and saw hundreds of black specks scattered between the tents that she realised were people – a great many people. Dear Lord, she thought: how on earth am I going to find my fellow Scottish women in all of this?

Arriving at the edge of the encampment, Elspeth saw a checkpoint manned by half a dozen Serbian guards who were directing the flow of traffic. Their lorry came to a halt and as Babov climbed down and began to speak to the officer in charge, a faint rumble of thunder could be heard from the Serbian hills behind them. The guards at the checkpoint stopped talking and turned towards the noise, which Elspeth knew was the sound of German artillery.

Babov climbed back into the cab and the lorry started up again. The driver now followed a route that led directly towards the encampment, before turning off onto a deeply rutted track that ran through the middle of the camp. The vehicle rose and sank on the uneven surface, almost as if it were a ship sailing through the throng of people. And in this vast sea of humanity Elspeth saw grannies dressed from head to toe in black, mothers wrapped in woollen shawls holding their babies close to their chests, younger women and girls wearing brightly coloured headscarves, men in grey overcoats and hats, smaller children – oblivious of the unfolding disaster – happily playing in the mud, all of these people milling together outside tents and campfires, or standing in small circles, or squatting on the muddy ground. There were also groups of soldiers warming their hands in front of open braziers, rifles slung over their shoulders, empty packing cases of ammunition stacked nearby. Scattered between the people, she saw animals: stray dogs scavenging for food, ponies, horses, donkeys and of course the ubiquitous Serbian oxen, most of them yoked to their wagons. There were also the vehicles, the carts and lorries – even an occasional bus and black taxicab – that had brought them all here. Underneath all of these people and animals and vehicles Elspeth saw mud, a thick glutinous sludge that appeared to stick to everything and everyone.

It seemed to her as if all of Serbia had been uprooted and brought to this spot, and she knew at once that this was a disaster, and that many would die from lack of food and hygiene. She was stunned at the terrible, awful scale of it all, this vast ocean of people. How desperate, she thought, for them to be forced to flee the comfort and security of their homes and end up in this barren place.

Their lorry turned off the uneven track and the drivers negotiated a way into an area of free space on the edge of the encampment. They parked the vehicles in a tight circle and Elspeth stepped down from the cab, her boots squelching in the mud as she surveyed the scene around her. Then something cold and wet landed against her cheek, and looking up at the leaden sky she saw flakes of sleet spiralling down.

Her priority now was to find the Scottish women as quickly as possible. Babov told her that the guard at the checkpoint had said they should ask at the general staff headquarters, a cluster of tents easily identifiable by a flagpole, he said. Looking over the heads of the refugees, Elspeth saw the Serbian ensign fluttering only a few hundred yards away, and she and Babov immediately set off towards it.

The sleet was falling a little faster now as they wove their way through the melee of people, Elspeth scanning the crowds, constantly on the lookout for grey and tartan uniforms. Carefully negotiating their way through the throng, they arrived at the flagpole and found two large marquee tents guarded by a ring of infantry. Elspeth waited. Babov spoke to the officer in charge and then followed him inside one of the tents, emerging a few minutes later accompanied by an older man, who was introduced to Elspeth as Colonel Gencic, the head of the Serbian Army Medical Service.

'My dear lady,' Gencic said to her in good English. 'Captain Babov has told me you've become separated from the other Scottish ladies.'

'Yes, Colonel. Captain Babov kindly brought me here,' Elspeth said, relieved to hear her language spoken. 'I understand that the rest of my unit were evacuated from Krusevac and may be in this camp?'

'That is correct, Dr Stewart,' Gencic said. Elspeth felt a wave of relief to know her friends were close by.

'Dr Curcin is leading a small party of your compatriots who have decided to leave Krusevac. However, I need to tell you that many of your colleagues have chosen to stay behind and are now prisoners of the Germans.'

'Oh.'

'Yes, not all of your colleagues are here. But fifteen of them are nearby...' – He frowned as he looked over Elspeth's head for a moment – 'it is easy to become lost in this place, so I will send a messenger to Curcin and he will come to collect you.'

She thanked the colonel and then turned to Babov. 'Goodbye, and thank you for your help, Captain. I couldn't have made it without your assistance.'

Gencic translated her words for Babov, who smiled and saluted her. Then the two men turned away and walked back inside the tent.

She waited for a while, and then saw a young boy – who looked about twelve years old – dart out of the marquee and run through the line of guards, disappearing into the crowds. As she waited for him to return, Elspeth began to fidget with impatience. She was curious to know which women had decided to stay behind and which had chosen to escape. Would Sylvia be here with them? She already knew that Dr Inglis would not – the departure from Kragujevac had almost been too much for her to bear, so she would surely have stayed with her patients in Krusevac...

'Ellie!'

Elspeth turned at the cry, just in time to see a figure in Scots grey striding towards her.

'Oh, Ellie, thank God you're all right.'

Vera – a light dusting of melting snowflakes in her close-cropped dark hair – flung her arms around Elspeth and pulled her into a hug before releasing her from her grip. 'We were so worried Ellie, what with you missing the train.' She drew Elspeth forward into another embrace, Elspeth grinning at the passion of her hold. As they pulled apart again, Elspeth saw Curcin standing behind Vera.

'Ah, Dr Stewart,' he said. 'We are very pleased to see you. Dr Inglis was most distressed that you missed the train.'

'I assume she has stayed in Krusevac.'

'Yes. She felt very bad about leaving Kragujevac, so she refused to leave Krusevac.'

Elspeth turned to Vera. 'Is Sylvie here?'

'No, she chose to stay behind.'

Elspeth felt a pang of disappointment as Vera continued.

'But Lydia is here, and Monica, and Aurelia and—'

'Where is everyone?'

'Come on,' Vera said with a smile as she took Elspeth's hand. 'I'll take you to see them. Everyone'll be thrilled.'

With Curcin walking alongside them, Vera led Elspeth into the crowd and between the makeshift tents until they arrived at the ambulance that Elspeth had last seen the evening of the evacuation from Kragujevac. Next to the ambulance were two uncovered ox wagons and a dozen of the Scottish nurses and VADs, who whooped with delight and ran across to greet Elspeth when they saw her.

As well as Vera and Dr Curcin, there were four nurses in the group – including Monica and Aurelia – and nine VADs, including Lydia. All of them crowded around Elspeth, their faces expectant as they pressed her for details of how she had escaped. Without mentioning Anya or her encounter with the German patrol, Elspeth told them only that she had made the first part of the journey from Kragujevac with a group of Chetniks, and the second part with Captain Babov.

'And here I am,' Elspeth said, after finishing all that she was prepared to say for now. 'But what happened after you left Kragujevac?' she asked Vera.

'Well, Sylvia and I managed to get the ambulance to Krusevac, while everybody else made it on the last train... except for you of course. Poor Dr Inglis and Dr Chesney were distraught when they realised you'd been left behind, but Sylvia and I thought you'd find a way out.' She grinned at Elspeth. 'Anyway, we arrived at the Czar Lazar Hospital, but after only one day were told that the German army was close to capturing the town. So Dr Curcin said we had two options: stay on at the hospital and become prisoners, or try to escape to Greece.'

'So you decided to leave?'

Vera nodded. 'I wasn't happy about leaving Sylvie, but it was decided we should take the ambulance, and as I'm the only driver I had to come. And now we've run out of petrol, we're going to have to leave her here anyway.' She looked sadly, almost affectionately, at the mud-spattered ambulance. 'And we're not sure how much longer the oxen can keep going. All the good animals have already been taken and these were all we could find.'

Elspeth eyed the four skeletal, droopy-headed beasts yoked to the wagons. 'And Sylvie?' she asked.

'Well, you know what she's like,' Vera said. 'She felt it was her professional duty to stay behind.'

Elspeth nodded, and felt the sickening wrench of knowing that Sylvia was now in enemy hands.

'Dr Chesney and Dr Wakefield have also stayed behind,' Vera added.

'And can you get to Greece?' Elspeth asked Curcin.

'No,' he replied, the melting flakes of sleet in his hair making him look even greyer and more sombre than usual. 'I just heard that the Bulgars have cut the road south to Salonika. We cannot get to Greece any more.'

Elspeth thought for a moment. 'Well, that means we're trapped between the Germans in the north and the Bulgarians in the south, doesn't it?' she said. Curcin nodded. 'So we'll have to surrender, won't we?'

'Not necessarily,' Curcin replied.

Elspeth felt her throat constrict. 'Surely you don't mean us to stay and fight?' she said, suddenly recalling Anya's words about a last stand. She turned to look at the hundreds of civilians standing around her, and saw one woman with two small children playing in the mud at her feet. 'We're vastly outnumbered... and all these people... it would be a slaughter...'

'No, no,' Curcin said reassuringly. 'We will not fight. We could not win against three armies. But we don't have to surrender. There is a third choice.' The women leant closer as he spoke quietly. 'Our people can leave Serbia.'

'Leave Serbia?' Elspeth said, an incredulous look on her face. 'You mean to flee the country?'

He nodded. 'Our people are Serbia's greatest asset. There is a rumour circulating that our army, and all men of fighting age – including all boys aged twelve or older – will be ordered to leave. And most people here will follow them.'

'But where to?' Vera asked. 'If the Germans are in the north, and the Bulgarians are in the south and east—'

'West,' Curcin said, 'across the Montenegrin Mountains into Albania.'

Elspeth turned to look towards Montenegro, where, just visible on the western horizon, a dark wall of rock lay below a high bank of cloud. She knew the fearsome reputation of those icy peaks: the black mountains as they were known, took their name for good reason.

'There is a pass through the mountains,' Curcin continued as Elspeth turned back to him. 'It will be dangerous. But it is our only chance.'

'But it's already snowing,' Elspeth said, 'and we've been told the mountains are almost impossible to cross even in good weather?' She looked at the civilians around her. 'To evacuate all these people – an entire nation – over those mountains, in winter – can it be done?'

Curcin shrugged his shoulders. 'What else can we do?'

'Many will die crossing those mountains—'

'But if we stay here, even more will die. Our soldiers and the chetniks might hold the enemy for a while, but eventually they would be overcome...'

At the mention of chetniks, an image of Anya reappeared in Elspeth's head. She put an arm around Vera and led her away from the wagons. Vera looked puzzled as Elspeth held her by the shoulders and looked her squarely in the eyes. 'Listen carefully, Vera: did Anya arrive in Krusevac?' she asked.

Vera blinked. 'Anya? What are you talking about?'

'Anya,' Elspeth repeated, shaking Vera's shoulders as if to wake her from a stupor. 'Did she come to Krusevac?'

Vera blinked, her mouth slightly agape. 'Have you gone mad, Ellie? Why are you asking about Anya?'

'Because I met her, Vera; she's here in Serbia.'

'Anya...' Vera said, a dazed expression on her face, 'in Serbia—?'

A shrill sound startled them both, and, turning towards the noise, Elspeth saw a bugler, who appeared to be standing above the heads of the crowd, near the headquarter tents. She stretched herself up on her toes and saw that he was standing on top of a wooden crate inside the back of a wagon, and beside him were several officers, one of whom was holding a megaphone as the bugler played a military call, the brassy notes strident in the cold air. Suddenly Dr Curcin brushed past her as he hurried towards the bugler.

'He plays an attention call,' Curcin shouted back to Elspeth. 'Will be important announcement...'

418

Elspeth saw that Vera was still stunned at the news about Anya, and so she took her by the hand, pulling her after Curcin. 'We'd better go with him, Vera, hear what's been decided. I'll tell you all about Anya afterwards...'

The sound of the bugle had already attracted a large crowd, which was pushing towards the source of the noise, and Elspeth followed Dr Curcin as he tried to squeeze through the throng. But the sheer number of people prevented him from going much further and Elspeth and the other women gathered around him as the bugler played his final notes, and then lowered the instrument from his lips. The crowd grew silent as Curcin turned around and whispered to Elspeth. 'This will be important announcement.'

The officer lifted the megaphone to his mouth and began to speak. The metallic echo of the speaker trumpet distorted his words of Serbian as Dr Curcin, furrowing his brow with concentration, translated each phrase.

'Soldiers and civilians of Serbia,' he began.

'We cannot defeat the Austro-Hungarians, the Germans and the Bulgarians.

'The Serbian General Staff have decided that the best hope for Serbia is for our soldiers to leave the country, then re-arm and return to fight another day.

'All roads south to Greece have been cut off by the Bulgars. The only possible route out of Serbia is over the mountains of Montenegro into Albania.

'The first part of the journey will be west, to the town of Pec at the base of the mountains.

'From Pec, we will follow the Rugova canyon between the mountains into Albania.

'In Albania, we will walk to Scutari and then to the Adriatic coast, where Allied ships will take us to Italy and Corfu.

'But we will return to Serbia, next year or the year after that, and we will retake our country from the invaders…'

As Curcin continued to translate, Elspeth looked at the faces of the Scottish women and Serbian civilians around her and saw their daunted expressions. Then she turned her gaze towards the Montenegrin mountains. The jagged snowy summits, briefly glimpsed through gaps in the heavy cloud, appeared like the black, broken-capped teeth of some terrifying leviathan. From here to the Adriatic, she knew, was a distance of almost two hundred miles, and everybody attempting to escape the enemy would have to walk up those fearsome-looking peaks and down again to the coast. As she looked at the rag-tag collection of people and animals, snowflakes gently settling on their heads, Elspeth wondered: was it really going to be possible?

5

Krusevac, January 1916

The train slowed as it approached the West Morava River, and then clattered noisily over an old iron railway bridge that spanned the two banks of the waterway. Gabriel looked through the carriage window and saw that both riverbanks were still white with snow, the fir trees sagging with the weight of icicles, which hung like melted candle wax from their branches. On the far side of the span the train passed small farm holdings and cottages, and then tobacco warehouses and factories as it slid through the suburbs and into the centre of town, before finally coming to a halt at Krusevac central station.

Gabriel reached up to the luggage rack and pulled down his leather holdall. It had been a long journey down from Belgrade, so it was a relief to stand and stretch the stiffness out of his legs. He stepped onto the platform and joined the other passengers queuing at the exit barrier. The train had been mostly full of German soldiers returning from leave, and a trio of Feld Gendarmerie – the officious-looking German military police – were meticulously checking the travel permits of all new arrivals. Gabriel patiently waited his turn and then showed his papers to a sergeant at the barrier, who took a fastidiously long time to read the documents before handing them back.

'Hm,' he said, looking Gabriel up and down dismissively. 'Your orders are authorised from Vienna, not Berlin.' The steel gorget around his neck was so highly polished that Gabriel could see his own reflection. 'You'll need to report to the garrison commander.'

'Where can I find him?' Gabriel asked.

'In garrison headquarters, inside the town hall,' the sergeant grunted, before grudgingly lifting the gate.

As he walked underneath the barrier, Gabriel contemplated the antagonism the sergeant had shown. It didn't really surprise Gabriel. The Germans, brought into the war in support of Austria, were in a bitter struggle against Russia in the east, and Britain and France in the west. And now they had to take on Serbia as well, in order to sort out what the Austrians had started but couldn't finish by themselves.

Outside the station Gabriel was surprised to see several taxi cabs waiting to pick up new arrivals. But after such a long journey down from Vienna he felt in need of some exercise, and so he asked for directions to the town hall from a passing German lieutenant, then hoisted the leather holdall and began to walk through the streets.

The town looked unexpectedly well maintained, Gabriel thought, as he strolled along pavements that had been scraped clean of snow, which now lay heaped in slushy grey piles on the street corners. He had been told that Krusevac was captured without a fight and all of the buildings he passed appeared undamaged, almost as if the war had not reached here. But then he turned a corner and came upon a market square, and saw the miserable items on sale: small potatoes, thin carrots, limp winter cabbages. A large number of peasant women wrapped in black shawls haggled over the price of this meagre fare, all clear evidence that the war had taken priority over the growing of food. He wondered if the Scottish women had been able to get enough food and firewood to cope with the harsh winter, and then he smiled at the thought of Elspeth, and the fact that very soon he would be seeing her again.

When the medical board in Vienna asked him to return to Serbia in order to escort the Scottish women to safety in Switzerland, it almost felt as if it was fate, as if it was predestined that he and Elspeth would meet again. Never before had he felt so certain of anything. He recalled the young reservist and his sweetheart in the café in Vienna just before he had departed for Sarajevo, and now he understood the feelings he had witnessed. On the train journey down from Belgrade he had thought long and hard, and had promised himself that he would not waste this opportunity: he would pledge himself to her. With her living in Britain and he in Austria he wasn't sure how it could be done, but somehow he was sure it would happen. He had felt excited and giddy at the prospect of trying, of having his life shaped by her presence.

Arriving at the town hall, he showed his orders to a sentry guarding the entrance and was directed to the garrison commander's office. After being made to wait for almost an hour, he was finally ushered into the room, where he saw a whey-faced German colonel with a Prussian-style haircut and moustache sitting at his desk. Gabriel saluted, placed the papers on the desk and then stood to attention. The colonel glared at Gabriel for a moment, then picked the papers up and shook them once to unfold them. He carefully adjusted a pair of pince-nez spectacles on the end of his nose and began to read, occasionally glancing at Gabriel over the top of his glasses.

Although he had not been given the command to stand at ease, Gabriel spread his feet and removed his cap just as the colonel finished inspecting the documents. With his red-rimmed eyes, offset against the pallor of his face, he looked eerily like an albino as he gazed at Gabriel with obvious disdain.

'So, you've been sent to relieve me of the Scottish women.'

'Yes, Colonel.'

'To escort them to Switzerland.'

'Yes, Colonel.'

'Hm.' The colonel clicked his tongue. 'And do you know why *you* have been selected for this particular task?'

The colonel's resentment was almost palpable. Careful, Gabriel told himself.

'Well, Colonel, I was captured and held prisoner in Kragujevac for most of last year. During the typhus epidemic several of the women fell ill and I helped at their hospital. So they know me, and I think they trust me—'

'Trust you?' Sarcasm dripped from his voice. 'You think the Austrian officer is more trustworthy than the German?'

Inwardly Gabriel groaned. He knew his arrival would be a sensitive issue, and had already been warned that where German and Austrian areas of control overlapped – as they did here – distrust and suspicion were common.

'Colonel, I mean no offence to any party here. I know how determined these women can be. As I'm sure you know, they can be very single-minded for the rights of their patients, whether they are Serbian, Austrian or German. I can see how difficult it must have been, to have had them under your jurisdiction—'

'*Difficult?*' the colonel thundered as he leant over his desk. 'You have no idea how difficult these blasted women are. Do you know,' he said, wagging a finger in front of Gabriel's face, 'that they refuse to accept that they are prisoners of war? They tried to lecture me' – he pointed the same finger at his chest – 'on the rules of the Geneva Convention, and have demanded receipts for every item they claim to have lost, telling me they will be asking for reimbursement after the war. They refused to sign a document which testified to the good behaviour of the German forces, saying it might be used as propaganda,' he clenched both fists in fury, 'and they even refused to look after a women's venereal disease hospital I opened, stating their priority was the wounded, and implying that the hospital had been built not for the benefit of women but to improve the health of my own soldiers.' He thumped the desk with one fist. 'They have even threatened to report me…'

As if realising he had lost his temper, he spluttered to a silence and then sat back in his chair. Gabriel waited until he was certain the rant was finished before speaking. 'I know they can be very demanding, Colonel.'

He shook his head. 'They're more than demanding, Captain. Those harlots are an undermining and pernicious influence in this town.'

Gabriel flinched at the insult. He felt the first stirring of anger but managed to stay silent as the colonel continued.

'To make things worse, when it was decided they were to be transferred to Switzerland, they insolently wrote directly to Vienna and insisted they be escorted by an Austrian, rather than a German officer. Well, Captain, I take it as a personal insult that they have gone over my head. Very regrettably, Viennese High Command has listened to their nonsense and forced Berlin to comply with this request. I find it impertinent that an Austrian officer is thought more suitable for this task.'

'Actually, Colonel,' Gabriel said, having reached the end of his tolerance, 'it was not Viennese High Command who sent me, but the Austrian Medical Board, who have taken responsibility for the women. And the women are correct: medical personnel *are* exempt from being taken prisoner and should be allowed to continue their work of tending the wounded unhindered. But the rest of what you have said is true – the women did send a request to Vienna that an Austrian should escort them to neutral territory. The reason the women gave for this request is they claim to have suffered verbal and physical intimidation by certain German officers.'

The colonel's eyebrows lifted with indignation, but Gabriel ignored him.

'Whether that is true or not, Colonel, is now a moot point, because Berlin has agreed to transfer responsibility for the safe repatriation of the women, and in my orders there is a letter from Berlin that orders you, Colonel, as commander of the garrison, to supply your *full* co-operation with this task.'

The colonel's facial pallor had disappeared, his cheeks scarlet as Gabriel continued.

'Now, as for why I was selected: I suspect the women's request must have arrived at the Austrian Medical Board's offices at the same time I was undergoing a medical examination to assess my fitness after being a prisoner. The medical board passed me fit to return to my unit, which is currently fighting in Italy, but at the end of the examination they asked me whether I knew the Scottish women and whether I would agree to act as their escort to neutral territory. I have agreed, Colonel, because I believe these women have done good humanitarian work for all parties involved in the conflict. Once these women are safely in Switzerland, my assignment will be over and I will return to my unit in Italy. Sir.'

The stress on the last word only emphasising his insolence, Gabriel held the gaze of the Colonel, who sat back in his chair and scowled, the muscles above his moustache tight with anger. After a moment he shook his head again, and then spoke quietly.

'You see, that's the trouble with you Austrians: too lax, too lenient. These women are not stupid. They know a soft touch when they see one.'

He roughly folded Gabriel's documents and tossed them across the desk towards him. 'I'll need travel warrants for all of the women,' Gabriel said as he leant forward to pick them up.

'My staff sergeant will give you what you need. Now get out of my office.'

Gabriel saluted, and with a smile he turned and left the room.

★★★

Gabriel obtained directions for the Czar Lazar Hospital from a clerk at the town hall, who told him it was only a five-minute walk away. As he walked through the streets, Gabriel felt his anticipation build at the prospect of seeing Elspeth again. Even just thinking about her made everything feel more alive. The bricks of the buildings he passed seemed redder, the snow whiter, even the grey piles of icy slush on the street corners seemed somehow more defined. He turned a corner and the crimson brick and concrete edifice of the hospital came into view.

Vienna had told him that the Czar Lazar had originally been built as a military barracks and training academy before being converted into a four-hundred-bedded hospital. He also knew that the scale of casualties meant that even more beds were required, and so the Magazine – a concrete bunker in the grounds of the complex that had previously stored explosives and ammunition – had been turned into three hundred extra beds, which were now under the care of the Scottish women.

Two German sentries were on duty at the main entrance to the hospital and Gabriel showed them his papers and then asked for directions to the Magazine. He was pointed towards a low, rectangular concrete bunker a short distance away. Stepping through the protective steel doorway into the bunker, he saw that the ammunition shelves that ran the length of the Magazine were filled with men lying on straw mattresses. A number of VADs who Gabriel remembered from his time in Kragujevac were attending the men, and one of them – he could not recall her name – glanced up at him, frowned, and then hesitantly approached him.

'It's… it's Captain Bayer isn't it?' she said.

Gabriel nodded and smiled as another VAD came and stood beside the first.

'Are ye here tae escort us to Switzerland?' she asked.

'Yes,' Gabriel confirmed, and both women grinned with delight as he continued. 'Is Dr Inglis here?'

'Och no, she's in our living quarters,' the first replied.

He looked around him but saw only the shelves lined with wounded men. 'And where are your quarters?'

'In the old office in the main hospital,' said the second woman, and as Gabriel gave a puzzled frown she smiled at him. 'Everywhere is so crowded, that the only space they could put us in used to be the administrator's office in the main building. There are fifteen of us living in that room. You'll find Dr Inglis in there, writing up her surgical notes.'

He thanked them, then left the magazine and crossed back to the main hospital building, where the guards at the entrance gave him directions for the administrator's office.

As he was walking along the hospital corridor he suddenly recalled there had been thirty Scottish women in Kragujevac, yet the VAD had just told him that fifteen women were living in the room.

What had happened to the others?

Before he could give this mystery any further thought, he found himself standing outside the door the guards had directed him to. The door had a frosted window panel. He tapped lightly on the glass and a voice from within instructed him to enter.

It was freezing cold inside the office and even smaller than he had expected. Light reflected from snow lying outside a window shone onto a mound of mattresses and blankets piled to his left. To his right was a dining table with folding legs and a stack of chairs propped up on either side of an unlit fireplace. Sitting in front of a small card table in the middle of the room was Dr Inglis, wrapped in an old Serbian army greatcoat, a pen in hand and an open ledger in front of her. On seeing him, her face broke into a smile, and, quickly recapping her pen, she stood to greet him.

'Captain Bayer,' she said, reaching across the table to shake his hand, her fingers icy cold in his grip. 'I'm so very glad to see you again.'

As he smiled back at her he noticed the redness of her nose and the blue tinge to her lips. 'I'm sorry about the temperature,' she said, as if reading his thoughts. 'But there's so little coal or wood. We only light the fire when everyone is back from work in the evening. But I could offer you some hot tea?'

He declined with another smile, lifted a chair from the stack by the forlornly empty fire-grate and sat opposite her at the card table.

'We are very grateful you have agreed to escort us to Switzerland,' Dr Inglis began. 'Initially the Germans appeared reasonably friendly and efficient – beastly efficient, as some of my girls have put it. But familiarity has bred contempt and as the weeks have gone by they have become increasingly insolent and, at times, frankly abusive.'

Gabriel smiled. 'Having just met the garrison commander, I'm not surprised to hear you say that.'

'Oh, he's quite a bully. Last week he asked us to take over the cholera sheds in this hospital – which of course we were happy to do. But some of my girls have not been inoculated against the disease, and when I insisted that they should be, I received a torrent of threats from him. In the face of such intimidation I sent a letter direct to the medical board in Vienna asking that an Austrian and not a German officer should escort us to safety. I was pleased that this was agreed and delighted that you were selected for the task.'

'I'm honoured to have been asked, Dr Inglis. Your unit's commitment has greatly impressed me and I'm only too happy to make sure you all get to safety.'

'Well, I never thought I would say it, Captain, but it will be a huge relief to get back to Britain. It has been very hard, looking after so many patients in such conditions. Getting decent food has been very difficult. The war has disrupted the harvest and all we've been given is a scanty ration of sour black bread, beans, rice and condensed milk.'

'Who will look after the patients once you depart?'

'A number of Bulgarian surgeons and orderlies will take over as soon as we leave.'

'Good. Well, please give me a list of names and I will have the appropriate travel documents authorised, today if possible. In which case, we should be ready to leave as early as tomorrow.'

'I have it all ready for you,' she said, turning the pages of the ledger. She removed a slip of paper and gave it to him. He looked at it for a moment and then frowned: he could only count fifteen names. And Elspeth's was not amongst them.

'If I recall correctly, Dr Inglis, you had thirty women in your group?'

'Yes, but half our number left before the Germans arrived. Dr Curcin is in charge of that party. They were trying to get to Greece, but we believe they may have joined the great exodus of Serbians over the Montenegrin mountains to Albania.'

'Oh, I see.' Gabriel felt a flicker of unease in the pit of his stomach. He had recently read a report in a Viennese newspaper of this 'Great Serbian Retreat', but had not considered that some of the Scottish women – including Elspeth – might be taking part in it.

'And sadly there have been two deaths.' Dr Inglis's face darkened. 'Shortly after Dr Curcin's party left us, we were told that Nurse Toughill was killed when a wagon slipped off the road into a gulley. I understand they buried her in a small village nearby. And then of course...' She paused to shake her head and sigh '... there was the tragic news about poor Elspeth.'

Her words struck Gabriel like a hammer blow to his chest and for a moment he was unable to breathe. There was a high-pitched buzzing in his ears, and although he could see Dr Inglis's lips moving he could not take in what she was saying. He blinked, forced himself to breathe, made himself listen to what she had to say.

'... and we heard that Elspeth missed the last train from Kragujevac, but managed to find a band of Chetniks that contained a woman she knew from London – Anya somebody. And it was this Anya person who came here a few weeks ago to tell us the tragic details...'

Keep breathing, Gabriel told himself as her words faded again from his ears. He felt numb, disconnected from the room and everything in it, almost as if he was watching someone else receive the news. Gripping the table edge in front of him, he made himself refocus on her words.

'... and so Anya told us she ran down the mountain trying to follow the wagon as it was carried downstream, but then found it smashed to pieces on rocks underneath a waterfall. She said she saw Elspeth's body wedged between the rocks...'

She stopped speaking as Gabriel leant forward and

covered his face with both hands. Listening to her was almost more than he could bear. After a moment he felt her touch his shoulder and he lifted his head to look at her.

'I'm so sorry, Captain Bayer,' she said. 'I'd forgotten that you and Elspeth used to work together.'

He could think of nothing to say and could not look her in the eye. The anguish he had felt on hearing the terrible news was already replaced by regret he had not insisted on going with her.

'If it's any consolation, Captain,' Dr Inglis continued, 'everybody felt the same when we heard the news and I bitterly regret allowing her to stay behind that last evening in Kragujevac. I should have insisted she go with us to the station, but Elspeth would not have had it any other way; that had always been her nature. And her sacrifice was not a futile one, because she did many wonderful things during her time in Serbia. She saved many lives and improved many others. We have seen so much death here, so many decent young women giving their lives to save others. Regardless of how they died – whether from disease or injury – their deaths were not in vain. We must hold on to that.'

He knew she was trying to console him, but her words seemed trite. Slowly he got to his feet, swaying before regaining his balance by grasping the edge of the card table. 'And Dr Stewart's friends?' he muttered. 'Sylvia...Vera?'

'Vera left with Dr Curcin's party before Anya arrived, so she doesn't know of Elspeth's fate. Sylvia, poor girl, was distraught when she heard. But like the good nurse she is, she carried on working. You might go up and see her if you like. The Bulgarians have asked her to help out in their surgical ward on the floor above us.'

Sylvia. He knew how close she and Elspeth were; she would be devastated at the news. He felt a desperate urge to see her – a last connection to Elspeth. But to do it he would have to pull himself together. Ignoring the pain inside his chest, he straightened up, then folded the list of names Dr Inglis had given him and put it in the breast pocket of his jacket.

'I will return tomorrow morning with the travel documents for your party,' he managed to say. 'Please have everybody ready.'

'Oh don't you worry, Captain Bayer: we'll be ready. Everyone is desperate to leave.'

★★★

Outside the office he slumped against the corridor wall. It took him almost a full minute to regain his composure, but after several deep breaths he managed to steady himself and stood tall again. His legs felt weak and when he found a staircase he had to grip the handrail hard to support himself. Ignoring the curious side-glances of Bulgarian nurses and Serbian prison orderlies who brushed past him he climbed the steps. He paused at the top of the stairs before walking along the corridor to the surgical ward.

The ward was – as expected – packed with casualties, attended to by a number of Bulgarian nurses and orderlies, but he immediately recognised Sylvia. She was dressed in a plain white blouse and grey skirt – as Elspeth used to wear – and was talking with a patient, a soldier with both legs in traction. He stood and watched her for a while. Then he saw her frown – almost as if she knew someone was observing her – and she turned towards him. Her eyes widened in recognition and a smile formed on her lips. But it lasted only a moment before it began to fade and he realised that she could tell he had already been told the awful news. She began to walk towards him, and he became aware that the other nurses, orderlies and patients were staring at him with curiosity. But he focussed only on her and saw the watery-eyed look of sorrow in her eyes as she arrived and stood before him without speaking, blinking as she tried to hold back the tears.

He did not know what to say to her and for a moment they stood there awkwardly, until she silently took hold of his hand and led him back towards a small door near the entrance and pushed it open to reveal a small galley kitchen. Inside the room were two Bulgarian orderlies, laughing at a shared joke as they sliced loaves of maize bread. However, on seeing Sylvia's face their smiles faded and they quietly laid down their breadknives and walked out of the room, closing the door silently behind them.

The kitchen was now silent, apart from an occasional rattle from a large copper samovar, which simmered in the corner. Gabriel watched as Sylvia fought to maintain her composure. And then she could no longer hold back the tears and went towards him; he enfolded her in his arms and held her close. She sobbed silently into his chest for a while, and then she took a deep breath and pulled away. As he gently released her, he saw the dark shadows underneath the soft green of her eyes, now red-rimmed and puffy.

'Dr Inglis told you?' she asked him.

He nodded. 'Are we sure it's Elspeth that's… that's…' He found he could not say the word.

'Luka came to tell us,' she whispered huskily and then sniffed back a tear. 'He and Anya told us the story—'

'I don't know who this Anya person is. Dr Inglis mentioned her to me, but I've never heard of her before.'

Sylvia took a deep breath before continuing. 'We both knew Anya in London, before we joined the Scottish Women's Hospital. She was one of our arson squad.'

Arson squad? thought Gabriel, and she saw his puzzlement.

'There are so many things about Elspeth you don't know, Gabriel—'

'But did Anya actually see it happen?' It helped to suppress his grief, by focussing on the facts, to activate his rational mind again.

Sylvia sniffed again and shrugged

'She told me she saw the cart that Elspeth was travelling in. It slid into a river and was swept away. She chased it downstream for more than a mile only to find the smashed wreckage lying on the boulders underneath a waterfall. She said she saw Elspeth, dressed in her cape and coat, wedged between the rocks…'

'So why didn't she try to retrieve her... her...?'

'It was too dark by then, Anya said. There was a whirlpool around the rocks and they were running from the Germans and Bulgarians... they couldn't delay. The next day they arrived here. Anya had hoped to see Vera, but she had already left with Dr Curcin's party. After telling us the news, Anya and Luka left with the rest of their Cheta to try and hold up the Bulgarian advance.'

Maybe I'm having a bad dream, Gabriel thought, a nightmare that will end with Elspeth walking into the room and smiling at us both. The wretchedness was welling up inside him, and so he re-focussed on why he was here, on what he needed to do.

'I don't know whether you've been told,' he said, 'but I've been assigned the job of escorting you all to Switzerland.'

'Yes, Dr Inglis told us.' She sighed. 'I can't say I'll be sorry to leave this place. It hasn't been easy, especially without... without...' She paused and took a deep breath before continuing. 'The Bulgarian doctors who have taken over the hospital have asked me to help with their surgical patients, but they're not up to your or Elspeth's standard.'

He half smiled at the compliment. 'I must go back to the garrison headquarters in order to arrange the travel permits and rail tickets. I'm hoping we can leave by tomorrow.'

She nodded, and then to his surprise she stretched up and kissed him lightly on one cheek. 'I'm glad it's you escorting us. I'm glad we got the chance to see each other again.'

He lifted his hand, and with a smile gently brushed the side of her face. 'I really must go.'

She smiled back, then opened the kitchen door and walked back into the ward. He followed her out, the other orderlies staring at him with puzzled expressions on their faces. Sylvia mouthed a silent goodbye at him and he bowed his head at her, then turned away and walked out of the ward.

6

Kosovo to Albania,
December 1915–January 1916

'It will be very difficult to cross the mountains wearing a skirt,' said Dr Curcin, sitting opposite Elspeth at a long table inside The Black Goat, a tavern on the outskirts of Pec. The other Scottish women at the table regarded Curcin with surprise. 'Parts of the Rugova canyon and mountain pass are very steep,' he continued. 'You should wear trousers.'

'Trousers?' Monica gave Dr Curcin a look of horror. 'Och, surely we can wear our skirts,' she protested. 'After all, a kilt is a skirt, and highlanders have been using them in the Scottish mountains for centuries.'

'The black mountains of Montenegro are different,' Curcin replied. 'There will be blizzards and deep snow. A kilt would not protect you from the cold in these conditions, and your longer skirts will not give you the freedom to climb the path.'

'Well, we can turn our skirts into trousers,' Vera said. As everybody else at the table looked at her in surprise, she stood and stepped back from the table. 'All we do is cut here,' – she drew a line with her finger down the front of her skirt – 'and here,' – she spun sideways and ran her finger down the back of the skirt – 'and then we sew the material around each leg.' She gathered the skirt tightly around her thigh to show what she meant.

'Good idea,' Dr Curcin said, nodding thoughtfully.

'Yes, excellent suggestion, Vee.' Elspeth rose from the table. 'I'll see if the innkeeper or his wife can lend us a needle and thread.'

She found the innkeeper's wife busy serving food and drink at the back of the tavern. Every hostelry in Pec, including The Black Goat, was full of refugees, and Elspeth knew that the Scottish women had been lucky to find a room, having arrived the previous evening after an exhausting ninety-kilometre trek, eight days after they had left the encampment near Pristina.

That first stage of the great exodus should not have taken so long. But two hundred thousand other civilians and soldiers were also trying to escape Pristina, and it had taken two days just for the women to find a place in the seemingly endless column of refugees on the road. This was more than an army in retreat, Elspeth thought as she scanned the slender line of humanity that stretched from one horizon to the other; it was as if the whole Serbian nation was passing into exile.

They mostly walked during those first few days, occasionally taking turns to sit amongst the food and hay in the back of the wagons. And as she trudged along the road, Elspeth saw many pitiful sights: peasants labouring through the mud in primitive straw shoes, old people hobbling along on walking sticks, lost or abandoned children sitting by the roadsides, ragged Serbian boys separated from their parents and sent on the march to avoid capture by the Germans. At night the women slept inside the wagons, covered with thin rubber sheets in an attempt to keep dry. The continually falling sleet was their biggest problem; it turned the road into a putrid, energy-sapping river of mud, through which the poor oxen struggled to pull the wagons.

After three days it turned colder and the sleet turned to snow and the mud froze. For a while it made things easier, as they were able to walk on top of the frozen road surface. But the drop in temperature took its toll and soon the oxen and horses began to die. Exhausted by the effort of pulling the overloaded carts and susceptible to the intense cold and lack of feed, they weakened and fell by the wayside. As soon as they perished, the animals were butchered by the side of the road and the meat given to anyone who happened to be close by.

And then the people began to die. Food was scarce and Elspeth saw how poorly clothed for the winter they were. Soon she came upon the terrible sight of dead civilians lying in ditches by the side of the road.

But after a week of hard walking they finally arrived at Pec, the gateway to the Rugova canyon and mountain pass they would have to negotiate if they were to make it to Albania. A short distance behind the town loomed the Montenegrin mountains, and Elspeth had gazed anxiously up at the intimidating mass of black rock – which dwarfed anything she'd seen in Scotland – and thought: are we really going to be able to do this?

It was Dr Curcin who had managed to persuade the innkeeper to give them a room in the tavern. This was no mean feat, Elspeth realised, as Pec – which normally held ten thousand people – had swelled by two hundred thousand more, who now occupied very available building while they prepared for the next stage of their journey.

The Scottish women had brought four oxen and two wagons with them, but after the trek from Pristina the animals were perilously close to collapse. In any case, they could not take the wagons into the mountains because the pass was too narrow, so Curcin traded the oxen for two miserable-looking ponies and a small amount of hay with the innkeeper, who seemed delighted with his end of the deal.

From here they would have to walk the rest of the way, Curcin said, along the Rugova gorge, a canyon that wove a route fifteen miles deep between the mountains, and then up a steep and narrow pass that zigzagged seven thousand feet to a plateau just below the highest summit. There was a timber hut on this plateau, which would provide shelter from the elements – if they could reach it. Then they would have to descend the far side of the mountains. After a further eighty-mile walk they would reach Lake Scutari and the Adriatic coast beyond. As the pack animals would have to carry all their supplies, each woman was limited to one rubber sheet and blanket, and a small supply of rice, cocoa and maize bread.

And now Curcin had told them they needed to wear trousers.

Well, it was just as well Sylvia wasn't with them, mused Elspeth as she returned to the table: Sylvia would have protested even more than Monica about trousers. Elspeth looked down at the women sitting around the table and held up a pair of scissors in one hand, a needle and reel of cotton in the other.

'Right,' she said. 'Let's go up to our room and make trousers.'

★★★

The freezing wind that howled along the mountain path was fierce, and Elspeth clung onto her hat with one hand as she tried to shield her eyes from the stinging sleet driven into her face. With her other hand she hauled on the bridle of the pack-pony. The heavily laden animal needed constant coaxing from Elspeth as it followed her reluctantly up the steep and icily rutted track.

The blizzard had struck the column in the mid-afternoon of this, their fifth day in the mountains. Thick sheets of icy sleet and hail pelted the brim of Elspeth's hat as she kept her head bowed, the wind howling past her ears like some demented banshee, the conditions the worst she had ever experienced. Visibility had deteriorated and rising ahead of her, seen dimly through the hypnotically swirling flurries of snow, she could only just make out the long column of refugees, soldiers, mules and other pack-ponies as they wound their way up the mountainside.

Dr Curcin appeared beside her, the officers' cap on his head white with snow, his moustache encrusted with tiny icicles. 'Let me take her,' he shouted, his voice almost lost in the force of the wind as he pointed at the pony.

Elspeth gratefully handed him the bridle and saw him slap the pony's rear. The animal's frost-tinged ears pricked up and it quickened its pace, trotting forward for a few steps before settling back into a slow walk again. A gust of snow temporarily blinded Elspeth and she dipped her head into the blizzard and tried to keep a steady rhythm on the icy path, one careful step after another. But the frozen rock was treacherous and she almost lost her footing just as another figure in scots grey drew alongside her.

'You all right, Ellie?' shouted Vera, pulling a scarf away from the lower part of her face, her eyebrows and lashes outlined with ice.

'Yes, fine,' Elspeth shouted back, blinking snowflakes away from her eyes as she regained her balance. 'It's just so slippery.'

'You're doing well; keep it up,' Vera said with a white-breathed smile of encouragement, then re-covered her face with the scarf as she settled into step beside Elspeth.

They had left Pec five days ago, first walking along a forest track towards the start of the canyon, the air growing colder and the snow deeper the higher they progressed. On entering the Rugova gorge, Elspeth saw the mountains rising up on either side, the daylight obscured by black rock, which arched overhead like a gothic vault, crested with icicles that hung down like the spears of a portcullis, giving the canyon a claustrophobic, almost subterranean menace. Ahead of her the refugees plodded steadily on as the gorge cut deeper into the mountains. As she watched the column disappear into the mist that first day, Elspeth had shivered with doubt. How on earth, she thought, could they make it through such difficult conditions?

The first night in the canyon they had dug snow holes into a drift underneath a rocky overhang. Wrapped in their blankets, the holes lined with rubber sheets, Elspeth and the others had spent a restless night trying to sleep before dawn finally broke. They had risen, taken a meagre breakfast of maize bread, and then started walking again. It had taken the whole of the second day to reach the end of the gorge and enter the mountain pass to begin the climb to the summit.

But the pass was a much more difficult proposition. At times it snaked between the crags, but at others it clung to the side of the mountain, and peering over the edge Elspeth had seen the sheer drop to a rushing torrent of a river that thundered far below. The heavy rain had swelled the tributary into a boiling, muddy maelstrom and she knew that any person or animal lucky enough to survive the fall would quickly be swept away.

And it was much slower going, as the path became narrower and bottlenecks began to form where pack animals had to be cajoled into continuing. At these hold-ups, the column ground to a halt and they would have to stand and wait in the cold until they could move again. Occasionally an over-burdened animal would slip and stumble over the icy track, and Elspeth would hear a sudden frantic braying and see a heavily laden mule or pony thrashing in the foamy brown water as it was washed downstream to an uncertain fate. On one occasion a horse slipped over the ledge, breaking its leg as it became trapped on a spur of rock a few yards below the path. It was a blessing when one of the officers agreed to put an end to its suffering, the crack of a pistol shot echoing mournfully between the mountains.

All that day they had continued in this way, making slow but steady progress, inching steadily higher and westwards.

And then, this afternoon, the blizzard had struck.

Elspeth kept her head bowed against the force of the wind, mostly looking down as she took one step after another, feeling the crunch of snow beneath her ice-crusted boots, trying not to think too much about the distance they still had to go. As the afternoon wore on, the wind and snow eased. But then the daylight began to fade and it soon grew dark inside the rock-enclosed pathway. Still they carried on walking, the path winding between the mountains as it ascended ever higher towards the distant summit.

Dusk had almost fallen, yet still Elspeth saw no sign of any place they might camp for the night. As she was squinting through the gloom in order to see the line of the path, a soft yellow glow appeared. One of the refugees in the column a few yards ahead must have lit a storm lamp, she thought. It was a relief to see a light, and relying on the feeble glimmer from the lamp, Elspeth and the others carried on walking.

After another hour, and with darkness now complete, the path began to level off. They rounded yet another curve, and from the light of the storm lamp she saw with relief that they had arrived at a broad, flat ledge enclosed on both sides by overhanging rocks.

'We can dig snow holes here,' said Curcin, pointing to a bank of driven snow on one side of the path. There were already a large number of refugees taking shelter there, but Curcin found a free area and was already digging in the snow with his gloved hands.

Elspeth was exhausted from the strain of walking in the dark, but helped the others clear a circle of snow, then watched Monica and Aurelia use the last of the wood and kindling to light a fire. Snow was melted and water boiled. And then, wrapped in their blankets, clustered together in a tight circle around the small fire, the women drank lukewarm cocoa and chewed a few mouthfuls of coarse boiled rice. Elspeth hugged her tin mug for warmth as she looked back down the mountain path and saw the flickering lights of campfires and storm lamps from other refugees. How many of them, she wondered, would survive this night?

After their miserable supper was finished, Elspeth watched the flames dwindle until the fire died and then followed Vera into their snow hole. With her head covered by another rubber sheet and wrapped in a blanket, she nestled up against Vera, closed her eyes, and promptly fell asleep.

★★★

Elspeth was the first to wake the next morning after another restless night's sleep.

Vera, curled up beside her, was gently snoring as Elspeth carefully lifted a corner of the rubber sheet covering their hole and brushed away the light dusting of snow that had gathered overnight. She poked her head outside. It felt colder than yesterday, but it had stopped snowing and the wind that had tormented them the previous day had disappeared. Although it was still night, the first hint of daybreak was evident on the eastern horizon and a star-filled cloudless sky told her further snow was not imminent. As it grew lighter, a diamond shimmer came from ice crystals on the rocks, and Elspeth watched the silly turn from black to purple and then blue, the rays from the sun picking out the subtle undulations on the rising path ahead. It was an absolutely still dawn – no hint of a breeze – and the vapour from Elspeth's breath floated in the cold air above her head like ectoplasm. There was something almost spiritual about this moment – sunrise in the mountains – which despite all the pain and horror of their exodus, filled her with hope. She heard whispering as others around her began to rouse, and then a sudden upward puff of snow came from nearby and the face of Dr Curcin appeared through the top of his snow-hole.

'Ah, a clear day,' he said as he stood and shook the snow from his greatcoat, grimacing as he stretched his back and swung his arms.

'I'm starving,' said Vera, who had woken as Elspeth climbed out of the hole and begun to stamp her feet against the numbness in her toes. The ponies were tethered together under the overhang, their faces and manes pitifully tinged with frost. One of them had been limping yesterday and Elspeth went across to brush the frost away from the poor creature's head, then gave each of the animals a handful of their dwindling supply of hay.

It was too cold to stand around for long, and after a quick breakfast of stale maize bread and melted snow they set off again. Her morale lifted by the clear blue sky, Elspeth soon felt warm from the exertion of walking, and her spirits rose even more as the pathway became steeper and she could instinctively feel they were nearing the summit.

All the rest of that morning and into the early afternoon they toiled upwards and onwards, travelling further west, deeper into Montenegro.

Then finally, late that afternoon, the mountains on both flanks fell away.

And Elspeth saw that they were now completely out in the open, a deep blue sky bright above their heads, the path no longer enclosed.

They had reached the top of the pass!

She spun round. Now she could see from one horizon to the other, the long undulating column of refugees coming up behind her, the mountain pass dropping away to Albania in front.

The wind on the exposed summit was strong now the mountainsides no longer sheltered them and Elspeth shivered as a blast of freezing air sliced through her greatcoat. With the fading winter sun at her back she hurried forward – Vera slightly ahead of her – and saw that the pass was widening into a snow-filled plateau.

'I can see a hut!' Vera shouted.

Looking past Vera, Elspeth saw a wood cabin standing on its own in the middle of the icy plateau. The building was very basic, little more than a timber-planked box with sloping roofs and smoke spiralling from a chimney. But it was a proper, man-made shelter, and from the delicious aroma blowing towards her, Elspeth knew that food was being cooked inside.

The breeze was whipping ice particles across the exposed escarpment into their faces as they hastened towards the cabin. Elspeth ducked behind the lee of one wall to escape the chill. Tied to a row of metal rings she saw half a dozen exhausted pack ponies and mules, heads down as they scavenged for scraps of hay that might have dropped from their last feed. Only a few yards away lay the butchered remains of a horse, the snow stained with blood, the rib cage pointing upwards, bones stripped of all meat.

After tethering the ponies to one of the rings and giving them the last of the hay, Elspeth followed the others inside.

'*Dobro vece!*' – Good evening! – said a ruddy-faced Serbian soldier standing just inside the door. Elspeth walked past him and was immediately greeted with the warmly acrid fug of tobacco smoke, wood smoke, and cooking, as well as the heady buzz and chatter of people happy to be indoors, away from the elements. On the far side of the cabin roared an open wood fire, the area before it packed with soldiers and civilians holding skewers of maize and horsemeat in the flames.

'I know Dr Curcin said the cabin could hold thirty people,' Monica said to Elspeth as the soldier at the door directed them to a far corner of the room. 'But there must be twice that number here.'

'Well, we're out of the cold,' replied Elspeth, 'and the greater the number of people, the warmer we'll all be.'

She sat down to remove her boots and then began to massage her feet, trying to restore her circulation and bring some feeling back to her toes.

'The smell of roast meat is driving me mad,' Vera said, squatting on the earth floor next to Elspeth. She was eyeing a soldier standing in front of the fire, two skewers of meat in his hands. Elspeth saw him look in their direction and then smile at Vera. Vera smiled back as she rose and walked across to him. A moment later she was on her way back to Elspeth with both of the skewers, the wood shiny with melted fat, the charred horsemeat still smoking. She carefully slid the meat from the sticks and handed a chunk to each of the women, before popping a small portion into her own mouth.

'Oh…' Vera's eyes rolled back in ecstasy. 'I'm in heaven…'

Elspeth blew on her piece of meat to cool it and then took a bite. Apart from maize bread and cold boiled rice, it was the first proper food she had tasted in more than a week and it was utterly divine.

They shared several more skewers of meat, and now

nothing in the hut – not the numbness in her toes, the smoke that made her eyes water, the smell of tobacco, or their unwashed neighbours – could mar Elspeth's contentment. That night, even though they were packed together so tightly that she could scarcely move, she had her first proper night's sleep for almost a week.

★★★

When Elspeth went outside the next morning, she saw that the pony that had been limping the previous day was kneeling in the snow. It was only with the greatest difficulty that she managed to coax it to its feet. She called Curcin out and they watched the poor animal hobble for only a few yards before it knelt in the snow again. Curcin looked at Elspeth and grimly shook his head. He went back inside the hut, reappearing a moment later with the ruddy-faced soldier who already had his rifle unslung. Elspeth looked away and then flinched at the sharp crack of the rifle shot. When she turned back, the pony was lying on its side, a crimson stain spreading rapidly through the snow beside it. The soldier leant his rifle against the side of the hut and pulled a knife from his belt.

'I've asked him to cut enough meat to last us three days,' Curcin said to Elspeth, as the soldier knelt beside the pony. 'The rest he'll distribute to the other refugees.'

She said nothing, but looked away as the soldier began his grisly task.

★★★

Elspeth had expected the journey down the mountain to be easier, but the iciness of the path made it more treacherous than she had anticipated. It took them a full day and a half to walk out of the pass, but finally they reached the valley at the bottom of the mountain, where they rested for a while, Elspeth looking back at the tattered refugees stumbling out behind her. She knew they still had another forty miles to go before they reached the town of Scutari, but they had made it through the most difficult part of the journey and now it was just a question of keeping on moving west towards the coast.

The following day they arrived at Lake Scutari, where they were forced to sell their surviving pony to the ferry master for passage to the town on the far shore. They had been told that a British Army supply team would be waiting for them in Scutari. However when they arrived at the refugee reception area outside the town hall, only one British liaison officer was there to meet them.

'I'm sorry, but this is all we have to spare,' the young lieutenant said, handing the women several boxes of army biscuits and one of tea leaves. Elspeth saw that the labels on the biscuit boxes were stamped '1901'.

'Yes, I'm afraid it's surplus hardtack from the last Boer war,' he said to her with an embarrassed smile. 'But they're still edible. If you soak the biscuits in hot tea, the weevils will come out and float to the surface where you can skim them away.'

'Where can we stay tonight?' Elspeth asked.

'The town is full of refugees,' he replied, 'but you

can sleep in the vestry of the town's Catholic church. My advice to you is to leave first thing tomorrow and carry on walking to the port of San Giovanni di Medua on the Adriatic coast. There's a British destroyer waiting in the harbour there and it'll ferry you across to Italy.'

The next morning they began the final stage of their journey. It was only twenty miles to San Giovanni di Medua, but it had begun to sleet again and soon the road was covered in mud, which hindered their progress. However, they were determined to reach the coast that day and so they kept on walking late into the evening. Then the sleet stopped and the skies cleared, and shortly before midnight the road crested a rise.

And there, lying sleek and dark under the light of a crescent moon, was the Adriatic sea, the lights on a destroyer in the harbour twinkling below them.

They had made it.

7

Bludenz, Austria, near the Swiss border,
January 1916

Gabriel stood patiently in front of the ticket counter inside Bludenz railway station. The station supervisor sitting at the counter took his time to study the travel permit, periodically glancing over Gabriel's head to count the Scottish women, who stood together in the middle of the station hall. Eventually, he handed the permit back to Gabriel.

'Your papers seem to be in order, Captain Bayer. You're not going with them, are you?'

'No. My escort duties finish here. We only need fifteen tickets.'

The supervisor counted out the tickets and slid them through the window on the counter. 'You can tell them that the next train for Zurich will arrive at the westbound platform in eight minutes,' he said.

Gabriel thanked him and walked back to the women. As they gathered around him, he saw their expectant looks.

'Not long to go now, ladies,' he said, handing a ticket to each of them. 'The train will be here in a few minutes.'

Their excitement was almost contagious, Gabriel thought, grinning at the expressions of glee that now enveloped him. He followed the women out onto the westbound platform and then stood for a moment by the platform edge, looking along the railway line towards Switzerland. It was a clear day, and in the far distance the slopes of the Alps glistened with snow, the sky above the mountain peaks cobalt blue. It would be a good day to travel, Gabriel thought, glancing enviously at the women around him, all of them visibly delighted at the prospect of leaving the war zone for neutral territory.

A wave of regret swept through him. He would miss the women and their commitment to the sick and wounded, their willingness to put a patient's needs ahead of their own, regardless of that patient's nationality. By comparison, his own work as an army surgeon seemed tainted. After he had seen the women safely onto the Zurich train, he would have to return to his unit on the Italian front and play his part in a war that seemed increasingly pointless.

Standing a few yards away from him, Dr Inglis was talking with Dr Chesney and Dr Wakefield, their battered leather holdalls resting by their feet. Further along the platform Sylvia was standing with Aurelia, and the image of the two women conjured a memory of Elspeth. The memory filled him with pain and so he forced it from his mind, instead proudly reflecting on the fact he had managed to safely escort the women thus far.

Their departure from Krusevac had not been without incident. Gabriel had reserved a railway carriage for the first part of their journey to Belgrade, but they were forced to spend the night in the station hall when the onward train was cancelled at the last minute. Then – as Gabriel feared might happen – they came upon a company of rough-speaking German infantry also waiting in transit at the station.

Several of the men appeared to have been drinking and started to pester the women. However, the officer in command – an arrogant-looking major – had only laughed when Gabriel asked him to control his men.

'Relax, Captain. My men are only having a little fun,' the major had said with a patronising smile.

But when the pestering turned to mocking and one of the infantrymen tried to touch one of the VADs, Gabriel had reacted furiously. 'My orders are sanctioned by German High Command,' he had said angrily, 'and if you do not control your soldiers, major, I will personally report you to Berlin.'

Reluctantly the major had called his men to order, but Gabriel had spent a restless night and was relieved when they were able to take the onward train early the next morning.

From Budapest they travelled to Vienna, where the women spent several days in a hotel on the Ringstrasse while Gabriel obtained the necessary documents for the next stage of their journey: a train to Innsbruck and then another to Bludenz, in the Austrian Alps.

Here – by order of the Swiss authorities – they were required to wait several days under typhus quarantine. Eventually, Gabriel received word they were clear to undertake the final stage of their that: crossing the Swiss border to Zurich, and then to Le Havre, in France, where a ferry would convey them to Southampton.

Gabriel flipped open the lid of his pocket watch – only four minutes until the train was due. He was suddenly aware of Aurelia walking past him, and looking back along the platform again he saw Sylvia standing by herself, staring towards the mountains, alone with her thoughts. He slipped the watch inside his greatcoat and walked towards her.

'They're magnificent, aren't they,' he said, arriving by her side.

She turned and smiled at him, the collar of her coat tucked high under her chin, her eyes green and steady below the fringe of blonde hair underneath her hat. In spite of her frayed uniform she looked beautiful, and the thought that he might never see her again felt unexpectedly painful.

'Yes, they are,' she replied, 'but I shall be glad to leave the mountains behind.'

He nodded, and then took a deep breath. 'Your train will be here in a minute… I just wanted to say thank you again for looking after me when I had typhus.'

'Oh, that's quite all right.' She thought for a moment. 'It seems such a long time ago now.'

'Well, anyway… I wish you luck for the future.'

Her look became serious. 'I'm sure we'll meet again, someday, after the war is over.'

'Whenever that will be,' he said, wryly.

'Well one day it will end, and then we can all get back to our normal lives.'

A normal life: he could hardly remember what his had been like. 'What will you do when you get back to England?' he asked.

She smiled. 'I'll spend some time with my parents. It's been hard work, so I'll allow my mother to pamper me for a while. I also need to find Vera, of course, to let her know about...' She faltered, but then quickly recovered. 'And then I'll come back to Serbia, if I can. The British and French in Salonika will retake Serbia next year, or the year after that. I would very much like to come back and finish what we started.'

He smiled at her confident expectation of an Allied victory, but then realised her certainty was justified: he could not see Austria and Germany winning this war.

'I'm sure you will be back,' he said.

'And what will you do?' she asked him.

'Well...' He chewed his lip and shrugged. 'I must go back to the Italian front. And if I survive—'

'You will survive,' she said firmly, and he smiled at her optimism.

'So – *after* I survive, after the war is over... well...' He paused. 'I haven't thought that far. I don't know what I'll do. Find a job, somewhere in Vienna, I suppose.'

She smiled but said nothing in reply, and he stood before her in an awkward silence. Despite her confident prediction that they would meet again, he knew this might be the last time he ever saw her. Soon they would be separated by several hundred miles, several countries, her language, his culture. He suddenly wanted to open his heart to her, to tell her how she and Elspeth had changed his life, of how the brutality of war had affected him, but how the selfless humanity of the Scottish women had healed him—

A piercing blast of a steam whistle echoed along the rail track. He saw Sylvia's eyes light up with excitement as she looked east along the railway line. He turned, saw the approaching locomotive and realised that all he might have said to her, would have to stay unspoken.

'Gather round, ladies,' Dr Inglis called across. 'We must stick together; all try to get inside the same carriage.'

The other women had already picked up their bags and were walking towards Dr Inglis as the noise of the approaching train grew louder, and then it arrived with a screech of brakes and a cloud of coal smoke and steam. A guard dismounted the rear of the train as several carriage doors clattered open and a scattering of passengers climbed down onto the platform. Gabriel saw that most of the carriages were occupied, except for one near the front of the train, which was empty except for an old woman sitting by herself.

'This carriage is free, Dr Inglis,' he called across.

Followed by the other women, Dr Inglis hurried towards him. There was a step below the carriage door, and Gabriel held his hand out to assist the women as they climbed up into the compartment.

The first was Dr Wakefield, who gave him a smile of thanks as she stepped inside. Next came Dr Inglis – who again expressed her gratitude for all his help – followed by Dr Chesney. Then Lydia, Aurelia, Monica and the other VADs and nurses, who wished him luck and hoped he would make it unscathed through the remainder of the war. And finally Sylvia. She took his hand like the others, but paused before going in.

'Look after yourself, Gabriel,' she said and then leant forward to kiss him lightly on one cheek. He smiled self-consciously as she turned away and disappeared inside the carriage.

He heard a whistle blow and slammed the carriage door shut behind her, then stepped back onto the platform. The guard waved his flag at the driver, who was leaning out of the cab at the front of the locomotive, and the carriage jolted into motion. Loss gnawed strongly in the pit of Gabriel's stomach as he realised this was probably the last time he would ever see these women.

The train had travelled halfway down the platform and was slowly picking up speed, when the window in the door of the women's carriage slid down and Sylvia's face appeared. She shouted something, but Gabriel could not hear above the noise of the train and so he broke into a run, sprinting along the platform towards her. But the train was accelerating and the platform end approaching fast…

'Haven't… address…' Gabriel could make out only a few fragments of Sylvia's speech before her words were scattered by the rush of air. He stopped running as he arrived at the end of the platform, then held up his hands and gave an exaggerated shrug to let her know he hadn't understood. He saw her shrug back at him and then she waved. He waved back, watching as she disappeared back through the window again, the train growing smaller as it headed west towards the Swiss Alps.

PART THREE

1919

A letter from Sylvia

To: Dr Elspeth Stewart, Bruntsfield Hospital, Edinburgh, Scotland

Sender: Sylvia Calthorpe, Leskovac Orphanage, Leskovac, Serbia

3 August 1919

Dear Ellie,

I'm really sorry I haven't written for so long but in the six months since Vera and I arrived back in Serbia, we have been hugely busy with the task of setting up our orphanage.

But the good news is that – after a lot of searching – we finally found a suitable location and we opened our doors to the first children four weeks ago. It was distressing to see these ragged, half-starved waifs, but we've now got ten orphans – three boys and seven girls – aged from four up to twelve. The farm we bought has suitable space and buildings that will, in time, allow us to care for up to fifty orphans. It is so very satisfying to help these poor children. I am sure that this is what I was meant to do, and I know Vera feels the same.

Of course our work was badly hampered by the influenza that swept through Serbia this spring. After all that this country has gone through during the past four years, it seemed such a cruel stroke. But I've heard that the numbers of new cases are falling every day, so we are hoping the worst may be over.

Mother and Father were instrumental in helping us buy the farm by releasing some of my inheritance early. But my intention is that we should become self-financing. This was a working farm before we bought it, with plum and apple orchards, goats, chickens, geese, ducks and enough acreage to grow vegetables and some cereals. So as well as a cook, laundress and cleaners, we've hired several farm labourers. Vera loves it here. She says it is good farming country and the soil is better than on her parents' farm in Oxfordshire. She and Anya tell the labourers what to do and they certainly jump to it – I think they're all quite terrified of Anya!

Mother has also been raising funds by holding whist drives and other charity events in London. She seems to have accepted me for what I am, and I think has given up her dream of trying to make me fit in with the 'Kensington' set. Since the exploits of the Scottish women were reported in *The Times*, I think she's secretly quite proud of what I've done.

Of course, Vera and I couldn't have done any of this without Anya's help. I don't think either of us expected to see her again. I most certainly did not. When Anya came to Krusevac that day – that awful day when she told me she thought you had drowned – she also told me that she and her Cheta were going to be part of the last stand against the Bulgarians. She didn't expect to survive, but of course she did. She told us that when she heard two English women were trying to set up an orphanage in Leskovac, she immediately thought that something as mad as that might be the idea of one of us(!) and so she came over to investigate. I don't think I'll ever forget the expression on Vera's face as Anya rode up to the farmhouse that day. As you might expect, she and Anya are now inseparable.

Talking of which, I hope you are sitting down when you read this, my biggest news yet…

I've met someone!

His name is Sasha: Count Sasha Djermovic. He's a colonel in the Serbian Army, but is also Serbian royalty and his family are distantly related to the Romanovs. He escaped into Albania like you and Vera during the great retreat, but came back last year when the Serbian army routed the Germans before their final surrender. I met him during the armistice celebrations in Belgrade and we instantly hit it off. He did some of his military training in Britain and speaks English fluently. I know it's only been a few months, but I've got a strong feeling it could be serious. He's even talked to me of marriage, and Mother would be as pleased as punch if that came off. He is as 'well connected' as a Serbian can be, and is going to help organise a royal visit at the orphanage from Crown Prince Peter later in the year.

And how are *you*, Ellie? I hope you're enjoying life in Edinburgh. I do so miss speaking to you. My only other regret is what happened with Gabriel, that we told him that you'd died, and that when we parted in Bludenz

I did not think to take his address. God willing he has survived the war. I know you must be so disappointed not to have had any reply to all those letters you wrote, to the Austrians, the Italians, and his father. Are you still planning to visit Austria when the blockade is lifted? I know you feel you can't move on until you know one way or another about him, so you are very much in my thoughts.

I will try to write to you sooner next time, my darling.

All my love

Sylvia

A *letter from Gabriel*

To: Dr Rudolph Fischer, University Hospital, Graz,
Sender: Dr Gabriel Bayer, Westbahnhof, Vienna

18 August 1919

Chief,

I am writing this to you as I sit in a café in the
Westbahnhof, waiting for the Vienna-to-Ostend express,
which will depart in one hour. I can't believe it's been
three years since we last saw each other. I would have
written sooner, but there seemed no point when the
British naval blockade was preventing any letters from
America reaching Austria.

Much has happened since you operated on me three
years ago.

The fractures have healed nicely, although I have a
slight limp and probably still have some shrapnel in my
left leg, from the Italian shell which you will remember
also took poor Klaus's life. A month after you sent me
home to convalesce, I was reviewed by the Viennese
medical board, who considered me unfit to re-join the
army and so I was medically discharged.

I had always thought of taking a post as a civilian
surgeon after I left the army, but first I went back to
Klagenfurt to see my father. After taking the time to

471

think about the things I had seen in the war, I eventually decided I did not want to stay in Austria any longer.

I remember once telling you about Dr Plotz, the young American who was researching a possible typhus vaccine. At that time America had not yet entered the war and Dr Plotz was still at the peak of his fame. My research on wound infection was relevant to other projects at Mount Sinai Hospital, so I wrote to him and he agreed to write a letter of recommendation and sponsor my journey to America.

So I travelled down through Serbia again, but this time I crossed the Greek border into Salonika, where I caught a liner and arrived in New York in September 1916. As promised, Dr Plotz found me a temporary research job at Mount Sinai while I prepared for the National Medical Board exams. I passed the exams, and then got a job as a surgeon at the German–American Hospital in Chicago.

It was wonderful at first. Chicago has a large Austrian community and I was made very welcome. But when President Wilson declared war on Austria in December 1917 and in view of my history of army service I was ordered to report to a police station. I was formally arrested and then escorted to an internment camp in Georgia, Fort Oglethorpe.

I spent more than a year as an internee, and it was not an easy time. A few months after I arrived, influenza struck the camp. More than half the inmates became ill and many died; the experience was almost as bad as the typhus epidemic in Serbia had been. I worked day and night in the camp infirmary, but this time I escaped infection and eventually the epidemic passed.

The second difficult time came in May of this year. A telegram from a neighbour of my father in Klagenfurt arrived, which said that my father had died from influenza. He had been in bad health for some time, but I was consoled by the fact that at least we had those precious few weeks together before I left for America.

I was released two months ago, shortly after the Versailles treaty was signed. My position as a surgeon in Chicago was still open to me, but first I decided to go back to Austria to settle my father's affairs. So, with other internees released at the same time, I sailed to Marseilles on the SS *Pocahontas* and arrived in Austria a month ago.

Among my father's papers I found an unopened letter. It was dated March 1916, but had been delayed by the naval blockade and only just arrived. The envelope had a British stamp and was curiously addressed – "To Herr Bayer, retired pastry chef and father of Dr Gabriel Bayer, Klagenfurt". When I opened it, to my amazement I discovered it was from Dr Stewart, the Scottish surgeon I told you about. I had been told that she had drowned, but to my great joy the letter stated she was alive and well, and working in London.

The London surgical conference takes place annually in August, so I sent the organisers a telegram, asking to be allowed to present the paper I was working on before the war broke out. I received a reply last week saying that, in the general spirit of reconciliation, if I could get a travel licence from the British Embassy in Vienna, they would allow me to attend. Armed with their reply and Harry Plotz's papers of endorsement, I approached the British Commissioner in Vienna. Because of my work as a surgeon with the Scottish women and in the Serbian First Reserve Hospital, he agreed to provide a licence for me to travel to Britain. The meeting starts in two days, which I hope will give me enough time to find her.

Well, the station clock is telling me that I must finish now and post this letter to you if I am to make the train and onward ferry connection to Dover. After the conference is over I intend to return directly to America. Maybe one day you and your family might consider visiting me in Chicago.

Once again, thank you for all your support and help over the years.

Gabriel

Edinburgh, Wednesday 20ᵗʰ August 1919

'Is it acute cholecystitis, Dr Stewart?'

Elspeth nodded. 'Well done, Miss Gillies.' The petite young woman in her short white coat, brown hair tied neatly behind her head, smiled with pride as Elspeth turned to the student standing beside her. 'Now, Miss Bruce: please demonstrate Murphy's sign for me.'

Elspeth knew that Miss Bruce was the least confident of the four women in the group, and she watched the slender red-haired girl nervously approach the bedside. The patient – a rotund middle-aged woman with thick blond hair – pulled up her surgical gown to expose her abdomen and then slowly lay back, clearly in some discomfort, thought Elspeth, judging by the expression on her face.

Miss Bruce knelt at the bedside and tentatively placed her hands on the patient's large belly. Elspeth smiled at the young student's timidity. She had a soft spot for Miss Bruce, who reminded her of how nervous she had been when she had been a medical student more than ten years earlier. Yet here Elspeth was, back at the Edinburgh Royal Infirmary and educating the next generation of women doctors.

Miss Bruce's hands were paddling uncertainly on the patient's upper abdomen, and Elspeth stepped forward to gently guide the student's fingers onto the inflamed gallbladder. The patient flinched at the pressure and a look of dismay flashed across Miss Bruce's face. But the patient quickly gave a smile of reassurance.

'Och, dinna worry about that, lassie; when Dr Stewart first examined me, I nearly jumped oot the bed!'

Miss Bruce finished her examination, then stood and thanked the patient before stepping back in line with the other students.

'Well done, Miss Bruce, we'll make a surgeon out of you yet,' Elspeth said, and then turned to Miss Gillies. 'So, Miss Gillies, how do we treat this acutely inflamed gallbladder?'

'Surgical removal, Dr Stewart?'

'Correct. Mrs Govan needs a cholecystectomy, and as her pain is not settling, the surgery needs to be done in the next twenty-four hours. Normally Professor Thomson or one of his team would perform the operation because, as you know, women surgeons are not ordinarily allowed to operate with the walls of the infirmary. But I am covering for Professor's team who are attending the London surgical conference for the next two days, so I'll be doing the operation tomorrow morning.'

The students' eyes widened with excitement as Elspeth continued.

'Now that's all for today, ladies. Tonight you should read the chapter on biliary anatomy in your surgical texts. Tomorrow you will be able to observe the operation and one or two of you may even be asked to assist. I'll meet you here in the ward operating room at seven-thirty sharp.'

Three of the four women curtsied and walked away, Miss Bruce waiting a moment longer to throw Elspeth a final smile of gratitude before following the others towards the ward exit.

As she watched the young woman leave, Elspeth fondly remembered Dr Inglis, who had taught Elspeth when she had also been a timid first-year student ten years earlier. She felt a twinge of sadness at the memory, because two years ago Dr Inglis had died after taking another Scottish Women's unit to Russia.

Elspeth had also considered going to Russia with Dr Inglis, but by that stage of the war so many male doctors had joined the army that there was a shortage of surgeons in Britain. So instead of going abroad again, Elspeth had gone back to work at St Mary's in London. And then, when her two-year contract had finished, she'd taken a post as surgeon at the Bruntsfield Hospital for Women and Children in Edinburgh.

As well as her surgical work at the Bruntsfield, Elspeth taught clinical skills to the female medical students. She loved tutoring her students, who were passionately keen about their studies. But she found it galling that the male students and their clinical tutors took priority for most of the learning opportunities. Women students were not allowed to attend post mortems or see major surgical operations, and male students had their ward teaching between the hours of nine and five, whereas Elspeth had to teach before breakfast or – as today – after supper.

She glanced up at the clock: half past seven. The new assistant surgeon had told her that there was an acute appendix to do that evening, but first she wanted to post the letter she had written to Sylvia that morning: a letter telling Sylvia that she still hadn't had any response to any of her requests for information on Gabriel's whereabouts. When her contract at the Bruntsfield expired in a month's time, she would travel to Austria to try to locate him. It was something she just *had* to do: find him, and let him know she was still alive. Even though it had been three years since she last saw him, she still thought about him, still could not bear the idea that he might go on with his life – if he *was* alive – not knowing she hadn't died. Because she still had feelings for him.

She went into the doctor's office, hung up her white coat, and from another peg took down her grey outdoor jacket. She left the ward, and at the top of the staircase to the ground floor almost collided with a petite, bright-eyed girl in a white coat who had come running upstairs.

'Oops, sorry,' said Dr Main, Elspeth's new assistant surgeon. She looked flustered and was breathing fast. 'The acute appendix is on her way up, Dr Stewart,' she said, breathlessly. 'Will you do the operation this evening?'

'When did she last eat?'

'Nothing since this morning.'

'Good, we'll do her right away then.' Elspeth sensed the young surgeon's nervous excitement. 'You've not done an appendix before, have you, Janice?'

'No, Dr Stewart.'

'Well, don't worry. I'll show you what to do today, and you can do the next one if you like.'

'That would be wonderful, Dr Stewart.'

She smiled at her enthusiasm. 'I'm just going out to post a letter, so I'll see you back here in ten minutes.'

'Thank you very much,' Dr Main said with a smile as she scurried towards the ward.

As she descended the stairs, Elspeth could not help but reflect on how ridiculous it was that women were not routinely allowed to operate in the Royal Infirmary. It was only two years ago, she recalled, that Dr Gertrude Herzfeld had become the first independent woman surgeon in Scotland, but she had only been permitted to operate at the Sick Children's Hospital. Even now, the only surgery that women were allowed to do were routine procedures like cholecystectomies or appendectomies, and these were generally restricted to the Bruntsfield Hospital. Yet when Elspeth had worked in Paris and Kragujevac, she had performed far more challenging operations than those. She knew the work of the Scottish women had advanced the suffrage cause and for ever changed the perception of female doctors. Yet in spite of the recently passed Equal Representation Act, it was clear to Elspeth that there was a long way to go before women, and women doctors, were treated as equals.

She arrived at the ground floor and walked through the wood-lined entrance foyer, past the gold-on-black panels commemorating donations from generous benefactors, her shoes echoing on the black-and-white chequered floor tiles.

'Dr Stewart!'

Startled by the call, she stopped and turned around. Behind the reception desk the hospital doorman was holding a small brown paper package. 'Yes, Jenkins?'

'A gentleman arrived here half an hour ago, asking to see ye, Dr Stewart. He was in quite a hurry, telling me he came up from London this morning but had to rush back to Waverley to catch the overnighter back to King's Cross. He's gone now, but he left this for ye.'

From London? Maybe it was one of Professor Thompson's team, back early from the conference? She went across and took the package from Jenkins and then frowned: the parcel was bound with string and her name was written in black ink on the front. There was a knot at one side and as she pulled at a free end to loosen it, Jenkins continued to speak.

'When I told him that he couldnae go up to the ward because visiting time was finished, he got a wee bit riled up. So I says to him, "If you don't calm down, Fritz, I'll have to ask ye to leave." But then he said he had to leave anyway, otherwise he'd miss his train.'

As she was pulling the wrapping paper aside, she suddenly stopped and looked up. 'Sorry, Jenkins – did you just say Fritz?'

'Aye, Dr Stewart. He didn't leave a name, but he sounded like a Hun to me.'

Elspeth looked down again. As the brown wrapping paper fell to the floor she saw grey moleskin. And now her hands began to tremble as she glimpsed, in faded gold lettering, the words "Romeo and Juliet, by William Shakespeare".

It was the book from the school library in Kragujevac. The book *he* had shown her four years ago!

'When... where...' she said, faltering with bewilderment. Then she shook her head to clear her mind. 'When did he leave,' she asked urgently, clutching the book as if her life depended on it.

The porter looked startled. 'Oh... only a few minutes ago—'

'Where did he go to?' she demanded, hurrying towards the entrance.

'To Waverley, I think, miss. The overnighter leaves at eight—'

But Elspeth was already through the door, slipping the book inside her jacket pocket as she strode down the steps, weaving a way between several startled-looking visitors and medical students in the infirmary forecourt. She hastened out into the street and turned right, in the direction of Waverley station, her heart hammering hard in her chest as her eyes scanned the pavement ahead.

Twenty yards in front of her, at the top of the narrow lane that led down to the meadows behind the infirmary, was the statue of a Unicorn atop a stone column. As she hurried towards the statue, Elspeth saw that someone was leaning against the column: a man dressed in a grey suit, a fedora hat pulled low over his brow, a walking stick in his left hand. She saw him raise the stick to signal a passing taxi, which swerved across the street and pulled up at the kerb beside him. The man limped forward to open the rear door and turned to speak to the driver.

And as he turned his head, his face came into profile.

Elspeth came to an abrupt halt, and for several seconds stood motionless with both hands pressed hard against her chest, holding her breath in case he was an illusion and might disappear if she were to inhale. It really *was* him standing there! There were several other pedestrians on the pavement, and one of them – a man with a highland terrier on a leash – glanced inquiringly at her as he strolled by, the terrier sniffing at her shoes. Elspeth could feel her heart pounding so strongly beneath her fingers that for a moment she thought it might burst through her ribs.

'Gabriel!' She heard herself shout his name, but it was almost as if she was floating above herself, listening to some other person call to him. She called again, but feared he could not hear her over the noise of the taxi, because he was removing the fedora and bending as if to climb into the back of the cab.

She called once more, and this time he froze and turned towards her. She saw him start with recognition and step back on to the pavement again, steadying himself with the walking stick. As she ran toward him he smiled at her, and when she finally reached him she flung her arms around his neck and felt his arms slip around her waist.

She wasn't sure how long they held each other, but at last Elspeth opened her eyes and drew back from him. As she studied his face, a wave of joy swept through her and she leant forward to hug him again, then pulled away once more, a serious expression on her face as she glanced at the walking stick in his hand.

'Have you been injured, Gabriel?'

But he was shaking his head with happiness and grinning stupidly at her as he stroked her hair. 'I thought I'd lost you, Elspeth,' was all he said, through gentle laughter.

'But you're limping—'

'It's nothing. Just a bit of shrapnel, a souvenir of the war. It's getting better every day—'

'Hey, pal,' shouted the taxi driver. 'Do you want this taxi, or no?'

She turned to look at the driver and only now realised that several pedestrians were gazing curiously at them. She didn't care – he had found her! – but Gabriel took a half step toward the taxi.

'Yes, please wait; I'll only be a minute.' Gabriel came back to her, gently leading her behind the stone column so that they were less visible to those on the pavement. With his free hand he pulled her close to him.

'It's wonderful to see you again, Elspeth. When I learned that you were still alive…' Again he shook his head as if in disbelief.

'How did you find out?' she asked.

'The letter you wrote to my father two years ago. It only just arrived—'

'I wrote so many letters, Gabriel. When Sylvia said you'd been told that I'd drowned… I feared…'

He grinned. 'What? That I might do what Romeo did?'

'No.' Then she smiled and shook her head. 'I don't know. At least you didn't run off with my best friend, as I suggested Romeo might have done.'

He laughed. 'I would never have done that.'

She thought her heart might burst with pure pleasure. 'Oh, it's so wonderful to see you again—'

'Are ye going tae be much longer, pal,' the taxi driver called across. 'Only, I've plenty of other customers I can take.'

'I'll pay you double the fare if you wait,' Gabriel called back.

'All right, pal, but you haven't long if you're to make the overnighter.'

'How did you get permission to come to Britain?' Elspeth asked as Gabriel turned back to her again.

'I managed to get a licence to attend the London Surgical conference, to present the research I did before the war. I arrived late yesterday and went straight to St Marys, where I knew you had once worked. One of the nurses told me you had left for Edinburgh, but didn't know to which hospital. This morning I registered for the conference, then slipped out and caught the Edinburgh train. I got here about an hour ago and tried the City Hospital first, and then the infirmary, but the doorman—'

'Do you really have to leave right now?'

He sighed. 'There is nothing I would rather do than stay with you, but my travel licence specifies I must present my paper at noon tomorrow and leave the country immediately afterwards. And I don't want to be made a prisoner for the third time in my life.'

'*Third*?'

He smiled. 'Another story, Elspeth, for another time.'

Her mouth felt suddenly dry at the thought of his leaving so soon. 'Will you go back to Austria?' she asked.

'No. I have a surgical job in Chicago.'

'*America*?'

He nodded and then she suddenly remembered. 'Dr Plotz?' she asked.

'Yes. He acted as my sponsor. I plan to settle permanently in Chicago. I'm booked on a liner that leaves Southampton for New York the day after the conference finishes.'

Permanently, he had said, and she felt an ache in the pit of her stomach. She glanced across at the taxi: the engine was still idling and the pungent smell of exhaust fumes was strong as the driver impatiently tapped his fingers on the steering wheel.

'In fact,' Gabriel continued, 'I must go now, if I'm not to miss my train.'

He led her out from behind the stone column and back to the taxi. As he opened the door, she felt an awful emptiness welling up inside herself, as if she was standing on a high tower looking down at the ground far below. He had only just arrived: to have waited so long to see him, and yet to know he would shortly be travelling to another continent – it was almost too much to bear.

He seemed to sense her unhappiness and held her close as he looked into her eyes. 'Living in America has made me realise how old-fashioned and inhibiting Austria is. The nation will change of course – the Hapsburgs have gone and there will be a republic – but it will take time, and I don't want to waste another moment of my life. I have an opportunity for a fresh start in a country unconcerned with the old conventions and traditions. And women doctors are readily accepted in America. There are already over a thousand women in clinical practice, and in Chicago there are even husband and wife surgical teams—'

'What are you saying—?'

'We need to go *now*, pal, or you'll definitely miss the overnighter,' the taxi driver barked.

'Yes, all right,' Gabriel said to him, then turned back to Elspeth and kissed her hard. Then he drew back. 'I must go now, Elspeth. Everything you need to know is in the book.'

And before she could say anything, he had ducked into the back seat of the taxi, slamming the door behind him. The taxi immediately accelerated away, quickly rounding a corner in the street and disappearing from view.

It had all happened so quickly that as she stood watching the empty space where the taxi had been, she wondered if she had been dreaming. But her bruised lips told her otherwise. She turned and began to walk back, stopping for a moment in front of a post box. She smiled: she would have to write Sylvia another letter, she thought, as she walked on and then turned back into the infirmary forecourt. Engraved in large gold lettering on either side of the doors were the words that she passed every time she entered the hospital:

"I was a stranger and ye took me in. I was sick and ye visited me."

She strode up the steps and through the door.

'Did you catch him, Dr Stewart?' Jenkins asked as she entered the foyer.

'Yes, thanks,' she replied with a smile.

In the empty doctors' office she took her jacket off and hung it on a peg. And then, finally, she pulled out the book.

She could see it had been well used: the moleskin cover was worn bare in parts, the spine cracked, several pages loose. She saw that there was a stiff white card tucked between the pages and held her breath as she carefully pulled it out.

The edges of the card were gilt-embossed, a white star on a red flag crest at the top. It was a ticket for the White Star liner the SS *Lapland*, due to depart Southampton on 5 September 1919 for New York. A name was stencilled in heavy black ink in the centre of card:

"Dr Elspeth Stewart".

She stared at the ticket for a long time.

After a while she sighed, then carefully tucked the ticket back inside the pages of the book and slipped the book into the pocket of her jacket. Then she walked back out onto the ward and towards the operating room, where she knew the evening's work was about to begin.

HISTORICAL NOTES

Frustration at the failure of the law-abiding suffragists to make significant progress led Emmeline Pankhurst to establish the militant Women's Social and Political Union (WSPU) in 1903, whose motto was 'Deeds not Words'. The campaign began modestly enough with the smashing of shop windows, but by 1913 had escalated to arson attacks and the planting of bombs. Nobody was convicted of the bombing of the Coronation Chair in June 1914, but newspaper reports stated that the police interviewed two suspicious women as they left the Abbey, and a feather boa, guidebook and silk purse were found at the scene. Other suffragettes were even more frustrated at the lack of progress, and National Archive records released in 2006 revealed that the police were warned about two suffragettes who had planned to assassinate Prime Minister Herbert Asquith.

However, the Great War gave women an opportunity to prove their worth in less violent ways, and the surgeons and nurses of the Scottish Women's Hospitals were one of several women-only groups who cared for Allied soldiers throughout Europe.

Dr Louisa Garrett Anderson was the chief surgeon of the Women's Hospital Corps, which established a hospital for wounded British soldiers inside Claridges Hotel in Paris in September 1914. She had been briefly imprisoned in 1912 for militant suffragette activities, but letters written to her mother from Paris show that she felt more comfortable doing good deeds more than violent ones. Based on her war experience, her methods of treating wound sepsis were published in the *Lancet* in 1916. The daughter of Elizabeth Garrett Anderson (the first woman to qualify as a doctor in Britain), Louisa never married, but instead chose to live with Dr Flora Murray, her physician colleague. They are buried together in Buckinghamshire and the inscription on their gravestone reads, 'We have been gloriously happy'.

Dr Harry Plotz qualified as a physician in 1912 and only two years later, at the age of twenty-three, claimed to have isolated the typhus bacillus. He did this by culturing blood taken from passengers arriving in New York from the Balkans who were unwell with epidemic typhus. The 'discovery' was publicised to great acclaim in the *New York Times* in 1914 and published in the *Journal of Infectious Disease* in 1915. That same year his findings were presented to the American Medical Association, where he received a two-minute standing ovation. Plotz named the organism *Bacillus Typhus Exanthematicus*, but as it had not been definitively proved to be the causal organism for typhus, most referred to it as the 'Plotz bacillus'. Plotz was able to grow cultures of the organism, which he then tried to develop into a vaccine against the infection. The Serbian government, desperate to stem the rising tide of deaths from typhus (more than two hundred thousand had died from the disease by early 1915), invited Plotz to Serbia in order to initiate a vaccination campaign. During the third invasion of Serbia, in October 1915, the Bulgarians captured him. However, his reputation as the 'discoverer' of typhus was well known and the Bulgarian authorities allowed him to continue his work unimpeded. He also went to Vienna to present his results to the Austrian medical establishment and then returned, as a medical hero, to New York in 1916.

Unfortunately within two years further studies revealed that the Plotz bacillus was not the cause of typhus, but merely a commensal bacterium living harmlessly inside humans. It was the Brazilian scientist Rocha-Lima who finally identified the true causal organism for typhus by examining the intestines of infected lice and he published his definitive results in 1916. He named the organism *Rickettsia Prowazekii* in honour of the two scientists whose earlier work had led him to make his discovery and who had both died from the disease. Plotz subsequently went to Paris to work for the Pasteur Institute, and later returned to America to lead the Virus Division for the US Army. He died of a heart attack working at his lab bench in Washington in 1947. A vaccine for typhus was not developed until the 1930s.

Oskar Potiorek had been a rising star in the Hapsburg Empire prior to 28 June 1914, but the assassination of Archduke Franz Ferdinand had a devastating personal effect on him. Serious questions were raised about his sanity in the weeks following the assassination, so it was a surprise to many when he was promoted to field marshal in command of the Austrian armies that invaded Serbia. After three consecutive offensives failed, Potiorek was dismissed from the army and went to live quietly in Klagenfurt, taking with him the Ottoman couch from the Konak and telling guests it was a reminder to him of the events of that fateful day in June. After the war a military commission was convened to look into his actions during the war, but many first-hand witnesses (General Appel, amongst others) had died of typhus and so the tribunal was limited in its conclusions. Although he was criticised for poor strategic decisions, no negligence could be attributed to his actions. Potiorek was known to dislike women and never married (there were rumours of a relationship with Colonel Merizzi) and he died in relative obscurity in 1933.

Bogdan Zerajic – like Gavrilo Princip a member of Young Bosnia – had attempted to assassinate Potiorek's predecessor, Governor Varesanin, in 1912, and committed suicide when the attempt failed. The authorities burnt his body, but his head was kept back and his skull used as an inkpot on the desk of Potiorek's chief of police.

Dr Elsie Inglis, the founder of the Scottish Women's Hospitals, did not approve of the militant actions of the WSPU. Despite her proposal being rejected by the British War Office, she established fourteen Scottish Women's Hospitals, which were sent to France, Serbia, Russia, Corsica, Romania and Greece, undoubtedly saving the lives of many Allied soldiers and civilians.

After her repatriation in February 1916, she took another Scottish Women's Unit to Russia to care for Allied troops fighting on the Eastern Front. Again the Scottish women performed magnificently in difficult conditions, but she fell ill and was diagnosed with advanced cancer. She returned to England in November 1917, and died only a day after arriving home. By that time the work of the Scottish women had been well publicised by the newspapers and she was lauded as a heroine. After a lying-in-state at St Giles' Cathedral in Edinburgh, and a memorial service at Westminster attended by both Serbian and British royalty, she was buried in Dean Cemetery in Edinburgh. Winston Churchill wrote of her: 'Her fame will shine in history.'

Dr Rudolph Fischer left Sarajevo after the war ended and went back to Graz to live quietly in retirement. He died in 1936.

The characters of **Elspeth, Gabriel, Sylvia, Vera and Anya** are fictitious and any resemblance to characters who lived at that time is purely coincidental. Although I have tried to synchronise my story with real-life events wherever possible, it must be remembered that this is a work of fiction and I have taken artistic licence in depicting events as they may have occurred. In addition, the characterisations and dialogue of real-life figures depicted in this story are also imagined, based upon my interpretation of correspondence and reports from that era.

ACKNOWLEDGEMENTS

Many thanks to my editor, Dorothy Pope, for her invaluable help with this second edition. Thanks also to Dr. Ana Wilson for help within the Serbian translation passages. As before, thanks to my wonderful family for their encouragement and support.